The Door

Copyright © 2020 Boris Bacic

All rights reserved.

ISBN: 9798697801963

TABLE OF CONTENTS

Prologue 5
Chapter 1 10
Chapter 2 29
Chapter 3 36
Chapter 4 40
Chapter 5 46
Chapter 6 51
Chapter 7 69
Chapter 8 76
Chapter 9 87
Chapter 10 98
Chapter 11 102
Chapter 12 108
Chapter 13 115
Chapter 14 128
Chapter 15 134
Chapter 16 143
Chapter 17 152
Chapter 18 159
Chapter 19 169
Chapter 20 181
Chapter 21 192
Chapter 22 202
Chapter 23 210
Chapter 24 215
Chapter 25 222
Chapter 26 227
Chapter 27 231
Chapter 28 248
Chapter 29 253
Chapter 30 266
Chapter 31 270
Chapter 32 279
Chapter 33 283

Chapter 34	297
Chapter 35	314
Chapter 36	319
Chapter 37	333
Chapter 38	339
Chapter 39	356
Chapter 40	363
Chapter 41	373
Chapter 42	388
Chapter 43	393
Chapter 44	398
Epilogue	420
Free Excerpts	432
Final notes	445

Thank you, Anonymous Military Advisor, for always correcting my erroneous military knowledge.

Thank you, Oli, for giving me valuable feedback about my novel. Without you, this book would have remained boring and predictable.

Gratitude to my fiancé Arijana, for constantly encouraging me to pursue my writing career.

Thanks DV Fischer for the amazing cover.

Big thanks to my editor, S. Williams, for going through the grueling job of correcting all my typos.

Huge thanks to my readers for supporting me and encouraging me to continue writing.

Prologue

"Hello?" Daniella shouted into the darkness ahead of her.

It was pitch black and she couldn't see her hand in front of her face. She took her phone out of her pocket and turned on the torch. It illuminated the dilapidated walls of the narrow corridor in front of her, which by logic shouldn't even be in front of her. The temperature was much lower here than it was back in the apartment and Daniella found herself shivering; and not just from the cold. Something was terribly wrong here and she could feel it in her bones, but she couldn't leave just yet.

She forced herself to take a step forward and after that, each subsequent step came naturally for her. The light of her torch barely penetrated the permeating darkness ahead and the deeper she went in, the more she became overwhelmed by a feeling of unease. She had no idea where she was headed and it was impossible to tell how far the corridor stretched on for. She glanced behind, just to reassure herself the apartment door was still open there. The idea of being trapped in this corridor, surrounded by such darkness, terrified her.

Come on, Daniella. Come on, you got this. Your sister's counting on you. She did her best to motivate herself, feeling her own breath uncontrollably tremble with each harsh exhale.

She quickened her pace a little. The steps she took up until this point were timid and short, but they slowly broke into a more confident stride, as the sound of her shoes echoed in the corridor with each step she took. Despite feeling less uneasy now, she kept glancing behind herself to make sure the door was still there, afraid it would somehow disappear, despite the corridor only going straight in a narrow path. The light which came from the apartment was now a small rectangle and Daniella was amazed at how much distance she put between herself and it.

The end couldn't possibly be far, right? The building wasn't that big, so whatever was on the other side must have been-

Her thoughts were interrupted when she heard a sound in the distance. She froze in place and perked up her ears. She stared down at the ground, since it allowed her to focus better, plus she couldn't see anything ahead of her from the dark anyway. Was it just her imagination? No, there it was again. Quiet, barely audible, but without a doubt, the sound of creaking, resounded in the distance.

It discouraged her, because she realized she probably had a long way to go yet. But then another terrifying thought occurred to her. What if someone else was in here? It made her pulse speed up and in the eerie silence of the corridor, she felt her heart thumping against her chest violently, all the way up to her ears.

"Hello?!" She called out again foolishly, knowing that she could potentially be putting herself in danger, as her voice echoed.

She didn't care about that, though. Right now she simply wanted whoever was there to respond, so that she knew if someone either was or wasn't there. This anticipation was only making her more nervous. She waited a moment, trying to catch even the faintest noise, her tremulous breathing being her only response.

"Come on Daniella, pull yourself together." she said to herself aloud this time, giving herself a mental shake and put one foot cautiously in front of the other.

She looked behind her shoulder. The light which provided solace to her was now barely a dot, a meager glimmer of hope in the ever-present darkness surrounding her. She turned back in the direction she was going, exhaled deeply and continued walking. The creaking noise from before followed her occasionally, but she decided not to stop and listen to it this time. After only a few more agonizing minutes which felt like hours, she started to notice something ahead of her. At first, she thought her eyes were playing tricks on her from being in such overwhelming darkness.

She put down her phone and squinted through the dark. It *wasn't* her imagination. There was a dot of light far ahead, just like the one behind her. It reinvigorated her and she broke into a light jog, as the torch of her phone violently bobbed up and down. And then she heard something that sounded like a moan, far ahead in the distance.

She gasped loudly and stopped to listen, breathless. Silence. She waited. And then it came again. A barely audible, feminine scream. A very familiar one.

"Michelle?!" Daniella shouted and broke into a sprint, "Michelle, hold on! I'm coming!"

The scream became louder and echoed throughout the corridor, as the creaking returned, now much louder than before, permeating the air both in front and behind her. The thought of her sister being harmed filled her with such primordial fear, that she forgot all about her own safety and threw herself in the path of danger to rescue her sibling.

"Michelle, hold on!" she shouted between sucking in shallow breaths, her voice drowned out by the creaking which was now so loud, that everything else became inaudible.

The dot of light in front of her grew and grew, until it turned into a rectangular, vertical slit and then took a clear shape of a door frame. *Just a little longer now, come on.* As she got closer, the source of light was somehow becoming thinner and she realized with dread that the reason for that was the fact that the door was closing. Terror coursed through her blood at the utter realization that the creaking came from the door itself and that it was slowly closing with each passing second, bringing her closer to being trapped inside this place.

"No, no, no, no!" she chanted repetitively to herself, as she sprinted towards the door.

But she was far too late. Just before she bumped into the door, the last vestiges of light disappeared and the door clicked loudly with an echo, instantly leaving her in complete and utter silence, save for her own panicked breathing.

"No! Open up! Michelle!" Daniella shouted, banging on the door with her palm as hard as she could, hysterically calling her sister's name over and over.

She fumbled for the doorknob, but found none. It was just a plain, wooden door with no doorknob and no lock. She banged on the door until her hands started throbbing with pain and when she finally stopped banging and the adrenaline subsided from her body, the meager panic which was previously present, gradually started to overtake her, building up like slow-boiling water.

Okay, okay. I'll go back to the apartment and then return and find a way to open the door. Then I'll find and rescue Michelle. She was starting to hyperventilate as she made that thought.

Her thoughts were interrupted when she heard the sound of steady footsteps echoing upon the concrete floor behind her, slowly approaching her. She froze in place, trying not to even breathe. The footsteps stopped right behind her and Daniella heard her own frantic breaths through her nose, as tears flowed down her cheeks.

She mustered all the remaining courage she had and ever so slowly, turned around, pointing the torch of the phone in front of herself with a jerky motion. There was nothing there. She stared at the encroaching darkness and slowly moved her phone down, revealing a set of footprints of what looked like pointy shoes on the ground, ending right in front of her. Footprints which came from a different set of shoes than hers.

She moved her phone back up, but before she could process what she was looking at, a face leapt out in front of her.

Chapter 1

"Piece of fucking shit!" Nathan shouted, as he tried to turn on the oven.

The interior light failed to turn on and he rotated the dial multiple times back and forth, hoping for a different result. This was the third time this month that the oven broke down. It was frustrating, because now he would need to fix a quick meal, instead of the healthy chicken and potatoes he'd originally planned on eating.

He leaned on the counter and exhaled in anger. His phone was within reach, so he snatched it up and started typing a message to his landlord:

Aleksei, the oven broke down again. I fixed it myself the first two times and I didn't mind paying for it, but this is getting ridiculous. Would you mind getting someone over here to fix it?

He didn't expect his cheap landlord to do anything about it, and sure enough, a few minutes later a message came in from him that said.

Ask Milo from building. He fix it cheaply.

Nathan scoffed and shook his head, as he heard his landlord's heavily Russian-accented voice in his head. He knew that arguing with him for a rent deduction based on the oven repairs would do no good. Aleksei was cheap on so many levels and it was starting to get on Nate's nerves. He somewhat understood his side, since Aleksei came from Ukraine, where tenants could easily damage the rental property and legally get away with it, but it still didn't take away from the fact that the landlord was a greedy piece of shit. He even tried to raise the rent once, until Nathan showed him the lease, in which it was stated that the price couldn't be raised mid-lease.

He scolded himself for jumping at the opportunity to move here. He was so eager to move out of the shithole he lived in before this, that he signed a lease right away upon seeing Aleksei's apartment. The apartment itself was nice at first glance, but that was just it – it was a look-but-don't-touch kind of place.

He dialed the number for Boss Café and waited for it to ring a few times.

"Boss Café, what can I do for you?" A perky female voice answered on the other end.

"Hi, can I get an order?"

"Sure thing. What would you like, sir?"

"Can I get uhhh… the chicken sandwich?"

He's been eating junk for the past few weeks and was intending to start eating healthy today. He was doing well until lunch time when the oven incident occurred. He opted for the chicken sandwich, since it seemed like the lesser evil, despite being tempted to order a pizza sandwich instead. He confirmed his address to the lady and she told him the food would be there in fifteen minutes or so. He thanked her and sat by his laptop, deciding to check Facebook for a bit. He scrolled through his news feed, when something caught his eye.

An ad with a picture of an array of buildings, with the caption under it that said *rent cheap apartments now!* He shook his head at the surgical precision Facebook displayed the ads they were showing him, and not just now, but a few other times in the past, too. One time, he was talking to a friend in person about a new donut place which opened in town and the moment he got home, he started seeing ads for the same place.

He was about to continue scrolling, when something clicked in Nathan's head. He's been living in this apartment for almost a whole year and the first few months were okay, but when he started calculating his expenses for utilities, repairs and other things his lazy landlord didn't want to maintain, this cheap apartment was turning out to be not so cheap.

He'd been sitting on the idea of moving into a new place for months now, but he was just too lazy to get up and actually do it. But he had to finally face facts that things weren't ever going to change. He wasn't going to let his landlord take advantage of his generosity any longer. He didn't mind paying for a more expensive apartment, but he wanted something that was actually functional. He clicked the ad, which took him to the website of a real estate agency.

He was immediately mesmerized by the myriad of apartments which were highlighted at the top and although some of them were far above his budget, he saw some really good-looking and moderately priced ones. He scrolled through, as he opened each apartment that caught his eye in a new tab, cluttering his browser with more and more tabs on top of the page. He had three candidates that he could potentially take a look at, so he put the tabs aside and continued scrolling through.

He was about to close the main page, when he saw one apartment that grabbed his attention. It was a two-bedroom apartment in the quieter part of town. Nathan knew that location and it was right across from a street which literally had everything he ever needed to leave his place for– pharmacy, bakery, restaurant, supermarket, butcher, etc.

Since he worked from home as a web developer and most of the locations were pretty close by to each other, he didn't need to worry about commuting time. He scrolled back up at the top of the ad. The price seemed abysmally low too, which didn't fit, because based on the pictures, the place seemed too good to be that cheap.

It looked spacious, fancily furnished, pristine-looking in the pictures and the layout of the rooms looked like someone had copy-pasted his own imagination of an ideal apartment. Nathan knew that the rental agencies polish the pictures to make the places look bigger and better, but something inside him told him that he should go for this one.

"Ah, screw it." he said and clicked on the option *schedule a tour*.

He bookmarked the other three apartment links, just in case this one was already taken, which he assumed was the case. It was too good to stay available for long, but Nathan hoped that he wasn't late. An abrupt ring at the doorbell jolted him out of his thoughts. He got up and opened the door.

"Hi." A young man carrying a wrapped sandwich greeted him "Sandwich for you."

"Hey, Bill. Been a while." Nathan greeted him and took the sandwich, while taking the cash out of his wallet to pay the delivery guy.

"Yeah, it's been like, what? Twelve hours?" Bill said with a grin.

Nathan chuckled and said.

"Well, don't wanna shock my body by cutting out all the good stuff, right?"

"Yeah. And not to mention you eating healthy is gonna be bad for our business." Bill winked.

"Well, you have a good one, Bill. Don't work too hard, yeah?"

"See ya, Nate."

He sat down and unwrapped his sandwich. The juicy aroma of the succulent chicken filled his nostrils and he practically started salivating, only now realizing how hungry he was. He was about to take a bite, when his phone started ringing. He sighed and picked it up, while putting the sandwich down. It was work.

"Hello?" He answered.

"Hey Nate, how's it going?" His manager Anthony asked.

"Fine, fine." Nathan responded.

He usually tried indulging in small talk, but right now he didn't want to ask Anthony how he was doing, because he knew he'd start talking a lot, and right now he really just wanted to eat his sandwich. There was an awkward pause on the line, before his manager said.

"Okay… well, the reason why I'm calling is because Ronnie needs some help fixing that one bug we talked about earlier. Do you think you could lend him a hand on it?"

"Yeah, sure. No problem. I'll do it as soon as I'm done with my own work."

"Awesome, thanks Nate. Have a good one."

He put his phone down and grabbed the enormous sandwich with both hands. He was about to take the first bite, when the phone started ringing once more.

"Well, that's just swell." He chuckled, hungry and a little frustrated.

He looked at the screen and realized it was an unknown number. He wanted to ignore it, thinking it might be one of those telemarketers, but then he remembered the apartment he scheduled for a tour. He quickly picked it up.

"Hello?"

"Hi, is this Nathan Sutherland?" A pleasant, female voice on the other end asked.

"Yes, it is. What can I do for you?"

"My name's Jessica and I'm calling from LiveBetter real estate agency about the tour you scheduled. Do you have a moment to talk?"

Nathan stood up, instantly forgetting about the sandwich.

"Yes, yes I do. Is the apartment still available for tours?" he asked impatiently, expecting to be disappointed.

"It is, actually." Jessica said "But we do have a lot of scheduled tours in the upcoming days, so the only time we'd be able to squeeze you in is today at 5:30 pm. Would that work for you?"

"5:30? Uhhh…" He glanced at his computer screen, trying to remember if he had anything at that time.

Video call with the team, dammit. Oh, well. He was just going to have to skip it, this was way more important.

"Uh, yeah. That actually works for me." he finally said.

"Great! I'll send you the address of the apartment via text."

"Sweet, thank you. See you then." Nathan said before ending the call with the agent.

A moment later, he received the address in the text. It shouldn't take him more than ten minutes by car to reach it. It was 2 pm right now, so he immediately sent a message to his manager that something urgent came up and he would not be able to make it to the meeting. Anthony was understanding and he said he would send the minutes of the meeting to him later on.

Once he sat down again, he grabbed the sandwich once more and contemptuously glanced at his phone, to see if it would start ringing. When it didn't, he was content enough to finally take the first bite. *It's even better when you postpone eating.*

Once he was done eating, he reopened the link of the apartment and viewed the pictures again. It looked perfect and it was no wonder that everyone lined up for a tour. Not only did it look good, but it also had additional benefits which he never had in this apartment, like a garage (*No garage,* Aleksei said), basement storage if he had a bicycle (*I use storage,* Aleksei retorted), allowing pets (*No filthy animals,* Aleksei remarked). He considered himself lucky to get first dibs on it.

He spent some time working until 5 pm and as soon as he closed his laptop, he put on his jacket and shoes, grabbed his keys and headed out. He would probably be early, fifteen minutes or so at least, but he always felt it was better to be early than late. He did not want to screw this up.

***

The traffic was abundant, as expected, since it was rush hour, but the city never had any jams, unless an accident happened somewhere on the road. He pulled over to the street mentioned in the address and stared in astonishment at the array of fancy buildings lining up. He hasn't been here in a while, so seeing these newly erected apartments was mesmerizing. He figured that one of these must have been up for renting, so if this apartment didn't work out for him, he could always look for another one in the area, even though it would probably cost him way more.

He pulled up in front of the building with the right number on it and immediately upon exiting the car, he saw a young woman standing in front. She had formal attire and by the way she immediately made eye contact with him, Nathan assumed she was Jessica.

"Hi. Nathan?" she asked with a toothy PR grin.

"Yep. I'm assuming you're Jessica?" Nathan returned the gesture.

They shook hands and she said:

"A pleasure meeting you. Right this way."

She led Nathan to the gate and input the 4-digit code on the panel next to it. The little red light turned green and a beep, followed by a click resounded. Jessica pushed the gate open and held it like that for Nathan. As he got in, he realized he was in the apartment complex's parking lot. His jaw dropped at the size of it. It was spacious enough for him to park a truck inside, let alone his car.

"About the parking." he asked, "The listing mentioned the apartment comes with a parking spot, right?"

"No, I'm afraid it doesn't." Jessica said, still smiling widely.

Nathan nodded disappointedly, until Jessica said.

"It comes with its own garage. Wanna see it?"

Fuck yeah, I wanna see it. Instead of voicing his thoughts, he nodded and followed her to the underground entrance to the garage. Nathan expected an enormous underground parking, however this place was barely big enough to fit the two cars which were already parked inside. Jessica said, as her voice echoed.

"The parking spots outside the garage are free for anyone to use, but..." She theatrically pointed to the rows of shutters lined up on the left, stopping her finger on the middle one, "This one right here comes with the apartment. So you'd never have to worry about not having a spot."

This was amazing. Right now, he used the free parking behind the building, which was a shitty excuse of a dirt-floored parking full of potholes and muddy water. And since it was free, he'd often have to drive around looking for available parking spots. More often than not, he'd just park somewhere on the side and leave a note with his phone number on the windshield, in case the person parked next to him needed to move.

He's had countless cases where he got a call from an exasperated person at 6 am, asking him to move his car, since it's blocking the way. His troubles would be resolved with this new parking and he wouldn't need to spend twenty minutes looking for a spot every time he went grocery shopping or anything else.

"Well, anyway. Let's go see the apartment, yeah?" Jessica said, elegantly climbing the slope of the garage entrance on her heels.

Nathan half-expected her to trip and fall at any moment, but she seemed to handle herself well, making him wonder if she often had to trek through inhospitable areas in those uncomfortable-looking shoes when showing apartments to potential residents. She led him to the building where the apartment was located and input another 4-digit code on the panel. It beeped and turned green and the door unlocked. Nathan noticed surveillance cameras placed around as well, so he said.

"Pretty tight security around here."

Jessica pressed the button to call the elevator. It displayed the number 8, which started to decrease.

"Well, one thing I should mention is that there was a burglary recently here. There used to be no passcodes, just doors with locks and no cameras, so someone was able to sneak their way in. Since then, security has been upped a little. There's even a guard in each of the buildings."

The elevator door opened and Nathan saw himself and Jessica reflected in the polished mirror inside. They stepped into the elevator and the agent pressed the button for floor 3.

"So, what's the landlord like? Hope he's not a miser like my current one." Nathan said.

"To tell you the truth, we don't know." Jessica said, as the elevator started moving.

"You don't know?" Nathan frowned.

"Yeah. Nobody in the company has ever met him, is the thing. He's verified and all, sent us all the relevant data, we just never met with him in person. I guess he's just a loner. Or too lazy to handle apartment renting."

"So, I'll never have to worry about him bursting inside the apartment for a surprise inspection, huh?"

Jessica chuckled.

"From what we were able to gather, all you need to do is pay the rent online and you'll never have a problem. I doubt a man who hired an agency to do everything, including tours for him, would be willing to waste his time to check up on the tenants."

"That… actually sounds awesome." Nathan smiled.

The elevator abruptly stopped and the doors opened. A middle-aged man standing in front of the elevator nodded to Nate and Jessica as they got out. Nathan couldn't help but admire the flawless interior of the building. It wasn't just shiny and clean. It looked sterile enough to eat off the floor. The walls were perfectly white and each apartment door seemed impregnably thick, despite only being made from wood.

"Here we are." Jessica said, as she pulled out her keys with a loud sound of jingling.

Nathan looked at the door which had the numbers 304 on. Jessica fumbled for the right key and unlocked the door with a loud click. The door swung open and she gestured for Nathan to go ahead first. Nathan nodded and stepped inside.

His eyes widened at the sight in front of him. Right from the position which he was standing on, he could see the living room. It was as ostentatious-looking as it was on the photos that he saw in the ad. The room was spacious, the furniture looked fairly new and the view outside the window on the other end was mesmerizing.

To say that he was impressed would be an understatement. He knew that the apartment would be good, but he expected it to be less so compared to the agency's pictures. It was as if the agency took the pictures and didn't even bother polishing them in Photoshop or any other program, as it already retained the highest possible quality. Nathan took a step forward and looked to the left, where the kitchen was, separated from the living room by a counter.

"Wow." He couldn't help but say aloud when he saw the beauty of the kitchen counter and all the things that came along with it.

"It's pretty cool, don't you think? You can even turn on some fancy lights here. See?" Jessica said and flipped a switch which turned on a bunch of bright-white lights on the ceiling above the kitchen, illuminating the area Nathan was standing on like an operating theater.

She continued.

"The oven and the fridge are fairly new as well, so you'll have no issues with them."

Funny you should mention this, Jessica. Nathan thought to himself, suppressing a laughter. He spent a moment admiring the touch-buttons on the surface of the cooking stove, before turning around.

"Shall we go see the rest of the rooms?" Jessica asked with a smile.

She took him to the window on the other side of the living room and showed him the view outside. The window overlooked the parking lot inside the apartment complex. Directly across from room 304, on the other side of the parking was the complex's other apartment building and Nathan could see rows and rows of apartment windows extending onto what he counted was nine floors.

Far on the left side where the parking ended, a park partially came into view, with neatly trimmed grass, a somewhat visible trail and a myriad of trees stretching high up.

"The fire escape is right here, but let's hope you don't need to use it. If you decide to rent the apartment, I mean." Jessica said, "And here is the bathroom."

She took him through the hall on the left side of the entrance, opposite of the kitchen. The bathroom was at the end of the hall on the right, and it was just as fancy and on par with the rest of the apartment, in term of space and equipment. It even had a radio built-in inside the shower. Opposite of the bathroom door on the left, was the bedroom.

The bedroom itself had a desk which could be used for work, Nathan thought. An enormous bed was in the room, right next to the giant closet. The nightstands on either side of the bed had fancy-looking lamps and the view outside the window offered the same view as the one in the living room. There was an oil painting on the wall above the desk, which depicted a lighthouse.

"Holy shit." Nathan shook his head in amazement at the whole apartment.

Something was wrong here. Why was a great apartment like this one so cheap?

It was almost thirty percent cheaper than its rival apartments, which weren't half as good as this one. He turned to Jessica and asked.

"Hey, so uh, the price I saw in the ad, is that the price for this apartment, or was that some sort of mistake?"

Jessica chuckled:

"That's the one, you're right."

"So… did somebody die in this apartment or something?" He scratched the back of his head, awaiting to see if the agent would laugh at his joke.

Jessica said.

"I know, you wanna know if there's a catch, right?"

"Well, uh…" Nathan fumbled, suddenly realizing he may have just come off as a douchebag "I mean… No, not that, just… Well, yeah. Just wanted to double-check, you know?"

Jessica chuckled and said:

"It's okay, I'd be suspicious too if I were you. I can assure you, though, there's nothing wrong with this apartment. If you do happen to have a problem, the landlord will cover all expenses for repairs or anything else."

"So then, is there a way to sign a lease, like, right away? I really want this apartment."

"I'm afraid not. We have to run a credit and background check and that usually takes a day or two. But if you fill out the application right now, you get top priority for it."

"That's great!"

Jessica pulled a folder out of her purse and opened it, to reveal a piece of paper. She handed it to Nathan and said:

"Alright, so I'm going to need your ID."

Nathan pulled out his wallet and handed the ID to her. She clumsily took it between two fingers with long, crimson-painted nails, which made Nathan wonder how she managed to hold anything properly in her hands. She smiled and said.

"Great! While you fill out the application, I'm going outside to make a call, be right back."

"Awesome, thank you." Nathan smiled and sat on the couch, placing the piece of paper on the coffee table.

He read through the application, which included basic information like his name, date of birth, occupation, etc. He was eager to have this apartment, but was still a little suspicious about the whole thing. The price, the secrecy of the landlord, something was off over here. But then again, he'd be paying a monthly rent, so if something really was wrong, he could just move out, no big deal. He was about to sign the contract at the bottom, when his gaze fell on something he didn't see before. Right in front of him, to the right of the apartment entrance and in the foyer was a door he didn't check. Did Jessica just forget to show it to him, or maybe this door wasn't important at all?

He tapped the pen on the table a few times, before dropping it and striding to the door. He heard Jessica's muffled voice to his right, outside the entrance, as she talked on the phone. He couldn't discern any words, but he didn't want to eavesdrop anyway. He grabbed the doorknob of the mysterious door in front of him and pushed it. He almost slammed face-first into it, until he realized it was locked.

He stepped back and stared at it, with his hands on his hips. What could possibly be behind this door? He tried to imagine the map of the apartment based on his orientation and since this room was connected to the bathroom on the other end, there was no way it could have been anything more than a tool storage, utility room or something like that.

His thoughts were interrupted when he heard something coming from the other side of the door. It was faint, barely audible at first, so much that Nathan thought it came from elsewhere. But the longer he stood in front of this enigmatic door, the more he became convinced that the sound was coming from inside the room. He tentatively took a step forward and turned his head sideways, to have his ear face the door. There was something that sounded like faint scratching coming from inside, but it was impossible to identify it over the cacophony of loud steps and murmured sentences that were coming from Jessica's direction.

He leaned in, but the closer he got, the more the sound seemed to fade away. He winced when he felt his ear touch the cold wood of the door. A moment later, he placed his ear against the door again and cupped it with his hand to block out any outside noises. The scratching got a lot clearer now and he was without a doubt, certain that the sound was coming right from the other side, as if whatever was there was slowly getting dragged across the wooden surface of the door with steady motion, before pausing for a moment and then continuing to repeat.

Suddenly, the entrance door swung open and Nathan recoiled in fear, stifling his scream, while his heart pounded a million miles an hour. Jessica stepped inside the apartment, looking at Nathan with a confused glance, probably realizing that he got startled. Despite that, she had her usual PR grin on her face, trying not to make a fuss over it.

"Great news, Nathan." she said after a moment of awkward silence, "Everything seems to be okay so far regarding the credit check, but we'll need a little more time for the background check and you're in the clear. Did you have a chance to fill out the application?"

Nathan was still baffled by what he had heard at the door, so he opened his mouth dumbly, before his delayed response came.

"Uh, no, not yet. I just got a few more questions to fill in, I'll wrap them up in it a moment, just…" He nodded at her, while his gaze inevitably moved towards the door.

Just a plain, wooden door, nothing more. He must have been imagining the sounds he thought he heard. Or maybe it was just bugs or something. Still, he wanted to know what the door was before he signed any lease, so he pointed to it and asked Jessica.

"Hey um, what's this door here?"

"Oh, right. I totally forgot to mention that." Jessica threw her hand up to her face disappointedly, "That is the storage room. At least that's what we think."

"You don't know what's behind the door?" Nathan raised an eyebrow.

"Yeah, we asked the apartment owner about it, but he says it's been locked since the start. Says it's rusted shut or something. He claims he tried everything to open it, but nothing worked and the only way apparently would be to take down the entire door frame, along with the wall, which would cost an arm and leg."

"Huh. I see." Nathan said, staring at the door in bewilderment.

"Is the door going to be a problem? If you need a storage, you actually get your own in the basement and it's big enough for bicycles or anything else you want to keep there."

Nathan looked at Jessica and smiled.

"No, no. Not a problem at all. I mean, I guess I understand now why the price is so low. He probably wants to make up for the locked door in the apartment, huh?"

"I guess so. So, about the application-"

"Yeah, lemme finish filling it out it right now."

Nathan got back to the couch and grabbed the pen. He hastily filled out the rest of the application and handed it back to Jessica with a courteous grin.

"Thank you." she said, "So, we'll be in touch. As soon as the background check is complete, I'll call you."

"Thanks for your time, Jessica. I'll put in a good word for your promotion." He winked and Jessica giggled like a schoolgirl out of flattery.

He left the place feeling hopeful.

Chapter 2

Nathan made a mental note to check the other apartments in a day or so, in case he got rejected for the dream apartment he went to see. He really hoped that wouldn't be the case, but he was ready for it. He got back home and when he checked his phone, it furiously vibrated with the notifications from work.

"Of course I'm needed at work the most when I'm away." he vocalized, as he tried to read the messages one by one, each subsequent message becoming more frantic and panicked.

He sat by his computer and started catching up with work. It was past 7 pm and he was nowhere near wrapping it up for the day, so he got ready to spend the night coding. He rubbed his eyes and realized he was hungry.

"Shit, I forgot to call Milo." he said, when his gaze fell on the broken oven.

He really wanted to be able to cook by tomorrow, so he decided he would visit the repairman, since he lived in the same building. He checked out the menu for Dennis Restaurant, since he felt embarrassed ordering from Boss Café twice in one day. Eventually, he opted for the Caesar salad from Boss Café and hoped he wouldn't see the same delivery guy from earlier.

After doing that, he got out of his apartment and went down to the first floor. Milo's apartment had the sign *REPAIR* on it, so that tenants would know where to look for him. Nathan heard loud classical music playing from the apartment as he neared the door. He felt sorry for the tenants that lived next to Milo, since this was a regular occurrence, but no one dared complain. They liked getting free repair services.

Nathan rang the doorbell for a prolonged moment and stepped back, waiting impatiently. There was no response. He knocked on the door three times so loudly that his knuckles hurt. Within seconds, the music got gradually quieter, until it became barely audible. Loud footsteps thudded inside the apartment and the sound of unlocking resounded moments later.

The door swung open on the inside and Nathan was met with a tall, overweight man with thick glasses. The top of his bald head glistened with sweat and he wiped it, as he leaned on the doorframe, holding a wrench in his hand. His shirt, which was not long enough to cover the bottom of his incongruously large belly, had an oil stain on it. Had it not been for the wrench, Nathan would have thought that Milo was dancing, hence the sweaty head.

"Hi, Nathan. Long time no see." he said with a deep, raspy voice while panting wheezily.

"Hey, Milo. I'm sorry if I'm interrupting you, but um, I have this thing that I was hoping you could help me with."

"Yeah, yeah. Not a problem. I was just fixing the sink. This old piece of shit building gets clogged a lot."

"Tell me about it. Every month I have something breaking down."

"So, what broke down this time?" Milo asked, wiping his forehead with his sleeve.

"The oven." Nathan said embarrassed, as he put his hands on his hips.

"Again? This is like the third time in two months."

"Yeah, I know. And I'm really sorry to bother you again with it. I asked my landlord to fix it, but he refuses to pay for any of the repairs, you know?"

"Yeah, I know. Those goddamn Russian commies."

Ukrainian. Nathan thought.

"Alright, let me get my toolbox and I'll be up there in a few minutes."

"Thanks a lot, Milo. I really appreciate it." Nathan grinned as the repairman nodded to him.

***

In a matter of minutes, Milo was in Nathan's apartment, with his head inside the oven.

"Huh, looks like the main fuse died again." he said.

"Shit. How? We replaced it last time." Nathan threw his hands up in the air.

He knew that this repair would be costly.

"Well, something in the oven must be frying it. I'm guessing one of the adjacent fuses. And since there's no way to test which one is faulty without frying the others, we'd need to replace all of them." He pulled his head out of the oven and wiped his hands on his shirt.

Nathan sighed and stared at the oven in frustration.

"You know what? Fuck it. I'll let Aleksei handle it. I'll be out of the apartment soon anyway."

"That so? Well look at you, Mister moving-up-in-the-world." Milo joked, "So where are you gonna move?"

Nathan shrugged.

"To tell you the truth, I don't know yet. I got a couple of places in mind, but I hope to get approved for this one place on the other side of town."

"Well, good for you. Your landlord is a greedy cuntbag, let me tell you that."

Nathan chuckled heartily.

"Thanks for checking out the oven for me, Milo." he said with a nod of approval.

"No worries, no worries. I'll be heading back now, then. Still gotta fix some stuff in my own apartment. If you happen to need anything, let me know."

"Will do, I appreciate it."

As Milo left the apartment, Nathan took a glance at the oven and shook his head, as he said in his mind.

Up yours, Aleksei.

***

A couple days went by and Nathan had started to lose hope about being approved for the apartment he applied for. He had woken up ready to browse some more apartments, not very hopeful about finding something as good as the one he saw. He had started to think about the trade-off and whether he should rework his budget to see if he could afford a more expensive place, even if it meant he wouldn't be saving that much. He wanted to one day have his own apartment, just like the one he went to see, but he would need to work really hard and then maybe he'd be able to get it in a few years, after he got promoted.

The question was, should he continue living in a dump like the one Aleksei so kindly provided to him and then save up some cash, or find a more luxurious place which will cut into some of his savings, but give allow him to live a more comfortable life?

Before he managed to answer that question, his phone started ringing. It was Jessica. He knew because he had memorized the 333 her number ended with. He hastily answered the call.

"Hello?" he asked.

"Hi, this is Jessica from LiveBetter, am I speaking to Nathan?"

"Hi Jessica, yes, it's me. How can I help you?"

"Nathan, I'm calling with some good news."

Before she even continued, Nathan mouthed a silent *yes* and pumped his fist victoriously. Jessica continued after a brief pause.

"We reviewed your application, ran a background and credit check and everything seems to be in order. So if you want to proceed with signing the lease, we will need a payment for the deposit and first month's rent. I'm sending you the payment methods on your email right now and you can do it at your leisure."

"Awesome, give me one moment, I'm checking it right now." He opened his email and clicked on the mail from LiveBetter, "Do you have a few minutes to hold on the line? I can proceed with the payment right away."

"Of course! If you run into any problems at all, let me know." she perkily said.

There were a few minutes of clicking through the silence on the phone, while Jessica patiently waited, despite Nathan uncomfortably saying 'just a moment please' every couple of seconds, or vocalizing what he was doing. Once the payment was complete, Jessica said.

"Alright. It may take a little bit until the payment goes through, so I will make sure to contact you as soon as it's confirmed and you can pick up the keys. Does that sound okay?"

"Perfect, thank you so much, Jessica."

He hung up, feeling ecstatic. This was it. No matter what came after this, he was ninety five percent sure that he would be out of this apartment. He tempered his expectations with those remaining five percent, in case something went wrong with the payment, or the landlord had a change of mind. That wouldn't be the first time it happened, either.

Due to his trouble finding a parking spot near the current apartment, he found one garage a while ago. Close by, good price. However, the minute before he could make his first payment, the agent got a call from the landlady of the garage and they had to scrap the deal. Turns out she changed her mind and wanted to sell the garage, instead.

After everything Nathan had been through with Aleksei, this was only a minor inconvenience for him.

Since it was still early morning and Nathan was about to start working anyway, he began doing some coding.

Chapter 3

Around noon, he heard a knocking on his door so loud, that it startled him enough to almost drop the cellphone out of his hand. He knew exactly who it was. Only one person knocked like that. Nathan strode to the door, while the loud knocking resounded impatiently again.

"Okay, just a second!" Nathan frustratedly said, as he unlocked the door and opened it.

In front of him stood a middle-aged man with thick eyebrows which merged into a unibrow, a stern look on his face above the double chin and a stale smell which permeated the air as soon as Nathan opened the door.

"Hello, Aleksei." He greeted him and gave him a fake smile, "What can I do for you?"

"You have time? We must to talk about problem." Aleksei said in his thick Ukrainian accent.

"You know, I'm kinda busy right now. I have this meeting in a few minutes and-"

"Just three minutes." Aleksei said, raising three stubby fingers to indicate the number.

Nathan wasn't really busy and he *did* have three minutes, he just didn't want to spend them on Aleksei. Those would be three wasted minutes of his life and millions of dead brain cells. In the end, he knew that Aleksei would persist, so he stepped aside and said.

"Alright, fine. Three minutes and then you have to go."

Aleksei waddled inside, his big belly coming in before he did. Even walking seemed to present a problem to him, as he started panting when he reached the living room. The first thing he did was point to the discarded containers of ordered food and said judgingly:

"You make mess here. Why you do not clean?"

"Well the mess has been here since yesterday, Aleksei. I can assure you that I always clean up after myself. And plus, this wouldn't have happened if the oven hadn't broken down. *Again.*" He emphasized the final word.

"How you manage to break it again?" Aleksei asked, waltzing over to the oven.

Nathan wanted to punch the fucker in the face, but instead gritted his teeth, as he impatiently said.

"I didn't break it, Aleksei. It kept breaking down ever since I mo-"

"What is problem with it?" Aleksei interrupted him and opened the oven.

"I already had Milo look it over. I don't think you'd be able to…"

But Aleksei didn't listen. He already stuck his head inside the oven and was checking it for faults. Nathan didn't even bother explaining, because he knew that the landlord would proceed to check it, despite not knowing shit about it. He was the type of person that would try out every solution that you already tried, while convinced that he would do it better and somehow manage to fix it. Still, every problem ended the same way, just like this one. Aleksei pulled his head out of the oven and said.

"Something wrong with oven. Did Milo come over to fix it?"

Nathan was getting increasingly frustrated by this point. He said.

"Yeah, he did. Listen, I really gotta go now, Aleksei. Is there anything you wanted to discuss, or?"

Aleksei kept staring at the oven and scratching both his chins and for a moment Nathan thought he didn't hear him. A second later, he turned to face his tenant and said.

"I came for rent."

"But you're five days early." Nathan frowned at the audacity of the landlord.

He was more than five days early though. Every few months he'd come one day early and it piled onto half a month.

"Yes, I must to travel back to Ukraine this week, so I will back in a week."

Nathan grinned, just about ready to kick Aleksei out of the apartment – through the window. He knew that the logical thing to do would be suggesting to pay *after* he is back from his trip, but that wouldn't fly with a gem like Aleksei.

"Yeah, okay. Fine." Nathan said and went to his closet, where he kept his rent money in cash.

He took the stack which he already calculated and separated beforehand and handed it to Aleksei. He said.

"Here. I counted it all, but you should count to make sure that-"

The landlord spat on his fingers and started counting the money before Nathan even finished. He made sure to count the money twice, before giving Nate a suspicious glance and saying:

"Okay. You call Milo to fix oven, yes?"

Nathan just smiled and nodded, fuming out of his ears, while Aleksei left the apartment. *Just you wait, asshole. I'll be out of here before you know it and you can go fuck yourself.* He thought to himself silently.

Chapter 4

Nathan didn't want to bother Jessica with incessant questions about whether he'd get approved for the apartment, since he knew that the process took some time. He was very eager to get out of his current apartment, even though it's only been two days since he met with Jessica, since more and more things kept breaking down. He still hasn't fixed the oven (he was intent on leaving that for Aleksei after he left, even if it meant having to go for a longer time without the food he usually made) and on top of all that, the toilet started to malfunction, with the flushing not working properly at times.

He had in mind to call Milo and actually pay for this, but he was feeling extremely petty towards Aleksei by now and the thought of the landlord paying for all the repairs in the apartment after Nathan left put a smile on his face. Besides, the toilet was still functional enough for Nathan to ignore the unpleasantries.

Either way, he had already browsed a few other apartments online and planned on checking them out, in case this one didn't work for him. *One of them has to work.* He thought to himself. He suddenly felt trapped in the current apartment, which was aggravated by the eagerness to move into the new one. For a moment, an illogical thought crossed his mind.

What if I don't find an apartment? What if none of the landlords want me as a tenant and I have to continue living here in this shithole? The logical part of him dismissed that irrational thought right away.

It wasn't until almost two weeks after his call with Jessica that he received a call from the agent. He hastily picked up the phone, dropping all the coding work he had been doing by then. This was more important than anything else right now, Ethan and Mike can wait for the debugging.

"Hello?" he answered.

"Hi Nathan, it's Jessica, how are you?" The agent's ever-jovial voice resounded on the line.

"I'm great, thank you." He wanted to ask her out of politeness how she was doing, but he was just too impatient.

After a moment of silence, she responded.

"Well Nathan, I have some great news. Everything seems to be in order, so you can come sign the lease for the apartment."

"Oh, that is so great, thank you Jessica." A goofy smile which he was unable to control was strewn over his face, "Thank you so much. When can we meet to handle all that?"

"Well, I'm available from now until 1 pm, or if you're too busy with work or something, we can meet after 5 pm."

"No, no, right now works fine. Do we meet in the apartment, or…?"

"Yeah, that way I can give you the keys and answer any remaining questions you have and then you can essentially move in right after we sign the necessary papers." Jessica responded.

This was it.

"Okay, okay. Cool. When do you think you can be there? I can leave work now and be there in around twenty minutes." He was so eager he could hardly contain it in his voice.

Jessica seemed to notice this, as she gave a slight chuckle, before saying:

"That sounds perfect, Nathan. I can be there earlier, so I'll be waiting out front."

"Thanks a lot. See you soon."

As soon as he hung up the call, he pumped his fist, just like during the last phone call and shouted.

"Fuck yeah!"

This was perfect. The apartment was cheap, so he would still have some savings and at the same time, he'd live comfortably, unless the apartment was really faulty in a way which wasn't noticeable the first time around.

It was 10 am and he was supposed to have a one-on-one meeting with his manager, but he sent him a message, apologizing for skipping it once again. He explained what was at stake and even though he could have just waited until he was done with work at 5 pm, he didn't want this opportunity to slip away. He knew that that kind of thinking was irrational, but there was no way he was taking any chances.

He wanted to whip out his phone and text Aleksei (with petty relish) that he's moving out, but a nagging feeling told him that he didn't want to make a fool of himself in case the lease didn't go through or something else went wrong. Once he had the keys of the apartment in his hands, he'd do that. His eyes fell on the broken oven once more and he scoffed, hoping it was one of the last times he'd see it in his life.

***

The traffic was non-existent and despite driving according to the regulations, he arrived at the apartment complex in around ten minutes, which was much sooner than he expected. As soon as he arrived, he saw Jessica in front of the gate, glittering as much as last time, with the makeup on her flawless face, pristine attire and a posture so elegant and balanced, that it made Nathan assume that she must have worked as some point as a sponsor girl or something similar.

She noticed him as soon as he exited the car and her smile widened even more. He wondered if it was a courteous grin, or if she genuinely smiled out of kindness whenever she met new clients.

"Hi, Nathan. Good to see you again." They shook hands.

She opened the gate and proceeded into the building and inside room 304. He was once again met with the godly sight of the dream apartment in front of him. It was probably his imagination, but it looked even better than the first time he saw it. Jessica told him to sit wherever he liked and whipped out a folder with papers. She gave him two copies and proceeded to hand him a pen.

"Please sign both copies here at the bottom. One is yours and one goes to the agency. Once that's complete, the apartment is all yours!"

Nathan smiled back and clicked the pen three times, out of habit. He carefully read through the lease to make sure he wasn't falling into any traps, like he did with Aleksei's apartment. He looked at the bottom of the text. On the right side was the signature of the agency, while the left side had a blank spot left for the tenant to sign. *Screw it.* He signed it hastily and handed the paper back to Jessica.

"Well, we sure handled this quickly, didn't we?" Jessica said, as she whipped out her keyring with a loud jingle.

She carefully detached three keys and one tiny remote and placed them neatly on the coffee table. She pointed to each of them one by one, as she said.

"This remote is for the gate and the garage door. I can't remember which button opens which one, so you'll have to try it out yourself. This key is for the mailbox and this one is for the apartment. And this last one is for the garage, in case there's no electricity or you happen to lose your remote."

"Got it." Nathan said, grabbing the apartment key.

"Oh, and if you need anything fixed, you can call… this number." she said as she took out a piece of paper and wrote a number on it "His name is Joshua and he's the superintendent of the apartment. If you happen to have any issues, you can call him. He also has spare keys of all the apartments in the building, so if you lose one, he can lend you one to copy it."

"Awesome, thank you." Nathan took the paper and placed it next to the keys on the coffee table.

"I… think that's it." Jessica said, raising the tone of the last word jovially, grinning at Nathan, "I'll take this copy of the contract. And this one is yours. You'll receive all the necessary info in your email in a bit and that's that."

She looked around and then back at Nathan, before saying.

"So, do you have any questions?"

"No, no. I think I'm good. If there's anything, I can always call you, right? Or the landlord?"

"You can call the agency. Since like I said, the landlord is a hermit of sort, so I doubt you'll get to meet him at all."

"Yeah, what is the deal with that, anyway?" Nathan scratched the back of his head.

Jessica shrugged elegantly.

"We think he's just really busy, probably has his own business he runs or something like that, no idea. Either way, you'll find it impossible to contact him, since he specifically asked us to handle everything related to the apartment. Anyway, in case you need anything, you have my number."

"Thanks again for everything, Jessica."

"Enjoy your new place!" Jessica waved and left the place with her signature elegant stride.

Nathan put his hands on his hips and sighed in relief, mesmerized by the beauty of the apartment. *His* apartment. He felt like a heavy load fell off his shoulders. Living here was going to be amazing, he was sure of it.

Chapter 5

"Hello, Aleksei?" Nathan said when he heard the click, which indicated that the person on the other end picked up.

He looked around his new apartment, at the half-opened boxes scattered around the room. He had taken his sweet time settling into his new apartment. He packed everything he wanted to move and got it to his new place by car. It was a long and tedious task and he had to take a day off from work, since he had ten big boxes and had to make two trips to get everything transported. By the time he was done with his old apartment, it looked miserly and empty, with just the old, torn-up furniture decorating it.

Even the humongous TV was brought to the old apartment by Nathan, since Aleksei had an old piece of shit that was used back in the 90s. Nathan proceeded to put the landlord's old TV on the bedroom floor, which Aleksei took as a sign that he wouldn't be using it and took it to his own home.

"Hi Nathan, what wrong?" Aleksei asked with his usual, skip-the-formalities tone.

"Well, I just wanted to let you know that I'm moving out."

There was a moment of Aleksei's panting being heard over the phone, before he asked:

"Move? When?"

"Well, I actually already found a new apartment. So, since the next rent is due in a little more than a month, I'll pay you for the remaining month, so you can find enough time for a new tenant." He had hoped that Aleksei would get the hint, which was *give me my deposit back*.

Another moment of silence ensued, as Aleksei breathed heavily over the phone, as if trying to wrap his head around what Nathan was saying. He took a deep breath and said.

"Okay. We must to meet and uh… how to say… check breaks…"

"Evaluate the damage. Yeah. When do you wanna meet?" Nathan impatiently filled in for him.

"I'll arrive 3 pm." Aleksei said.

"Alright, see you later, Aleksei."

He knew that the landlord wouldn't let things go so easily and would try to find some reason as to why he should keep the deposit or deduct money from it, so Nathan prepared a bunch of counter-responses to it. He was by no means greedy, but when it came to Aleksei, he would fight until the last penny, just so that bastard wouldn't have it.

And that's exactly what he did, come 3 pm. He went back to his old apartment, scolding himself for ever being able to live in a place like that. Moving out was an eye-opener which allowed him to realize just how shitty that place really was. It was like a toxic relationship. Once you get accustomed to it, you feel like it's normal until one day you finally get out of it and ask yourself, why the hell did I put up with that?

That's what his best friend Sam explained to him as an analogy multiple times. *Shit, I gotta let him know the news.* Nathan thought to himself. It's been a while since the two of them spoke, due to their busy schedules, but this was definitely something he would want to know.

As he expected, Aleksei started inspecting every nook and cranny of the apartment, trying to find the slightest blemish or fault. Nathan stopped him in his tracks though, and hired a cleaner to take care of everything right after he took his things out. He told the cleaner to take notes of anything that may have been damaged and luckily, nothing like that was found, save for the toilet and the oven, which were really not his fault and he had already reported to Aleksei and Milo.

Still, he allowed Aleksei to carry on with his inspection, without uttering a word. He knew that trying to convince him that everything was fine besides the aforementioned things would be futile. When Aleksei finally arrived to the toilet and tried flushing it, he said.

"Toilet broken." He accusingly pointed to it.

"Yeah, but it broke before, remember? And you refused to fix it, so I had to call Milo. And *pay* for the repairs out of my own pocket. Remember?"

Aleksei scratched his double chin, not responding to this. He continued to the kitchen, where he whipped out a crumpled piece of paper with Ukrainian words and numbers next to them, after which he opened the kitchen drawer and started counting the utensils. This was surprising even for Nathan, the fact that Aleksei had a specific number of silverwares written down. Aleksei would probably find it surprising that the number was higher than whatever was on his list, especially for the knives, which Nathan had to buy to replace the dull ones which were in the apartment.

After he was done silently counting, the landlord didn't utter a word. Of course he didn't. He would probably want to keep the surpluses, the cheap motherfucker. Once he finally reached the oven, he said.

"You broke oven."

"I told you, Aleksei. That oven is a piece of shit, it keeps breaking every month or so. I had to pay at least three times to get it fixed."

Like with the toilet, Aleksei ignored Nathan's response and instead waltzed over back to the paper he had brought with him. He flipped it on the other side and pulled out a pen from the chest pocket on his shirt. He breathed heavily, as he wrote something in silence in Cyrillic letters, putting numbers next to names, which clearly indicated costs.

Once he was done, he showed the paper to Nathan, as if he would understand Ukrainian language and said.

"Oven and toilet broken. It take about 500 dollars to fix."

"I'm not paying for that." Nathan flat-out said, not even caring about being polite to this greedy bastard anymore, "I paid for repairs a dozen times. The washing machine, the sink, the oven, the toilet. I'm done paying, Aleksei."

"Then I keep deposit. I have to pay repairs." Aleksei said with a shrug.

"That's your problem. You can keep the deposit, but then you won't get your rent money. Or if you prefer, we can call the inspection, so they can decide who's in the right and wrong here."

This was a bluff, but he knew that Aleksei would refuse involving any third parties into this.

"No inspection. You pay repairs and rent and I give you back deposit." Aleksei sternly said.

Nathan stared at him for a moment, before smiling widely. He gently tapped his hand on the kitchen counter and said.

"Okay, Aleksei. Okay. I'll pay for the repairs. But if you insist I do that, then I'll be calling the IRS, so we can see if there's something amiss over here."

Aleksei widened his eyes at this and scratched his fat cheek, as his forehead visibly started glistening from the sweat that began beading up. Nathan detected frustration on his face. Finally, the landlord crumpled up the paper and said.

"Okay, Nathan. You were good tenant. No need to pay repairs. I'm good man, I will pay."

"Alright. Then you can keep the deposit as my last month's rent, how does that sound?" Nathan asked, unable to contain his smile.

Aleksei nodded docilely, his double chin shaking like pudding.

"I have to repair apartment. You go out now." Aleksei said and pointed to the door.

Nathan victoriously nodded and strode out of the apartment, not even dignifying Aleksei of a proper heartfelt goodbye.

Chapter 6

Nathan wanted to add some personal décor to the apartment, but it already had its own touch, like the oil painting of the lighthouse in the bedroom, or the strange humanoid-looking figurine on the living room coffee table. He felt as if adding more décor to the apartment would only clutter it, despite it being just spacious enough for him to do a backflip in the living room (not that he could). Even the TV, which he loyally used for years was obsolete, with the giant, flat-screen mounted on the wall of the living room.

He decided he would just unpack and leave things the way they were for now and if he felt like it was missing a personal touch, he'd add something to it. Once all the moving boxes were empty, he stacked them inside each other and went out to throw them into the dumpster behind the parking lot. As soon as he opened the door and stepped outside into the hallway, he saw another tenant, an elderly lady with grey hair tied into a bun. She was standing in front of the door of apartment 303, which was just across the hall from 304. The keys jingled in her fingers and Nathan could see her wrinkled, veiny hands shaking. He made a step to the right and turned to face her.

"Hi, ma'am. I'm the new tenant of 304." he said with a grin.

The lady looked in his direction, making brief eye contact just for a second, before turning back to face the door without a word, her hands shaking even more fervently now, as she tried to stick the key into the lock. She looked anything but talkative, but then again, she looked very old, so Nathan assumed that she simply may not have heard him.

"My name's Nathan. I just moved in and just wanted to-"

Before he could finish his sentence, the lock loudly clicked throughout the hallway and the old lady swung the door open. She stepped inside her apartment and slammed the door in Nathan's face, a little too fast for someone who displayed such fragility just a moment ago.

Well, that was rude.

He raised his eyebrows in confusion more than annoyance and ultimately decided to shrug it off. As he carried the boxes to the elevator, he couldn't help but remember the story his ex-girlfriend once told him about a neighbor next door she had. She said that there was this crazy old lady in the building who kept running around with scissors and one time even cut the internet cord. She never hurt anyone aside from that, but it was still an inconvenience.

He wondered if this old tenant from 303 caused equal amounts of trouble and if it had anything to do with the fact that the price of the apartment was so low. Deciding that all of that was foolish thinking, he shrugged it off. This was his new place and today was the first day. There was nothing that would stop him from having a good day.

He continued down the hallway with the boxes in his hands. When the elevator door opened, a mesmerizingly beautiful, redhaired girl greeted Nathan with a smile, shyly glancing at him, before looking down. When Nathan stepped inside with the boxes in his hands, he looked at the girl and asked.

"Going down?"

The girl nodded, clasping her hands together in front of herself at the waist. The door closed and the elevator stood still for a moment, before it started descending.

"My name's Nathan. I just moved in." He wasted no time introducing himself.

"Maria. Nice to meet you." she said in a soothing tone.

"So, do you live in the building, Maria?" Nathan asked.

"No, I was actually just visiting my boyfriend." she replied with a smile.

Dammit. Nathan thought to himself as his hopes of getting to better know a hot neighbor were flushed down the drain instantaneously. The door of the elevator opened too soon for his liking and Maria gave Nathan another enchanting smile, before stepping out and saying.

"See you around, Nathan."

Nathan waited for her to get a head start, so that he could avoid the awkward situation of walking along with her after they've clearly said goodbye. The elevator door tried to close again, before Nathan hastily put his foot inside, causing it to reopen. Since the coast was clear enough to go now, he proceeded outside and tossed the boxes into the dumpster.

The morning was sunny, albeit a little chilly, and since the park was practically his backyard, he thought about going for a walk later. Unfortunately, it was a work day and he wouldn't be done until at least 6 pm, due to the myriad of bugs his team had been facing, and by then it would already be dark.

Maybe a night walk, then?

He went back to his apartment and that's when his eyes inadvertently fell on the door to the right – the storage. He had been so busy with moving that he hadn't even paid attention to it until now, but now it stuck out like a sore thumb.

It was a plain, brown, wooden door. It looked fairly new, with only a few tiny scratches here and there, but it in no sense looked like it was as sturdy as Jessica mentioned it was. He figured he'd try to open it himself and if that didn't work, he would just hire someone to do it. And if they couldn't do that either, then what can you do, it's just a storage anyway? Nathan assumed it was barely big enough to fit a broom inside, so he wasn't overly concerned with it. Still, he couldn't let go of this nagging feeling of wondering what was behind it. He was compelled to find out, even though he knew that in reality there really wouldn't be anything interesting or of use to him inside.

As he sat down to begin working for the day, he glanced at the door one last time and thought to himself.

I have a toolbox in the car. I can use that to pry the door open.

The morning was uneventful, but at 3 pm he had a remote brainstorming session with his team. He joined 5 minutes earlier and his manager Anthony greeted him. They made some small talk and Nathan moved the laptop around to show him the fancy new apartment. Anthony produced sounds like 'wow' and 'oh' in amazement. Other team members started showing up then and they started talking business.

Since the meeting took longer than they expected, Anthony gave the members a 5-minute break. Nathan muted his microphone and got up to go to the bathroom. As he was taking a leak, he heard something nearby that sounded like very faint, barely audible scratching, coming from the wall between the bathroom and the storage. He stopped doing his business and perked up his ears to hear better, but the scratching was gone. He got closer to the wall to figure out if he was just imagining things, but he couldn't hear anything else.

His thoughts were interrupted when he heard Anthony's voice coming from the laptop's speaker.

"Nate, you ready to join?"

Nathan flushed and washed his hands. He heard the cacophony of his coworkers calling his name multiple times with a hint of impatience in their voices.

They sure are in a hurry.

He sat back in front of the laptop. He realized that all of his coworkers were already back, so he unmuted his mic and asked.

"What's with the rush?"

Anthony said.

"Oh, we saw you standing in front of the laptop for a few minutes, so we called out to you to see if you're gonna join back. I guess you didn't hear us"

Nathan shook his head.

"I just came back from the bathroom this second."

"Oh, then it must have been someone else we saw just now."

Nathan frowned and said.

"Uh, no. I live alone, so…"

Still, something about what Anthony said made Nathan feel a cold shiver run down his spine. Anthony waved his hand dismissively and said.

"It was probably a camera glitch or something, then. I thought I saw someone's legs in front of the camera before they moved out of sight. I assumed it was you."

"I thought it was him, too." One of Nathan's coworkers said, "Hell, I even saw his laptop move slightly."

"Well, maybe the laptop was just placed awkwardly and slipped slightly or whatever." Another coworker added.

"Maybe his apartment is haunted." His Korean coworker Taedong said.

The majority of the group burst into a laughter. Even Nathan chuckled at the remark, but he wasn't sure if it was due to the humor or to hide his concern. He wanted to ask them what exactly they think they saw, but before he could say anything more, Anthony interrupted the murmurs of the group and said.

"Alright guys, let's get back to business. So, about that client bug we've had…"

Nathan couldn't properly focus for the rest of the meeting. He felt like he was being watched and although that idea seemed absurd, he kept glancing around the room suspiciously, but in a subtle way that wouldn't give him away to his coworkers. He tried to remember how he left his laptop and if it really moved and even glanced at the storage door, but eventually, he dismissed the theory as ridiculous.

***

Come 7 pm, Nathan wrapped up his remaining tasks and made a light dinner (in a perfectly functional oven). After that, he took a short break watching some TV. His gaze kept falling on the storage door, which he knew he had to fix, but his body just wouldn't let him get up. Just 5 more minutes turned into an extra hour and by the time 9 pm rolled around, he figured that it was too late and that the other tenants may not appreciate him making loud noises at this hour.

Guess I'll do it tomorrow morning. He thought to himself as he yawned. He knew he'd be too lazy to go down to the garage in the morning, so he went down now and brought the toolbox back upstairs. He put it next to the storage door and hoped he wouldn't bang his shin on it in his groggy state after he woke up. Just then, his phone started to ring. It was Sam. He didn't even have time to say hello after picking up, when he heard Sam's obnoxiously loud voice.

"What's up, you overtime-loving fuck?"

"Hey, come on. I don't work that much overtime." Nathan lied, as he sat down in front of the TV.

"Dude, you said you had over two hundred fifty hours of work last month."

"That's how it is with adult life, man. You'll understand when you grow up."

"Hardy-fucking-har." Sam said, "Anyway, haven't heard from you in a while, how's everything going?"

"Well, I just moved into a new apartment." Nate proudly proclaimed.

"No freaking way. You left good ol' Aleksei? *But who pay rent now?*" He imitated Aleksei's accent with the final sentence and laughed out so loudly at his own statement, that Nate had to move the phone away from his ear.

"Fuck that guy." he responded after Sam stopped laughing, "He can find someone new to live in that shithole."

"You didn't even invite me to a housewarming party. Not cool, bro."

"I'm inviting you now. Wanna come over tomorrow night?"

"Yeah man, I do. Just shoot me the address via text, because I'm real forgetful."

"I know. And it keeps getting worse every year."

"Fuck you." Sam chuckled.

They exchanged pleasantries and news on the phone for a while. Sam was a manager in a big company which sold concert tickets and despite him and Nathan having very different career paths and busy lives, they still found time to catch up. They've been close friends since middle school and Nathan went so far as to call Sam his best friend, which really meant a lot, since Nathan carefully selected his friends.

Sam often said that their friendship would last forever, because they became best friends in times of trouble. It all started when Sam plastered a sign that said KICK ME IF YOU THINK I'M GAY on Owen, the nerdy kid. After getting his round of kicks from the other students and even going into the classroom with the sign on his back, Mrs. Amstadt put together why everyone was giggling.

Since Nathan was in the front row and the most obvious one laughing, the teacher asked him if he did it. He said no, and when she asked him who did it, he shrugged. Mrs. Amstadt threatened to send him to the principal's office, to which Sam swiftly stood up and took the blame.

They were both sent to the principal's office and received detention, all the while laughing at Sam's clever prank. Ever since that day, they were inseparable. When he thought back to it, they both agreed that it was a cruel prank, but luckily Owen held no grudge against them. They were friends on Facebook and from what Nathan could tell, he was pretty successful running his own startup.

"Alright, well, I'll see you tomorrow then. I'll bring some beer or whatever. Sleep tight." Sam said when they were finally finished reminiscing old times and exchanging jokes.

***

He woke up in the middle of the night, drenched in cold sweat. He had no reason to be awake, and yet for no apparent reason, his eyes shot open, as he lay there on his side. He stared at the meager ray of moonlight that gleamed in through the portion of the bedroom window which wasn't covered by the blinds. He flipped over to his back and exhaled deeply, realizing he must have just had a nightmare. He tried swallowing, but his throat was so dry, that he may as well have had sand in there.

He fumbled for his water bottle on the nightstand, almost knocking it over in the process. Once he grabbed it and felt how light it was, he tossed the empty bottle on the floor and got out of bed with a frustrated groan. He went to the kitchen, turned on the lights and poured water into one of the big Viking-like mugs he bought in Prague. It was the most satisfying thing taking big gulps from it, letting the water sloppily slide down the sides of his mouth, especially when he was parched like now.

His stopped his loud gulps abruptly, when he heard something. He slowly moved the mug away from his mouth and gently placed it on the kitchen counter, while perking up his ears. There was a scratching sound coming from somewhere. Nathan made a few tentative steps towards the living room and flicked on the light switch. Bright lights immediately illuminated the living room, and as he darted his eyes around the floor, one thought crossed his mind.

If this apartment is infested with rodents or bugs, I swear to god I'm burning the place down.

The floor had nothing on it, but the scratching persisted, sounding like a rat gnawing on something. Nathan recognized the sound, because his parents had mice in the attic and sometimes he'd hear them in the walls, scraping and scratching. They never got inside the house, but it was still unnerving hearing them scurrying around at night.

He took a few steps further into the living room, confusedly looking around and trying to figure if the sound was getting louder or fainter. It was really hard to tell where the source of it was, so he turned around and walked back towards the kitchen.

The sound was now coming directly to his left and as he turned his head in the direction of it, he reprimanded himself for not realizing it sooner. In his groggy state, he hadn't even realized that the sound was coming from the storage door – just like it was on the first day when Jessica was with him.

He felt his heart beginning to race a little, as he held his breath, slowly taking a step towards the door, careful not to chase away whatever was in there. Once he was close enough, he slowly placed his ear against it. The sound was right in his ear now, steadily going downward with each motion. It was consistent, each scratch and pause in between lasting a precise amount of time.

Scratch. Pause. Scratch. Pause.

It was hypnotically deliberate, which made Nathan think that this couldn't possibly be an animal. And yet, he couldn't move his ear away from the door.

Scratch. Pause. Scratch. Pause. Pause.

The scratching stopped. Nathan just then realized that he was holding his breath and that his entire body was stiff. He stood still in anticipation, unsure if whatever was on the other side had heard him and decided to scurry away. The silence was unnerving. It was so quiet that he heard his heart beating in his chest at a rapid pace.

BANG!

Suddenly, a loud thud resounded on the other side of the door, so loudly in Nathan's ear that he felt the impact of the hit, making him recoil backwards and almost stumbling on his ass.

"What the fuck!" He muttered between breaths, as he felt his heart beginning to race a lot faster now.

Another bang resounded on the door, this one much louder and more sinister. Nathan's panic kicked in and all he knew was that he needed to get the hell out of there, so he turned towards the exit and bolted towards it. He swung the door open and brushed past the elderly man who was standing right in front of his door.

"Hey, what gives?!" The man took a step back in surprise, giving Nathan a contemptuous glance.

Nathan stopped by the wall opposite of the door and pointed towards his apartment.

"There's… there's something in there!" he said, his chest heaving from the lack of breath.

The old man frowned at Nathan and then looked at the apartment, before he himself pointed inside and asked skeptically.

"What, in there?" He raised his eyebrows.

"Yeah, they're right in there! I just heard them!" Nathan craned his head to peek inside and pointed towards the storage door.

The old man scratched his thick, white mustache and stepped inside with such confidence and authority, that Nathan immediately thought that he must be ex-military or police. The man stopped in front of the storage door with his hands on his hips. He looked at Nathan and pointed one finger towards the door.

"You mean in here?"

"Yeah, right there." Nathan felt a little more daring (and embarrassed) with the old man taking lead like that, so he got back inside and stopped next to him.

The old man looked at Nathan with what he detected was pity, as he scratched his cheek uncomfortably.

"Right, the storage room. They probably didn't tell you." The old man said.

"Tell me what?" Nathan asked.

"Mice." He grabbed the knob and tried to turn it demonstratively, before stepping back and saying, "The door to the storage is probably rusted shut or stuck somehow. It's been like that since the start. Probably the fault of the construction workers. Anyway, mice probably found their way inside through a hole or something."

"Wait a minute. Mice?" Nathan asked, making a disbelieving grimace.

"Oh, don't worry about it." The old man vaguely smiled at Nathan, probably seeing the distress on his neighbor's face, "They only live inside the walls, they won't be bothering you in the apartment. There was probably a hole somewhere in the basement when they built this place, so they managed to get through it or something. But there's no way they can get inside your place, this building is high-quality. Lived here for over three years."

"No, wait a second. That couldn't have been a mouse. I mean, there was a slam on the door. A loud one. They-"

"Mice." The old man interrupted Nathan and nodded, "They can get really big. You may have scared the little bastard, so he hopped or something. If they scare you, you can get a cat. This is a pet-friendly place."

Nathan frowned at the old man, offended by his statement.

"I'm not afraid of mice, thank you."

The old man raised his hands in defense and said.

"Hey, sorry. I meant no offense, kid. Anyway, just came to see what was going on in here. I heard you pacing around the apartment. I live below in 204, so it was really loud. I wanted to ask you if you could keep it down, it's kinda late."

Nathan looked at the floor, as if hoping to notice some phantom footprints on the floor.

"Sorry, I must have been walking a little louder when I woke up to get a drink of water from the kitchen." he said.

The old man chuckled.

"Well, this was *really* loud. I mean, it sounded like you were doing aerobic exercises in your boots here. I don't mind it personally, but my wife Margery is a really light sleeper, you know?"

Nathan dumbly opened his mouth to protest, but didn't know what to say. There was someone else in his apartment, jumping around in a heavy pair of boots? That didn't make any sense. The old man was probably just exaggerating.

"Are you sure it was coming from here? I mean, I live alone here." Nathan finally said.

The old man stared at Nathan for a prolonged moment, as if searching his face for something, before dismissively waving a hand and saying.

"Ah, you're probably right, could have been some other apartment. This building has real thin walls. Sorry about that."

"Don't worry about it."

The old man nodded and said.

"Well, it's pretty late, so I should get back."

He got past Nathan and exited the apartment. He stopped in front of the entrance and turned back around to face him, as he said.

"My name's Vincent, by the way."

"Nathan."

"Pleasure meeting you, Nate. You sleep well now, son." Vincent smiled under his bushy mustache, waved and disappeared down the hall.

***

Morning came and Nathan droopily dragged himself to the bathroom. After he was done with his morning routine, he was awake enough to notice the toolbox he so cautiously laid on the floor in front of the door and immediately remembered his duty. It was only 8 am, but he still had time before he had to start working, so he decided he would make breakfast and then start tinkering with the door.

He made some eggs and bacon, which he brought from his old apartment when moving and after getting reinvigorated by the first meal of the day, he finally felt motivated enough to try and open the door.

"Alright ma'am, let's try and crack you open. Don't worry, I'll be as gentle as I can." he said to the door comically.

The first and most obvious thing he tried was opening it by twisting the handle. As he expected, the door wouldn't budge. He tried pushing the door, but that didn't work, either.

"So you like it rough, huh?" He stepped back and nodded resolutely.

He braced himself and took up a position with bent knees, which gave him more stability. With as much force as he could muster, he rammed the door with his shoulder. He did so a few times, each time with more force. It was to no avail and by the time he was done, his shoulder was throbbing and the door hadn't budged an inch, not even during the moment of the impact. It was as if he was ramming a wall.

Since his shoulder couldn't bring down the door, he started kicking it. Again, no dice. What was this thing made of? The entrance door of his apartment was sturdy and there was no way he would be able to breach it, but this was just a plain, wooden door, in no way supposed to withstand a lot of force and yet, it didn't budge an inch.

"Okay. Okay. No problem." Nathan said, as he knelt down and opened the toolbox.

He glanced at the door, as if it were a person and smiled.

"Girl, you're about to get roasted." he said, as he started pulling out various tools.

He wanted to unscrew the hinges, since then he could just pop the door out of the frame, but the problem was, the door opened to the inside, so the hinges were inside the storage. He inspected the doorknob to see if there was anything that could be done about that, but no luck – he was too much of a layman for tackling more complex work. The worst thing was the fact that there was no keyhole, so the door probably had no key to begin with.

When all his options were exhausted, he decided to try and wedge a screwdriver into the gap between the frame and the door. The screwdriver couldn't fit in there, so he took out a hammer, as he said:

"Alright, we'll do this the forceful way, then."

He placed the screwdriver's pointy end to face the extremely thin crack between the frame and the door and carefully hit the back part of the screwdriver with his hammer. That did practically nothing, so he tried hammering with a lot more force. The screwdriver practically bounced off the door with a loud scratching noise, sliding down the frame.

"Shit." Nathan cursed, as he leaned in to inspect the damage done to the wooden surface.

He couldn't see anything with the naked eye, so he ran his hand across it to feel any irregularities. It felt smooth. He suddenly felt like he had pushed it too far with trying to open the door, that he meddled with things which he was not experienced with. He felt grateful for avoiding damage to the door, which could have easily been caused by his carelessness.

Defeated, he nodded at the door silently and packed up his tools. It wasn't over yet, though. This was a job for someone who was trained for it.

Chapter 7

"How's it going, Nate?" Sam grinned with a smug face when Nathan opened the apartment door.

"Sam?" He raised his eyebrows.

He glanced at his watch and realized it was 7:30, a little earlier than he expected him to arrive.

"Come on in. How did you get past the gate code?" He gestured for his friend to come in.

Sam stepped over the threshold, gently cradling the bottle of wine with both hands.

"There was a polite old lady who was just entering the building when I arrived. I asked her to hold the gate for me and she was happy to oblige. We actually rode the elevator up to this floor and made some small talk along the way. She was really nice and all, told me about her grandkids and then when I told her where I'm going, she just got serious all of a sudden."

That caught Nathan's attention. He asked.

"Wait, was it the lady from across the hall? 303?"

"Yeah, that one. Pretty weird. But anyway, who cares."

Sam proceeded into the living room, leaving Nathan with a confused frown. He started to connect the dots and whatever was going on with that old lady, somehow it seemed that she didn't have a problem with Nathan, but with the apartment and those who lived in it.

Sam's amazed whistle came from the living room, as he shouted.

"Damn, quite a place you got here, Nate. Where'd you find the leprechaun?"

Nathan joined in and told Sam to make himself at home.

"I actually got this place pretty cheap. I was surprised, too." he said with a chuckle.

Sam sat in the sofa in front of the window and put his feet on the coffee table.

"Take your goddamn feet off the table." Nathan warned him.

Sam grumpily obliged, rolling his eyes.

"You told me to make myself at home."

"Yeah, that's my bad. I forgot what you're like."

Nathan grabbed two wine glasses from the top drawer above the kitchen and a corkscrew from the bottom and took them to the living room. He sat on the couch and placed the items neatly on the coffee table.

"So, what's the deal with this place? Someone die in here or something?" Sam asked, with a mischievous grin.

"You wish. To tell you the truth, I don't even know, myself. I suspect there may be one reason why they lowered the price, but it just makes no sense to lower it so much."

He looked at Sam, who now stared at him with a grievous expression in anticipation. After three or so intense seconds passed, Sam turned his palms upwards and shook his head with an I-don't-understand grimace, before saying impatiently.

"Well, what's the reason?"

Nathan looked at the door of the storage room and pointed towards it without uttering a word. Sam snapped his fingers, before raising his index and saying.

"Right, gotcha. You got a dead body in there."

"You know, I would not be surprised if that were the case. But seriously though, the problem is, the door can't be opened."

"Huh." This seemed to intrigue Sam.

He hastily stood up and walked over to the door, stopping inches in front of it, with one hand on his hip and the other on his chin, in a thinking posture.

"Can't be opened, you say?" he asked with an arched eyebrow.

Nathan stood up and raised his palms, shaking them at Sam.

"No, Sam. No, no, no. I know what you're thinking, but trust me, it won't work. I already tried opening the bastard. It won't budge."

Sam turned to face Nathan and smiled.

"I see. Yeah, I understand. You probably tried everything, yeah?"

Nathan nodded and continued silently staring at Sam, suspecting that he was not done putting forth his suggestions. His fears came true a moment later, when Sam shouted.

"But you didn't try the *Samwich Kick*!"

As he uttered the final word, he performed a spin-kick towards the door. As his foot connected to the door with a loud thud, he suddenly lost balance and fell on his face with an even louder thud.

"Ah, Jesus fucking Christ." He muttered on the floor, touching his teeth with his fingers to see if anything was broken.

"Jesus, Sam. Are you alright?" Nathan knelt down, worried that his friend may have injured himself.

"Yeah, yeah. I'm fine. Am I bleeding?" He looked at his fingers as he ran over his teeth.

"No, you barely even hit the floor, you moron. What were you thinking?"

"Ah, fuck." Sam groaned, as he propped himself in a pushup and then got back up.

Nathan got up as well, in time for Sam to turn back towards the door.

"Impossible. My Samwich Kick didn't knock the door down. My Samwich Kicks always knock doors down."

"That was years ago, back when you were still in training and more agile than a tortoise." Nathan chuckled.

"Well, shit. You're right, then. If my kick didn't bring this bitch down, then it's impregnable. What is it, anyway?"

"Just a storage room. I've never seen inside, obviously, but it's not an important place in the apartment. Anyway, the agent who got my lease said that the price was probably lowered because of that. Which is pretty neat, if you ask me."

"Well, whatever. That head bang nearly killed me. I'm just gonna sit this one out and take some painkillers in the form of red liquid."

Nathan couldn't help but laugh again at Sam's idiocy. His friend didn't find it so interesting, however. The next couple of hours were spent drinking and talking. Sam did most of the talking, as he was generally like that. When he drank however, he was more so talkative. He proceeded to tell Nathan about the girl at work called Cindy he was hitting on, and how she was giving him the cold shoulder, pretending to be hard to get, but that he was convinced that he would get on her good side.

Nathan warned Sam about getting in trouble with HR over it, but Sam seemed confident enough in his charm. Their conversation subtly transitioned into marriage and kids and despite all of their high school and college classmates being married and with kids, Sam and Nathan felt that they weren't ready for such a commitment. Nathan had short-term relationships here and there, but he wanted to focus on his career more first, find some stability, then find a girl that would be special to him and gradually build something meaningful from there. Sam on the other hand, wanted to bang chicks with daddy issues and low self-esteem until he was ready to settle down.

Despite their differences, they supported each other vehemently. Sam looked like a sociopath on the outside, but when it came to his friends, he was capable of showing strong empathy. When Nathan started liking Amy from art classes in high school, Sam encouraged him to ask her out. He did, and they ended up dating for a few months. When Nathan was on the fence about quitting his old job to join the current company, Sam encouraged him to do it, despite everyone else telling him to settle for what he had. The bottom line was, if it weren't for Sam, he would have missed out on some of the things in his life and for that, he was abundantly grateful to him.

When Nathan finally asked Sam what he really wants in life, Sam thought for a long time, before saying.

"I wanna quit my job and travel the world, man."

Nathan was about to laugh, when he saw how serious Sam was.

"Quit your job?" he asked.

Sam nodded.

"Yeah. I've been saving up some money and I think I'll do that in a year or so. I've been delaying it for such a long time, but not anymore."

For a moment, Nathan was overcome with a moment of profound sadness. He realized how old the two of them were getting and wondered if they would remain in contact after Sam left for his trip.

Once they were done with the serious topics, Sam told Nathan how he started listening to old songs a lot more often lately. When Nathan asked him to confirm if he was referring to old songs from their childhood, Sam shook his head. He whipped out his phone and tapped on the YouTube icon. He typed something in and a moment later a song started playing. It was *Born Free* from Matt Monro. As soon as the introduction music was done and the lyrics started, Sam started to sing along with his hands raised high up.

Nathan reminded him to keep it down, since the others were probably sleeping, to which Sam obliged unhappily. He proceeded to tell Nathan more about some of the songs he liked and about a playlist he insisted on sending to him.

It was almost 2 am when Sam glanced down at his watch and realized that he had work early tomorrow. Nathan had to wake up early as well. It was a Thursday night and he hadn't planned on having Sam stay over for so long, but when they started talking, he forgot about the time. As Sam waddled to the exit, he gave Nathan a layman military salute and said.

"Well, see you around, Nate-man."

"Try not to get yourself killed, Sam." Nathan saluted back.

Sam turned around and Nathan closed the door.

"Born freeeee, as free as the wind blooooows…" He heard Sam singing out in the corridor, as he made his way out of the building, wondering of any of the neighbors were woken up by his enchanting voice.

Chapter 8

Time went by slowly the following day. Nathan only got about five hours of sleep and hated himself for not predicting that a friend like Sam might end up staying later. He felt good after catching up with his friend though, so he had no regrets. Around noon he finally snapped out of his groggy state and managed to pick up the pace. Every time he got up to go to the bathroom, the storage door would come into sight. It bothered him a lot more than he wanted to admit to himself.

He decided he would call someone over to take a look as soon as he was done with work. He got back to coding, but whenever he'd look up from the couch, his gaze would inadvertently fall on the sturdy door, which mockingly stood in silence.

Eventually, he decided to go to the bedroom desk, telling himself that it's better to work from one spot which is only used for that purpose. And it was the truth. He loved working from his bed in the past, but when he finished listening to the TED talk which explained that your brain gets confused if you use one place for multiple purposes, which thus results in sleep disorders, he tried to always work from home by designating a certain workspace.

Working was much more convenient when he didn't need to worry about shitty insulation. Here, he comfortably worked in his t-shirt, something which would not be possible in Aleksei's apartment. His thoughts came back to the winter days he spent in his old apartment, when he needed to wear a jacket and double socks, just to get the feeling back in his toes, sniffling as he typed on the keyboard. Or the summer days, when he couldn't stop sweating like a pig, despite the air conditioner blasting away all day. It turned out later that the AC was faulty - just like everything else in the apartment - and couldn't go below a certain temperature. Aleksei of course, refused to fix that as well.

Once Nathan was done with work, he looked up some door repair services online and called a few of them, until he finally got one that actually picked up the phone.

"What?" The guttural voice on the line answered.

Nathan was taken aback by this rude attitude, but decided to give them a chance before he jumped the gun.

"Hi, I saw your website, it said you specialize in door repairs."

"Yeah." The man answered so briskly, that Nathan paused for a moment, expecting a follow-up.

When none came, he continued.

"Well, I have this door which needs fixing. Can you send anyone to take a look at it?"

The man muttered a barely audible 'mhm', after which he remained silent some more.

"So… do you have anyone or…?" Nathan asked awkwardly.

"Hold on, I'm checking the schedule." The man said, "When do you want it fixed?"

"I dunno, as soon as possible, I guess. Do you have any availability today?"

"Today... oof... going to be hard to do it so soon. I would need to finish one other place earlier-"

"That's alright, if you can't do it, I'll look up someone else, thank you." Nathan cut the man off, fed up with his attitude.

As expected, the man quickly interjected.

"Now, hold on, hold on. I just realized there's one slot available, so I can squeeze you in there. How does 7 pm sound?"

"Perfect. Here's my address."

"Alright. Our guy will be there soon."

Nathan grinned on the phone complacently, proving once again to himself that if someone is a piece of shit, you need to treat him as a piece of shit to get respect or proper treatment.

***

Although the door service guy was thirty minutes later than he said he should have been, Nathan didn't mind. As long as he got someone to look at the door. The repair guy was a skinny-looking man around Nathan's age, who had a thick New York accent. He was surprisingly polite and talkative, despite Nathan expecting someone as grumpy as the guy on the phone.

"So, where seems to be the problem?" he asked with a smile on his face, as he stepped inside the apartment, looking around in fascination.

"Right here." Nathan pointed to the storage door "I can't get this bastard open. I tried a little of this and that, but it just doesn't wanna budge."

The repair guy laid his toolbox down and tried the knob, as if that would just magically get the door open. *Oh, there you go, problem fixed, sir. That'll be $300.*

"Well, let me try and pry it open." the guy said, "I may or may not damage the door a little bit when opening it and in the worst case scenario, the lock will have to be replaced, just so you know that these things are unavoidable sometimes."

"Yeah, no problem, man. You do what you gotta do, I don't care how you do it, I just really want it open."

"Right-o. Let me see what I can do here." He reached down into his toolbox and started pulling out various tools which Nathan wouldn't even know how or when to use.

"Can I get you something to drink? Coffee, or some juice or something? Beer, maybe?" Nathan asked, standing behind the crouched repairman rummaging through the toolbox.

"No, thank you, I'm fine. Actually…" He looked up at Nathan, "Can I get a glass of water, please?"

He asked so politely, that it'd be impossible to say no. Nathan wondered how a guy like that worked for an asshole like the one he talked to over the phone, but he quickly reminded himself that his boss may have just had a bad day – maybe an Aleksei-type customer, maybe a frustrated housewife complaining about something not working, or about the outrageous price, or demanding to speak to the manager.

"Do you want some ice with that water?" Nathan asked.

"No, no, just water please. I have a very sensitive throat, you know. A little colder than usual and I can't speak properly the next day. It's really a shame, because I usually have to drink cold beer slowly and that's no enjoyment for me."

"Yep, I know how you feel about that. I just drink it and regret it later." Nathan said with a grin, to which the repair guy chuckled, as he stood up with a vice-like tool in his hand.

Nathan handed him the glass of water, which the man thanked him for and took a few sips, before giving it back to Nathan.

"I'll leave the glass here on the counter, you feel free to refill it whenever you want." Nathan said.

He placed the glass down and got back to the guy, who was now doing something with the aforementioned tool, which looked like measuring the door.

"So uh… can I help you in any way?" Nathan asked.

"No, no, it's fine. This can only be done by one person, so I'll try some things out and let you know in a bit how it goes."

Just then, Nathan's phone vibrated and upon unlocking it, what he dreaded came to pass. There was an urgent task that his team needed help with.

Better get to it, then.

"Alright, well you feel free to do whatever is necessary. I'll be in the other room, gotta get some urgent work done. If you need anything, feel free to come in." Nathan said to the man.

The next thirty minutes or so Nate spent in the bedroom, trying to figure out what caused the bug and how to fix it, while the sounds of banging intermittently came from the other room, distracting him and often startling him. He knew that the repair guy had to do it in order to get the door open, so he wasn't irritated.

He started contemplating what he should tell the landlord once the door was opened. Nathan would cover the costs of the repairs himself, but how would the landlord feel about the whole thing? Maybe telling him about it would be a bad idea in itself. His thoughts were interrupted by three steady knocks on his bedroom door.

"Come in!" Nathan shouted and faced the door.

The repair guy tentatively peeked inside, before stepping in and saying.

"Hi, um. There seems to be a problem here. The door is a lot tougher than I initially thought. So I may have to resort to some other measures, with your permission."

"What kind of measures?" Nathan frowned, not liking the direction which this was going in.

"Most likely, I'll have to saw my way through the door to get to the other side. It will completely damage the door, but at least you'll be able to get in. Is that okay with you?"

It was okay with him, but his thoughts again returned to how the landlord might react, and that was the only thing stopping him from just telling the repair guy to go ahead and do his thing. He thought for a moment, before concluding that he really, *really* wanted the door open. He wanted to be sure about the tradeoff however, so he asked.

"Well, how much does it cost to replace an entire door?"

The repair guy crossed his hands and tilted his head.

"Well, that depends on the kind of door you're looking for. It can range from $80 to over a thousand. Our company can get doors installed for you at an average price of about $300. All I would need is to get the measurements and we'd be able to get it done for you in a couple of days, as soon as the door arrives. Hell, you can even choose the color and type."

That was a relief.

"Alright, you got me. If you gotta break down the door, then do it. How long will that take?"

"Shouldn't be too long. Just gotta make a hole big enough to reach inside, is all." The man smiled.

Nathan nodded.

"Well, I'll be here if you need anything else."

The man nodded back and left the bedroom, gently closing the door behind him. Nathan was pretty much done with the bug he had to fix by then, so he slumped down on the bed and browsed Facebook a little. The electrical sawing noise started then and it was ear-piercingly loud enough to wake up the dead. Nathan felt bad for the neighbors having to endure this annoyance, but he hoped that they wouldn't complain, since it was 8 pm – therefore not too late or too early.

He tried to block out the outside noises by scrolling through memes and interesting posts, until he got to one news article which caught his eye. It had a picture of a coin with two faces on it and underneath it said *'Janus was the God of doors, gates and transitions. He represented the middle ground between abstract dualities such as life/death, beginning/end, youth/adulthood, rural/urban, war/peace, etc.*

Underneath the picture was an actual link which said *These were the gods in Roman Mythology*. The god of doors… Nathan shook his head, bemused at the fact that Facebook had once again proven its surgical precision at stalking people and tailoring content for its users based on their browser history. He *was* interested in mythology though, so he clicked the link.

There was a numerical list of gods which Romans used to believe in and Nathan skimmed through the article, but the one that really caught his eye was the one he saw in the thumbnail – Janus, the God of doors and gates. It said the following:

It seems like the ancient times had a god or goddess for everything: Poseidon, god of the sea; Venus, goddess of love and beauty; and Apollo, god of the sun. In Roman mythology, Janus was the god of doors, gates, and transitions. Janus represented the middle ground between both concrete and abstract dualities such as life/death, beginning/end, youth/adulthood, rural/urban, war/peace, and barbarism/civilization.

Janus was known as the initiator of human life, transformations between stages of life, and shifts from one historical era to another. Ancient Romans believed Janus ruled over life events such as weddings, births, and deaths. He oversaw seasonal events such as planting, harvests, seasonal changes, and the new year.

It is further emphasized that Romans believed that special doors and gates would open only during certain times, or when certain conditions were met (appeasing Janus with a proper sacrifice, etc.). It was believed that these doors would go through what we know today as 'limbo' and ultimately lead to the Underworld.

There was another knock on the door, startling Nathan out of his focus on the article. He hadn't even realized that the sawing and buzzing had stopped.

"Yes?" he shouted and the door opened.

The repair guy timidly stepped in, with an uncomfortable expression on his face.

"Hi, sorry to bother you again. We uh… we seem to have another problem."

"What is it?" Nathan stood up from his bed.

"Come with me, I'll show you." The man said, pursing his lips.

Nathan followed him to the door, where he saw a plethora of tools strewn on the floor. His eyes fell on the electrical saw, whose blade looked like it had been badly damaged.

"So, uh. I can't get through the door." The man said awkwardly.

"What do you mean you can't get through? It's just wood there, right?" Nathan asked.

He looked at the door and realized that he saw not a single scratch on it. It looked as pristine as the first day he came to see the apartment.

"That's the thing." The man shrugged, "I don't think this is actually wood. I mean, it feels like it, it looks like it, but…"

He knocked on the surface of the door three times loudly, which in turn produced a woody, hollow sound.

"But nothing seems to be able to get through. It's like it's made from material I've never seen before. And trust me, I've seen all sorts of things in my eight years of work."

"So, what's the next best thing we can do to get it open?" Nathan sighed in disappointment.

What was the deal with his impregnable door? He ironically pondered calling the SWAT unit and telling them that there's a hostage in the storage and watching them scratch their heads as they were unable to breach the door even with their explosives.

"Well, that's the thing. I've never had it come to this point. But apparently, when worse comes to worst and the door won't open, the only remaining thing to do is to break down the wall. But repairing it will cost an arm and leg."

"Dammit." Nathan cursed, now finally beginning to understand why the landlord kept the door locked.

Well, of course he did, if he had found a way, he would have opened it earlier and raised the price of the apartment. This was it, then. Nathan would just have to live with the fact that the door was inaccessible. It wasn't important, anyway. It's like Jessica said, he could always use the storage in the basement. So what if he had to walk all the way down to retrieve some items? It was worth the low price of the apartment. Now that he thought about it, the last thing he needed was the landlord to get angry over him fixing the door or deciding to raise the rent because of that.

"Alright, let's just leave it how it is, then." Nathan said, "How much do I owe you for this?"

"That'll be $150 for coming out, nothing for repairs. I'm really sorry that I have to charge you for not being able to help you with it, but it's company policy."

"No, it's fine. I totally understand. Thank you for coming out on such short notice."

Despite not having to do so, Nathan tipped the door guy $20, to which the man thanked him politely. As soon as he was out, Nathan locked the door and got back to the storage door. He put his hands on his hips and shook his head in disappointment.

"I guess you win. You can keep your secrets." he said, as he turned around and went back to sit on the sofa.

Chapter 9

Nathan woke up in the middle of the night, drenched in cold sweat. It was his first nightmare since he moved to the new place, not counting the one from a few nights ago when he woke up panting. He couldn't even remember when was the last time he had a bad dream. In fact, he couldn't clearly remember what the nightmare was about, until he exited his bedroom to grab a glass of water and gazed upon the locked storage door.

Fragments of the dream started to come back to him, like forgotten images resurfacing from his childhood. He remembered standing in a dark place, in front of a giant door. He couldn't remember anything more than that, but all he knew was when he woke up, his heart was pounding against his chest rapidly and he was drenched in cold sweat.

"Stupid." he said to himself as he gulped down the water and placed the empty glass in the sink.

He staggered out of the kitchen, dismissing his dream as a projection of stress from work. Still, he couldn't help but stare at the door as he made his way around the corner. *It's just a stupid door, nothing more.* He glanced at his watch and realized it was 3:43 am. He still had time for a few hours of sleep before he needed to get up. Without even finishing his thoughts properly, he drifted back into sleep.

***

The following day was uneventful and he started to feel a little claustrophobic for not leaving the apartment in days, so he decided it was time to stock up on food and other supplies. He worked until only 3 pm, so he had the freedom to spend the rest of the day productively (which he ended up not doing.). As he was about to leave the apartment, he got a call on his phone. He expected another call about an urgent issue at work, so he was surprised when he realized the call was from Jessica.

"Hello?" He picked up the phone tentatively, already bracing himself for trouble.

"Hi, Nathan. It's Jessica. How are you?"

Small talk first, okay.

"Hey Jess. I'm good, just finished work for the day, so I'm going grocery shopping. What's up?"

"That is great. How's the new apartment?"

"Great! Everything is in working order and I'm making it homier, the place is really great, I love it."

"I'm really happy to hear that. I'm actually just calling to see if everything is okay with the apartment and if you needed help with anything."

That's it?

He chuckled into the phone, scolding himself for being so paranoid. He was so used to getting calls from Aleksei only when something was wrong, that a call from Jessica to just check up on him felt strange.

"Yeah, everything is great! I got no complaints whatsoever!"

Not even about the door? A nagging thought in his mind said, but he quickly pushed it back.

"I'm so glad to hear that. If you happen to have any problems at all, don't hesitate to call me. The agency will handle all the necessary repairs or anything like that." She paused for a moment, "Except that one pesky door. That one can't be opened at all."

"Yeah, I know. I tried calling someone over, I mean, I was going to cover the costs of the repairs, but they literally couldn't saw through the door."

"Huh." Jessica said curiously, "Was there by any chance any damage done to the door or the frame?"

"No, nothing like that. The repair guy threw everything and the kitchen sink at it and it didn't so much as make a scratch. Say uh, Jessica, you said you never saw what's behind the door, right?"

"No, it was like that when I first saw it. I've been an intermediary for that apartment for about two years now and the door has been closed since. Other tenants tried opening it too, but they were stumped."

"I guess everyone new who moves in decides he's gonna be the big hero to pry open the door, huh. Maybe the door is like Thor's hammer, you know like, it won't open to anyone who isn't worthy."

Jessica chuckled heartily at the nerdy joke, which was a pleasant surprise to Nathan. His jokes would often leave people with blank stares, not understanding that he was being sarcastic. *Gotta work on that punchline,* he often told himself. Jessica continued.

"Alright, well that's all, then. Again, if you happen to run into any kind of problem, don't hesitate to contact me. I usually work until around 6 pm and can be there within ten minutes or so, depending on the circumstances."

"Thank you, Jess. I really appreciate it. Have a good one."

The call with Jessica left Nathan feeling good. He'd never had a landlord who was welcoming and kind, so to have someone call just to check up, like Jessica did, made him feel appreciated as a tenant – even if calling was just part of the agent's job.

Once he left the apartment and got downstairs, he saw a resident of the building his own age checking the mailbox.

"Hi there." he said to the neighbor.

He was about to exit the building, when he saw the old lady from 303 walking in. He stepped aside and held the door open for her.

"Afternoon, ma'am." He nodded.

She looked down the entire time, as she silently strode in.

"Hi, Jimmy." She pleasantly said to the man at the mailbox who just finished grabbing a bunch of envelopes from his mail.

"Good afternoon, Mrs. Rogers." He replied.

The old lady got up the stairs and disappeared out of sight before Nathan could say anything more. He opened his mouth dumbly and pointed towards the stairs, as he looked at Jimmy and said.

"Did you just see that? She outright ignored me."

Jimmy shrugged.

"Maybe she didn't hear you say hi or something."

"I thought that, too. But this is the second time she just ignored me. Maybe she just doesn't like me." Nathan said, still holding the door open.

"No, that can't be." Jimmy called the elevator, "Dolores is the sweetest old lady you'll ever meet. She doesn't not like anyone."

The elevator door opened and Jimmy stepped inside.

"Well anyway, gotta go. See you around, buddy." He waved.

Nathan waved back and went out to buy groceries.

***

It was almost 8 pm when he returned to the building. While he was out, he stopped at a restaurant to have a well-deserved, fancy meal, after which he actually went to buy groceries. He started to feel slightly nauseous while at the restaurant, which he assumed was from the food, however he got better almost as soon as he got back home.

He stumbled into the elevator with the paper bags he was barely able to hold and fumbled for the third floor button. He ignored the urge to put down the bags, despite his fingers burning from the weight. He scolded himself for stocking up on so much food, but as the elevator door opened, he thought to himself.

My momma didn't raise a two-trip grocery bitch.

His footsteps echoed as he made his way to his apartment. Once he stopped in front of the door, he had no choice but to put the bags down in order to grab his keys, which he silently sighed in relief for. He bent down and gently placed the bags on the floor, careful not to break or squish anything that found itself on the bottom. He was about to straighten his back, when he heard it. A sudden, muffled thud coming from inside his apartment.

He instantly froze, perking up his ears, as he stopped breathing at the same time. It was eerily quiet. It sounded to him like the noise which pesky kids make and then try to be as quiet as possible, because they realized they've been heard. Nathan slowly straightened his back, becoming painfully aware of the loud, rustling noise his jacket was making in the process. He turned his head to the left and slowly leaned in closer to the door with his ear, to see if he could hear anything.

Nothing. The sound of his own heartbeat pulsing all the way up to his head was the only thing he was able to hear, as he did his best not to breathe, unaware a couple of times that he was running out of breath, until he forced himself to inhale slowly once again.

Thud.

Another sound came from inside, followed by a quick pattering of footsteps, maybe five of them, before they abruptly stopped. Nathan recoiled, stifling a gasp. Someone was definitely in there.

"Hey, is anybody in there?" He shouted at the door.

Silence was his response. Whoever was in there was probably aware that they were really loud, so they abruptly stopped making noises. But how did they get inside in the first place? There was no way the intruder could have entered, unless he had a spare key. Windows were out of the question.

"I'm calling the police!" Nathan shouted and stepped away from the door.

He didn't know if the burglar was armed and he didn't want him to panic and go guns blazing, so he opted for allowing professionals to handle the situation. He took out his phone and dialed 911. The operator answered almost instantly.

"911, what is your emergency?" A female voice asked on the other end.

"There's a burglar in my house. I live on 47 SW Morrison Street, Apartment number 304."

"Sir, are you in danger right now?" The operator asked.

"Yeah, I'm just outside my apartment. But I can hear him in there."

"Sir, please keep your distance from the apartment. A patrol unit has been dispatched and will be there in a few minutes. Do you need me to stay on the line with you?"

"No, it's fine. Thank you. I'll wait for the officers in front of the building."

He hung up and hesitantly looked at his groceries, before deciding to leave them there. There really was only one way out of the building and Nathan doubted the intruder would be waltzing out of the building with a bunch of grocery bags. He raced downstairs and got in front of the complex gate, swiveling his head left and right, on the lookout for any police cruisers.

They arrived only a minute after he did and parked their vehicle elegantly in front of the building. Nathan half-expected the police to roll in with blaring sirens at a screeching halt, but that was of course only happening in movies and TV shows. Two officers stepped out of the vehicle and approached Nathan.

"Good evening, sir. You called about the burglar?" The older policeman asked.

"I did, officer. Right this way."

"Have you already been inside?" The younger police officer asked.

"No, I just heard some noises, like footsteps."

Nathan led them inside the building. They entered the elevator and got up on the 3rd floor, where Nathan pointed them in the right direction towards the apartment. The officers stepped around the grocery bags and approached the door and knocked three times authoritatively.

"This is the police! If anyone's in there, come out with your hands in the air!" The senior police officer shouted and waited.

A moment later, he nodded at the younger cop and drew his gun. The younger officer leaned in to his radio and informed dispatch that they're going in. The older cop tried opening the door, but it was locked. Nathan quickly fumbled for his key and handed it to the officer. He unlocked the door with a painfully loud click which echoed throughout the entire corridor. If the intruder wasn't aware of the police by then, he definitely was now.

"Wait here, sir." The younger police officer raised his hand at Nathan in a halting gesture, as he followed the senior cop inside the apartment, slipping out of Nathan's side.

Nathan anxiously tapped his foot on the floor. He looked behind and saw that his neighbor from 301 was timidly peeking in curiosity through the crack of his open door. Nathan pursed his lips and nodded to him as a greeting, before turning back to face his own apartment. He felt a mixture of impatience and nervousness, as he wondered if the burglary would turn into assault and possibly things escalating even more from there.

"Sir? Can you come here for a moment?" One of the policemen shouted from inside the apartment.

Nathan rushed inside, not sure what to expect. He saw the two officers with their guns holstered, hands on hips, as they stared in fascination at the storage door. When the senior cop saw Nathan, he pointed to the door and asked.

"Can you get this open for us?"

"Oh, right. That door can't be opened. Been stuck ever since I moved here."

"Hm." The officer let out the sound through his nose, as he looked back at the door, "Well, we checked the premises thoroughly and there seem to be no signs of burglary. Can you check if anything is missing?"

Nathan nodded and started skimming through his apartment valuables. There really weren't many precious things that could be stolen, save for his laptop and the huge TV he brought with himself and left in the bedroom (the one in the living room which came with the apartment would be hard to unmount from the wall). Once he was sure that all the important things were safe, he returned to the officers and said.

"Nothing valuable seems to be missing, officer."

The older officer nodded, as he scratched his cheek. He and his partner exchanged enigmatic glances, before the senior one faced Nathan again and said.

"And you're sure you heard sounds coming from *in here*? The sounds seem to be transferring a lot in this building, it's quite possible you heard it coming from another apartment. Upstairs, maybe?"

The condescending tone insulted Nathan.

"No. I'm positive it came from in here. I listened carefully."

The officer raised his eyebrows.

"Well, there are no signs of forced entry, the windows are all closed and we checked all the potential hiding spots. Now, unless your burglar someone managed to get… in here-" He tapped on the storage door twice with the palm of his hand, "Then you didn't hear it right."

Nathan looked at the door and then glanced around the apartment one more time, desperately looking for something that could help his argument. He heard the sounds inside the apartment, there was no doubt about it. The thudding, the footsteps, they all sounded like they were directly in his ear. The officer probably noticed the confused look on Nathan's face, so he said.

"Listen, if you happen to find anything missing, let us know and we'll see if we can't launch an official investigation."

"Yeah, I, uh…" Nathan's gaze inadvertently fell just behind the officer's feet, at the bottom of the storage door.

He saw something down there that he hadn't seen before. He blinked and squinted, trying to make out what he was looking at.

"Sir? Are you okay?"

Nathan snapped his head back to the police officer. He looked back at the bottom of the door, but nothing was there.

"Yeah, okay." He said, "Sorry to bother you like this. I'll call you if I find anything suspicious."

The officer tentatively nodded with a suspicious, penetrating glare.

"Alright. Well, you have a good night, sir."

They left the apartment and the younger officer shouted back from the hall.

"Don't forget your groceries, sir."

Nathan couldn't help but stare at the storage door, more baffled now than he was when he heard the footsteps ten minutes ago. He squatted down to inspect the bottom of the door once more. Nothing. It was as pristine as it was the day he moved in. But he was sure he saw something for that split second when the officer was talking to him.

Something that looked like four, tiny, crude scratch marks, starting on the floor near the door and disappearing under the bottom.

Chapter 10

"Wait. What?" Sam asked over the phone with a slight chuckle.

"I'm not lying, man." Nathan replied, as he put the chicken and potatoes in the oven and turned the dial, "I was right outside my apartment when I heard someone from the inside. It sounded like something was knocked over, or something like that. And then there were footsteps."

"Shit, man. Well, maybe that's why the price is so low. They didn't tell you that it was haunted." Sam made a high-pitched *boooo* ghost sound, before he burst into laughter.

"Stop kidding around man, I'm serious."

Nathan wasn't amused. *I guess this is payback for me laughing at your failed Samwich Kick.* He thought to himself.

"Alright, alright, sorry. Anyway, I'm sure it must have been nothing. In some buildings, sounds travel through pipes and it sounds like it's coming from somewhere else, you know?"

It was surreal to hear Sam coming up with such logical explanations, especially given the fact that he was a paranormal enthusiast. When he first told Sam about the strange occurrences with the door, he thought that his friend would lose his shit about it being something paranormal. The lack of Sam's response was… not Sam-like.

"Yeah, I guess that must have been it." Nathan said, "I mean, there was no way that someone was inside. And there's no way that someone is like, squatting inside that storage room. I'd smell something for sure. And not to mention that it wouldn't be stuck so well, unless he welded it shut, and even then it's questionable."

"Yeah, I hear ya." Sam replied, "You know I think you're probably just overthinking the whole door thing. It's just a door, that's all."

"Maybe. But it's not just the sounds coming from the door, either. I still don't understand how the repair guy was unable to breach the door. I mean, it literally damaged his tools."

"Shit. Well, maybe it's made from some super strong material. Like, titanium or some shit."

Nathan stopped in front of the locked door with the phone in his hand. He carefully ran his fingers over the smooth surface, trying to feel any irregularities. He glanced down at the bottom, where he saw the scratch marks last night. Was that his imagination, or did he really see it?

"No, that makes no sense." He said to Sam, "Something really weird is going on here."

"Hm." Sam was obviously speechless and probably skeptical at Nathan's assumptions about the door, "Well listen, I gotta get back to work. I'll talk to you later. Don't stress about the damn door, man."

"Yeah, I should go, too. Have a good one, bro."

The rest of Nathan's day was uneventful and he was feeling pretty tired by the end of it. He was having a lot of trouble sleeping since he moved in, which he attributed to him not being used to the new bed yet. He never had any trouble sleeping in new places before, but maybe this bed just didn't suit him. It was around 10 pm when he decided to go to bed.

***

He found himself entrenched in the same nightmare from a few nights ago. He had completely forgotten about the dream, until he found himself immersed in it once again. In it, he was in a pitch-dark place, surrounded by what looked like fog. In front of him was a giant door in a frame, standing in the middle of the darkness. It towered above him threateningly like a skyscraper, obscuring his view. For some reason, he couldn't compel himself to move. He just stood there, mesmerizingly staring up at the door in a trance.

And then, the door started to creak as it began to open. It creaked so loudly that it permeated the entire room menacingly. The gap between the door and the frame grew wider and wider and Nathan was able to see inside, but the only thing he saw was more darkness. And then, when the gap was wide enough, something emerged from within. Four grey, bony fingers wiggled their way out and grabbed the edge of the door, their jagged long nails visible even in the permeating darkness of this place. The creaking got louder and louder, and then…

Nathan shot his eyes open. He realized that he was staring at his bedroom ceiling. His heart was pounding and he had difficulty breathing. He was drenched in cold sweat and a sudden realization hit him – the creaking persisted, even now when he was awake. It was loud enough to send a cold shiver down his spine and as he lay there listening to it, he realized that it was the same door creaking that he heard in his dream. And it was coming from outside his bedroom.

It only lasted for one prolonged moment, before it slowly dissipated and then completely stopped. Nathan wondered if he had imagined the whole thing in his groggy state, but there was no doubt about it – it wasn't just in his dream. He glanced at his watch and realized it was 2:20 am. Slowly, he got out of bed and went out to see what was going on.

He knew that there was no possibility for an intruder to be inside, so whatever this was, he wouldn't be able to go back to sleep until he checked it out. He peeked outside of the bedroom towards the living room, but saw nothing there, even with the meager light from the streetlamps shining through the window. He slowly stepped outside the bedroom and took a few steps forward. He instinctively peeked left around the corner and what he saw there made him gasp audibly. The storage room door was wide open. He swiveled his head left and right to make sure he was alone in the apartment, and when he realized he was, he tentatively stopped in front of the storage door, peering inside. But what lay beyond wasn't a storage space.

It was a long, dark hallway.

Chapter 11

Nathan felt like he was still in that same dream, as he stood transfixed at the door. There was no way what he was staring at was real. The corridor in front of him, despite being abnormally dark, stretched way beyond what a normal storage room should be. He couldn't see far, but from what was visible in the dim apartment, Nathan saw dilapidated concrete walls, floor and ceiling, barely wider than the door frame, enough for one person to fit in.

He suddenly felt an irresistible urge to step closer to the corridor, go inside and explore it, but he just couldn't will himself to make that first step. The darkness ahead was so permeating and threatening that it seemed sinister enough to devour anyone who stepped inside. Nathan had to know what was in there. He rushed to the light switch and flipped it, instantly illuminating the entire living room with a blinding light which hurt his eyes momentarily. He stepped right in front of the storage room once more and frowned when he realized that turning on the living room lights did nothing to break away the darkness inside the corridor. It was as if the light from the apartment couldn't penetrate past the threshold of the door.

What *was* this room, anyway? Was it some kind of optical illusion? The corridor led directly towards his bathroom, so the wall of it should have been right there, and yet instead it extended further than his eyes could see. Baffled by this whole thing, he rushed inside the bathroom and looked to the right. The toilet seat and the bin for laundry were right there, by the wall. He approached and reached for cold surface, half-expecting his hand to simply fall through. When he felt the cold surface on his fingertips, he chuckled at his own absurdity. But that still begged the question – what in the hell was that storage room exactly?

He happened to glance at his watch as he held his hand on the wall and realized it was 2:35. Somehow, it's already been 15 minutes since he woke up. Where did the time go? Has he been staring at the door for that long in his trance?

He rushed back outside and stopped in front of the door once more. He held his breath, as he heard something from the inside, in the distance. It sounded like very faint creaking. It lasted only for a short moment, but it immediately reminded Nathan of the nightmare he had about the door opening and the skinny hand reaching inside. Was there another door somewhere inside? None of this made any sense.

"Hello? Is anybody in there?" He daringly asked, hearing his own voice cracking from the dryness.

His voice echoed, but silence was his response. He glanced at his watch again. 2:48. The longer he stood there, the stronger the urge to go inside got. The corridor was beckoning him, tantalizing him like a mermaid luring a sailor with her song - and he was about to answer its call. Blanking his mind, he took a step forward across the threshold. He immediately felt an unnaturally cold air enveloping him. There was a clear threshold in temperature of the living room and the corridor, like an invisible wall that couldn't be penetrated. It felt like stepping outside of a sauna during winter.

Nathan put his left hand on the door and pushed it. The door wouldn't budge. He put both his palms on the door and tried pushing with all his might, stepping over the threshold now entirely. A shiver ran down his spine as he felt the cold go over his entire body like a freezing wind. The door wouldn't budge even when he pushed with his entire strength. Pulling didn't help, either. It was as if it was stuck in place. For some reason, that didn't surprise him. The utter realization started to hit him that whatever was going on in this apartment was not scientifically logical.

He turned to the side to try and get past the half-open door, before a terrifying realization hit him. What if the door closed on its own while he was still inside? He glanced at his watch again. 3:03. Where did the time go so quickly? It was as if the door somehow hypnotized him, making him lose track of time.

As much as he was tempted to explore the corridor, he still had his ability to think rationally, despite it being so late. He didn't have the proper equipment to go inside and he had no idea how far it would extend. At the back of his mind, he knew that the corridor couldn't extend too far, but then again, there shouldn't have been a corridor there in the first place, so he had to be ready for anything once he broached the doorway. And the last thing he wanted was to get stuck inside the place without any proper light sources, food or water, unable to open the door.

He shuddered at the thought that the banging and scratching he heard earlier from inside may have been from a victim who got trapped inside. He leaned across the threshold, feeling the cold wrap around his arms once more and grabbed the door's edge with both hands. He tried pulling it once more, but the result was the same as before.

Defeated, he returned to the living room and sat on the couch, facing the door. As he tried to swallow, he felt how dry his throat was, so he quickly stood up and strode to the kitchen. He poured a glass of water, cautiously glancing at the door every second or so. He didn't want to admit it to himself, but he felt vulnerable turning his back to the door. He felt like he was being watched by someone… or something, from the darkness of the mysterious corridor. His mind unconsciously kept returning to the nightmare about the door that creaked open and the bony hand which wiggled its way inside.

He stared at the door with a penetrating gaze while drinking his glass of water in three big gulps. He loudly slammed the glass on the kitchen counter while still looking at the door. This was a mistake, because he accidentally slammed the glass upon the edge of the counter and it toppled over and broke on the floor with a loud shattering sound.

"Shit! Goddammit." Nathan said, as he stepped over the shards of the broken glass, careful not to cut himself.

He went to the bathroom to retrieve the broom and dustpan, while not taking his eyes off the storage room. When he accidentally almost bumped into the wall, he realized it was time to focus. He retrieved the items and returned, checking the gap at the door and trying to compare it to when he got outside. The door was still wide open. He got back to the kitchen and swept up the broken shards of glass, carefully disposing of them in the trash can. He put the broom and dustpan next to the bin and approached the door once more. After observing it carefully, he returned to the couch and slumped down on it. He became aware of his heart racing and chalked it up to excitement, rather than fear. He glanced at his watch.

3:12.

Nathan nervously tapped his fingers on the armrest, doing his best not to blink too frequently, afraid that he may miss the door closing. Time went by painfully slowly as he glanced at his watch every minute or so. At 3:15 he stood up and approached the door again. *Maybe it opens only during certain hours? Or during certain nights*? He suddenly remembered what he read earlier about Janus, the god of doors. The urge to go inside was almost irresistible now, but whenever he felt tempted to step inside, he reminded himself that there might be a maze in there, with no other way out.

3:16. He sat back on the couch.

3:17. He nervously tapped on the couch armrest, intermittently glancing from his watch to the door.

3.19. The sound of creaking began reverberating throughout the living room so loudly, that it made Nathan's heart jump into his throat. He looked up wide-eyed and realized that the creaking was coming from the door, as it was closing. He stood up with explosive speed and stared in bafflement, as the gap between the frame and the door grew ever smaller.

Click. The lock of the door resounded loudly when the door shut. Nathan blinked fervently a few times, before standing up and approaching the storage door. It was closed completely. He tried turning the knob and pushing the door, but just as he expected, it wouldn't budge, leaving its undiscovered secrets unearthed.

He asked himself silently why the door opened now and if he would ever see it open again. He has lived in this apartment for about a week now and he has never heard the door creaking or anything similar happening, so his assumption was that he was either a heavy sleeper, or the door hasn't opened until tonight. He had to know what was inside, though. All the noises he heard from before started to make more sense now, which terrified him. That day when he heard footsteps and called the police, someone was in his apartment. And they probably got in from the mysterious corridor.

Chapter 12

It was his day off, so he slept until noon. When he woke up, he was relieved to realize that it was all a nightmare. He staggered over to the bathroom and after he was done with his business, he went to the kitchen. He took out some eggs from the fridge and cracked them into the frying pan. After he got four of them opened, he put the shells into one another and tossed them into the trash bin.

He was about to turn around and turn on the burner, when his eyes fell on the broom and dustpan next to the trash.

"Oh shit." He mumbled to himself at the utter realization that last night was in fact, not just a dream.

He jerked his head up in the direction of the door. It was closed. Of course it was. But it definitely opened last night, he wasn't imagining it. And there was a long-ass corridor inside, not a storage room. What time did the door open? 2 something? 2:20, yeah, that was it. The door opened at 2:20 and closed at exactly 3:19 am. If it always opened and closed at the same time, then it meant that Nathan had only one hour to explore. That may be enough, depending on the length of the corridor. But it was impossible to tell just how long it really was.

He grabbed his phone and set the alarm for 2:15 am. He felt a little ridiculous going on this sort of expedition, but he just had to know what was in there. He wondered if the landlord knew anything about this and that that was the reason why he lowered the price. Anyway, it didn't matter. He'd wait and see tonight if the door would stay open for the same amount of time and if it did, he would go in and check it out himself the following day. But he couldn't do it without proper equipment, no he needed to be prepared. He would go out today and buy some supplies. A flashlight, because he couldn't rely on his phone which had such rotten battery, especially with the torch on. And some long ropes. If the corridor actually twisted and turned, then he could easily get lost, but tying a rope around his hand and on something in the apartment would help him find his way back if he got out of sight of the door.

He felt feverish at this new adventure he was about to embark on. He was somewhat daunted, yes, but his excitement for exploration outweighed his fear. As a kid, he always played around in the backyard of his home digging holes, pretending to be an archeologist. And whenever his parents would take him to playgrounds, he'd go inside the big tubes and pretend to explore uncharted areas, rather than play with the other kids on swings and see-saws. Although he chose a different career path, since being an archeologist was less lucrative and adventurous than Indiana Jones implied, his passion for exploring never dissipated.

In fact he used any chance he could when he went on vacations to go trekking in areas off the beaten path, or visiting historical landmarks and learning about ancient culture. He once even took a cable car to Mount Hua in China to go on what was considered the most dangerous plank hike in the world. The trail on the side of the mountain face was so thin, that travelers had to be harnessed to avoid falling and just looking down made Nathan feel dizzy. He made it halfway through, until he got too tired and decided it was time to go back. He ignored the laughs of elderly Chinese people who chugged along the path like it was nothing.

This whole thing with the door brought him back to his childhood and reminded him of how he abandoned the career path he was passionate about over one that was more fruitful. Still though, as excited about exploring the corridor as he was, he couldn't help but notice a sense of dread which gradually grew inside him, like a seed that slowly sprouted. This corridor was unnatural, there was no doubt about it, but what exactly was it? A portal to another dimension? If that were the case, then he could be in a lot of trouble if he got lost there. He tried not to think about it, as the feverish excitement in anticipation of exploring took over his rational thinking.

He knew that he had to prepare well for it though, so he had to get in contact with someone who was somehow connected with the apartment. He couldn't possibly be the first one to see the door open. Since the landlord was in hiding, he decided he would call Jessica and see if he could get any more information about the previous tenants from her. She probably wouldn't just give him the information, so he devised a plan.

He picked up the phone and scrolled through his call list. He didn't have Jessica memorized in his contacts list, but he still remembered which number belonged to her. It was the weekend, so he was on the fence about calling someone during their off time, but he had to get some info before tonight. He then also he remembered that Jessica told him not to hesitate in case he ever needed anything, so he dialed her number. *I'll make it quick.*

She picked up after just two rings.

"Hello?" She answered in a more casual tone than what Nathan was used to.

"Hey, Jessica. It's Nathan."

"Nathan, hi!" Her tone immediately got more perky and formal, "How's everything going?"

"Good, good. Listen. Sorry to call you on the weekend like this. Do you have a moment to talk?"

"Yeah, not a problem. What can I do for you?"

The abrupt shift in her tone from something that felt human to customer support-like didn't sit well with Nathan. He felt like he was talking to an automated machine, which already had programmed responses. He tried to ignore that thought as he paced around his living room and stopped at the window. He for some reason had a habit of always looking through the window whenever he had a conversation on the phone that he had to focus on. He said.

"Well, uh... I wanted to ask you about the previous tenant."

"Previous tenant?" Jessica sounded confused.

"Yeah, I uh... I found something in the apartment which I think may belong to him. So I was wondering if there's s way for me to contact him, so I can give it back to him?"

"Huh, that's... strange. I thought we cleared out the whole apartment. What did you say the item in question was?"

"Oh, it's uh..." Nathan quickly looked around his living room, trying to find something that he could throw in to pass as a missing item.

Idiot, not thinking ahead.

His eyes fell on the little Buddha statuette that his mother gave him for his birthday a few years ago.

"It's uh, some kind of a statue or something. A pretty small one, so…"

"I see." Jessica said somberly and paused for a moment, "Well, what we can do is we can send someone to pick it up and give it to her."

Her? So the previous tenant was a woman? That's a start.

"Oh, I don't wanna bother you guys. Is there a way that I can give it to her personally? I could call her to pick it up or something."

"I'm afraid not." Jessica said with fake sadness in her voice, "We have a strict company policy not to reveal any information about the previous tenants, so the only way we can do it is if we take it to her."

"I see." Nathan said, as he stared at the crowded parking lot outside his window, not sure what to say next, "You know what? I'm sure it's not that important. If she starts missing it, she'll call you guys, right?"

"If you think that she may come looking for it, then I can come pick it up and give her a call, it's not a problem for me."

"No, no, it's okay." Nathan said, starting to feel a little uncomfortable now.

His plan backfired and if worse came to worst, he'd have to give up his Buddha statue, playing dumb and pretending it's the lost item of the previous tenant. He really didn't want to give up his mother's gift, but if it came to it, he'd have no choice now that he screwed up with his dumb tactics.

"Is everything else okay?" Jessica asked.

"Yeah, everything is fine. I also just had one question about the storage door. Did the landlord ever mention it opening at any time, like ever?"

"Not that I know of. He told us that the door has been stuck since the beginning and that he tried opening it, but that nothing worked. We never tried opening it ourselves and the few tenants who lived there before you asked about it, as well. But unfortunately, no luck opening it."

"The few tenants? I thought this building was pretty new."

Jessica paused for a moment before answering.

"Yeah, it is. The tenants usually found new places or moved out of the state due to new jobs, or some other things that came up for them." She quickly recited.

There was something in the way she said it. Her tone was too serious, contrasting the typically jovial intonation she usually had. And the way she uttered the sentence was too smooth, as if she rehearsed the line to perfection. *Maybe I'm just overthinking things.*

"I see. Alright, well thank you, Jessica. Sorry again to bother you."

"Not a problem at all. Call me if you need anything else." Her tone returned to its perky self.

"Thanks. Have a good one."

He mumbled a barely coherent *dammit* under his breath as soon as he hung up. He sat down on the sofa, staring at his locked phone, his thoughts wandering elsewhere. He suddenly remembered Janus, the Roman God of doorways. He wondered if the Romans were actually on to something with their knowledge about traveling between worlds, if the corridor behind his storage door was just a pure coincidence. Sam knew more about these things. He was fascinated by mythology, the occult, the unexplained, paranormal, etc. He could ask him.

Without hesitation, he dialed the number. It rang five times before Nathan hung up. If Sam didn't answer by the fourth ring, he wouldn't answer at all, since he always had his phone on him at the ready. He could try again later instead. For now, he had to go buy some supplies for his expedition tonight.

Chapter 13

The building was quiet when he made his way out to buy the things he planned. He browsed long and hard at the convenience store, while the employee breathed down his neck the entire time. Eventually, Nathan asked him what he would recommend him to bring in case he had to go down a chimney. The employee initially suggested calling a chimney service, but when he saw how determined Nathan was about doing things himself, he offered to sell him a 200 foot-long rope. Nathan decided to buy four, much to the bewildered expression of the clerk. And then the look in his eye changed. Nathan saw that look before – in Aleksei's eye, when they were bargaining for rent. It was the look which said 'this guy is a sucker, so I should try and swindle more cash out of him'.

Sure enough, the clerk offered the most 'durable' aka the most expensive rope there was, claiming that buying anything cheaper was not worth it and risked snapping, especially under more weight. Nathan frowned at the man, before deciding to go for the one which cost half the price, just to spite the employee. Next, he bought a flashlight and five packs of batteries. Again, the clerk recommended the $180 heavy-duty torch, which would not only illuminate, but blind anyone staring directly at it. Once again, Nathan politely declined and took the regular one.

Once he paid, the clerk thanked him with a smug smile on his face, which unmistakably told Nathan that he fell for the man's trap and bought exactly what the clerk intended him to buy. It was an age-old trick – offer something way out of the customer's price range and then show him something significantly less expensive, but still expensive.

Feeling like a fool for the second time today after his call with Jess, Nathan grabbed his things and stormed out, not even dignifying the clerk with a proper goodbye.

***

He had started feeling nauseous again while driving back home. It only lasted for a very short time and ended before he returned to the apartment. He scolded himself for eating all the junk food for so many consecutive days in the past few weeks and swore to himself that he would lay off for a while.

When he returned, the building was equally quiet as when he left. It was past 3 pm, so he figured that most of the people were napping. It was a cloudy, gloomy day only meant for sleeping anyway and Nathan himself felt the weight on his eyelids as he unlocked his apartment and stepped inside.

He barely managed to lay out the items he bought on the kitchen counter, admiring their pristineness, when the doorbell rang. He jerked his head towards the entrance, half-startled at the sound.

Another neighbor here to complain? He thought to himself as he grabbed the doorknob and swung the door open. In front of him stood the old man from two nights ago, Vincent. He had a serious expression on his face (at least Nathan thought it was serious, but he couldn't see under his thick mustache). When he saw Nathan, his cheeks puffed up, which Nate realized was him smiling.

"Hey, Nathan. Am I interrupting anything?"

"Mr. Vincent, good afternoon. No, not at all."

"Just Vincent." It sounded like an order, not a request.

"Vincent." Nathan emphasized with a nod, "What can I do for you?"

Vincent raised one hand dismissively and looked down for a brief moment, before looking back at Nathan and saying.

"I just wanted to introduce myself properly. I realize that I may have been a little harsh last night when we just met." He looked at something behind Nathan, before saying, "Do you mind if I come in for a few minutes?"

Nathan was taken aback, but he couldn't think of an excuse on the spot, so he stuttered, before saying.

"Uh, yeah. I mean, not at all. Come on in."

He stepped aside and Vincent nodded, as he walked in. They went into the living room and the old man stopped in the middle, putting one hand on his hip and using the other to scratch his chin. Nathan couldn't help but notice the bulging veins on Vincent's biceps below the sleeve of his shirt. The old man had to have been pushing 60, but he'd still be able to kick Nathan's ass with no trouble whatsoever, he reckoned.

"Really nice place, I gotta say." Vincent said, taking in the view.

"You haven't been in here before? While the other tenants lived here?" Nathan asked.

"No, never even stepped on this floor until you made me do it."

Nathan thought that the old man was angry, until Vincent turned around to face him and smiled once more. His eyes fell on something behind Nathan once more and Nathan suddenly realized that Vincent was staring at the kitchen counter and inevitably at the items that rested on top of it.

"Going on a hike somewhere?" he asked, pointing behind Nathan.

Nathan looked behind at the items, feeling like a kid who was caught red-handed doing something wrong. He felt the need to justify his actions to the old man, just like he did to his parents when he was a kid, but he quickly dismissed that ridiculous thought the next moment, remembering that he was a grown-ass adult and didn't need to explain himself to anyone, let alone his neighbors.

"Uh, yeah. The weather was nice the past couple days and I've been real lazy working from home, so, you know." He shrugged.

Vincent nodded.

"Must be some extreme hiking, if you need a rope and flashlight, huh?" Vincent frowned.

The way he stared at Nathan made him feel like he was being interrogated, rather than questioned.

"No, not at all. But I *am* going on a night hike, so that's why I made sure I had a flashlight."

"And the ropes? Kinda looks like you're getting ready to climb Mount Everest." He chuckled heartily.

Nathan returned the chuckle, practically feeling Vincent's invisible prodding fingers.

"No, just going to the park nearby. But I like to be ready in case I ever run into any dangers." he said.

Vincent nodded, raising his eyebrows as if to gesture that he understood what Nathan said. He turned around and took a few slow steps around the room, glancing at the furniture.

"Which trail are you going hiking on?"

Fuck, I don't know.

"Trail 3." he quickly uttered, as he stepped behind the kitchen counter and poured a glass of water.

"3? I thought that one was closed." Vincent frowned, suspicion returning to his face as he faced Nathan.

Nathan took a long gulp, giving himself the time to think about his next response. When he was done, he said.

"Is it? I didn't hear about any closures."

Vincent turned around and made his way to the sofa, as he said.

"Yeah, apparently something happened there. No idea what, but the trail just abruptly got closed." He sat down and looked at Nathan with an intense stare.

He felt uncomfortable under Vincent's commander-like stare. He never enlisted in the Army, but he felt that this is what it probably felt like for soldiers to undergo morning lineup and inspection. It made him feel like the old man could read his thoughts and would call him out on it any moment. He continued playing along and hoped that all would work out okay.

"I see." he said, "Well, guess I'll just try another trail instead. Anyway, you want something to drink?"

He quickly tried to change the topic, feeling immensely uncomfortable. Vincent dismissively waved his hand and said.

"No, no. I gotta get back soon, my wife Margery is gonna kill me if I'm late for our Skype call with our nephew from Wisconsin."

Nathan's phone started ringing suddenly, to which he gave a silent prayer. *Saved by the bell.* He pulled it out of his pocket and said to Vincent.

"Hold on, I gotta take this real quick."

"No problem, son." Vincent said, as he pulled out his own phone from the back of his jeans and started texting someone.

Nathan thought to himself how this old man was so multi-practical about things. His own grandpa didn't know how to send a text from one of those old, big brick-like phones and Vincent here was texting on his touchscreen so rapidly that it would make any young social media-addicted person envious.

Nathan looked at his phone and realized that the call was coming from Sam. He swiftly swiped the green dial button to accept the call and said.

"Hey, Sam. Hold on just a sec, I'll call you back later, alright?"

"Yeah, no prob, bro." Sam said, before they ended the call.

Vincent was still texting, the loud noise of typing permeating the room. Nathan put his own phone back in his pocket and waited for the old man to finish texting.

"So, how do you like your new place, son?" Vincent asked, still typing vigorously.

"It's great. I mean, it was pretty cheap and you can see how nice it is. Are all the apartments in the building like this?" Nathan asked, as he sat down on the couch.

"Yep. Yep." Vincent nodded, as he stopped his texting just long enough to utter the sentence, "The place is fairly new, so all the apartments are luxurious."

He continued typing, as Nathan said.

"Well, this apartment is amazing. I can't for the life of me figure out why the old tenants left this apartment. You didn't happen to meet them, did ya?"

Vincent abruptly stopped texting, but continued staring at his phone. He raised his head to look at Nathan with apprehension in his narrowed eyes, as he pursed his lips and slowly shook his head.

"Afraid not. Like I said, I never even stepped on this floor, so I never got to talk to any of them."

"I see." Nathan tapped his fingers on his thigh.

Vincent brought down his head and continued texting a little more. A brief moment later, he slapped his knees and looked at Nathan, as he suddenly got up.

"Well, I'll have to get going now, Nate. I can call you Nate, right?"

"Sure, everyone does." Nathan stood up himself, "You sure you don't want to stay a little longer? I mean, I got some beer if you like."

"I'd definitely love to share a beer with you over a game or just on a lazy Sunday afternoon, but I really have to go. Thanks for the hospitality, though."

He brought his hand forward in a handshake, and Nathan took it, feeling the bone-crushing squeeze of Vincent's grip. As Nathan tried to pull away subtly, the old man leaned in a little closer to Nathan and said.

"Listen, Margery makes the meanest stew you'll ever try. So if you're ever up for it, feel free to stop by. I'm sure my wife would love to meet you."

He winked and finally released the grip, leaving Nathan with a throbbing hand. He turned around and opened the entrance door, as he waved and said.

"Be seeing you around, Nate. Be careful on that night hike of yours." He winked once more connivingly.

Nathan waved and closed the door. Despite being a stern guy and having a gaze that could burn holes in titanium, Vincent seemed pretty nice. Nathan wouldn't mind getting to know his neighbor better over a beer, like the old man suggested. As long as he wasn't around when Sam arrived – something told Nathan that the two of them, being so disparate, Vincent as an authority figure and Sam as someone who willfully disobeyed one – would not get along.

He called Sam back, who picked up before the first ring ended properly.

"Hey, bro." he answered jovially.

"Hey, Sam. Sorry man, a new neighbor stopped by to introduce himself. Pretty cool guy, but not your type of friend."

"Why?"

"I think he's ex-military or law enforcement or something. I mean the guy looks so tough he may have been a Navy SEAL, for all I know."

"Oh, brother." Sam sighed, "A brainwashed jarhead, huh. I do not understand why someone would willingly subject themselves to-"

"Sam, Sam. Sam. That's not why I was calling." Nathan interrupted him right away, knowing where this was going to lead.

He knew that if he let him get on his high horse, he'd start the same old topic about how all soldiers are brainwashed puppets of the government, waging war in a politician's name against falsely proclaimed enemies of the state. He heard that story a million times before, each subsequent time in a more detailed way.

"Alright, let me just tell you." Sam insisted, "There's this one guy on Instagram-"

"Goodbye, Sam."

"No, wait, wait, wait!" Sam quickly recited into the phone, falling for Nathan's bluff.

Nate couldn't help but stifle a peal of laughter.

"Alright, what did you want to talk about?" Sam asked.

"Well, it's gonna sound kinda weird, but. You know a lot about the paranormal and that kinda shit, right?" He faced the storage door, frowning as he spoke.

"Do I know about the paranormal." Sam sarcastically repeated what Nathan said, "Nate. Nathaniel. Nathanson. I am the king of the paranormal, the occult, the otherworldly and otherwise unexplained." he proudly proclaimed in a theatrically exaggerated manner.

"Alright, king. What do you know about doorways?"

Sam suddenly got serious, entirely contrasting his usual self. Nathan was always amazed at how serious he could be when it came to paranormal topics, whereas he was a goofball in any other situation.

"Doorways? When you say doorways, what do you mean exactly by it?"

"I mean, shit, I don't even know what I mean. Like, doors in our world that lead into other dimensions, portals maybe? Some doors which may twist our reality somehow or distort it? Like, remember that one documentary we watched about the pilot who claimed he went through a vortex in the Bermuda Triangle?"

"Oh, yeah. He claimed that his plane flew through a long corridor of some sorts for about 5 minutes, before he emerged at his destination. And technically speaking that was impossible, because he was hours away from it."

"Right, that one. What was that called again?"

"Wormhole." Sam exclaimed as soon as Nathan asked.

"Right, right. That's it. So, wormholes. What do you know about them?"

"Not too much, but enough to give you some basic info. Space agencies have been theorizing about them for years and claim that should one be discovered, we could travel long distances over short periods of time, because apparently, wormholes distort time and space and can either compress or stretch a portion of our plane."

"So… they could act like some sort of portal?" Nathan turned away from the door and stepped into his bedroom.

He sat by his desk, where his laptop lay on top of the smooth surface. He opened it and turned it on, the bright light of the screen casting a meager light in his dark room. Sam continued to speak.

"I wouldn't call it a portal. It's more like a fast lane, but imagine it being thousands, maybe millions of times faster. You enter a wormhole in Portland and boom. You emerge in New York a few seconds later."

"Huh. Interesting. But this is all just theoretical for now." Nathan said, as he opened up his browser and typed *wormholes* in the search bar.

"Yeah. Apparently, wormholes are really volatile and extremely small. But hey, scientists were wrong about a dozen other things they theorized about space. So, who's to say they aren't wrong about this, too."

"I see. Hm." Nathan tapped his index finger on the side of his laptop, staring at the Google search results in front of him.

"Why are you asking about all of this, Nathan? I never thought you were interested in- Wait. It's the storage door in your apartment, isn't it? Did something happen to it?

Did you manage to open it?" The excitement in Sam's voice was palpable over the phone.

"No, nothing happened with the door. I was just curious, is all. I read an article a few days ago about Roman gods, and one of them was Janus, the door god."

"The door god?" Sam chuckled wheezily into the phone, "Those guys had gods for everything, didn't they? God of war, god of wine, god of garbage bins…"

"Yeah, well. Anyway, Janus, the god of doors would open doorways which would connect our world with the world of the dead and the Romans believed that they could get the doors to open with proper sacrifices." Nathan shared that last bit of information, because he knew that Sam would be interested in it.

"Well goddamn. I gotta read up on that." The excitement in his voice showed no signs of subsiding.

It wasn't one of those bullshit 'I'll put it on my list' excuses. Nathan knew Sam long enough to tell that he was legitimately interested in the whole door ordeal. Sam cleared his throat and said.

"Alright, listen man. I'm going to investigate what I can about supernatural doors and portals, so we can see if we can't crack that baby open. Who knows, maybe there's something paranormal right behind the door, bro!" Sam's excitement only grew every passing second and Nathan knew that any second now, his friend would say that he needed to go and head off to read up on paranormal doors.

"Thanks, Sam. Let me know if you find anything interesting." he said and ended the call.

He started to feel a pang of guilt for not telling his friend the truth. He couldn't risk it, though. Sam would insist going on the expedition with Nathan and the corridor was too narrow and probably too dangerous. He couldn't put his friend in that kind of danger. He would explore the corridor on his own and if he deemed it to be safe, he would tell Sam and invite him for a tour.

Chapter 14

Nathan shot up, wide awake, as if he had been electrocuted. He glanced around and realized he was on the sofa of his living room. He was feverishly gripping the armrests of the sofa, breathing heavily. Once his haziness cleared out, he leaned back, wiping the sweat off his forehead in relief.

"What a nightmare." he whispered breathlessly to himself.

But he couldn't remember what the nightmare was about. Something was chasing him, that's all he knew. The rest was blurry. He raised his left arm and glanced at the watch. It was 10:24 pm. He must have dozed off some time ago, because he noticed that his phone still had Facebook open. He rubbed his eyes, realizing that he could sleep some more if he wanted to, since he had enough time. But as groggy as he was however, he didn't want to sleep anymore.

Upon swallowing, he realized that his throat was dry, so he went to the kitchen and gulped down the entire 15-ounce mug of water, making a splashing mess on the floor along the way. He heard his stomach rumbling and the inevitable feeling of hunger followed along with it. He felt too wobbly from sleeping to cook, so he instead ordered pizza from Boss Café. He spent the next half an hour or so browsing the internet, still too lazy to move from his chair.

Two minutes past eleven, he got a phone call from an unknown number. He suspected it was delivery from the restaurant, so he picked it up.

"Hello?" he said with a cracking voice.

"Hi, I have a delivery for Nathan. Are you home right now?" A male voice, who he recognized instantly as Bill asked on the line.

"Hi, yeah. Go right ahe- Oh. Shit." A horrible realization suddenly hit him, "You're at my old apartment, I forgot to update my address, fuck."

Bill remained silent on the phone, which only intensified Nathan's anxiety. He exhaled deeply and said.

"Alright, listen. I'm on a new address. I forgot to update it in the system, I'm so sorry."

"It's not a problem. Just give me the address and I'll be there."

Nathan slowly recited the address to Bill, emphasizing the code for the gate for him. Bill lethargically said he'd arrive in about fifteen minutes and hung up. He felt like shit for giving him the wrong address, especially since the guy was usually really busy with other deliveries. This at least, helped wake him out of his stupor and he felt more than ready for the storage door to open.

Ten minutes later, the doorbell rang and Nathan quickly got up to open it. He braced himself for Bill's judgmental and aggravated reaction, but he was instead greeted by the delivery man with a smile, balancing the pizza in one hand.

"Hey, Nathan. New place, huh?" he asked.

"Bill, I'm so sorry, man. I just woke up from a nap, I completely forgot to update my address."

Bill closed his eyes for a moment and waved his hand dismissively.

"Not a problem at all. I don't have any other deliveries right now, so you're good. That'll be $12.50."

"Shit, let me just get my wallet real quick." Nathan said, feeling even more like a klutz.

He took the pizza from Bill, the cheesy aroma filling his nostrils, which instantly made him salivate. He placed the pizza on top of the kitchen counter next to the ropes and torch and rushed into his living room. He scanned the furniture for his stray wallet, but was unable to locate it anywhere.

"Just a sec." He raised an index finger to Bill and made his way into the bedroom.

When the realized that the wallet wasn't there either, he checked the pockets of his messily splayed pants and jacket on the floor. No dice. He practically ran into the bathroom in a panic, hoping against hope that he may have left it on the laundry machine unconsciously. He glanced at the top of the machine, but all he found was toilet paper and a small basket filled with bathroom items.

He turned around, ready to get back to the living room to check it out, when his eyes fell on the sink. Inside the sink, contrasting its pristine, glowing whiteness was the brown square-shaped object, which he instantly identified as his wallet. The faucet was slowly dripping every few seconds right on top of the wallet. Instead of grabbing it, he squinted, leaning forward to see if he was losing his mind. He tentatively reached for it and grabbed it with the tips of his fingers, feeling its weight from the sogginess. He raised it up, watching in fascination as the water dripped slowly from it.

"How in the fuck did it end up over here?" he asked himself, as he shook the wallet violently a few times, straining it and making the water splash the sink.

He opened the wallet and realized that most of the items inside were unsullied by the water, as it was facing the away from the faucet while in the sink.

"Un-fucking-believable." he murmured, as he pulled out a twenty.

He strode out of the bathroom, waltzing towards the entrance.

"Hey Bill, sorry to keep you wa-" He froze as he rounded the corner, because he saw Bill inside his apartment, standing right in front of the storage door, staring at it with wide eyes.

Bill didn't seem to notice Nathan and continued staring at the middle of the door, seemingly enthralled. Nathan cocked his head, curiously looking at Bill, who didn't even seem to be blinking. His eyes were transfixed on one spot on the door.

"Uh… Bill?" he asked.

Bill showed no signs of noticing Nathan, as he made no movement whatsoever. Nathan started freaking out by this point. Something was terribly wrong here, but he couldn't tell what exactly. Bill's behavior shouldn't have been worrisome, especially since he could have simply heard the mice scratching inside and yet, Nathan had this feeling of dread slowly boiling inside him and steadily reaching to the top. Whatever it was though, he felt for some unexplained reason that he couldn't let Bill stare at the door any longer. He forcefully put his hand on Bill's shoulder and shouted.

"Bill! You okay?"

This finally seemed to snap Bill out of his trance and he jerked his head towards Nathan. He looked confused, as he darted his eyes around the room from Nathan to the door.

"Uh, sorry for the delay. Here's $20. You can keep the change for all the trouble." Nathan said and handed the cash to Bill, eyeing him carefully.

Bill looked down at the twenty bucks, before he hesitantly took it with extremely shaky hands and nodded multiple times in frenzied motion. Without a word, he just turned around and got out of there. Nathan raised his eyebrows, staring at the outside darkness of the hallway through his open apartment door, not sure what he was feeling. He looked at the door, but nothing seemed off about it. It was still the plain, wooden door it had been all these days. Except it wasn't and he knew it. Something was extremely unnatural about this door and not in a good way. Bill could feel it too, Nathan was sure of that.

It couldn't have been just scratching that he heard, because Bill looked scared shitless. He was pale and his eyes so wide that they looked like they could pop out of his skull. He must have heard something in there, something that terrified him. He couldn't be bothered with that right now, though. Whatever it was, maybe he would find out tonight.

Despite suddenly losing his appetite, he decided he needed to get his strength up for his exploration tonight.

He hastily closed the door of his apartment and locked it with a loud click. He took one already cut slice of pizza, trying to sever the cheese which held itself together over the top like glue. He was able to eat two, before his brain registered that he was full. The extra cheese was a mistake and the abundance of food he ate made him feel bloated and sleepy.

He allowed himself to drop on the couch and give himself some time to digest the fatty food. He glanced at his watch. It was 11:20 pm. He had three hours until the door opened, so he allowed his heavy eyelids to shut. He set the alarm for 2:15 am anyway, so it would wake him up a few minutes before the door opened. Even if it opened at a different time, he would hopefully be woken up by the creaking of it. Before he knew it, he fell asleep.

Chapter 15

A loud blaring of his phone alarm woke Nathan up. He opened his eyes widely and instantly jumped into a sitting position. He snatched the phone and looked at the screen. 2:15 am. He turned off the alarm and immediately looked at the door. It was still closed. He placed the phone back on the table and leaned back against the couch.

Oh crap, forgot to check the equipment.

He stood up and rushed to the kitchen counter, feeling excitement surging through him. He felt like he could run for miles, although he was well acquainted with that adrenaline-like experience and he knew that it would dissipate soon.

He flicked the torch on to see if it worked. It cast a large beam of light towards the ceiling and Nathan flicked it off. The flashlight looked like it could penetrate the darkness for quite some distance, so Nathan hoped he'd be able to see more in the corridor this time. He nervously glanced at his wristwatch. It was 2:17. *Just three more minutes.* He felt the same nervousness that he had before his first date, back in high school. Holding the flashlight firmly in his sweaty hand, he strode back to the couch and took a seat, since he had a clear view of the door from there.

2:18. Any minute now. He nervously tapped his foot on the floor, producing a rhythmic sound. He was in so much anticipation that he almost felt feverish.

3:19. He suddenly started pondering how he should have bought a remote toy car or a drone that he could attach cameras to and send into the corridor. It was really stupid of him not doing so, but if the door really opened every night, he would have plenty of chances to send drones in there.

Still 2:19. Time went by so slowly.

Click.

Nathan stood up and focused on the door. The click at the storage which distinctly sounded like the door unlocking echoed so loudly, that it resounded in the entire apartment. And then there was silence, like in a suspenseful moment of anticipation, or rather as if the ominous click of the door silenced everything around it.

And then the creaking started. The door began opening with such a loud creak that it pierced Nathan's eardrums. Slowly, the gap between the door and the frame widened, revealing more of its impregnable, devouring darkness inside. Nathan could do nothing but stand and stare at the door with a rapidly thumping heart, waiting for it to fully open and reveal its dark secrets.

When the dark corridor was fully in sight, the incessant creaking which stirred with it a cacophony of terror and annoyance inside Nathan finally stopped, leaving the apartment in utter silence once again. In his petrified state, Nathan only just then remembered the flashlight. He clumsily flicked it on and pointed it at the corridor, the beam bouncing violently up and down from his shaking hands.

Despite the flashlight having an extremely strong beam, it wasn't able to illuminate much. All he saw were grey concrete walls and then more darkness extending ahead, way further than any room in an apartment should have. Steadying his breathing, Nathan willed himself to take a step forward and then another, slowly approaching the enigmatic door, until he was standing right in front of the threshold.

Even from here, with the flashlight pointed directly down the corridor, he saw nothing but darkness ahead. It was as if the dark ahead was so thick, that even the beam of his light couldn't penetrate it.

"He-hello?" he shouted into the daunting corridor timidly, his voice slightly echoing inside.

Silence. He squinted and pointed his flashlight in various corners of the corridor, as if that would illuminate it more. There was nothing but absolute darkness there. The place was beckoning him, calling for him to come and explore its uncharted corridors. Maybe he could go inside for a little bit and come back if it turned out to be too much for him? He glanced at his watch and realized it was 2:21. He swiveled his head towards the kitchen counter, ignoring the pizza box and focusing on the stack of ropes in the bag. He looked back at the corridor.

Fuck it.

He walked over to the counter and pulled out one rope. He impatiently unrolled one of them and held it by one end. He frenetically looked around, until his eyes fell on the leg of the coffee table in the living room. It was a sturdy and extremely heavy table, so not only would it be able to hold the rope without sliding across the room, but if it *did* happen to slide, it wouldn't fit past the storage door. Nathan knelt down to the closest leg of the table and tied a layman knot as best he could. He grabbed the edge of the table with one hand and used the other to tug the rope with all his strength, in order to make sure it wouldn't come loose.

He tugged it a few more times and when he was satisfied enough with its stability, he stood up. He clumsily found the other end of the rope under the pile and tied it around his left wrist. He made the knot gentle enough not to scrape against his skin, but firm enough not to come loose. Just like with the table, he grabbed the rope with his free hand and yanked it, while providing resistance with the tied hand. Once he was sure it wouldn't come off, he turned his wrist towards himself and glanced at the watch. It was 2:25 am. He didn't have much time, but he figured he'd go exploring until 2:40, while keeping an eye on the apartment behind him. That would give him enough time to get back. He ran to his foyer and put on a pair of sneakers.

He knew that the apartment could be deceptive though, so he set his wristwatch alarm to the aforementioned time. He got ready to step inside the corridor, when he realized how parched he was. Feeling a little frustrated and impatient now, he ran into the kitchen with the rope around his hand and gulped a few big sips from his mug. He was now officially ready to go inside.

He stepped in front of the door, facing the darkness ahead. He pointed the flashlight in front, hoping for a different result this time, but the thick darkness still heavily hung in the air. He took a deep breath. Something was holding him back. It was a weird feeling. It was like the corridor was calling to him, but at the same time, something else was holding him back from entering. The one calling him was a temptation, while the one holding him back felt like a warning.

"Come on, Nathan. Don't be a pussy. Fifteen minutes. In and out." he said to himself.

Before he could give himself more time to think it over, he lurched forward and stepped inside, feeling his entire body getting shrouded in an inexplicable winter-like cold which made him shiver for a moment. He exhaled and saw his frozen breath in the air. Once his body got past that initial dive through whatever the invisible barrier between the apartment and the corridor was, he no longer felt cold. It was much colder in here, yeah, but not so much that he was freezing.

He looked back at the apartment, glancing at the living room and kitchen which he could see from here. It felt surreal, staring at his apartment from this angle. It was as if he entered a mirror world and stared at his place from behind the mirror.

Dismissing that minor fascination, he faced forward and started walking. He kept his flashlight pointed in front of him, illuminating every crack and blemish on the corridor floor and walls. His footsteps echoed steadily with every step he'd take and every time he'd glance down at the dusty (and probably the immensely cold) floor, he was sure he did the right thing by putting his shoes on.

He glanced back at his apartment. He was a solid dozen feet away from it now, the light from it barely illuminating a small portion of the corridor near the entrance. Seeing his apartment from there was calming like a lighthouse in a tumultuous sea and he felt reassured every time he'd glance back at it. He slowly continued walking forward, as his light seemed to have more trouble illuminating the area in front of him. The beam was getting shorter, as if the darkness was thickening and condensing into an impenetrable fog. Nathan couldn't help but remember that quote from Nietzsche about staring into the abyss.

He glanced back at his apartment for reassurance again and saw the doorframe, now tiny and so far away that he couldn't make out the furniture inside it anymore. He raised his hand and looked at the wristwatch. 2:31 am. He still had time. He turned back towards the darkness and continued walking, now even more slowly, afraid he was going to bump into a wall or something like that.

He stopped every few seconds to perk up his ears when he thought he heard something, only realizing a moment later that it was his own footsteps echoing. Whenever he glanced back at his apartment, it slipped further and further away, becoming less discernible in the darkness, but still glowing in the distance like a beacon of hope. The door now seemed like a faraway, vertical rectangle, a small glimmer of light in a place shrouded in utter, devouring blackness.

A distant creaking suddenly came, long and loud enough for Nathan to hear properly and recognize as the sound of a door opening. Or closing.

His heart suddenly jumped into his throat and he quickly turned around, muttering a barely audible *oh no* to himself. *The door is closing!* He thought in a panic. The creaking stopped, but the rectangle of light was still there.

"Oh, shit." Nathan chuckled to himself in relief, steams of breath leaving his mouth in the process.

He felt his legs cut off belatedly and then slowly regain their feeling. It's been a long time since he had that feeling, but he remembered it well. It was the same feeling when the bully Jordan told him he would wait for him after school to beat him up for accidentally bumping into him and making him spill his juice over himself. Nathan still remembered how he froze when he saw Jordan standing at the bike racks with his two lapdogs, Michael and Christopher, all three of them equally burly and intimidating.

The feeling in his legs went away when Jordan got into his face and pushed Nathan on the ground. He ordered him to apologize and Nathan obliged, knowing full-well that if he didn't, he was just going to get beaten up, just like Scott did. Jordan made Nathan say something down the line of "I'm sorry for being such a loser and spilling your juice" loudly. After the thugs had their laughs, they left Nathan there in the dirt.

Jordan got expelled from the school a few months after that. Apparently, he beat up a kid and he and his friends pissed on the poor kid. Years later, Nathan ran into Scott in the subway, who told him that Jordan was in prison for stabbing someone to death. Christopher admitted to the two of them stabbing the person over a dispute in the bar and now he's serving a twenty-year sentence, while Jordan got life in prison. Michael's whereabouts were unknown and Nathan sincerely hoped that he turned his life around and didn't follow the same path that Jordan and Christopher did.

Another creak resounded, this one a lot shorter and more distant. The thought of being stuck in here with only a limited source of light from his flashlight – which couldn't illuminate shit – terrified the hell out of Nathan. He looked at the time and realized it was 2:34. That was enough exploration for one night. He would come back tomorrow, better prepared. He started walking back towards the apartment, slowly reeling in the rope as he went.

His spirits were raised as he saw the rectangle slowly growing in size and more and more discernible objects inside the apartment becoming apparent. About five minutes later, he was in front of his own apartment.

He stepped over the threshold and felt a wave of warmth hit him as he did so, like entering a well-heated building during winter. The sensation was so strong that he couldn't inhale for a moment. A second later, his body adjusted to the temperature in the apartment and he sighed in relief.

He looked back at the door, admiring its darkness. It was scary, knowing from this point of view how deep inside the corridor he was just five minutes ago. Nathan felt like he was actively putting himself in danger going inside, but as much as it scared him, it also exhilarated him. He couldn't help but feel a sense of pride, as he stared at the disheartening blackness ahead. He wanted to explore deeper. But it was too late now. It was almost…

His watch started beeping to signal it was 2:40. He swiftly turned it off, placed the flashlight on top of the coffee table and untied the rope from his hand with more effort than he expected would be necessary. He allowed it to drop on the floor, not even bothering to untie the other end from the coffee table.

"So, you open up on your own terms, huh?" Nathan scoffed and shook his head at the door.

He sat on the couch, contemplating buying some more things for his exploration, but he didn't know what else to bring. Maybe he could get some chemical lights, just in case he went in too deep. And maybe a backpack for some extra things like water, etc. The harder he thought about it, the more tired he got. He wanted to go to bed, but he couldn't. He had to wait and see if the door would close at the same time as usually. Truth be told, he was actually feeling uneasy of falling asleep with the door open. Although he didn't run into anyone or anything in there, something was definitely unnatural about it and he felt vulnerable every time he looked away. It was like a stalking predator, just waiting for him to drop his guard.

So he instead decided to sit on the couch with the TV on, until the door closed. A movie played on the screen, which Nathan didn't even pay attention to. He tried to focus, but the harder he tried, the heavier his eyelids got...

He opened his eyes suddenly when he heard the door beginning to creak loudly. Just as slowly as it opened, it closed, narrowing the gap and concealing the darkness, until it was completely out of sight. Once the door finally closed, it clicked, to indicate that the lock was set in place. Nathan rubbed his eyes. He must have dozed off while watching the TV. He realized that the volume was pretty low and he frowned. He didn't remember turning down the TV.

I must have turned it down in my half-asleep state. He thought to himself.

Or maybe the apartment wanted you to fall asleep. A second thought came through, but he quickly dismissed it.

Either way, it didn't matter. He was ready to finally go to bed and tomorrow, he'd be back to explore the corridor. This time, much deeper.

Chapter 16

He hated himself in the morning. He was he unable to fall asleep properly after his short expedition, and now he was so tired that he could barely keep his eyes open. He woke up at 9 am and continued sleeping until 2 pm and he still felt like he needed more sleep. He finally understood what his friend Brian was talking about when he said that sleeping in the daytime can never replace sleeping at night. Nathan always laughed at him, saying that his job as a security guard was a joke – sleeping on the shift a couple hours, and then sleeping after the shift in the morning for 6 or so hours. But now he got it. Losing out on sleep was no joke.

At around 3, he got a call from Sam. He ignored it at first, since he didn't feel like talking to anyone in his zombified state, but when he saw that Sam wouldn't let up until Nathan answered, he grumpily picked it up.

"Yeah?" he groused.

"Nathan, me boy! How's it going, Nate-man?" Sam amiably said into the phone, completely contrasting Nathan's serious mood.

"Fine, Sam. What about you?"

"Great. Listen. I spent the night looking into paranormal doors and that sort of shit. I found a lot of interesting theories, you got time to talk about it?"

This grabbed Nathan's attention, immediately giving him a small boost of energy. He knew that Sam did more than just his homework and probably found out a lot of things related and unrelated to the doors. This could prove to be useful, but Nathan didn't want to fall down the rabbit hole of researching things that he didn't need for this case. He knew that Sam was about to pour all the information onto him, so he made a mental note to stop him when he got off track.

"Alright, hit me." he said.

Sam barely even waited for Nate to finish that sentence, before he began.

"Well, listen up. Here's what it says. Hold on a moment." There was a moment of pause while Sam stayed on the line, "Okay, this was written by a user on 4chan called shortboy69. He says the following." Sam's speaking tone changed into a reading one, "My grandma's house used to be haunted. She lived in the countryside and whenever I'd visit her for a sleepover during Christmas, my bedroom door would open on its own. I'd be sleeping, sure that I left it closed and I'd see it open in the morning. The thing is I asked my grandma about it and she says she never entered my room during the night. This went on for a few nights in a row and I obviously didn't believe her.

I set up a camera to record it and sure enough, when I checked out the footage in the morning, it showed the door opening at 3:12 am. No one was standing there. I continued recording for the next couple of nights and the door always opened, always at the exact same time.

One night I stayed awake and when the door opened I went outside to check out what was going on. Now, as soon as I stepped out of the bedroom, I got this awful feeling I couldn't describe, like something was really wrong. I went to check up on my grandma and she wasn't in her room. I checked out the rest of the house, calling out to her and she was still nowhere to be found. It was around this time that I started to realize what exactly was making me feel so nervous. It was quiet. Like, really quiet. Usually in my grandmother's house I could hear the fridge buzzing or the boiler making some noise, but now, there was nothing. Not even my footsteps, which are usually really loud, were heard properly.

And my voice - whenever I would call out to my grandmother - would immediately be muffled. It's hard to describe it, but it felt like the sound coming from my mouth would only travel an inch or so before coming to a full stop. I ran back to my bedroom and stayed awake for the rest of the night. In the morning, my grandmother found me in there, scared out of my wits.

When I asked her where she had been, she said she'd been asleep in her bedroom the whole time. Needless to say I noped the fuck out of there and never came back. To this day I still don't know what the fuck is wrong with that house, but I assume it's haunted or possessed."

Sam finished reading and cleared his throat, before a moment of silence ensued. Nathan turned his palm to face upwards in a quizzical gesture.

"Is… is that it?" Nathan asked.

"Yeah, that's his comment." Sam confirmed.

"Then we gotta find that guy immediately! Who could possibly be more credible than shortboy69?" Nathan said with a higher pitch.

"Very funny, Nathan."

"Come on, man. That's not even close to what I need. My door can't open. I don't have doors swinging open on their own in the middle of the night." His skeptical glance fell on the storage door, as he bit his tongue.

"Okay, well how about this one? This is a post on Reddit's true encounters forum. His post is called *Door opening on its own in my new house* and here's what this guy wrote." Sam cleared his throat and started reading with his robotic, reading tone once more, "Guys, I need your help. I moved into a new house recently and there's something weird going on. Before you jump into the comments and start saying it's a haunted house, just hear me out.

First of all, to give you some backstory, I moved into this house three weeks ago and everything was fine at first. The entire house is great, with the exception of a shed outside, which I couldn't get to open. The previous owner told me the door was stuck and he never bothered to try prying it open. I didn't really care at the time, because I wouldn't allow some shitty tool shed to make me miss my opportunity at getting his dirt-cheap amazing house, so I bought the place."

Nathan sat at the edge of the couch, now fully and breathlessly paying attention. Sam continued.

"Ever since I moved in, I had some difficulty sleeping and frequent nightmares, but I had those in my old place as well, so I didn't really think much of it. At first, I tried opening the shed door multiple times, but nothing ever seemed to work. After some time, I just gave up on it. I do need to mention that I tried *everything* and literally nothing worked when it came to opening the shed. Now fast forward two weeks after moving in.

I woke up at around 2 am to hear my dogs barking their throats out. It sounded like something was really agitating them, so I got dressed to check it out. When I got outside, I couldn't believe my eyes. The shed door was fucking open. I tried anything and everything in the past few weeks to pry the door open and couldn't so much as put a dent on it and now it was simply wide open. My two dogs were right in front of the shed, barking at it so angrily that I expected them to lunge inside.

I couldn't see inside, since it was so dark in there, and fearing that it may have been a burglar or squatter, I shouted 'who's there?', but no one answered. I ordered the person to step outside, but he refused. I told them I'd call the police, but there was still no response. I heard something clatter inside, as if something got knocked down and I saw a pair of garden shears drop on the ground in front, where they were illuminated by the porch light. The dogs became even more berserk and I commanded them to get back, afraid the intruder would try to strike them in a panic. I had my phone on me, so I turned on the torch and pointed it at the shed.

It was fucking empty. I saw some old rusted tools and dust-covered shelves, as if no one had stepped inside for a long time. I should also point out that the dogs immediately stopped barking as soon as I pointed the torch there. It was like the light dispersed or chased away whatever was inside. I got back to bed and in the morning, the shed was closed again.

I tried opening it a couple more times after that and even called someone to tear the whole fucking thing down, but for some reason no one was ever able to do it. Either their tools just broke, or they came to the house and then ten minutes later they'd pick up their stuff, all pale as if they've seen a ghost, saying they wouldn't be able to do it. I went out again a few nights ago at 2 am and sure enough, the shed just opened on its own. I didn't want to step inside out of fear of getting trapped in there, but one thing is for sure – something unnatural; is going on here.

Have any of you experienced anything similar before?"

Sam stopped reading and took a deep breath. Nathan found himself holding his breath as he listened to Sam. He got goosebumps all over his body from that story.

"Wow." he exclaimed, pondering the uncanny similarities between that random stranger's case and his own.

"So, Nate. You need to figure out if the door opens at any *specific* times. Are you sure you've never seen it open, during night when you went to the bathroom or something?" Sam asked ecstatically.

No, I'm not.

"Yeah, I'm sure, man. Don't you think I'd, I dunno, notice when the only locked door in my apartment opened all of a sudden on its own in the middle of the night?" He chuckled awkwardly as he proclaimed what he thought was a smooth lie.

He was tempted to tell Sam, but he knew that his friend would insist on joining him on the journey. He had to make sure that it was safe first. Sam seemed to buy his lie, as he said.

"Hey, I actually know a medium. I think I told you about him before. He's gonna be in town in a few days and maybe he could-"

"No." Nathan briskly cut Sam off, "We don't need a medium for this."

"Alright, if you're sure."

There was a moment of silence, before Sam continued.

"Alright, well here's what one of the comments says. In certain religions and cultures, it is believed that doors can serve as portals into another world. For example, Romans believed that the god Janus was responsible for opening doors when adequate sacrifices were made, allowing the subjects to go into the underworld. In ancient Egypt, doorways were built to allow free passage for the soul. All in all, everyone agrees that doors can represent one of the following: beginnings, transitions, gateways, thresholds or endings."

Sam's reading tone ended here and he spoke normally.

"Each of these words he mentioned are hyperlinked and lead to another website."

"Can you click on the 'threshold' word?" Nathan asked, trying to sound as neutral as possible.

"Alright." Sam said and went silent for a moment, before saying, "Alright, it took me to this website about symbolism. Let me see, let me see… Okay, so here's what it says."

At this point, Nathan leaned on the back of the couch and ran his fingers through his hair. Sam's tone changed again to the one of him reading.

"A threshold is typically a boundary between a point at which two places meet. It is where two worlds come together and provide a point of passage. Reaching or crossing the threshold is often associated with rebirth and leaving the past behind, but it is often seen as revisiting the past, too. A door can be used as a type of threshold to symbolize a boundary and separate two distinct places."

He paused for a long moment, which Nathan took as a sign that he was finished reading.

"Is there anything more specific on it?" He asked.

"No, just a bunch of basic information and symbolic mumbo-jumbo. But anyway, coming back to the main point, there are a few things I'm able to surmise from all of this."

"And that is?" Nathan asked.

"Well first of all, you may need to try and provide some sacrifices or offerings to see if the door opens." Sam said, "Like, some guys here on Reddit said it can be a goat sacrifice, like blood in a bowl and-"

"Okay, getting a goat inside the apartment to slit its throat may be a *little* harder than they suggested." Nathan interrupted Sam.

"Okay, then there's the second solution, and that's to see if the door opens at any time during the day or night. Set up a camera or something to record it during the night and check the footage in the morning. If it opens, then you gotta see how long it stays open. The guy who posted that thing on Reddit said the door usually stays open for 20 minutes."

"Hypothetically speaking, what if it does open? What then?" Nathan asked, doing his best to hide his curiosity, even though he could barely omit the excitement in his voice.

Sam said.

"Well, the first thing you gotta do is, you need to determine why the door is opening, which could be for two possible reasons. The first reason could be because the passage always existed there, intertwining with our plane of reality and the door just happened to be placed conveniently there, offering a passage into another world. Chances of that happening are extremely low, mind you, so if that's the case, we're talking about like, one in a million."

"Alright. Let's say that that's not the case. What would be the second reason?"

Sam sighed deeply.

"Something really bad happened in that place, either in the building or before it was built. And now some malevolent being from another realm may be trying to make their way into our world."

Chapter 17

It was only 1:15 am and Nathan was already having trouble keeping his eyes open. The conversation he had with Sam stuck with him throughout the entire day, but he wasn't going to let the creepy experiences of other people deter him from exploring the tunnel. He would do the same thing as last night – go in as soon as the door opens, walk for around fifteen minutes this time and then go back.

He knew he'd hate himself in the morning again for not sleeping enough, especially since It was a workday, but this felt just as important as work. Something revolutionary could be in there. Something that could shape all future studies about the multiverses, about life and death, hell, maybe even about time travel. He didn't really care about fame or having his name plastered on any Nobel prize (even though he thought it would look good on his resume), he just wanted to explore and unearth the secrets untouched by any other living human for ages.

At 2:19 am, the door lock resounded, startling Nathan. The loud creaking ensued and in seconds, the door was open. This time, he was ready. He had already tied all the ropes together and placed them on one big stack right next to the coffee table. His flashlight was at the ready and he had a bottle of water prepared to gulp down before leaving. He hadn't bought anything else for his trip, since he was too lazy to leave the apartment to buy something he may not even use and eventually rationalized that backpacks and other survival equipment were of no relevance in a place like this one.

The rope was already tied to the belt of his jeans for better mobility and his alarm was set for 2:35 am. He was ready to go. As he stepped over the threshold and felt the cold wave wash over him in a familiar sense, he uncontrollably shivered for a moment.

"Never gonna get used to that." he said, hearing his own voice echo inside the corridor.

He started striding forward more confidently this time, knowing what awaited ahead for at least the next five minutes of walking. He thought about using a sharp object to carve something into the walls or floor as a landmark, but he figured he would just measure the rope when he returned.

Every few minutes, he glanced at his watch which dimly glowed in the darkness of the corridor, as he quickened his pace more every time he saw how little time he had left. At 2:25 am, the corridor started showing signs of disrepair, with visible cracks showing up and parts of the concrete walls being peeled off. At first they weren't very obvious, but the deeper Nathan went in, the more they got apparent. At one point, there appeared to be something that resembled scratches on the floor, walls and even the ceiling in uneven manners. Nathan couldn't help but stop and stare at them for a prolonged moment, likening them with an unease to the scratches he saw under the door that night when he called the cops

Those scratches didn't look like they were naturally made. They were too long and deliberate, meaning that someone must have them. He thought about rats, but that couldn't have been it, because what he saw resembled claw marks. This made him feel a little paranoid, so he shone his light around just to make sure he was alone. So far he didn't feel like he was in any danger and for all he knew, whatever animal made that, may have been here years ago. That's at least how old the walls looked like.

He turned around to look back at the door of his place once more. The apartment was still there, albeit barely visible as a distant dot of light. He continued going when he suddenly felt his phone vibrating in his pocket.

Who the hell could it be at this hour?

He pulled it out and saw Sam's name on the call screen. He answered it.

"Hello? Sam?" he asked.

There was no response.

"Sam? Can you hear me?" Nathan asked.

There was a sound of loud static, which made him recoil for a moment.

"Na… going on…. out me?" Sam's barely audible voice came through the cacophony of crackling.

The static was so loud that Nathan practically had to shout into the phone to hear his own voice.

"What? You're breaking up, Sam! Listen, I think the connection is not good!"

And then the static stopped and Sam's voice came through as clear as day.

"Going into the corridor without me, huh?"

It took Nathan a moment to process what he was hearing and once he did, a cold shiver ran down his spine. He instinctively turned back towards the apartment, expecting to see Sam's silhouette standing there, but the small dot of light was still unobscured.

"Yeah, I know what you're doing, Nathan. You could have called me over there. I thought we were friends."

Nathan opened his mouth dumbly, dumbfounded beyond words.

"Sam, I-"

His watch started beeping, signaling it was 2:35 am.

"Shit." Nathan nearly jumped at the sound, as he scrambled to turn it off.

He quickly placed the phone back on his ear and said.

"Sam, you still there? Listen, I didn't mean to cut you out, I just-"

"That's okay. Keep going forward." Sam calmly said.

Nathan kept silent again for a moment, not sure if what he was hearing was correct. By this moment he was starting to get a little freaked out. Something was terribly wrong with this entire phone call. This wasn't Sam's usual way of speaking. And why was he even calling at 2 am? And how in the hell did he know what Nathan was up to?

"Nathan, it's okay." Sam said, "You gotta go exploring further. Go forward, don't worry about it."

"No, no I can't do that, man. The door is gonna close and-"

"Keep going, Nathan. You gotta keep exploring. Go forward."

"No, I-I can't. The door's going to- it's going to close, I can't risk it, I-I'm, I'm going back." His voice now trembled prominently and he felt cold sweat enveloping him.

At this point, the static started once more, first in the background, barely audible, but slowly grew louder, until Sam's voice was barely heard once again.

"Nathan. G… ward. Do… op… ing."

"Sam? Sam, you're breaking up. Sam!"

The sound of distant creaking resounded somewhere in the distance at this point and Nathan's flashlight started flickering, intermittently leaving him in complete and utter darkness.

"No, no, no. Not now, dammit." He hit the flashlight with his phone a few times and it flickered back to life.

He glanced at his watch and realized it was 2:38 am.

"Shit, I gotta get back," he said to himself.

He couldn't stay here any longer tonight. Something was wrong. He couldn't tell what or why, nor could he explain what he felt, he just knew that that feeling of not being in imminent danger was now completely gone and he felt like a sitting duck being stalked by a predator from the darkness. He placed his phone back on his ear and said through the static.

"Sam, I don't know if you can hear me, but I can't talk right now. I'll call you later, alright?"

He hung up and started jogging his way back, not caring about folding the rope as he ran. The dot of light which represented his apartment never felt more welcoming than now and his hope grew by the second along with the light of his living room. Once he was finally through the door, he stopped and turned back to face the corridor, panting and sweating.

"Ah, holy shit." He groaned between breaths, as he leaned on his knees.

It was 2:44 am when he glanced at his watch, so he started reeling in and folding the rope. It took him about ten minutes to finish folding it up and once he had the last bit sorted, he stacked it next to the coffee table. His breathing had normalized by then, so he picked up his phone and called Sam.

It rang four times, before a groggy Sam answered.

"Hello?" It was evident that he was woken up by this call.

Nathan started speaking quickly, trying to explain as much as he could in one breath.

"Sam, listen. I'm sorry about not telling you. I can explain why I hid it from you. I didn't know if the door was dangerous and going in there-"

"Nathan, Nathan. Whoa, hold on. What are you talking about? Bro, it's almost 3 am for fuck's sake." His voice still sounded croaky, but less so.

"Yeah, but you called me just twenty minutes ago. What were you even doing awake at this hour?"

"Nate, are you smoking some weed, man? I've been asleep since midnight."

"No, no. That's not true. You called me, you told me to go forward, you said-"

He stopped mid-sentence, feeling like something was very much off over here.

"Wait, hold on." he said as he turned on the speaker and entered his call history.

The last call on the list was from Sam, but it was earlier that afternoon. Nathan scrolled through the rest of the call history, but all the other calls were from earlier and different callers.

"Nate? You still there?" Sam asked.

"Uh, yeah. I'm still here, Sam." Nathan said, exiting the call logs.

"Look, I gotta work in the morning, let's talk tomorrow, yeah?"

"Sure, Sam. Sorry. Sleep well."

He hung up, staring at his phone. He looked back at the corridor, at the infinite abyss ahead. The sense of unease washed over him at the thought that someone could be in there right now, watching him.

Chapter 18

Four days had gone by since that night and Nathan hadn't stepped into the corridor since, rationalizing that he needed more time to prepare properly. In truth, the logical part of him was telling him that going inside would be dangerous.

He got a call from Sam two days after that night, who asked him if he managed to find any solution to the door. He didn't remember their call at 2 am, so Nathan decided not to mention anything. He kept the call as brief as possible, uncomfortable discussing the topic, so he just said he tried recording and offering some items to the door like raw meat and nothing worked. Disappointed, but determined, Sam said he would get back to him with some more solutions soon. Nathan couldn't help but admire Sam's dedication to finding a solution.

Nathan wasn't done with the corridor, yet. He kept telling himself that it would take more than just one creepy occurrence to dissuade him from exploring further. He just needed a break, is all. He decided that his work was suffering too much due to a lack of sleep and he needed to set his priorities straight.

He still wasn't able to sleep, though. At night, he'd wake up just before the door opened, as if being tantalized by it and he wouldn't be able to fall asleep again until that peculiar sound of the door locking resounded. On top of that, when he did manage to get some meager sleep, he was plagued by horrid nightmares of running through maze-like corridors shrouded in dark fog, while something chased him. He never saw or knew what it was, but all he did know was that the sound of doors creaking constantly followed right behind him.

He started to understand why the previous tenants may have left the apartment and why it was so cheap. He was sure that the landlord knew exactly what was going on and probably wanted to get his money's worth from the apartment, as low as it was. Maybe he even tried resolving the issue, but to no avail.

Nathan had to find out who the landlord was and ask him some questions. Maybe he would get some insight into the whole door situation, understand how it all began and then help Sam narrow down the possible solutions. He just needed to know what he was getting into, in case it was dangerous.

The past few days he was busy catching up with work and napping in-between, but today he was done earlier and he had to make this call. He had to do it before he got too lazy again. He dialed Jessica's number and waited as it rang.

I would be annoyed with a tenant like myself. he thought to himself candidly.

"Hello?" She picked up.

"Jessica, hi. It's Nathan."

"Hey Nathan, how's it going?" She sounded perky, which alleviated his tension a little.

"Good, thanks for asking. Listen, I'm sorry for bothering you so often with insignificant things, but I-"

"Not a problem at all, go ahead."

"Yeah, so. I was wondering. Is there a chance I could get in contact with the landlord? It's really important."

"I'm really sorry, Nathan. The landlord gave us strict instructions not to give the tenants any personal information. Apparently, they've had issues with some tenants in the past. Is there a problem?"

Nathan hesitated. *Should I tell her or not?* For all he knew the landlord ordered the agency not to tell the tenants anything about the door, but as far as he knew, the agency was obliged to warn the tenants about such a thing if they knew about it. And what if Jessica didn't know about the door and then asked the landlord about it? He could see Nathan as a threat and kick him out, and he couldn't leave before he was done exploring. Would Jessica even believe Nathan about a door that seemingly opens on its own? The last viable scenario could be that the landlord himself didn't know about the door. It was a stretch, but not impossible.

"Nathan? Can you still hear me?" Jessica asked.

"Yeah, I'm here, Jessica."

"Okay. So, why do you need the landlord? I'm sure our agency can help you with anything related to the apartment."

Nathan bit his tongue.

"It's the storage door." he blurted and silence ensued on the line.

"The storage door?" Jessica asked.

"Yeah. I keep hearing some sounds coming from the other side. I think it might be rats or bugs. Probably rats, because they sound pretty big."

Jessica let out a muffled 'mhm', before saying.

"Can you give me more details about the problem you're having?"

"Yeah, I mean, I hear loud scratching a lot of the times, especially at night, it's really hard to sleep. And on top of all that, I think there's some damage to the door because of that. Could you by any chance contact the landlord about it and see if he can come check it out? I'm sure he'll know what to do."

Jessica's voice sounded rather exasperated now.

"Alright, I'll get in touch with the landlord and let you know as soon as I find something out, okay? But there's really not much we can do. If it's rats, the landlord can choose to break down the wall and fix the problem. But if he refuses, we can only void the lease and give you your deposit back."

"Can you please just try and get him to contact me or get over here to assess the problem? Please." Nathan said with his persuading voice as best he could, smiling into the phone, despite Jessica not being able to see his face.

"Nathan, I…" Jessica sighed, and Nathan couldn't tell if she was frustrated or just perplexed about what to do, "I can get in touch with the landlord, but I can tell you right away that he doesn't want anything to do personally with tenants or the apartment. He's a complete hermit and strictly told us not to allow tenants to get in contact with him anyhow, under any circumstances."

Nathan sighed in disappointment.

"Alright, I understand. But please, just try to explain the situation to him and see if he agrees to meet with me. If not, totally okay, we can just forget about the whole rat infestation, I'll just…" He looked in the direction of the door, "I'll just learn to live with the scratching, not a problem."

"Alright. I'll get back to you as soon as I manage to get some info."

"Thank you, Jess. I really appreciate it."

Poor Jessica.

Nathan really didn't want to bother her, but from what he figured, he had no other choice right now. The landlord probably knew something about the door. Why else would he be hiding like this? Nathan had to find him, just to have a short conversation with him about it, that's all. As he lay on the couch to give his aching back a short break, he felt his eyelids becoming heavy suddenly. Maybe he could take a short nap.

***

He was jolted awake by something. By what? When he came to his senses, he realized he was on the couch of his living room, in almost complete darkness. He saw a faint glimmer of light falling through the window, probably coming from the adjacent building.

Jesus. How long have I been sleeping?

He glanced at his watch and horrified, realized it was 2:31 am. A batter of footsteps echoed somewhere to his right, fading away in the distance. He jerked his head towards the storage door instinctively, but couldn't see from the dark.

"Hello?" he asked, instantly sitting straight up, all of his senses alert.

He fumbled for his phone on the table, accidentally knocking it on the floor. He felt the ground with his hands, all the while staring in the direction where he thought the storage door was in the dark, until the shape of his phone came into contact with his fingers. He quickly unlocked it, breathing shallowly and turned on the torch. The light illuminated a big portion of the room, immediately giving Nathan a sense of sanctuary and safety.

He pointed his light towards the door and there it was. Wide open, just waiting for him to get inside. As if hypnotized, Nathan stood up and slowly made his way to the door, until he was right in front of the threshold. There was a faint creak somewhere in the distance, barely audible, but still there.

He flipped the switch next to the door to turn on the light and turned off the torch on his phone. He felt as if he was out of his body, as he put his shoes on and as he grabbed the end of the rope and tied it around his wrist and as he took the flashlight and flicked it on and as he stepped inside the corridor, not hesitating for a moment.

A voice at the back of his mind told him this was all wrong and that he shouldn't be here. But that voice was only a whisper now. His desire to find out what was ahead was stronger than his fear of danger. He started walking slowly, his footsteps echoing throughout the corridor and step by step, he left the solace of his apartment further behind, entering the decrepit corridor deeper by the second.

Despite the feeling of being guided by an otherworldly force, he still possessed enough rational thinking to glance at his watch every few minutes, careful not to go too deep. The distant sounds of creaking resonated occasionally throughout the corridor, sometimes barely audible, and sometimes very close, almost as if they were only inches away. Nathan ignored them as best he could, focusing on putting as much distance as he could into the corridor.

He stopped only when he felt his hand being tugged from behind. He shot around, heart pumping, when he realized that the rope on his wrist was hanging tightly in the air.

"Shit, it's not long enough." he said to himself, pointing the flashlight at the front which he still wanted to explore.

He contemplated untying the rope and continuing without it, but ultimately decided against it. The corridor ahead was somehow even darker, if that was even possible and Nathan felt that the deeper he went in, the more useless his flashlight was becoming. The corridor showed no signs of ending any time soon and he couldn't risk getting stuck in here.

Not satisfied at all with the current situation, he turned around and started jogging back. He would pull the rope out once he was out. It was extra work, but at least he'd be out of the corridor faster.

Once he was back in the apartment, he started tugging the rope, reeling it in little by little. It was way more work than he initially suspected and his arms were starting to get tired.

I need to go to the store tomorrow and buy more rope. I'll buy three more stacks, that should be enough to get exploring for a while. But I won't go to that same store from last time. There's a good one on the-

His thoughts were interrupted when he pulled in another piece of rope. His eyes focused on the rope that just fell loosely on the floor of his living room. His brain didn't even process what he was staring at, at first. He got closer and just then realized what it was. The end of the rope.

That was wrong, there wasn't supposed to be an end of the rope at all. It was supposed to connect with the end connected to the table leg. Maybe it untied from the rest of the ropes somehow?

He squinted and just then clearly saw that the rope was severed. He wasn't sure if it was cut or it got lacerated somewhere along the way, but he felt the hairs on the back of his neck stand straight. He bent down and picked up at the rope, inspecting it from various angles. He glanced at the corridor, at the omnipresent darkness and suddenly felt like something would lunge from within the depths at him.

No, the rope was just torn. The floor is all cracked, it probably got snagged along the way, that's all. Despite saying that, he felt no calmer. He grabbed his flashlight and pointed it at the corridor, illuminating almost nothing in the process.

He waited in front, glancing at his watch every few minutes, until the door closed. Almost as soon as the click resounded, he felt the weight fall from his shoulders. He went to bed and slept surprisingly peacefully for the rest of the night, as if nothing happened. He kept telling himself in his mind that he would no longer be going to the corridor, but he knew that he was lying to himself.

From that night, he explored the corridor with every chance he got. He bought five extra ropes and tied them all together, hoping that that amount would be enough. He tried not to think about the corridor stretching infinitely or something otherworldly sabotaging his rope. He tried getting a drone inside, however almost as soon as it would put some distance in the corridor, it would start to lose signal, which Nathan assumed may have been electromagnetic interferences. So the bottom line was, it had to be him who would explore.

He tried to go just a little deeper every night, addicted to that sense of accomplishment and exhilaration of the unknown. He tried to imagine what was on the other side, which motivated him to continue going. Maybe a mirror of his own apartment. Maybe a completely different apartment. Maybe a completely different world.

He almost completely swapped sleeping at night for sleeping during the day and his work productivity suffered due to it. His teammates got worried about him, that he was going through a rough time and needed help, but he assured them that he just had trouble adjusting to his new apartment. They were understanding about it, which greatly helped him share the load with the rest of his team members.

Sam called him a few times, too. He tried to give Nathan some insight about what he learned and what they could possibly try to open the door, but Nathan would always find an excuse to end the call, stating he was either too busy or too tired. He promised Sam that they would try something though, as soon as both their schedules aligned.

He knew he couldn't keep this facade up forever. He had to finish exploring the corridor and get back to his normal life as soon as he possibly could.

The thought of that somehow terrified him, that sense of normalcy and mundane routine. For now, he just wanted to savor exploring the corridor and finding out what was on the other side. One dreadful thought kept plaguing his mind thought. As he moved deeper inside the corridor, it got progressively more dilapidated and even treacherous, as the ground had more and more cracks and even small potholes.

Whatever was on the other end, it would probably not be a pretty sight and he wasn't sure how he felt about it. Did he want to find derelict, abandoned ruins which he could explore all to himself, or would he rather find an apartment like his own, with someone living in there? That latter statement made more logical sense, which would also explain all the footsteps he heard a few days ago. But at the same time, running into another person in such a peculiar place wasn't a comforting thought.

All those worries, all those doubts, would disappear whenever the creaking of the door would resound in his apartment and he found himself in the narrow corridor once again, unearthing its long-forgotten mysteries.

Chapter 19

Vincent stood at Nathan's door with a warm smile. He was leaning on the doorframe with his elbow, while holding a case of Budweiser in the other.

"Hey, Nate. How you doing, son?" he asked, still grinning under his well-coifed mustache.

"Hi, Vince. Come on in, you aren't interrupting anything." Nathan stepped aside and gestured for Vincent to come inside.

Vincent pushed himself away from the frame and got inside, placing the beer on the kitchen counter. He looked around the apartment, his gaze focusing a little longer on the coffee table. The table which seemed pushed out of place a little, standing annoyingly diagonal in contrast to the rest of the furniture. Nathan forgot to move it back from that one night when he tugged the rope's end a little. He gave himself a silent pat on the shoulder for remembering to remove the ropes out of sight, though. He had no particular reason to do it, he just suddenly got an urge an hour ago to do so, so he listened to his gut feeling. Turned out, he was right to do so, because not long after that, Vincent came for a visit.

"Well go on, sit down. Make yourself at home." Nathan said, as he got to the kitchen counter and said, "Let me just find a bottle opener here."

"Oh, no need. Watch this." Vincent said and approached the counter.

With a smooth motion, he pulled out one bottle and placed the cap on the edge of the counter. Nathan watched in trepidation as Vincent slapped the bottle cap with the palm of his hand, ever so gently, and it came off with a loud pop.

"I definitely wouldn't wanna try that myself. Or else we'll have beer spraying like a geyser all over the place." Nathan said.

"It's not that hard. Come on, let me show you." Vincent said as he took a sip from the opened bottle and placed it on the counter.

He pulled out another bottle, practically tossing it in the air before catching it and placed it on the counter with a loud, glassy thud.

"Come on, take it." he said.

Vincent was smiling when he said it, but the way he was menacingly leaning over the counter with his buff arms, it may as well have been an order. Nathan tentatively grabbed the bottle and tried to imitate Vincent's movement. He placed the cap at the edge of the counter.

"Now, hold the bottle firmly, but don't push it upwards." Vincent said, "And now take the root of your palm and hit the cap, as if you're trying to slap the bottle out of your hand."

Nathan raised his hand and brought it down, slamming it upon the bottle cap. The cap slipped under the counter, but remained on top of the bottle.

"Dammit." Nathan said.

"Try it again. You got this." Vincent nonchalantly said as he took another sip.

Nathan looked at Vincent with bemusement and placed the bottle back at the edge of the counter, shaking his head. *It's not gonna work.* He repeated the same movement from before and this time, the cap fell off with a loud pop, clattering down on the kitchen floor and rattling in circles, until it completely stopped.

"Shit, it worked." Nathan said in surprise, as he bent down and picked up the cap, placing it on top of the counter.

Vincent raised his bottle and clashed it against Nathan's, as they both took a sip. Vincent turned around and made his way to the couch, as he said.

"OSP."

"I'm sorry?" Nathan asked.

Vincent sat down, leaned back, stretched out his legs and said.

"On-site procurement. In my unit we had training for utilizing whatever you can find in the field to survive. No water canister? Put a condom in a sock. No can opener? Use your knife. No knife? Well… you better start using your wits to survive, then."

Nathan tantalizingly waved his index finger at Vincent, as he smiled.

"I knew it. I knew it. I knew you used to be military. You have this authoritative attitude about you that just gives it away immediately."

Vincent glanced down at the coffee table and nodded with a chuckle.

"Marine Corps. Twenty-five years."

"Have you served anywhere?"

"Yeah. Two tours in Afghanistan, two in Iraq. One in Yugoslavia." Vincent looked at Nathan and took another sip of his beer.

Nathan mirrored Vincent's movement and went to sit on the couch.

"Damn. You're like a real-life Rambo." he said awkwardly, not sure how to respond to such a hardened war veteran.

Vincent chuckled.

"There's no such thing as Rambo. You gotta work with your fellow soldiers in order to stay alive. No heroics, no one-man army, nothing like that. That's just dramatized by Hollywood." He looked nowhere in particular and chuckled to himself, as he said, "You know, I remember when *Rambo* premiered in the theaters. I was already married to Margery and I told her, I said 'Margery, we gotta go see this movie. It's about this soldier who takes on an entire town by himself, I wanna see those skills for myself'. Margery really wasn't in favor of watching these guns-blazing action movies, but I was intrigued by it. I was already a marine by then for almost four years and I thought maybe this Rambo would utilize some good tactics for survival which we didn't learn about in the Corps."

He laughed again to himself and shook his head, as he said.

"Let me just tell you, if anyone ever tried to be like Rambo, he'd be dead in a jiffy."

"I know, right?" Nathan laughed along with Vincent, "I mean, who the hell shoots from their hip with such accuracy and doesn't get shot by one of the hundreds of oncoming assailants?"

"Well, that's Hollywood for you. But let me tell you, back when that movie came out, there had been a surge in applications to the Marines and the Army for a while, because they wanted to be like Rambo. Most of them failed the medical and physical tests – and thank god – because those kids would have gotten themselves killed on the battlefield." Vincent said as he brought the beer bottle to his mouth.

There was a brief moment of pause, before Nathan spoke up.

"Do you uh, have any kids, Vincent?"

Vincent gave a mild smile and said.

"Yeah. I have a daughter. Her name's Sarah." He took a long gulp from his bottle, "What about you? You got a family, Nate?"

The way he asked the question so quickly made Nathan follow the old man's pace, despite wanting to ask more about Sarah. He shook his head in response to him.

"No, not yet. I mean I got a mother in Idaho and a dad in Colorado. I don't talk much to my dad, though. He uh... he wasn't really around when I was younger and we kinda drifted apart, you know. As for starting my own family, I'm not in a hurry to get married."

Vincent nodded and quirked his lips curiously, as he raised his bottle and said.

"Well, if you wanna take my advice, don't get married at all." He winked.

Nathan genuinely smiled. He started to see Vincent as more than just a hardened killing war machine. This old man was capable of humor and emotions and was unlike anything he thought soldiers were whenever he saw them on the streets or on TV; serious expressions, authoritative tones, kind of like robots without emotions. Vincent, although authoritative, was nothing like a robot.

"So, how'd your hike go?" he asked Nathan, which completely caught him off guard.

Nathan opened his mouth and did his best to force his brain to conjure up a lie on the spot.

"I... actually... ended up not going. I had a lot of work during the weekend and I was just, you know, too tired to do it."

"Mhm." Vincent nodded, not taking his eyes off Nathan.

They both took sips of their drinks, as Vincent asked.

"What do you for a living, Nate?"

"I work as a programmer. I work for a company in New York, but since they have no offices in Oregon, I work from home."

Vincent nodded and asked.

"Is it like... coding, creating what do you call it... software, and that sort of thing?"

"Something like that, yeah. A bunch of uninteresting technical mumbo-jumbo. Nowhere as exciting as the life of a soldier."

"Marine." Vincent corrected him with a smile.

"Sorry. So, how long have you been living here?" Nathan asked.

"Not long. Maybe a few years. This building is pretty new and we invested in an apartment right around the time construction started. It's a lot cheaper getting apartments that way."

"Did you have to wait long until the whole thing was finished?" Nathan asked with fascination, suddenly getting an idea of doing the same thing himself.

"No, just four years. It all depends on the contractor, though. Some people need to wait up to ten, and a minority even get their money back after a long time waiting, since there's not enough investment and the companies just bail on the whole project. But Margery and I weren't worried, we're young and ambitious, got our entire lives in front of us." He winked, as he downed the bottle and placed it on the coffee table.

Nathan laughed at his final sentence. Vincent stood up and said.

"I'm gonna grab another one, if you don't mind."

"Hey, it's not like you brought it." Nathan said sardonically

Vincent popped open another bottle with an equally precise motion as the first time and swallowed a sip. He wiped the suds off his mustache and looked at the storage door.

"Are the mice still bothering you?" he asked, as he pointed to the door with his bottle.

Nathan took a long gulp of his beer, while he thought about what he should tell Vincent. After he separated the bottle from his mouth, he shook his head and said.

"No, they appear to have gotten bored. I mean, I don't wanna jinx it or anything, but they're gone for now. They'll probably be back, though. I know mice aren't that easy to get rid of."

Vincent nodded. He slowly paced towards the living room, as he said.

"Well, this door is notorious in this building. Everybody knows it as 'the door that won't open'. Hell, you don't even need to explain the whole thing. You can just say 'the door' and people will know what you mean. That night when you and I first met, when I got back to Margery, she asked me what was going on. And I just told her, I said, 'Oh, we have a new neighbor upstairs. And he's having problems with *the door*'."

He chuckled, but Nathan simply nodded. He suddenly felt like he was out of loop for a joke that everybody else knew about. Chances were that Vincent knew a little bit more about the whole situation, though.

"So, do you know who the landlord of this apartment is?" He asked, suddenly intrigued.

"I've seen him around a few times, but that's it." Vincent shrugged.

Finally, we're getting somewhere.

"So, do you happen to know his name or anything?"

"All I know is he's around your age, but I've never spoken to him or anything. Why do you ask?" Vincent frowned.

Nathan was skeptical about talking to Vincent about these details, but he felt that he old man meant no harm. He felt like he could trust him with such details.

"Well, I've never actually seen or met him. Hell, I don't even know his first name. Apparently, he asked the real estate agency to hide his information, since he's had these..." Nathan scoffed, "...problems with previous tenants."

Vincent kept frowning, as he took another sip of his beer, not taking his eyes off Nathan. The speed at which he consumed alcohol told Nathan that the old man's liver was as resilient as he himself was. Vincent finally shrugged and said.

"Well, I honestly haven't even noticed the tenants coming and going. How many did you say there were before you?"

"No idea. The whole thing is really cloak and dagger, it seems." Nathan shrugged.

"I wonder what could be chasing them away so frequently. They might be afraid of those rats inside." Vincent said as he pointed behind himself at the storage compartment.

"So, does the landlord come here often?" Nathan asked.

"I've only seen him come here twice or three times in the past couple of years. So I wouldn't get my hopes up of meeting him. He might just unexpectedly pop up at your door, but I reckon he only arrives when there's an emergency." Vincent said.

"Well, anyway. As long as he's not as bad as my previous landlord, I think I'll manage." Nathan said, trying to change the topic a little bit.

He proceeded to tell Vincent everything about Aleksei and all the problems he'd been having while living there. Vincent supported Nathan's decision to leave and added that he would kick all those abusive immigrants who try to exploit the honest American system out of the country. He explained that he was no racist or anything like that, but that he hated greed and people who valued money over other qualities. His final statement was:

"Well, good luck to your landlord finding another good tenant like yourself. He's probably going to spend the next few months going through tenants like dirty socks, regretting ever letting you go."

He proceeded to tell his own story about a greedy landlady he had, who used to pop into his apartment on the 1st of every month at 6 am, demanding to have the rent money. She'd proceed to make her way inside the apartment and count all the items in the apartment. When Vincent said all items, he literally meant *all* items. The lady apparently had a list of everything, including silverware, glasses and cups, furniture, even the toilet, to which Vincent remarked a few times to her that he'd have a hard time ripping it out of the ground and selling it for beer money.

She never let up, though. And when Vincent finally decided to move in with Margery, he told the landlady to keep the deposit. She called him a week later, stating that there's huge damage to the sofa and that she needed more money to fix it. He politely declined, to which she continued pestering him, until he blocked her number.

"Landlords should go through psychological evaluation before taking the job, I tell you." Nathan shook his head, laughing.

Vincent smiled. The two of them kept talking for an hour or so about casual things, until Vincent's phone started ringing. As soon as he pulled it out of his pocket, his eyes widened and he jumped off the couch, saying.

"Oh, shit. Margery's gonna kill me. I was supposed to be home half an hour ago. Hello?" He brought the phone to his ear panicking, "Yes, honey. I'm coming home. Nathan just needed some help with the sink."

He paused for a moment.

"Yeah, something was wrong with it and I wanted to help him with it… Yeah, I know the casserole is getting cold, I'll be down there in a minute… What? No, no we weren't just drinking. We were fixing the sink… I don't know if he can come over for dinner."

He looked in Nathan's direction, who made a grimace and shook his head. Vincent looked away and said.

"Sorry, Marge. He's too busy… Yeah, I know. Well, maybe next time, alright? Okay, see you soon."

He hung up and put the phone back in his pocket. He looked at Nathan and put his hands on his hips.

"Well, Nate. This was a pleasure."

Nathan stood up.

"Yeah, we should do this more often. Whenever you wanna stop by after 6 pm or so, feel free to do so."

They shook hands and Nathan felt the old man's familiar vice-like grip, but tried not to allow his face to contort into a grimace. Vincent said.

"Oh, no no. Next time it's your turn to come to my place. Margery is dying to meet you."

That works even better.

As much as he trusted Vincent, he felt like the old man could sniff out danger easily and would quickly catch on with whatever was wrong with the door, so being away from it worked excellent for Nathan.

"Alright, I'll make sure to stop by as soon as I find the time."

As Vincent left the apartment, Nathan felt refreshed. He hasn't had a good conversation like this with anyone besides Sam in a long time. Despite running on fumes due to the lack of sleep, he felt much better and energized all of a sudden. He and the old man clicked so well that an hour went by without him even noticing it.

He took a mental note to start hanging out with him more often.

Chapter 20

The door opened with its loud creak, beckoning Nathan inside. He rubbed his eyes and glanced at the watch. As if he had to. It was exactly 2:19 am and he had one hour before the door closed. He took the rope and tied it over his belt at the back. He tugged it a few times to make sure it was secure and grabbed his flashlight. He flicked it on, allowing the beam to fall upon the darkened corridor and light his path. Not hesitating anymore like he did the first couple of times, he stepped over the threshold and began striding.

He wanted to walk until 2:55 tonight, if possible. He would jog back to make it in time before the door closed. He made his way through the familiar cracks and scratches on the floors and walls, listening to the occasional creaking in the distance. He often thought about those sounds, whether they were coming from some other doors in the distance. He always remembered the multiverse theory and tried to imagine the corridor branching out into countless other corridors, each one having its own door, leading to its own universe. Maybe in one of those universes, he would find himself, but different. Maybe he would find a world where he still lived in Aleksei's apartment, or a world where he never even lived in his apartment, or a world where he had a good relationship with his father, or simply wore a different-colored shirt, or poured milk first and then cereal, etc.

The thought fascinated him, but he tried to push it back. He had to keep his expectations in check and focus on exploring, otherwise he could miss something important.

2:31.

The flashlight flickered a few times, leaving him for a few split seconds in complete darkness. He stopped until the light stabilized and then continued going forward. He had already gotten used to this occurrence. As he went deeper inside the corridor, the flashlight would flicker more often and there was nothing he could do about it. Even changing the batteries and flashlight itself did no good, so Nathan concluded that there must have been some electromagnetic (or paranormal) interference inside the corridor.

He remembered his ex Natalia, who he used to date for a brief period. She adamantly believed that she had some paranormal powers. She said lights would often flicker as she passed under them and Nathan would play along, pretending to believe her, until it actually happened. They were walking in the park and one of the lampposts blinked for a moment. Natalia coldly looked at him and said like it was the most normal thing in the world.

"See? There it goes."

Nathan doubted her up until that point though, because she seemed a little looney with all the things she told him. While they were sitting by the Oswego Lake, she tried convincing him that the lake had a dangerous underwater creature living in the waters, and that that was the reason they didn't drain the dirty water and replace it with clean. She also told him about her brief encounter with an alien and about the demon which haunted her parents' house.

Nathan was convinced about the flickering lights, but not about the other things. It bothered him so much, that he had to google it and found out about something called streetlight interference phenomenon. The information was scarce though, so he decided to believe that Natalia may have just had something in her body that caused the lights to flicker, rather than a ghost haunting her.

"Come on, work dammit." he said and tapped on the flashlight with his palm a few times when it went out for more than a few seconds.

The flashlight stopped flickering in response and illuminated the floor in front. Nathan was about to continue ahead, but instead froze in place. Was it simply his imagination, or did he just see something moving right at the edge of the light, for a split second? He pointed the light up and illuminated the path ahead.

"Hello?" he said with a croaking voice, trying to squint through the darkness which his torch couldn't reach.

His brain must have been playing tricks on him in such darkness. He read that people can hallucinate in places where their senses are deprived and over here, without his flashlight, he was in utter darkness, save for the tiny, barely visible dot of the door far behind him.

Now more hesitant, but still determined to explore, he continued walking forward. By this point the corridor was barely recognizable compared to what was closer to his apartment. The concrete walls were completely covered in cracks and holes and pieces of the ceiling were scattered all over, making Nathan produce loud, echoing, cracking sounds whenever he'd take a step. He glanced at the watch and realized it was 2:53 am.

Dammit, already?

He looked back and had to squint to see the little dot of light which represented his apartment. He glanced at his watch again. 2:54 am. Maybe he could go forward just five more minutes. He would run back, twenty minutes would be more than enough. He didn't need a lot of convincing and before he knew it, he was back on track, moving forward again.

His phone buzzed once, but he ignored it. Might be a message or something, so he could check it out later. The air got significantly colder now and Nathan began shivering. He would need to remember to bring a jacket next time. The creaking also got louder now. It sounded like it was only a few dozen feet away from Nathan, but no matter how deep he went, the sound would always be away the same distance. He quickened his pace, in hopes to catch the sound before it could 'move' once again. His phone buzzed once more. Half-irritated and half-amazed that he even had a signal inside a place like this, he decided to ignore it and move on.

2:56 am.

His phone started buzzing again, this time for a call.

"Okay, who the fuck?!" He pulled out his phone in frustration and saw unknown caller on the screen.

He swiped the green answer button and put the phone up to his ear. He was about to say hello, but something stopped him. Even before he put his phone to his ear, he heard something coming from it. At first it was hard to discern what it was, but after a brief moment of focusing, he was able to figure out that the sound coming from his phone was actually whispering.

The words were inaudible, but from the way the voice came out, the fast and hushed whispering, made Nathan's hair stand on the back of his neck. It distinctly sounded like someone was trying to convey secretive information without being heard by someone else. There were no pauses in the whispering, though, not even for a split second. The person was breathlessly speaking for a solid twenty seconds or so, until Nathan finally spoke up.

"Hello?" he said, his voice cracking.

As if on cue, the whispering abruptly stopped. Not like they stopped because they heard Nathan and were suddenly aware of his presence. It was as if someone pressed a mute button on the TV remove. There was an agonizingly long pause, before the sound of the call ending resounded in Nathan's ear.

He moved the phone away from his face and glanced at the screen. It said *call ended 03:19*. Has he been on the phone for three whole minutes? He realized that he had five text messages, so he quickly opened them. They were all from the same unknown number.

D_n't.

*G# %!*4*

...

!o b<ck!

Above you.

Nathan froze. He stared at the last message. He reread the two words of the final message over and over, but they still remained the same. Just then, a slow and steady creaking came right from above Nathan. He felt his entire body going tense. He couldn't force himself to look up, even though he knew he had to. He felt his breath beginning to quicken along with his heartbeat and yet he was rooted.

He began pointing his flashlight up, ever so slowly, the beam bouncing up and down violently from his trembling hands. He illuminated more and more cracks on the ceiling and then… nothing. There was nothing there. Simultaneously, the creaking stopped as well, as if his light silenced it.

Nathan loudly sighed in relief with a quaky breath. He had to go back, it was already late. He shifted his weight from one leg to another and felt something on his belt. A tug.

His first thoughts were that the rope reached its end, but then another gentle tug came. And another. He was frozen in place, unable to turn around. Something was behind him, he just knew it, but couldn't force himself to turn around. At the back of his mind, if he didn't face whoever was behind him, they wouldn't see him. But he couldn't go forward, either. The rope slowly began tightening against his pants. And then, it yanked him so hard, that he almost fell backwards. It was now violently trying to yank him back and he was slowly being pulled back. During all that commotion, he looked behind himself, but saw nothing discernible.

In a fit of panic, Nathan quickly undid his belt and pulled it off his pants, allowing the rope to come loose and disappear out of sight.

"What the fuck!' he said breathlessly, as he kept his flashlight pointed where the rope had been a second ago, the beam of it trembling violently.

And then, the creaking came once again, this time right in front of him, just out of his light's reach. His flashlight started acting up again, flickering on and off.

No, come on!

In a panic, Nathan hit the torch with his palm a few times. The creaking was getting closer by the second.

He saw something in the split seconds when the light was working. A hand. A pale, bony hand appearing just at the edge of the light, feverishly clawing at the floor with its jagged nails. And it was pulling itself closer to him. The light went out and came back again and now Nathan saw the other hand, reaching further into the light in front of the first one, its wrist and forearm so skinny that the bones protruded prominently, the nails on the fingers equally jagged and broken as on the other hand.

A mass of black hair appeared between the arm and hand, falling on the floor messily and Nathan realized he was staring at a woman, an emaciated woman, crawling on the floor, with dirty, ragged and ripped clothes. The creaking got louder again and all Nathan could do was stare, rooted in place, not sure if he was morbidly fascinated or petrified with fear.

The light continued blinking and each time it did, the woman got closer and closer, now only inches away from Nathan, the sound of creaking so loud that it drowned out all the other noises. The woman moved one hand in front of the other, clawing at the floor with her broken nails so hard that Nathan saw them getting bloodied and leaving scratch marks on the floor.

She stopped and started to raise her head, ever so slowly, leaving the messy strands of hair hanging on the ground.

The light went out completely for a few seconds and when it came back, Nathan screamed.

He was face to face with the woman's face, but it was unlike any face he could ever imagine. The woman's emaciated face was pale as a sheet of paper and scratched all over, as if clawed by a cat. The most terrifying thing about her though, were her eyes – or a lack of them. Instead of eyes, there were two, black, sunken holes and yet despite that, Nathan could tell with absolute certainty that the woman was staring directly at him.

She opened her mouth, revealing another black hole similar to the one in her eye sockets. And then, the creaking sound came, directly from her open maw. It was all Nathan could take.

He turned around and started running in the opposite direction. He didn't care what was on the other end or the fact that he was moving further away from his apartment. All he wanted was to get the hell away from that woman. Nothing in the opposite direction could be as horrible as the sight he just witnessed.

He ran as fast as he could, panting and violently swinging his flashlight up and down, its flickering light bobbing from ceiling to floor repeatedly. The creaking got a lot faster and a lot louder now and it was right at his heels. He felt his lungs and legs burning after only a dozen seconds of sprinting, but he knew he couldn't stop, otherwise the woman would catch him and do god knows what to him.

Just when his hope started to wane, he saw something in the distance. Something that looked like a dot of light. Although pale, in this darkness and in such a perilous moment it seemed like the most welcoming sight ever.

Nathan got a sudden surge of energy and he ran faster, quick-approaching the light, which grew more and more, until it started to become apparent that it was a door. A door, his salvation, his way out of this hellhole, curse him for ever wanting to explore this goddamn place.

The door was clearly in sight now and although Nathan couldn't see anything more than a pale yellowish light on the other side, he didn't care. He found a way out of here. A terrible realization hit him however, when he heard an additional creaking not just behind him now, but also in front of him. The door was closing.

No, no, no, no, no.

Despite being unable to inhale more than a tiny gasp of air and his entire body burning from the sprint, he pushed on. He couldn't stop now. The door was halfway closed already, but the fact that the creaking behind him was no longer so close gave him the strength to run on. Summoning the last vestiges of strength he jumped through the door and into the blinding light and hit the hard, cold floor, just in time for it to shut behind him with a loud bang and click.

He got into a sitting position and looked at the door, scooting backwards until he hit a wall with his back. The sound of creaking was now muffled, but getting closer rapidly. In mere seconds, a dangerously loud bang resounded on the door - enough to make Nathan jump back at the wall he was already against - and then intermittent creaking, until it slowly faded away. It was replaced by scratching, which gradually got louder and louder. And then it just stopped completely. Eerie silence filled the entire room, allowing Nathan to hear his own panting and whimpering. He slowly stood up, not taking his eyes off the door.

"What the hell is that thing?" he said to himself between breaths, as he took one tentative step forward.

He just then realized he was staring at a very old, very worn-out looking door. Its wooden surface was massively damaged, the white paint on it only sticking to a few spots. The wood seemed to be half-rotted and the knob was missing. Nathan looked around and realized he was in an apartment, but it looked abandoned and ruined beyond repair.

The walls were dilapidated, similarly to the ones in the corridor, with the exception of some remnants of now-turned-brown paint sticking to some parts, dimly illuminated by the sickly yellowish light hanging from the ceiling. The furniture and carpet which apparently belonged to the living room were musty and torn, while dust collected on shelves and on the kitchen counter.

"You fell for it too, huh?" A voice came from behind.

Nathan screamed, turning around and recoiling in fear. He then remembered that he inched closer to the door and took a step to the side. He was staring at a man around his age, with slick, shiny hair and big, round glasses. He was clean shaven and his face looked so smooth and flawless that it would make every face cream company jealous. He wore a white shirt and a black vest over it, with black pants and shiny shoes under, which completely contrasted the dilapidated apartment. It made Nathan wonder if the man was worried about dirtying his wear.

A smile stretched across the man's lips and he adjusted his glasses, as he clasped his hands together in front of himself and said.

"I'm… afraid you won't be able to leave now."

Chapter 21

"Who are you? Did you see that thing out there?" Nathan pointed at the door, violently jerking his head in the direction of it, before looking back at the man.

The guy couldn't have been more lethargic, contrasting Nathan's panicked state. He put one hand on his chest and chuckled, as he said.

"I'm so sorry, rude of me not to introduce myself. My name's Martin. A pleasure to meet you, Mr.…."

He outstretched his hand in an elegant manner, gesturing Nathan to introduce himself. It took Nathan a moment to realize what the man wanted, until he finally spoke up with a scarcely perceptible voice.

"Nathan."

"Nathan." Martin repeated, "Well, I'm really sorry to have to welcome you in such conditions."

He took a few random steps around the room, glancing around the apartment and said.

"This place isn't in perfect shape, but a little more fixing and it should be ready." He grinned widely, showing off pearly rows of teeth."

Nathan scoffed, not sure if the guy was joking or really oblivious to his surroundings, but after what he saw back in the corridor, he wasn't sure what to believe. He turned his palms upside down and shook his head in astonishment.

"Are you for real? Do you see this shit? What is this place and what's going on here?"

Martin's grin disappeared and he frowned as he crossed his arms over his chest.

"I'm not sure what you're referring to, Nathan."

Nathan opened his mouth in disbelief, before pointing at the door again and asking.

"You saw that woman back there, didn't you? The one with the creaking voice and with… with no eyes. Right?"

Martin stared at Nathan with a blank expression, as if trying to comprehend what he was saying.

"Listen, Nathan. They're waiting for you. We really don't have much time. Follow me."

He gestured Nathan to follow him and strode to the entrance.

"Hey, wait!" Nathan reached out to him in futility, since Martin was already through the door and out of sight, "Goddammit."

He glanced back at the door one more time, suddenly feeling like a sitting duck all alone here. He needed no convincing to follow the mysterious man. Even before he stepped out of the apartment, he saw the corridor outside – it was as wasted as the apartment inside, only much darker. Nathan took a step outside, thanking god that he still had his flashlight with him.

"Martin?" He looked to the left and his words caught in his throat.

Something about this place felt oddly familiar, as time-worn and damaged as it was, he just couldn't put his finger on it. He looked behind at the door of the apartment he just came out of. There was a rusted 102 on it, with the zero hanging upside down woefully. He started walking down the corridor, past the other apartments. Most of the doors were badly damaged, and the door to room 104 was knocked off of its hinges, splayed on the floor of the entrance, revealing an equally musty and dirty interior like in 102. Along the way, he saw cryptic messages crudely carved on the walls on both sides.

WHO IS HE???

CANT FIND

As he made his way further through the long corridor, the messages got more difficult to read, as if they were written in a hurry or panic. He tried to shine his light on them and read as he made his way through, but at the same time, he didn't want to linger in one spot for too long. His heart was beating against his chest and he held his breath, as he kept shining his light behind him, paranoid that someone was following him.

TRICKED

CANT LEAVE

HELP

The messages said on the walls.

"What the hell is this place?" Nathan whispered to himself, hearing his own voice quiver.

As he neared the end of the corridor, which forked left and right, a faint, greyish light suddenly started gleaming in from the right side, right around the corner. And then, it suddenly hit him. He looked back once more and then became certain as the light he saw. This was his apartment building. It was damaged beyond recognition, but it was definitely his building. Was this really on the other side of the corridor?

A universe in which the building was abandoned and left to decay like this? Did he somehow travel into the future? Before he could finish his thoughts, he heard a voice coming from around the corner, where the light was.

"What's your name?" It was a deep male voice, which seemed to echo ominously in the corridor, loudly enough for anyone outside of their apartment to hear.

"Michelle." A gentle, female voice responded.

Nathan quickly turned off his flashlight and stretched out his right hand to his right. He felt the cold, uneven surface of the wall and used it to slide his hand across it and tiptoe his way through the place, careful not to make too much noise.

"Nice to meet you, Michelle. My name's Vincent." The male voice responded.

Vincent? My neighbor Vincent?

Nathan stopped right at the edge of the corner, leaning against the wall with his back. He felt the cold, sweaty shirt press against his back uncomfortably, but ignored it.

"I live in 204." The male voice said, "If you ever hear any screaming coming from my apartment, don't worry about it. That's just my wife Margery shouting at me for screwing something up."

That's definitely Vincent.

The female voice chuckled, just in time for Nathan to recklessly jump around the corner and step into the grey light. Standing right next to the letterboxes was Vincent, leaning against the mail with his elbow in his signature pose. He was facing away from Nathan, but the muscly stature made it obvious it was the same Vincent. Standing right in front of Vincent was a woman, but he couldn't clearly see her features, since Vincent was blocking her.

"Vincent! Holy shit, am I glad to see you!" Nathan said and let out a laughter of relief.

"I hope she's not too hard on you." The woman said.

"That's every woman in marriage for you. But I wouldn't trade her for any starlet in the world." Vincent responded to the lady and let out a dry chuckle.

"Hey! Vincent!" Nathan frustratedly said, louder this time, "Do you he-"

He took a step forward and tried to grab Vincent's shoulder, but his hand fell through and he lost his balance, stumbling forward and almost falling down face-first. Shocked, he turned to face Vincent and Michelle, who continued speaking to each other, as if Nathan wasn't even there.

"You should come by for lunch sometime." Vincent said, "She is one mean cook, that one."

"I'd love to." Michelle said with a smile.

Nathan looked at her and just then noticed her features for the first time. She couldn't have been older than twenty. She had blond hair and what in this dim light looked to

Nathan like brown eyes. *Smiling makes her look pretty*, Nathan thought. As if on cue, the smile faded from her lips and she looked to the right for a moment, frowning, as if she was thinking about something. Nathan's heart jumped when he realized that she may have been staring at him, but his hope died when Michelle turned back towards Vincent and said.

"Hey, um, Vincent. Have you ever noticed anything um… weird about this building?" She said it so hesitantly, that it seemed as if she was trying to choose her words carefully.

Vincent raised his eyebrows and turned down his lips. He shook his head and said.

"No, nothing in particular. Weird how?"

At this point, Nathan swiped his hand across Vincent's head, expecting his palm to connect with the back of the old man's head. The hand simply went through as if it were thin air.

"Well, um…" Michelle puckered her lips, staring at the ground, "It's nothing, actually. Forget it, it's no big deal." She smiled.

"Well, if you ever happen to need some fixing, you can either call me or the super. He's better than me though, and always willing to help, so don't hesitate to call him if you need anything."

"Thanks, Vincent." Michelle smiled.

Nathan moved his gaze back towards Vincent and realized that the old man was staring at Michelle. He looked back at Michelle and saw that the smile was still plastered to her face. Both of them were frozen in place. Nathan cocked his head in fascination, his brain unable to process what he was seeing.

He got closer to Michelle, until he was only inches away from her face. It felt like staring at a super-realistic life-sized doll. He reached out with his hand, slowly inching them closer to Michelle's arm. Despite somehow knowing what was going to happen, he wanted to see if she was as transparent as Vincent was. He was about to touch the fabric of the shirt on her forearm, when he felt a strong grip on his wrist.

Michelle's hand moved so fast, that he didn't even realized she was holding him until he blinked a few times and saw her fingers feverishly gripping his wrist, turning his skin white from the pressure. Startled, Nathan recoiled and pulled back, but Michelle held him firmly in place. He panicked and grabbed his forearm with the other hand and tugged, failing to budge even an inch.

His eyes happened to fall on Michelle's face and he realized she was now staring directly at him with a serious expression on her face. This petrified him and he stopped yanking, staring back at her wide-eyed. And then she spoke.

"You have to find me." she said with a trembling voice.

Her entire body and even head were completely still like a statue, but her mouth was moving and her widely opened eyes and raised eyebrows expressed fear. Nathan started pulling again, desperately trying to break free, but only managing to produce searing pain in his wrist.

"Please. You have to hurry." Michelle said.

Her eyes got fixated on something behind Nathan and widened even more, as she said.

"Oh, no. She's here."

That's when the creaking began. Low, perceptible just enough to grab Nathan's attention. Tentatively, he turned his head around and looked down the darkened, dilapidated corridor. Crawling out of one of the apartments, just barely visible at the edge of the light, was a figure. It was a very familiar figure to Nathan – as soon as he saw the tattered clothes, the black hair and the bony arms, he stifled a scream and started tugging his arm even harder.

"Run!" Michelle shouted.

He tugged twice fruitlessly and the third time, he felt the vice grip on his wrist disappearing just like that and found himself falling down on his back. He quickly got up and looked in the direction of the woman down the corridor. She produced another low, creaking sound, which could have easily been mistaken for a door creaking. She slowly turned her head towards him and he was once again faced with those vacant black holes for eyes.

She started creaking much louder, which Nathan took as a sign that he's been spotted. She started crawling towards him at an impossible speed, defying all logic of physics and her frail body. Nathan turned to the left and started running once more, fear quickly overtaking him and his fight or flight instinct kicking in immediately.

He found himself running down the corridor which he came from, but it was much longer this time. It seemed to stretch endlessly, disappearing in the darkness ahead. One of the doors on the right side of the wall far ahead swung open so violently that it banged against the wall and Nathan saw a source of sickly, brownish light gleaming in from inside. Just as the creaking started closing in on him and he expected a bony hand to wrap around his ankle, he jumped through the light, instantly getting blinded.

When he opened his eyes, the blinding light was gone and he found himself back on the floor of the musty apartment which was 102. He quickly looked back and realized that he was once again in front of the storage door, even though that couldn't possibly be the case, since he fell in front of the entrance door.

"What?" He vocalized aloud to himself, as he stood up, "That's not…"

He looked at the battered door and then turned his head in the direction of the entrance. He screamed and fell down on his ass when he saw a person standing there. A moment later, he realized he was staring at Martin. Martin sighed and shook his head, as calmly as a few minutes ago when they first met.

"I'm afraid visiting hours are almost over." The man said woefully, clasping his hands in front of himself.

Nathan propped himself on the dust-covered coffee table and got up, too afraid to take his eyes off Martin. The longer he stared at the man, the more confused he got. He was just standing there, as if nothing even happened, all formal and calm. Was Nathan dreaming?

"Where am I? What the hell is this place?"

He took a few timid steps towards Martin, but before he was able to react, Martin raised one hand and elegantly pushed Nathan with his palm. The motion was gentle and yet Nathan lost balance and felt himself falling backwards. He hit the floor with his back and quickly stood up, ready to defend himself.

But Martin was gone. In fact, the entire place was gone and Nathan was back in the living room of his apartment. He spun in circles, calling out to Martin, but silence was the only response he got. The storage door was closed and when he glanced at his watch, he realized it was 3:19 am.

Without further thinking, he clambered up to his feet, grabbed his keys and wallet and power-walked out of the apartment in search of the closest motel.

Chapter 22

As Nathan picked up the mail from his letterbox, the rude lady from 303 strode inside the building. It was morning, so he assumed she must have been up since early sunrise, doing whatever it was retired people do to pass the time.

"Hi, sweetheart." she said with a big smile.

Nathan raised his eyebrows and looked in her direction.

"Hi, Mrs. Rogers. Went out for a walk?" Another female voice on Nathan's right side replied.

Of course she's not talking to you.

"Oh, yes. I need to stay in shape, don't you think?" The two ladies chuckled and Nathan felt like a moron for thinking even for a second that Mrs. Rogers would dignify him with a glance, let alone greeting him.

"Well, see you later, sweetie." Mrs. Rogers said and entered the elevator.

As soon as the doors closed and Nathan heard the elevator ascending, he turned to the other neighbor. It was a woman in her early thirties, dressed in formal attire. She had a nametag hanging around her neck, so Nathan assumed that she worked as a customer representative, or worked in a bank. Either way, something that required a lot of interaction with people. He couldn't see her name on the tag though, since it was flipped the other way.

"Hi." he said to her with a smile.

"Hi back." She grinned a PR smile and Nathan's suspicion of her working with people got confirmed as he likened her to Jessica, "You're the new guy in 304, right? I'm Valerie."

They shook hands and Nathan said.

"Nice to meet you, Valerie. I'm Nathan. Say, um... how well do you know Mrs. Rogers?"

Valerie's smile remained on her face, but the expression in her eyes seemed to change to somewhat confused with a barely visible frown.

"Just her name and face. Why?" she asked quizzically.

"Oh. Well, it's just, we live across from each other, but she seems to hate me."

Valerie chuckled.

"Oh, that can't be true. Mrs. Rogers doesn't hate anyone or anything. What makes you think that?"

"Well, I tried striking up small talk with her, but she never actually responds. Just gives me the angry stare, you know?"

"Hm." Valerie said, the smile now disappearing from her face.

She tapped her index finger on her chin and said.

"Well, come to think of it, she never was on good terms with anyone from 304, except that one girl from about a year ago. And there have been at least a few people who came and went in the past few years after her. Maybe after the girl left, she just started feeling like all the other tenants were intruders. I don't know."

"She was actually friendly with someone from my apartment? Do you happen to know her name?" Nathan suddenly got intrigued.

Valerie shook her head with a sad expression.

"Sorry. I only know Mrs. Rogers by her name."

"I see."

"Well, I would love to chat some more, but I have to get going now. Duty calls."

She smiled again and waved her fingers to Nathan, making her way out of the building.

***

Nathan rubbed his eyes, while clutching the knife with the other hand. It was almost time. He spent the previous few nights in a nearby motel, for obvious reasons and the bed wasn't comfortable enough to give him peaceful sleep. He didn't have anywhere else to go and he didn't want to get Sam involved in this. It was obvious that the apartment was dangerous, and telling Sam about it would only put him at risk. His friend would be adamant about going in there, even if Nathan told him there were booby-traps with poisonous darts set all over the place.

His friend wasn't so keen on exploring, as he was fascinated by paranormal occurrences. Whenever they went camping with friends and stories were told around the campfire, urban legends about ghosts and such, everyone would listen in utter silence and anticipation, at the edges of their seats. Many of the girls (and some guys) would even scream during an occasional story. But not Sam. He'd have a goofy grin plastered across his face the whole time and even ask for details afterwards, asking the storyteller if the tale he told was true or not.

There was one particular story that Sam once shared and as far as Nathan was aware, it was the story that got him interested in the whole paranormal shit. This story supposedly happened way before Sam was born, according to what his father told him about it. Apparently, in a small town where Sam grew up, there was an old lady whose name nobody seemed to know. This in itself was weird, because the town was extremely small and everybody knew everybody.

This one particular day, Sam's dad planned on driving out of town to a lodge in the words he used to own. He brought his dog, Mr. Potato with him on the journey, since he planned on being away for the weekend. On his way out of town, he saw the old lady standing by the side of the road, just staring at him silently. Mr. Potato started barking viciously by this point at the lady. Sam's dad ignored the barking and sped up, until he got to the gas station. She was there again. There was no way she could have gotten there before him, because the station was in a straight line of driving around 5 minutes away – and Sam's father drove fast, according to him.

Upon seeing the old woman at the gas station, the dog started barking once more. Sam's dad was afraid Mr. Potato would jump out and bite the old lady, but as soon as he opened the car door, the dog started whimpering and put his ears down.

The granny stood at the edge of the gas station, again, just staring at the car silently. A little creeped out now, Sam's dad tanked and bolted out of there. It started to rain heavily along the way and the sky darkened. It was weird, since it was still the afternoon around 5, mid-spring, so there's no way it should have been dark, but Sam's dad swears these dark clouds covered the entirety of the sky, making it seem like it was midnight.

He somehow got to the lodge and got inside, getting completely drenched even from the short distance from the car to the inside of the lodge. That's when things started to get even weirder. Apparently, only a few seconds after he got in, he heard loud knocking on his window. He faced the direction of the sound and realized it was the old lady from the town. Sam said that the lodge itself was in an area which is pretty open, so there was no way you wouldn't see someone approach you, let alone surprise you once you're inside. And not to mention this old lady was way behind at the gas station, making the journey on foot. Sam's dad even watched in the rearview mirror as he drove off and she was far behind, before he made a turn.

Sam's dad shouted at the woman to go away, but she just kept knocking louder. Mr. Potato started growling and barking more violently than before and suddenly the air was filled with the cacophony of rain, thunder, barking, knocking and shouting. The woman ignored the warnings and continued knocking. The window glass shattered under her incessant knocking, but she continued doing the knocking motions, as if the glass was still there. Sam's dad fumbled for the fake floorboards where he hid his rifle and pulled it out. But when he turned around to face the woman, she was gone.

Not only that, but the rain had completely stopped, the sky was clear again and all that was left as evidence of the entire encounter were the shards of broken glass on the floor of the lodge. Nathan has been skeptical of the entire story for years, even though Sam told him about it over and over. He was once even told the story from Sam's father himself, but remained somewhat unconvinced.

He was open to *something* unexplainable happening there, though. Sam's dad was of sound mind and wasn't the type to make things up or share unreliable information. If he said that the woman was for sure behind him with no way of getting to the station before he did, Nathan believed him.

The creaking started. Nathan clutched his knife firmer as he stared at the door. More precisely, he stared at the wardrobe he so clumsily dragged across the living room and placed in front of the storage. Behind the wardrobe, he heard the door opening, its incessant creaking resonating painfully, bringing with it the unmistakable presence of evil.

When the creaking finally stopped, Nathan felt no relief. On the contrary, the eerie silence felt like an ominous calm before the storm. He stared at it for what felt like hours. When he glanced at the watch, he realized only two minutes have gone by.

I just gotta stay awake for an hour, come on.

He encouraged himself. He thought about getting a gun, but he didn't trust himself with it. What if everything he saw in the corridor wasn't real? What if all of this was some elaborate prank for some reality TV show? He's seen videos of pranks gone wrong; people getting shot, punched, hit by cars, pushed off buildings, etc. He didn't want to risk going to prison over some idiot who thought it would be funny to prank him like this, as unlikely as it probably was.

If it wasn't a prank though, the question still remained if all of this was real. What if he was just hallucinating and the door never actually opened? He suddenly felt a strong urge to tell Sam about the whole thing. He wanted to call him right now and invite him over, so that the two of them could go exploring the corridor together.

No, that wasn't his wish. It was the apartment's. It wanted Nathan to lure his friend inside. He wasn't sure for what purpose, but he knew that whatever it was, it couldn't have been to share a frosty beer over a night of scary storytelling.

He started to feel tired from standing, since he had been standing in the same position for over half an hour. He sat down on the sofa, still clutching his knife. He never for a moment took his eyes off the wardrobe, especially making sure to monitor the edges of it, in case something tried to crawl out without him noticing.

He knew that a wardrobe wouldn't stop whatever was in there, but it would at least buy him some time to defend himself. Whenever the image of the eyeless, creaking woman bursting into his living room and jumping on him popped into his mind, he pushed it back. He rationalized that there was a reason he was still alive. She probably couldn't get inside, or maybe didn't want to. She could have killed him all those nights since he moved in, but she didn't. And he never once saw her close to his own apartment, so maybe she just wandered in the further reaches of the corridor.

His thoughts were interrupted when he heard something from behind the wardrobe. It was a voice.

"Nathan?" The gentle, female voice asked in a muffled manner right behind the wardrobe.

Nathan immediately recognized the voice, but he couldn't believe what he was hearing.

It was his grandmother.

Chapter 23

"Grandma?" Nathan asked with a trembling voice.

"It's me, Mr. Adventurer." The voice responded.

It can't be.

His grandmother used to call him Mr. Adventurer or Nathan the Adventurer all the time, because of his constant pretending of exploring uncharted places. Her husband, Nathan's grandfather Joshua died before Nathan was born, so he never had a chance to meet him. His grandmother had four kids, all of whom had their own children and yet out of all the grandchildren, she favored Nathan.

She even told him so openly all the time whenever he came to visit her. She'd always hold his side whenever his parents would scold him over not doing his homework or making a mess when playing Nathan the Adventurer. And she'd always help him find the lost cities and other forgotten places. She'd sometimes go out of her way and organize an entire treasure hunt, in which Nathan had to solve clues to find the hidden artifact.

"Nathan, sweetie." The voice said gently, "I knew you'd come see me again. You always were my favorite grandchild. That's why I always save the special desserts just for you."

Nathan suddenly felt like a kid again, like he was back at his grandma's house, playing games, eating her homemade apple pies and having a time of his life. He missed those times. The simple times, back when the biggest concern was how to find the imaginary treasure. Back when he could come to his grandmother, whenever he needed sanctuary from the real world, whether it was cruel or just boring.

He approached the wardrobe, tears welling up in his eyes.

"Grandma? Is that really you?"

"Mr. Adventurer, I've found a very rare pirate treasure map here, but I can't show it to you like this. Won't you come here and see it?" His grandmother asked in a playful tone.

Nathan wasn't thinking. Without hesitation, he got to the side of the wardrobe and pushed it, leaving a small gap between it and the doorframe, revealing the dark corridor ahead.

"Grandma, where are you?" he said, his voice echoing inside.

"This place is so big, Nathan! You're going to love this! Why don't you come here so we can explore it together? And later you can have some chocolate chip cookies I made."

The smell of freshly baked cookies suddenly permeated the air, filling Nathan's nostrils. His smile widened at this. He squinted through the darkness and asked impatiently.

"Grandma, where are you? I can't see you."

Grandma replied.

"Come on in, Nathan. I have a very rare pirate map."

The voice seemed to grow distant, which immediately made Nathan's smile drop and his unease grow.

"Grandma?" he shouted after her.

"Nathan, come on, sweetie! The treasure's waiting!" The voice was even more distant now, indicating that Nathan's grandma was moving away from him.

"Grandma, wait!" Nathan shouted, but there was no response.

He rushed over to the coffee table where he left his flashlight and snatched it. He flicked it on and shone it inside the corridor.

"Grandma? Where are you?" he called out to her.

"Come on, Nathan! Adventure awaits!" she giggled in the distance, her voice echoing.

"Grandma, it's so good to hear your voice again. I haven't seen you since-"

He took a step forward, stopping right at the threshold of the door. His words got caught in his throat, which suddenly felt as dry as a desert. Something inside him screamed at him to stop right where he was and not take a step further. He wasn't sure what, but all he knew was the hairs on the back of his neck stood straight, as he stared at the corridor.

"Come on, Nathan! I have a very rare pirate map!" The voice of his grandma shouted back once again.

"G-grandma?" Nathan called out to her, shining his light in various corners of the corridor, hoping to catch a glimpse of anything other than the permeating darkness.

"This place is so big, Nathan! You're going to love this!" His grandmother simply responded.

"Grandma, why don't you come out here?" he said with a hoarse voice.

"Nathan, come on sweetie. The treasure's waiting!"

There it was again, that same response. He hadn't realized it until now and suddenly he felt debilitating fear unlike any he felt before. Those sentences that his grandmother was uttering were on a loop. Same sentence, same intonation, to the letter.

"This place is so big, Nathan!" The voice came again from the corridor.

Nathan slowly backstepped and grabbed the edge of the wardrobe. Steadying his breathing as best he could, he pushed the wardrobe back in its place in front of the door, as the voice of his grandmother continued to haunt him playfully, as if nothing happened. Nathan ran into the kitchen and grabbed the biggest knife he could find. He glanced at his watch. 2:24 am.

He was behind the kitchen counter the entire time, while his grandmother's voice tantalized him incessantly, always uttering the same couple of phrases, sometimes closer, sometimes further. Nathan ignored the voice, feeling like he was on standing on needles the entire time.

At around 3 am, something changed. The voice got much closer, as if it was right behind the wardrobe. It also got louder and more agitated. It uttered the same sentences, only this time the tone was higher-pitched and the way it spoke was faster. Nathan sensed anxiety in the voice. Or maybe it was anger. He couldn't tell with certainty.

By 3:15 am, the voice of his grandmother was so loud that it was practically shouting hoarsely. Nathan expected some of the neighbors to come complaining about the noise. He hoped that would happen, because sitting here and listening to it was hell. He could have just left, but something kept him there. He couldn't tell what it was, but he was sure that it was the same thing that constantly tempted him to go inside the corridor.

3:19 am.

The door started creaking, indicating that it was finally closing.

"WHY WON'T YOU COME?!" The guttural, deep voice no longer belonging to his grandmother, but rather something more malevolent shouted with utter finality, making Nathan jump back and knock a plate on the floor, shattering it in pieces.

Despite that, he never took his eyes off the wardrobe, afraid that something would just jump out as soon as he turned away. The door clicked with a loud locking sound and he was finally able to breathe a sigh of relief. He wiped the sweat off his forehead and tentatively went around the wardrobe and into his bedroom.

As he lay in his bed, he thought about what had just happened. Whoever that voice was in there, it wasn't his grandmother, because his grandmother had died over ten years ago.

Chapter 24

Despite not getting nearly enough sleep again, he felt okay in the morning. He read somewhere that this was a trick that the brain plays on the host when there's a lack of sleep. The first couple of hours the person feels great and energetic and then their energy suddenly plummets. To avoid getting burnt out, he went to buy some coffee and a load of Monster Energy drinks. He didn't even like energy drinks, but he needed them right now.

When he sat down by the desk and chugged the can in less than thirty minutes, he started to realize how much his life was spiraling out of control. He could just up and leave the apartment. Fuck all of this stress, fuck the paranormal bullshit inside it, he could just void his lease and find a normal apartment, even if it was as shitty as Aleksei's.

Except no, he couldn't. Otherwise he would have just left already. Something was keeping him here. It wasn't as simple as just leaving. It was like Martin said.

You won't be able to leave now.

What did he mean by that? He probably already knew. For days, he tried going out of the apartment, but whenever he'd go further than two blocks, strange things would happen. It all started whenever he tried to leave the apartment. Whenever he would get too far from it, he'd start to feel nauseous. The first time he tried to get out of town for a few days, he suddenly started feeling sick and was unable to get out of bed. The next time when he managed to drag himself into his car, he lost consciousness in the garage and woke up to an empty tank.

He tried calling a cab to give him a lift, but whenever he did it, either the line was busy, or the operator said they dispatched the cab driver, who never actually arrived. Even the motel he managed to get to a couple nights ago was very close by, literally two blocks away, and it still made him feel somewhat nauseous during his stay. It was as if the apartment knew exactly when he planned on leaving. So whatever was going on here, he was stuck. And he knew exactly what he needed to do to get out.

The apartment wanted to be explored. He avoided the answer for as long as he could, but it was clear. He had to find the girl named Michelle, the one he saw inside the otherworld of the apartment and there was no getting around it.

At exactly 3 pm, there was a knock on his door. Nathan was in the middle of some work, so he frustratedly got up and went to the entrance door. He swung it open, almost slamming himself in the head in the process.

"What's up, fuckboy?" Sam stood grinning in front of him.

Next to him was a buff, serious-looking man in his forties with slick, grey hair and a shiny leather jacket.

"Sam? What are you doing here?" Nathan asked, glancing at the man only momentarily, who stared ferociously at him, before he moved his gaze back to his friend.

"Decided to give you a little surprise visit. Since you kept finding excuses to ditch resolving the you-know-what issue."

Nathan opened his mouth in an attempt to tell Sam to shut up, when Sam dismissively waved his hand and said.

"Oh, don't worry. This is Nigel. He's the medium I mentioned over the phone."

Nathan looked at Nigel. The man gave a meager nod to Nathan, his serious facial expression never changing even the slightest. Sam clapped his hands together and said with a smile.

"So. You gonna let us in, or?"

Nathan scoffed. He was caught off guard and didn't want any fake psychic prancing around his apartment, looking for anomalies and ghosts.

"You know, I'm kinda busy with work right now, so…" Nathan said.

"Oh, come on. It'll be quick. We just need a few minutes, Nate. I promise you, you won't regret it."

Nathan knew full-well that those few minutes could easily turn into an hour, but he was well-aware that Sam wouldn't let up until he had his way. So he stepped aside and silently gestured them to get in.

"Great!" Sam said, not wasting one second.

Both he and Nigel walked in, not bothering to take off their shoes, Nigel's timbers leaving prominent, muddy imprints on the carpet.

"Hey, I'm just gonna need you to take off your… yeah, never mind…" Nathan tried saying, but the two guests were already in the middle of the living room.

Sam faced Nigel and said.

"Now, Nigel. Do your thing. I want you to really focus and tell us if you feel anything strange."

Nigel nodded and lifted his chin slightly, slowly glancing from one end of the wall to another. Sam tip-tied next to Nathan, leaned in and said.

"Now, watch this. I haven't told him anything, he doesn't even know what to look for."

"Oh." Nigel said grievously, his face changing from serious to a grimace, as if he had just tasted a lemon.

"Something wrong, Nigel?" Sam asked, nudging Nathan with his elbow and winking at him playfully.

"This place… I sense strong negative energy here. Oh my… I haven't felt this kind of thing in a while. Oh, dear."

Seriously?

Nigel raised one hand and put it up to his temple, as he slowly rotated in one spot. He raised the other hand and pointed his index finger at Nathan. Nathan looked at Sam in confusion, but a moment later, Nigel continued rotating to the left, still pointing his finger straight, until he was facing the storage door.

He then stopped and made a wincing sound, as if he just burnt himself. He eyed the door up and down and slowly approached it, lowering both his hands. He stared at it with his mouth agape for a prolonged moment. He raised his hand, which Nathan noticed was trembling violently. This seemed to get aggravated further, the closer his hand got to the door.

When the tips of his fingers finally touched the surface of the door, the shaking seemed to stabilize. He gently proceeded to place the palm on the door. He held it like that for a few seconds, and then he yelped and recoiled, holding his hand as if he had been pricked.

"What in God's name?" he said, intermittently looking at the door and Nathan and Sam.

Sam clapped his hands again and leaned on his knees, laughing violently, seemingly in happiness. He patted Nathan on the shoulder with great force and pointed a finger at Nigel and said.

"Ha! See, I told you! Nigel is the real deal."

Nigel seemed to look as bemused as Nathan, with Sam's jovial behavior contrasting the two of them. Nigel reached into his pocket and pulled out a handkerchief, and wiped the beads of sweat off his forehead. Nathan looked at Sam, beginning to think that he and Nigel were fucking with him.

"Samuel, this is a serious matter." Nigel said, turning his palms towards Sam, "I can't do anything about this, no, no, no. This is way beyond my power. We need to call a priest for this."

"A priest?" Nathan raised his eyebrows.

"Yes, a priest. This-this… door, or whatever it is, is a source of evil. Have you stepped inside?"

Nathan was taken aback. He looked at Sam and realized that all eyes in the room were fixated on him in silence.

"Please, tell me you didn't step inside." Nigel said as he took one menacing step towards Nathan, with worry in his eyes.

Nathan took a deep breath and said.

"No, I didn't step inside. The door's been locked since I moved here." He gave a fake smile to Nigel.

"Oh, thank god." Nigel wiped the newly formed sweat off his forehead, "You have to understand, this is an immensely evil place. To tell you the truth, it's a miracle you're still alive. Have you noticed anything strange lately? Some unexplained sounds, things moving around, waking up with scars or bruises you don't remember getting, a feeling of immense paranoia, like someone's watching you, etc.?"

Nathan's hairs on the back of his neck stood straight. If Nigel and Sam were in on this, this was an extremely fucked up joke. But Sam would never prank Nathan with a thing like this. Would he?

"Nigel, Nigel." Sam said loudly, trying to grab the medium's attention, "How do we open this sucker?"

"You don't!" Nigel looked offended, "And why would you wanna do that anyway? No one should be living here in the first place. This entire apartment should be burned down to the ground!"

"Alright, that's enough." Nathan finally interjected, much to the silence of the room which unpleasantly ensued, "We are *not* calling a priest."

He looked at Nigel and said.

"Thank you for coming, but that will be all. No, I haven't noticed anything weird. So I'm sorry to say, but you're wrong about your psychic bullshit. Now, if you would kindly leave my apartment, both of you, I would really appreciate it."

He wasn't angry, but he did feel upset. At first, he wasn't sure why, though. The mixture of them making their way inside and Nigel confirming his suspicions… yeah, that must have been it. The fact that the truth was actually confirmed.

Sam shrugged and said.

"Alright. Alright, Nate. But you and I are not done with the door, yet. We'll figure something out."

Nigel returned the handkerchief back into his chest pocket and suddenly seemed composed again. He looked at Nathan and said.

"Thank you for your time."

He outstretched his hand for a shake and Nathan tentatively took it. The moment he did, Nigel pulled him in and hugged him tightly. He held him like that for a long moment, before Nathan pushed him away.

"Get off me, man! What the fuck is your problem?!" he shouted, just about ready to punch Nigel, "Get. The. Fuck. Out."

Nigel nodded and he and Sam were through the door in seconds. Sam turned to face Nathan inside the apartment once more and said.

"Nate, Nate. If I can just-"

Nathan slammed the door in his face and locked it loudly. He expected Sam to knock and call out to him, but that never came.

Chapter 25

Jessica unlocked her apartment door and stumbled inside. She was dead tired and desperately wanted a glass of wine. The whole day of taking clients on tours of apartments was draining of her energy, especially Mr. Wilson, who asked a million ridiculous questions about the apartment.

He was an elderly man, who insisted that the radiator in the apartment be dismounted and replaced with what he had, since he believed it was more cost-effective. Then he asked if the trees blocking the window view could be chopped down. When she said no, he wondered if any of the other apartments in the building were available instead. It took everything in her not to break out of her role and snap at him.

When she first started doing this job a year ago, her face muscles would cramp up from all the forced smiling she did. Eventually, she learned to do it habitually and it even became like a reflex to her. Her family members and friends told her a few times to stop being fake with them with all the grinning, but she could never help it.

"Professional deformity."

She called it that way, having read somewhere that we bring our work inadvertently home with us. She had a friend who used to work in call center as a customer representative and since she used Dutch at work, she'd often start conversations in Dutch before correcting herself.

Jessica took off her shoes, feeling the pain in her heels and toes as she stepped barefoot onto the wooden floor surface.

She turned on the lights and dropped her purse on the bar-like chair next to the kitchen counter. She went inside the kitchen and flicked another switch.

Fancy, purple lights lit up the counter from above, casting violet shades down. She placed a pre-readied wine glass on the counter and opened the Chloe Rose. She poured the pink liquid into the glass, until it was half-full.

Half-empty, she thought to herself and poured another half, considering herself deserving of such a reward. She closed the bottle and placed it back under the counter. She picked the glass up and brought it up to her mouth. She smelled the aromas of watermelon and raspberries, savoring them. She'll wait until she's in a more comfortable position. She went over to the sofa and sat down.

The remote was positioned facing the TV, so without even picking it up, she pressed the power button and the gigantic UHD TV mounted on her wall flicked on. An episode of *How I Met Your Mother* was on, just in time for Barney Stinson to make a joke at which the audience laughed. Jessica leaned back on the sofa, crossed her legs and took a small sip of her wine.

She immediately felt herself relaxing both mentally and physically. This was her zone. She closed her eyes and laid her head back on the headrest of the sofa, listening to the jovial conversations of the show's characters and the exaggerated laughter of the audience. She could fall asleep easily like this, but it was still too early. If she fell asleep now, she'd get all groggy upon waking up and she would have an irresistible craving for sweets. She was already crossing her calorie intake with the wine, so she didn't want to screw things up further with chocolate she so cunningly hid from herself in the top drawer of the kitchen.

Her work phone suddenly started ringing from her purse, snapping her out of her half-sleepy state. She opened her eyes and leaned forward. She muted the TV with the remote and still holding the glass, she stood up with a sigh and approached the bar chair. She placed the glass on the counter and with finesse, fumbled around the purse cluttered with various items like makeup, medication and hygiene products, until she found her phone.

"Jessica speaking, how can I help you?" she said, grinning into the phone.

Professional deformity.

"Hi. I was told you were the one in charge of handling my apartment." A stern, male voice answered on the phone.

How rude of him not to even introduce himself. Was she supposed to magically read his thoughts on who he was, among the fourteen clients she was handling?

"Hi, which apartment is that, sir?" she asked politely, bringing the glass of wine to her mouth.

"SW Morrison Street, Apartment number 304." the voice said.

Jessica was about to take a sip, when she stopped. She felt her hand trembling, so she hastily placed the glass back on the counter with a loud slam. Did she hear that right?

"Did you say SW Morrison Street, sir?" she asked.

"That's right."

"Oh, well it's an honor to finally speak to you, sir. I didn't think you would ever call us like this, so I'm a little surprised."

"Yeah." The mysterious man on the other end said.

There was an awkward pause, so Jessica decided to kill it by saying.

"So, what can I do for you, Mr....?"

"I'd like to keep my identity a secret."

"Um. Yeah, of course." Jessica cleared her throat and asked, "So what can I do for you... sir?"

"I just wanted to check in and see how things are going with the new tenant. Is he uh... causing any trouble?" The man tentatively asked, as if probing to see what Jessica would say to his enigmatic question.

"No, not that I'm aware of. I mean, he's naturally interested in the door, like anyone would be. But other than that, he seems like a good tenant, good record and all."

"That's not what I'm interested in." The man swiftly responded, "Tell me, has he asked about me or any former tenants?"

Jessica was somewhat taken aback by his response, but she was used to working with rude clients by now, so she simply said.

"Now that I think about it, he has. But I told him I didn't know anything about you and that all the information about the other tenants is confidential."

"So, I take it he doesn't know about the previous tenants going missing?"

"No, not that I'm aware of. He asked a few questions about them, but I think he doesn't know. I told him that-"

"You *think*?" He interrupted her.

Jessica opened her mouth dumbly, not sure what to say. Maybe it was the fact that she's already had her patience tested today, but she felt like she was bursting at the seams with anger. Through her teeth, she uttered.

"Well, I mean… I don't know if anyone else told him anything. If he does know something, he didn't learn it from me."

"Alright. That's all I wanted to know. If he asks any more questions, just tell him what you've been telling him so far. Oh, and please don't try calling me on this phone. Have a good evening, Jessica."

"Oh, before you go, the tenant asked me to-"

The man already hung up and Jessica was left feeling perplexed and frustrated.

Chapter 26

"Yeah bro, don't worry about it, Nathan's cool. He's just probably having a bad day." Sam said to Nigel, as they shook hands with a firm grip.

"Alright. Well, uh. Listen." Nigel said hesitantly, as he scratched his cheek, "I uh… I really think you should be there more often for your friend. He uh… I don't think he's just having a bad day. I think it's that place. It may be affecting him badly."

Sam crossed his arms and frowned. He completely believed what Nigel was saying, but he was wondering if the medium dramatized it a little too much.

"Nigel, what did you feel back there?" he asked more seriously than he intended to.

Nigel sighed and scratched the back of his head. He looked extremely nervous, as he pulled out his handkerchief and wiped the newly formed beads of sweat off his forehead.

"Well, um." he said, "It was like I was standing in the middle of a torture chamber and there were dozens of people screaming in agony. I've never felt anything like that before."

Sam nodded. He was a firm believer of these things and never joked about them. He and Nigel went way back, when they met at a mutual friend's party. Sam was usually dismissed when talking about ghosts and other paranormal things, so he decided to keep it to himself when meeting someone new. However, when he met

Nigel and he told him that he wanted to get into the paranormal business, the flood gates opened.

Sam told him about his sleep paralysis and how he woke up with bruises on his arms once and Nigel told him about his ability to see his dead grandmother in his house. They bonded over their strange experiences and the following day after the party started sending each other various articles, videos and investigations about ghostly occurrences. From there, they met up and began hanging out.

This didn't last for long though, because Nigel soon found a guy in Idaho who claimed he could teach him more about his 'gift' and how to use it. Although Sam was sad to see Nigel leave, he was more than happy for him and wanted to know all the details about his work.

Sam never told Nathan about Nigel before, except in passing as 'a guy who he met a long time ago and spoke to occasionally'. He knew that Nathan wasn't a believer in these things and only talked about it on the rare occasions to indulge Sam. Over the years, he tried to convince Nathan of the most evident experiences and stories and his friend would listen and nod, but Sam wasn't an idiot. He knew Nathan long enough to figure when he was unconvinced.

But this door, there was something going on with it. When Sam was there for the first time and Nathan went to the bathroom, he thought he heard voices from behind the door. He wasn't sure if it was his imagination, so he got up and approached the door. When he heard what sounded like playful whispering between two girls, he knew that he wasn't imagining it. Of course, he didn't want to tell that to Nathan, to avoid getting him to panic or worse, dismiss his claims once again. So he kept it to himself, but was adamant about investigating the phenomenon. One thing was for sure though – whatever was in there could not be good and he felt it for himself.

Sam, who firmly believed and even craved seeing with his own eyes something otherworldly, didn't want anything to have with this door. So he contacted Nigel. Luck had it that Nigel was visiting Portland for the week and Sam grabbed the opportunity to get him to visit Nathan. When they went to his place earlier, Nathan looked like a wreck. He looked like he hadn't slept in days and was erratic and easily aggravated.

If he knew one thing about Nathan, it was that he would never talk about his problems. If he really was experiencing something paranormal which affected his life, he would probably not tell Sam about it, mostly because he didn't like burdening others with his issues. But Sam wouldn't give up so easily. Whatever was behind that door, they would find out together.

He thanked Nigel for all his help and apologized for Nathan's behavior and they said goodbye to each other. He went back to his apartment and opened a bottle of beer. He took a sip and placed it next to his desktop PC. It was already on, so he pulled the chair out and sat down. He double-clicked on the browser and opened the link he bookmarked earlier.

It was an article about limbo, which basically connected the world of the living and the dead. He was halfway done with it yesterday, before he got too tired to read on. He hastily found the sentence he left it on and continued reading. It usually took him a long time to finish something, since he would find distractions if it got too boring. This article however, was extremely captivating and had he not felt sleepy the previous night, he would have finished it in minutes.

Essentially, the article was explaining about the existence of limbo and how, although only theorized, has been reported by a plethora of individuals who claimed to have walked through various types of limbo. One person reported going into a house of mirrors in the amusement park, and upon exiting, everything was reversed. The article went on to say that he went back inside the mirror house and upon exiting a second time, everything was back to normal.

Other cases reported opening doors in their houses and finding themselves in a different version of their homes. Most of the people were too freaked out to go exploring this limbo or new world and would therefore backtrack, thus returning to their own world. Sam shuddered at the thought that there may be unreported cases of people who got lost in there forever.

One common thing that people report about these limbos is the fact that they needed to open doors to get to them, or that the doors opened on their own at certain times on their own. Tomorrow he would call Nathan, so that they could discuss the details more. There was no way he was letting him handle this alone. He closed the website down and checked the remaining pages he bookmarked. Five more sources. That'll probably be a rabbit hole leading to more sources.

He took a sip from his cold beer, already feeling refreshed.

Buckle up, Sammy boy. It's gonna be a long goddamn night.

Chapter 27

Nathan hadn't planned on using the rope. He had already stowed it away in the closet in his bedroom right after that first fateful night when he encountered the horrors inside, when something tugged his rope and him along with it. When he came back to his apartment that night, the rope was neatly stacked, like he never even touched it.

He knew what was on the other side, so he didn't need a rope. He did feel like he needed a weapon though, so he took the kitchen knife and held it firmly in his right hand, ready to slice away at that creaking bitch if she appeared.

The door opened at the usual time and Nathan had a feeling of dread as the dark corridor appeared before him, beckoning him once again. He took a deep breath, as if readying himself for a dive and stepped over the threshold, the familiar cold air washing over his entire body.

Yep, that's the feeling right there. he recalled.

He tentatively illuminated the ceiling and path ahead. For some reason, he had the impression that the woman from the corridor could scale ceilings and walls with no problem, considering how quickly she moved despite her body being so frail and defying all logic and reason. Then there was also that message which warned him to look above. It was clear that something was fucking with him in here, but he wasn't sure if someone was warning him, or if it was his own head playing tricks on him.

He barely had time to walk for fifteen minutes, when he saw a light ahead, much brighter and closer than last time.

This was all wrong. He checked his watch and realized that it was still 2:19 am. Not only was the time on his watch wrong, but he couldn't have reached the other side so quickly. Maybe time flowed differently over here. He suddenly remembered the whole wormhole conversation with Sam and wished that he could be here with him. Sam would have joked about the whole thing all the way through, even when staring the monstrosities in the face, Nathan had no doubt about that.

He stepped into the bright light, getting completely blinded by it. he closed his eyes firmly, but the light was too strong, so he shielded his face with his hands, rays of white still penetrating between his fingers. And then they disappeared.

Nathan gradually opened his eyes and lowered his hands. He realized that he was back in apartment 102, or the otherworld version of it. It was as decayed as he remembered it from last time and immediately he got a bad feeling washing over him, when he recalled his last visit here.

"I can see you're becoming more acquainted with the corridor and overcoming your fear." A familiar voice said next to him.

Nathan instinctively shone the flashlight to his left and came into view with Martin, the mysterious man from his last visit. Martin seemed unfazed by the beam of flashlight being pointed directly at his face, as he continued smiling, the bright light casting creepy-looking shadows above his eyes.

"Jesus, you scared me." Nathan said, suddenly feeling his heart begin thumping faster in a belated manner.

He put his flashlight away and Martin put a hand on his chest and slightly bowed his head.

"My apologies. I sometimes forget how stressful this entire ordeal can be."

Nathan continued staring at Martin in silence, expecting more to the answer. Martin seemed to be aware of this, so he opened his mouth dumbly, before closing it again. He stepped aside and gestured for the door elegantly and said.

"We have limited time, Nathan. Shall we?"

"What if... what if I run into that dangerous woman again?" Nathan asked hesitantly.

Martin straightened his back and frowned at Nathan.

"I'm afraid I don't know what you're talking about. This is just a residential building and all the tenants are friendly. I can assure you there's no one dangerous here. Now, please. You need to go and see her." He gestured to the door once more in the same elegant manner.

Nathan tentatively looked at the door and then back at Martin, who remained in the same position. Who or what in god's name was this person and why was he so kind and oblivious? Was he just pretending, or did he really not see what was going on here? Either way, Nathan knew he couldn't waste any more time.

He walked past Martin and opened the door, revealing the darkness of the corridor outside. He clutched his knife more tightly and swallowed, feeling how dry his throat was. He timidly shone the flashlight left and right, to make sure nothing or no one was there. As he stepped outside, he saw no light this time coming from the corner where the letterbox was. He had a strong urge to call out to someone out there, but he knew that could only be a bad idea.

He wasn't even sure what he should do, but something told him to go to his own apartment, to room 304. Maybe that's where he would find Michelle. He decided to go by his gut and started walking down the corridor towards the letterbox. He illuminated the walls and the crude messages once more, but this time they seemed to be different. Among the messages, it said:

DONT

STUCK

YOUR FAULT

CANT BREATHE

Nathan looked to the right around the corner and gasped when he realized that the exit was chained shut. There were heavy, rusted links connecting with each other wrapped around the double-door handles tightly, with a heavy, equally rusted padlock hanging from the lower side. The glass on the doors also seemed to be changed, as it had tiny metal bars across it, much like in a prison. And beyond them - darkness. There was no way Nathan could get through there, but not that it was his intention anyway.

He turned in the opposite direction and looked at the elevator on the left. The doors were just as rusted as the walls were decrepit and the button to call the elevator seemed to be missing. Despite that, Nathan was still able to push the inside of the button, not expecting the elevator to work, feeling something slimy get stuck on his finger.

Disgusted, he wiped it on his jeans, doing his best to fight to urge to illuminate the substance. His heart skipped a beat when the elevator whirred to life from somewhere above.

The sound steadily turned into a humming noise which lazily began descending. Nathan took a step back, as he impatiently waited for the doors to open. He pointed his flashlight down the corridor where he last saw the woman appear, breathing a sigh of relief when he realized it was empty this time. The humming reached the elevator in mere seconds and then stopped. Eerie silence permeated the air for what felt like minutes, until a startling thudding sound came from inside. It was followed by a rusty scraping, as the doors of the elevator slightly opened and got stuck.

"What? Come on." Nathan said to himself, as he took a step forward.

He pointed his flashlight at the gap between the doors and gasped, stopping dead in his tracks. Something was inside. He pointed the light down and saw a trail of dark red liquid leaking out from the bottom of the gap towards him in a thin stream. He pointed his flashlight in the direction of the elevator doors, focusing on the middle. There was definitely something inside.

He couldn't tell what it was and he dared not go closer, but from what his flashlight was able to illuminate, it looked like some sort of a fleshy, reddish substance. It was prominently pushing on the elevator doors from the inside, partially sticking out through the gap in various places. Nathan squinted, slowly moving his flashlight further upwards. There was one place where a small lump stuck out through the gap more than the rest. Nathan screamed and took a step back when he realized it was a human finger. He would have fallen on his ass, had there not been a wall behind him to support his back.

The beam of his flashlight violently bobbed up and down, when he illuminated a blue eye near the top of the gap. It blinked and Nathan just about lost it when he saw the pupil darting in various directions, either voraciously searching for something, or silently pleading for help in desperation.

He pushed himself away from the wall and ran down the corridor where he knew the stairs would be, his heart thumping against his chest. After he was halfway through the corridor, he stopped and looked back, panting and panicking. That thing wasn't following him. Of course it wasn't. Whatever it was, it was stuck inside the elevator. It actually looked like it was suffering. It even made a moaning noise while he was there, or so he thought.

What in the whole hell is this place?

He reprimanded himself for falling into the trap and going inside in the first place. But he didn't have a choice and there was no way he could go back now.

He faced the direction which he initially ran in and pointed his bobbing flashlight at the walls and ceiling, to make sure no abominations were lurking up there. Once he was convinced that he was safe, he apprehensively continued forward. The stairs were supposed to be just at the end of the corridor on the left side. He had to reach them, since the elevator was no option, unless he wanted to share it with that thing inside.

Hey, you mind scooting over a little? I'm heading to the third floor, what about you? Oh, don't worry, the elevator can comfortably hold five people, I think. He almost laughed hysterically at the joke he made in his mind.

On his way to the stairs, he carefully pointed his flashlight at every door. Every few seconds, he'd spin around, just to make sure nothing was there. To say he was paranoid was an understatement. One of the apartment doors on his left was open and he illuminated the interior. He was unable to see anything besides the devouring darkness, so he hastily walked past it.

Much like in the corridor, the apartment building got progressively more decrepit the further he went. The walls and ceiling looked like they were barely holding up and the floors had bigger potholes on them. Near the end, he illuminated something on the floor that looked like a trail of dark, viscous red liquid. It was probably once formed as a pool, as it was big and round. When Nathan moved his flashlight further up, he realized that the splotch of blood, if that's what it was, looked like something was dragged on the floor.

His heart began racing once more, as he pointed the flashlight into the darkness ahead. He timidly tiptoed forward with a hesitant movement, steadily following the sloppy trail of blood. It curved to the left and continued up the stairs. The stairs.

This was not a good idea. What was he thinking coming back here? If there's blood here, that means that someone got killed, because there was no way someone with so much blood loss could have survived. And if someone was killed here, that could potentially mean that he was in danger, too. He clutched the knife with his sweaty hand so firmly, that his fingernails started digging into his palms.

As if on cue, a heavy pattering of footsteps resounded upstairs, from right above Nathan and fading in the distance. Nathan instinctively pointed his flashlight at the ceiling, his hands trembling violently. He then suddenly felt vulnerable with the light not covering the area around him, so he pointed it at the stairwell, carefully scrutinizing the red trail which went up the stairs. He had to go up there, there was no other choice. Or was there? Maybe he could just go back.

"It's okay, Nathan." Martin's voice came from behind.

Nathan jumped and screamed, raising his knife and pointing the flashlight at Martin's ever calm face.

"Jesus Christ, Martin! What the fuck were you thinking?!" he said in a hushed tone, hesitantly glancing at the stairs once more for a brief moment.

"It's alright, Nathan. This place is perfectly safe." Martin calmly said.

"Safe? Do you see this? Someone's been killed here! And what about that… tha-that thing in the elevator?!" He pointed his knife behind Martin down the corridor.

Martin seemed unfazed and entirely bemused by Nathan's anxious behavior. He smiled and said.

"Come on. We don't have much time."

With that, he walked past Nathan and started going up the stairs.

"Martin, wait goddammit! You're gonna get yourself killed!" he said, trying to be quiet again, in case the person upstairs was listening.

It was futile. Whoever, or whatever was upstairs would have heard Nathan speaking so loudly anyway. Martin disappeared behind the corner and Nathan heard the echo of his shoes, as he climbed each step. If the shouting hadn't alerted the person upstairs, Martin's footsteps definitely would.

"Martin!" Nathan shouted again, suddenly feeling a surge of adrenaline.

He got to the bottom of the stairs and looked up at the darkness they ended in. He pointed the flashlight upwards, illuminating the wall which wound along with the stairwell to the left. Without thinking, he used the adrenaline rush to climb up the first set of stairs and then swung around and climbed the second set, all the while following the trail of blood which stretched across every step, trying not to think what awaited at the end of it. He stopped as soon as he made one step on the floor upstairs. This place… was different.

Nathan shone his flashlight around and realized that the walls here were moving. His eyes couldn't understand what they were seeing at first. He thought his mind may have been playing tricks on him, that he was getting dizzy or something. But then he shone his light on the wall right next to him and he stifled a scream.

"Oh, jesus, fuck!" he screamed and ran back to the stairs, almost tumbling down in the process.

Maggots.

Thousands, no probably more like millions of maggots covered every inch of every wall and ceiling, wiggling grotesquely and climbing over each other in what looked like orchestrated movement. Nathan shone his flashlight right above him and saw that the maggots squirmed on top of the ceiling, impossibly holding themselves glued to the wall. He pointed his flashlight to the floor and realized that not a single maggot was down there. He couldn't believe what he was seeing with his eyes.

He'd think that with all the squirming and slithering they did across each other, at least some would fall down on the floor, but no. It was as if the floor had something toxic that the maggots were trying to avoid. Their numbers ended right at the edge where the walls and floor met and not a single one touched the ground. It was the most disgusting, but also the most fascinating thing Nathan had ever laid his eyes upon.

"Fuck. What the fuck?" he managed to gasp out, frantically pointing his light in various direction.

He suddenly felt itchy all over his body and began imagining the maggots crawling inside his shirt, pants and hair.

"Fuck. What the fuck is this fucking place?!" he said, scared, frustrated and confused, all at the same time.

How did he ever get himself in this fucking mess? Why didn't he just stay in Aleksei's shitty place and make his peace with the broken oven and bouts of heat and cold during summer and winter? He wished more than anything that he could go back to that life right now, when things were simpler, when he got eight hours of sleep and did his boring job and got drunk with Sam. He wondered what Sam was up to right now and what he would have done in this situation. A vague smile inadvertently stretched across his face when he imagined Sam being all ecstatic over the wall of maggots phenomenon.

The thought gave him a slight boost of courage. He exhaled, a little calmer now. He had to go through here. It was either going through the maggot-infested hall, or going back to that amalgamation in the elevator.

He took a slow and hesitant step on the floor of the second floor, shining his light at the ceiling to make sure no maggots would fall on his head. A moment later, he figured he'd much more hate them falling onto his face or in his mouth as he stared up, so he tightly pulled his shirt down, grateful that it had no collar which the maggots could fall into. Stiffening his neck and not daring to look up every second despite the strong urge, he turned left and pointed his light at the stairwell which was supposed to lead up to the third floor.

It was blocked. At the bottom of the stairwell was a set of rusty bars, stretching from top to bottom, with no visible way to open them.

"Fuck." Nathan said, as he pointed his light through the bars at the top of the stairs.

"Holy shit!" he screamed.

Something was there. He couldn't tell what exactly, but for the split second that his flashlight illuminated the top, a skinny, pale creature came into view, before it scurried around the corner.

"What the hell was that?" Nathan asked, his heart beating violently in his chest and shivers running down his spine.

He felt somehow better when he spoke to himself aloud like that. He felt less alone in this god-forsaken place. Whatever that thing at the stairs was, he couldn't go its way anyway, to what he gave a silent and thankful prayer. He turned left towards the corridor and pointed his torch down it, partially illuminating the wiggling walls of maggots. He knew that the fuckers were right above him, but he tried not to think about it actively or imagine them squirming their way onto him.

"Martin? Are you there?" he asked in a somewhat hushed tone.

There was no response, which he pretty much expected. He started walking down the hall. As he did, he started seeing the apartment doors on both sides. Amazingly, they were untouched by the maggots, as well. Just like with the floor and walls, the maggots verged just on the edge of the doorframe, but dared not touch the door itself.

Although the tiles of the floor looked cracked and dilapidated, Nathan couldn't see the walls and ceiling over the abundance of maggots covering them. The doors however, confirmed his suspicion that this floor was just as old as the one below. As he got to room 202 on the left side, he saw that it was left slightly ajar. Nathan pointed his flashlight at it and the door slammed shut with a loud bang.

He jumped back with a panicked scream and then froze, remembering that the maggot wall was right next to him, almost brushing against it with his shoulder.

What in the holy fuck was that? This place is fucking with me, no doubt about it. It's just... it's just fucking with me.

Where the hell was he even going? The stairwell was blocked and the elevator was… occupied. There was no way to get to room 304 from here. And then he heard it.

Voices, coming ahead. It sounded like two people were having a conversation, but he couldn't tell what they were saying. Their voices carried throughout the corridor and Nathan followed the sound. The voices gradually got louder and Nathan was able to discern a female and a male voice coming from room 204.

Wait. That's Vincent's room.

Nathan tip-toed his way in the direction of the sound, trying to muffle the noise of his footsteps upon the broken tile floor as much as he could in order to try and discern any notable words or sentences. He pointed his flashlight at the door of 204 and realized it was propped widely open. Maggots crawled all around the doorframe, just like with the other apartments. This room however, entirely contrasted the rest of the doors, as this one emanated a faint, yellowish light from the inside.

Nathan slowly got closer, while swerving around to see if anyone or anything was following him. The voices were gradually becoming clearer and Nathan thought he heard distress in them.

"What do we do now?" The elderly female voice came clear as day from room 204.

Nathan stepped in front of the door, pointing his light inside. He saw the foyer and further beyond that the living room. They were in pristine condition; fully furnished, clean, kept up.

"We'll have to keep it secret for now." A rough male voice came with an echo and Nathan instantly recognized it as Vincent's.

Feeling a surge of hope, he ducked under the doorframe (even though his head was way below it even when standing) to avoid the maggots and stepped inside the apartment.

"But what if they find out about it?" The female voice came again and it sounded like she was on the verge of tears.

"Hello?" Nathan called out, suddenly feeling safe in this apartment.

If Vincent was here, Vincent would protect him. Nothing could go wrong with a hardened veteran like him around, right?

"They won't find out." Vincent said.

Nathan presumed that the voices were coming from the room to the right, so he peeked around the corner. He was staring at a tiny, neatly decorated kitchen with a table barely big enough for two people to eat. Vincent and a woman around the same age who Nathan assumed was his wife Margery were sitting across from each other at the table. Margery had her face buried in her hands, while Vincent stared at her with his fingers crossed, a grievous expression on his face.

Heavy bags were under his eyes and he looked like he had lost 20 pounds. He was entirely different than what Nathan saw in person.

"Vincent?" he gently called out to him.

Neither of them responded. Margery put down her hands, revealing a tear-smeared face. She looked at Vincent and asked.

"I just… I don't know what we should do. Maybe she'll come back."

"No, she won't come back, Margery." Vincent shook his head, "Listen, I know this is hard. But let me handle the whole thing."

Nathan got the urge to call out to them once more, but he knew that it would be futile.

"But what if someone finds out about it? If the neighbors find out that we knew something, but kept quiet-" Margery asked again, until Vincent interrupted her by putting his hand on hers firmly.

"They won't find out. Margery, look at me." Vincent looked stern, but compassionate at the same time.

Margery looked at him, with her lips trembling.

"They won't find out." Vincent said.

And then they froze. Vincent held his hand on Margery's so firmly that his fingers turned white. He had a slightly concerned expression on his face, which Nathan had not seen before in him. Margery's face was contorted into a painful grimace, as she probably tried doing her best not to break down entirely.

What were they talking about? What exactly were they hiding from the others? Did Vincent know something about what was going on in apartment 304? Or maybe something was wrong with the entire building? What if everyone had a locked door and they just simply hid the existence of it from one another?

Nathan's thoughts were interrupted when he saw something drop on the kitchen table with a wet thump, right next to Margery's and Vincent's hands. He squinted at what looked like a tiny clump of something. And then another one fell down. And then ten more, twenty and more and more little pieces of something slowly falling down one by one on the table and beside it with wet splotching sounds.

It took Nathan a moment to realize that he was staring at maggots. His eyes widened and he looked up. The maggots were right above him, covering the entire ceiling, just like outside. They weren't there a minute ago and now they were squirming above on the ceiling, falling one by one. Nathan felt one fall on his shoulder, and he screamed, swatting it off.

It was futile, because more kept falling and he felt them touching his neck, hair and arms, even managing to wiggle their way inside his shirt. At the exact same time, the maggots began falling in waves, beginning at the other side of the kitchen, massively plummeting, as if someone was pulling off a band-aid off the ceiling.

A big, fucking maggot-infested band-aid. He managed to think to himself in that whole mess.

Nathan screamed when he saw the wave falling towards him and turned around. He began running, stomping on the maggots on the floor in front of him with squishy sounds, but within seconds, the wet globs of the maggots overwhelmed him. He slipped on the slimy, slippery stains of the maggots he stampeded on and fell head first. He could barely see anything from the larvae. He felt them wiggling their way into his shoes and pants and then ears and mouth and he screamed, rolling and swatting at his head.

And then the sensation suddenly stopped. Nathan continued rolling in panic and dared open his eyes for just a moment. He was back in his apartment. He got up in a sitting position and looked down, frantically touching his face, neck, and arms. There were no maggots. He happened to glance at his watch and realized it was 3:19 am.

And the door was closed.

Chapter 28

Nathan felt itchy the entire day. Although he wasn't sure if the whole maggot experience was even real, it felt as real as it gets and it was traumatizing. He went as far as to lift his pillow and turn it over before going to bed, in case there were any stray bugs on it. Every sensation he felt made him paranoid while trying to fall asleep. He didn't have good experiences with bugs in the past, so he assumed that the apartment may have been playing tricks on him based on his fears.

Back when he was around 6 years old, he woke up to find a giant fucking cockroach right next to his open mouth. He screamed so loudly that his dad ran inside with a baseball bat. When he realized that it was just a bug, he shook his head and killed the bug for him, but not before patronizing him and telling him that bugs weren't that dangerous.

And then when he was 10, he went to visit his grandpa, who made him eggs and bacon. When he lifted one part of the eggs with his fork, he saw a bug wiggling under the egg on its back. He lost his appetite, even though his grandpa tried telling him that it was just a harmless fly which probably fell off the ceiling while he was cooking. That was no fucking fly.

Nathan's experience didn't get any better when he moved into his first apartment after growing up and getting a serious termite problem. And from there, it only got worse with the revolution of the internet and the more widespread sharing of creepy pictures related to deadly flesh-eating bugs, or gigantic spiders, spiky, venomous centipedes and other such abominations.

As hard as it was to get the maggots out of his head, it was even harder to get the sight of Vincent and Margery out. If the conversation he heard was real, then Vincent was hiding something, but what? What could he possibly be hiding, which had anything to do with the apartment, save for the fact that he knew about the corridor?

Maybe, just maybe, he knew something about the previous tenants. He did seem suspicious when Nathan asked him about it. But why would he hide it? Something terrible must have happened to the tenant, if it was worth hiding. He had to know what.

Without wasting any time, he got out of his apartment. He saw Mrs. Rogers from 303 unlocking her door in a hurried manner.

"Ma'am, wait." Nathan said, no longer able to keep silent.

She ignored him and rotated the key, while a loud clicking sound resounded. Nathan got to the right of her and said.

"Ma'am, I just want to-"

"Stay the hell away from me." She tersely retorted and looked at Nathan so angrily, that he had no choice but to oblige.

She turned to the door and grabbed the doorknob, twisting it in the process. Nathan opened his mouth again.

"I just need to know some things about my apartment, that's all."

The woman held her hand on the doorknob firmly, staring blankly at the door.

"Your apartment?" she asked, turning her head towards Nathan once more.

"Yeah. Listen, I know it sounds crazy, but my life may be at stake here. You must know something about… whatever is going on in there. Please." Nathan said as politely as he could, searching Mrs. Rogers' face for any kind of compassion.

She slightly turned her head towards him. There was something in her eye and it wasn't hate or annoyance. Nathan felt that there was some sympathy. Before he could decipher it further, the lady turned back to the door and said.

"All I'm going to tell you, is that you need to get out of that apartment, if you value your life. Now leave me alone."

Before Nathan could say anything else, she got inside and slammed the door shut in his face, much like in their first encounter. What did she see that made her so afraid of in apartment 304?

There was no use dwelling on it, so Nathan instead decided to focus his attention where he could actually get some answers. He climbed down to the second floor. It was 12 pm, so he hoped he wasn't interrupting anything. Vincent was retired, so he could hardly catch him working or whatever. When he got to the door of apartment 204, his heart sank. There was a note plastered on the door, which said in crude letters.

GONE FISHING. BACK IN A FEW DAYS.

Nathan began grinding his teeth in frustration. Against good judgment, he rang the doorbell, hoping against hope that someone would be there. When no one responded, he pressed his ear against the door and held his breath, listening for any noise coming from inside. Nothing.

He pressed the doorbell again, holding it annoyingly longer this time. If anyone was inside, they would have heard it and opened the door by now already. He ran his hand downward across his face in anger and strode back upstairs. His phone buzzed and he pulled it out of his pocket with frustration, as he closed the apartment door behind him.

He expected it to be work, but it was an unknown number. A message flashed across the screen that said:

YoU hAVe tO fInd ME

The message seemed to have various strange symbols and dots around the letters, as if it was glitched. And then another message came through from the same number.

Yo CanT s%4E H*m.*

Nathan's heart began beating faster. He called the number without further thinking and turned on the speaker. For some reason, he was too afraid to put the phone up to his ear. It took the phone a moment to connect and then it began ringing.

After only two rings, it sounded like someone picked it up, but there was no sound on the other end.

"Hello?" Nathan said, staring at the phone, while his hands were trembling.

A loud, creaking sound came from the phone so abruptly, that Nathan dropped it on the ground and gasped. As the phone fell on the carpet, the screen pointed upwards, the creaking ceased for a second, before continuing again. And then the call ended.

"What the fuck." Nathan said, hesitating to get near his phone.

He tentatively bent down, observing the locked screen with caution. No more sounds came from the phone.

Chapter 29

Nathan told Anthony that he desperately needed a few days off, despite initially refusing to use his PTO. He wasn't sure what was going to happen next, but he did know that he wouldn't be able to focus on work until this whole door thing was resolved. He prayed that the entire ordeal would end by the time he had to go back to work.

I'll solve the mystery of the door and then get back to work in a few days. I'll work really hard, overtime probably, but I can still earn that promotion. He kept telling himself in desperation, despite not believing it himself. In truth, he really just wanted his life back to normal now.

He hasn't been inside the corridor last night. He felt like he was being drained of life every time he did go inside and maybe that was exactly what the apartment wanted.

He went down to Vincent's apartment at around 9 am after having a meager bagel for breakfast, which he bought in a nearby bakery. He was pleased to see that he could at least get that far without any strange occurrences. The GONE FISHING note was still stuck to his door and upon ringing the doorbell, Nathan got no answer. He was starting to get impatient.

What would he ask Vincent, anyway? What was it that he and Margery were hiding? It's not like he could ask him something openly, just like that. Vincent was definitely hiding something, though, and although Nathan had no concrete evidence, he knew it had something to do with either the apartment or the building. Something happened and they swept it under the rug. He could start by asking him about Michelle, the girl he talked to in the apartment's vision. For some reason, she was important for Nathan to find, he just couldn't connect the dots yet.

He went back upstairs, feeling defeated. As he inserted the key inside the lock from the fourth try, he heard a door open behind him. He ignored it, not even bothering to greet his neighbor, as he knew it was Mrs. Rogers and she was probably going out somewhere.

"Young man?" her voice came from behind.

It was soft, just like when she was speaking to other people and it surprised Nathan so much, that he was compelled to turn around. Mrs. Rogers stood at her door, leaning on the doorframe, with a tentative smile on her face.

"Do you want to come in for a cup of coffee?" she asked.

Nathan opened his mouth, taken aback by this question. Did he hear that right? Was his neighbor from 303, the one who refused to even look at him from day 1, calling him inside her own place for a cup of coffee?

"Well, come on, boy. I don't have all day." Her tone returned to the usual stern one, which snapped Nathan out of his trance.

"Uh, yeah. Yes, I'd love to." He clumsily responded, as he scratched the back of his head.

"Come on in, then." She turned around and went inside her apartment, leaving the door open.

Nathan quickly followed, afraid that she may change her mind if he lingered outside for too long. The foyer was dim, casting a depressing, orange light on the room. It immediately reminded Nathan of his dad's place. The entire studio where his father lived was dimly lit and unkempt, with empty takeout containers and beer cans scattered all around the place. Nathan knew that the light had almost nothing to do with it, but stepping inside Mrs. Rogers' apartment brought back that bad feeling from when he visited his father the few times he managed to make the effort.

Mrs. Rogers went into the living room and waited for Nathan by the door. Nathan took off his shoes, feeling like he was walking on needles from the old lady's unrelenting gaze.

"Come on in, make yourself at home. You can sit on that sofa there." She pointed at the old-looking sofa behind the coffee table and went into the kitchen.

Nathan nodded and sat down, glancing around the room. He could tell that an old person lived in this apartment, from the black and white photos on wardrobes, old-fashioned tables, etc. There were also unsightly oil paintings on the walls, of things Nathan couldn't even begin to describe. He further surmised that Mrs. Rogers was religious, because there were a number of crosses on the walls and shelves, as if she was trying to sanctify the entire apartment.

The only things that made the apartment look somewhat new was the fact that the walls were pristinely pink, most of the furniture looked ten years old tops, entirely unlike the World War II era style furniture his grandmother used to have and on top of that, Mrs. Rogers had a flat-screen TV. The apartment at least *looked* cozy. And it probably didn't have any doors leading into a nightmarish world. Mrs. Rogers shouted from the kitchen.

"I'll be in there in a minute! Do you prefer coffee or tea?"

"I'll have whatever you're having." Nathan hollered back.

The sound of drawers opening and closing resounded from the kitchen, followed by a clatter of dishes. Nathan's eyes focused on one photograph in particular, of a young woman in a wedding dress and a handsome-looking man. They were smiling.

"That's Harold, my late husband." Mrs. Rogers said, to Nathan's surprise as to how she appeared in the living room so stealthily.

"I'm sorry." he muttered.

"Don't be. We had a happy life together. Watched our children grow up. Managed to say our goodbyes before he…" She stared at the photo, as if reminiscing.

Nathan detected a glint in her eye. Mrs. Rogers got in front of the sofa opposite of Nathan and slowly sat down, supporting herself with her arms. Prominent blue veins bulged from her hands, as she did so.

"How many kids do you have, Mrs. Rogers?"

"Dolores. You can just call me Dolores. And I have three kids." She looked to her left at the non-black and white photograph, which had two teenage girls and one young boy in it, "They're all grown up now. Sally has two beautiful boys and Victor and his wife are expecting. As for Anna…" Dolores chuckled, "That one just wants to enjoy life. I can't blame her. But I hope she decides to settle down before it's too late."

Nathan nodded. There was an awkward silence between them where he didn't know what to say. What did he have to talk about with an old woman that would work well as an icebreaker, before he moved on to the main questions?

"What about you, young man? And what is your name?" Dolores asked with a lazy smile.

"Nathan, ma'am. And I have no wife or kids. I like to believe that I still have time to start a family in the future." He smiled.

Dolores leaned back in her sofa.

"I noticed you've been hanging out with Vincent from apartment 204 lately. He is a nice man." she said.

"He sure is, ma'am."

"Dolores." She corrected him.

"Dolores, right. Sorry. I really admire him, being in the Marines and all, it really is impressive. I can see him as being a stern, commanding type."

Dolores let out a laughter. It was surreal to see the old lady laughing.

"Oh, Vincent just looks scary. But trust me, he is as harmless as a kitten. He likes to put on this act of being a tough guy, but I can see right through him. My Harold was like that, too. Acting all macho, especially in front of other people. But us women have our ways of controlling men without them even realizing it. You can ask Vincent's wife about it." She chuckled.

Nathan felt like the mood was being lightened. This was good, he needed Dolores to be as relaxed and as open as possible, although he assumed that she invited him because she wanted to talk about more serious matters anyway.

"Well, he could have fooled me." Nathan said.

Dolores stood up and said.

"Excuse me, I need to get the pot of water off the stove. I hope you like chamomile tea?" she said, as she slowly shuffled out of the room.

"That'll be fine." Nathan said.

He was indifferent to any kind of tea and only drank coffee when he felt like he really needed it, but for now, as long as it took him a long time to drink it, enough to get all the answers he wanted, it would be fine.

There was another sound of clattering coming from the kitchen and then brief silence. Moments later, the clattering began again, much more unsteadily this time and Dolores emerged out of the kitchen with an entire tea set, the pot and stacks of cups shaking dangerously with rattling noise. Despite looking unsteady, Dolores managed to place the tea set down on the coffee table with finesse and sit down on her sofa.

She took a cube of sugar and plopped it into her cup.

"Be careful, it's very hot." she said.

"Thank you." Nathan said and tossed in two cubes of sugar inside his own cup, watching with relish as they slowly dissolved in the orange liquid.

He touched the outside of the cup with his hand and removed it when the heat started to burn his fingers. He always got his tongue burnt from hot drinks, because he was too impatient to wait for them to cool off. Waiting for the drinks to cool off worked well in his favor this time, though.

He leaned back in the sofa and cleared his throat, as Dolores put a spoon in her cup and stirred it with a slight circular motion. She mirrored Nathan's movement and leaned back, placing her hands in her lap. Nathan suddenly became aware of her penetrating gaze once more, so he awkwardly cleared his throat again and leaned forward to toss in one more cube of sugar inside the cup.

"So, you plan to stay here for long, Nathan?" Dolores asked.

"You mean here in your apartment, or…?" Nathan connivingly asked, to which they both chuckled.

There was a brief pause between them, as the clock on the wall ticked loudly with each passing second.

"So. Apartment 304." Dolores said in a theatrical manner, nervously tapping her index finger on her lap.

Nathan looked up at her with raised eyebrows.

"Very strange apartment, that one." she said, "Very inhospitable."

She didn't move her gaze away from Nathan for one second. Despite the cup being warm, Nathan took it by the delicate handle carefully and sipped a tiny sip, feeling the warm water burning his mouth. He placed the cup back down and said.

"I'm not sure what you mean, Dolores?"

Dolores scoffed and shook her head.

"Oh, come on. Don't play dumb. Everyone in the building knows about the locked door. And a few know that it's not just a regular door." She raised her eyebrows pointedly.

Nathan leaned on his knees and frowned, as he asked.

"What do you know about my apartment, Dolores? Have you seen anything in there?"

She shook her head.

"No, not seen. Just heard." She leaned forward and took a sip from her tea, her hands now visibly shaking, but Nathan was unsure if it was because she was old, or something else.

"Heard what?" Nathan asked.

Dolores placed the cup back down and stared at it, before saying.

"Voices. They often come from the apartment. When I first moved here, I thought there were more people living in there. But the apartment has always been occupied by one person at a time. And then whenever they would go out somewhere, I would still hear someone speaking inside. And then when the tenants left for good… the voices remained, even though it was locked up tightly and no one was inside."

She ran her hand up and down her shoulder, as if she was cold and looked at Nathan. Nathan scratched his cheek. He knew that Dolores didn't just hear any voices in there, otherwise she wouldn't have been this distressed. What she heard inside must have been something far more unnerving.

"I know you probably don't want to talk about it, but I need to know what you heard in there, Dolores."

Dolores looked to her left at the photo of her and Harold. She took a deep breath and sighed. She looked back at Nathan and shifted in her sofa uncomfortably.

"The voices themselves aren't really what bothered me that much. I would hear them often, yes. And they would always speak in a hushed tone, as if they were trying to avoid being overheard. But they always spoke loudly enough for me to hear them. And then as soon as I would put my ear against the apartment door, they would stop. You see, it's unnatural. Because, there's no way they heard me, there's just no way. I snuck over to the door at least a few times, but as soon as I would press my ear against the door, they stopped.

But not like normal, you know how when the teacher catches you talking to your friends in class and you go quiet, but your friend still continues speaking for a moment or two before he realizes the teacher caught you? Well, these voices… it's like they all heard me at the exact same time and then decided to go silent.

And I could never tell what they were talking about. They just… they just sounded like they were panicked. Or plotting something important. I could never tell which one of the two it was."

Nathan felt a shiver run down his spine. Dolores cleared her throat and looked at the photo once more, before continuing.

"As scary as the voices were, they aren't what frightens me about that place." Dolores took a sip of her tea and looked at Nathan.

She smiled at Nathan and asked.

"Tell me, Nathan. Do you believe in God?"

"I do. I'm not an overly religious person and I don't go to church, but I was raised a Catholic and I believe in God, yeah."

Dolores nodded. She looked at her lap and asked.

"And what about the devil?" She raised her gaze back up, with a serious expression on her face.

Nathan frowned.

"I... I'm not sure."

"We were taught that the devil disguises himself and tries to make things look appealing. If he waltzed around in red skin, with a pitchfork and evil laughter, no one would ever give in to his temptations. But as a pleasant sight to the eyes... he ensnares us in his trap and he drags us into hell after we die. If there is hell here on earth however, then it is apartment 304, Nathan."

Nathan was on the edge of his seat. Dolores uncomfortably shifted in her sofa again. She sighed and began her story.

"About a month ago, in the middle of the night, I heard someone calling my name while I was sleeping. At first, I thought I was dreaming, but the voice continued, calling my name softly. Even when I opened my eyes, the voice persisted. It kept saying 'Dollie. Dollie, wake up." Her voice started trembling by this point and she put her hand on her mouth.

Nathan saw a new glint in her eye. She removed the hand from her mouth and continued, with a somewhat calmer voice now.

"Only one person called me that. My Harold. And Harold died 12 years ago from cancer. I missed him so much, that in my excited state, I didn't even stop to think about that fact. At the back of my mind, I was making excuses as to how he survived. You know? Maybe he never died and was in hiding or something. I don't know. I was making up these stupid excuses in my mind."

Her voice trembled uncontrollably as she spoke now, so she cleared her throat and wiped at the tears trickling down her face, continuing to talk, despite seemingly barely able to utter sentences without breaking down.

"Anyway, I heard him calling me. Now, you have to understand that the walls here are very thin. Your neighbor can cut onions and you will start to cry, is how thin they are. I got up and opened my front door and then I heard his voice much more clearly. He said 'Dollie, I'm in here. Come to me, sweetheart.'.

It was clearly coming from 304 and I thought it would be locked, because no one lived there at the time, but it was unlocked. It was *unlocked*. I pushed the door open, revealing a dark apartment. As soon as I stepped inside, the ecstatic feeling no longer overwhelmed me. Instead, I felt cold, physically and emotionally. It's hard to explain. It's like I was suddenly walking into a dead place which had no hope of anything good or alive ever being inside it.

At first it was quiet, and then I heard it again. Harold's voice, gently calling out to me, telling me to come to him. I wasn't exactly sure where the sound was coming from, until I got to the door near the kitchen. And then I heard him clearly on the other side. Now at this point, all the barely sparked hope I had of seeing Harold had vanished and was replaced by this… dreadful feeling and this fear which I never felt before. I asked him if it was really him, leaning against the door. He said that it was and that he missed me a lot. He said that we could be together now again, all I needed to do was open the door.

I grabbed the doorknob and a part of me wanted to turn it, but something told me to stop. Everything sane in me was screaming at me to not open the door. I mean, just then my senses started to return properly to me. Harold was *dead*. I watched him die. I watched him get buried. There was no way he was behind this door. This realization suddenly hit me and I felt so foolish for even thinking that that… thing inside could ever be my Harold.

Whatever was in there sensed my hesitation and it urged me to open the door, becoming increasingly violent. I stepped back and Harold, or that thing impersonating him began cussing at me, calling me a whore, telling me he never loved me and that he couldn't wait to die to get away from me, and other such horrific things.

I ran out of there as fast as I could and locked my apartment door. I ran into my bedroom, covered myself with my blanket over my head and recited the Lord's prayer over and over. But I heard his muffled voice calling out to me the entire night. Eventually, some time before dawn, it stopped."

She looked at Harold's photo once more and then back at Nathan with finality in her eyes, as she said.

"I haven't been able to sleep well since then. I've become more religious and I try to go to church as often as I can. Whenever I open the door, the sight of 304 scares me. But I know I am safe in here. While the previous tenant lived in 304, she and I were good friends. She always offered to help carry my things, bring me groceries, and so on. But as time went on, she became more closed off. At first, I thought she was getting annoyed with me, or hiding something, or just tired. She was a student after all. But later I began to realize there was much more to it."

Nathan's eyes widened. Someone actually knew the previous tenant from apartment 304. He can finally get some information. So he asked.

"You actually knew a tenant before me?"

Dolores grinned.

"Oh, not just knew her. She became like a daughter to me in the six months that she lived here."

"So, who was she?" Nathan impatiently asked.

"Her name was Michelle." Dolores smiled.

Chapter 30

"Well, let's hope they bite better today." Vincent said, as he swung the fishing rod.

The line flew ahead with a reeling noise, followed by a distant splash as the hook hit the water.

"It's almost 6 pm, so the fish are probably hungrier." Vincent's friend Brock said, as he sat in the wooden chair.

He was holding a cigarette in his stubby fingers and had his shirt unbuttoned, prominently displaying his beer belly and hairy chest. Sunglasses covered his eyes and the top of his bald head glistened from the sun. Vincent sat on the wooden chair next to him and gently placed the rod on the prop in front.

The lake was peaceful and not a single voice could be seen or heard. A red sun gleamed between the branches of pine trees that occupied the horizon. Vincent looked at the orange sky, feeling a sense of tranquility. He hadn't started going fishing until he retired. Having been in the military for 25 years, he always needed something to occupy himself. There was always a lot of work around the house where he and his family lived before, but soon that work became scarce and he had to find another hobby.

Brock suggested that he come fishing with him. Brock was an avid fisherman and even though he and Vincent knew each other for a solid five years, they never went fishing together, mostly because Vincent always politely declined. He considered fishing boring and uneventful. He wouldn't have gone at all, had he not been bored out of his mind the one day Brock invited him again.

At first, he regretted it, but once he started appreciating the silence and the peacefulness, he started to understand why Brock did it so often, despite his wife's protests.

"So, Loraine isn't angry with you?" Vincent asked.

"What do you think?" Brock responded with a smirk.

Vincent smiled and shook his head. He leaned aside and grabbed the bottle of beer he previously left next to the chair. He took a sip and held the liquid in his mouth for a moment, savoring the taste. He kept his eye on the line, to see if it was moving in any way.

"What about Margery?" Brock asked, blowing a plume of smoke out of his mouth.

"She's taking a walk, picking some mushrooms nearby. She used to be really into that kind of stuff when she was younger."

"Isn't that dangerous? What if she picks a poisonous one?"

"She knows what she's doing. Hell, she and I used to do it together before. But then when we moved to Portland, we weren't exactly close to any places that had wild mushrooms, so this is a treat for her." Vincent said, taking another sip of his beer.

Brock put the cigarette in his mouth and inhaled. A moment later he blew out the smoke and said.

"Back where I come from we have a story about that."

"Oh, yeah? Which one?" Vincent asked.

He placed the bottle of beer down and tapped the fishing rod, in hopes of attracting some fish. Brock nodded.

"Yep. There used to be a married couple in my middle school, teachers. They were biology teachers, if I remember correctly, and they used to go mushroom picking together. One day they accidentally picked a poisonous mushroom, apparently it resembled the edible one in some way. They hadn't realized what they did until they ate it for dinner and poisoned themselves. The police found them dead in their bed, as if sleeping peacefully."

"So they died in their sleep?" Vincent asked.

Brock chuckled.

"That's where the funny part comes in. Apparently, they realized they poisoned themselves after eating dinner and they were so pissed, them, a couple of biologists to accidentally eat a poisonous mushroom, that they wrote a letter in which they said goodbye, saying they knew they were poisoned, but refused to call an ambulance out of pride. Ain't that the craziest shit?"

"Jesus. And Marge says that *I'm* stubborn." Vincent shook his head, unable to contain his laughter at the absurdity of the situation, "Could have called an ambulance. At least that way they'd be embarrassed, but alive. Like this they are dead and everyone still apparently knows the story."

The two of them kept quiet for a long moment. Vincent thought about the fact that they had to go back home in a couple days. He enjoyed these peaceful fishing moments, but he felt uneasy leaving the apartment like that for too long. He had to check up on it soon and see if everything was okay.

"You know, I met a guy in my apartment building a few days ago." he said, "Pretty cool guy, I think you'd like him. Maybe we can invite him to go fishing with us sometimes."

"Well, depends. Does he know anything about fishing?"

"Did *I* know anything when we first started?" Vincent looked at Brock with a smirk.

"Good point. Sure, he can tag along, as long as he's not one of them vegans who bitch about destroying nature and killing animals."

"I don't think he's vegan." Vincent said definitively.

The top of the rod began tipping slightly. Vincent quickly stood up and reached for it.

"Looks like we got a big one!"

Chapter 31

"I'm sorry, you said her name was Michelle?" Nathan asked, staring wide-eyed at Dolores.

"Yeah. She was such a sweet, young girl. She used to be an art student, you know? Aspired to become a great painter someday. She even drew a picture of me once and it was really impressive, almost like someone just snapped a photo." Dolores let out a peal of laughter and shook her head, as if reminiscing.

"So, what happened to her?"

Dolores looked at Nathan with confusion.

"Wait, didn't they tell you?" She frowned.

"No, tell me what exactly?" he asked.

Dolores leaned forward and took a sip of her tea. She gently placed the cup back down and leaned back in the sofa. She put her hands on the armrest and said.

"About two months after she moved in, she began experiencing… strange occurrences. She complained of constant nightmares and claimed that there was something wrong with the storage door in her apartment. Back then I didn't know anything about it, mind you. I knew there was something wrong with the apartment, yeah, with the voices and all, but I chalked it up to my old age and paranoia. Oh, I wish I helped Michelle somehow." She shook her head mournfully, before continuing.

"Anyway, Michelle became more erratic as the months went by. She lost a lot of weight and barely managed to get more than a few hours of sleep. Despite that, she still always had a smile on her face and was as cheerful as ever when talking to me. I asked her if anything was wrong, but she'd always tell me it was nothing and that she just had trouble sleeping, the poor thing.

She visited me almost every day for the first few months and then just stopped completely. Shut herself inside her apartment. It was hard for anyone to get her to even open the door, let alone go out and do something. I tried inviting her over, but the few times that she did open the door for me, she barely just poked her head out to tell me she was really busy with her studies. By then she already looked like a skeleton and had huge bags under her eyes.

I knew that it wasn't healthy, but I didn't want to pry and shove my own suggestions down her throat. So I left her alone and it's a mistake I regret to this day."

Dolores stared at Harold's photograph in silence with a sorrowful expression on her face. Nathan didn't want to interrupt her moment of lamenting. When she looked back at him, she smiled bitterly and said.

"Sorry. It's really difficult, when you blame yourself over what happened. I first did it with Harold for many years, until I was able to come to terms with his death. And now Michelle."

Nathan nervously tapped his foot on the floor, patiently waiting for the continuation of the story.

"Michelle eventually stopped opening the door to anyone altogether. The superintendent got really worried when he got a call from her parents, who claimed that she never answered her phone. He took the set of spare keys that he had and opened her door and…" Dolores stifled a weep, "And she was gone. Just like that."

A tear rolled down her face and she wiped it away and said with a shaky voice.

"All of her things were there. Her art, her clothes, her half-eaten food. But she was nowhere to be found. It was as if she vanished without a trace. Her apartment was locked and the keys were on the kitchen counter, which left the police scratching their heads. I got in touch with Michelle's parents once and they told me that the police deduced that Michelle must have run away, which of course is absurd. She had no reason to run away."

"So, what do you think happened to her?" Nathan asked, now unconsciously fidgeting his fingers.

"Oh, don't play dumb with me, young man. You know darn well what happened to her." Dolores sternly said, looking down at him with red-rimmed eyes.

"The… the door?"

Dolores nodded.

"Whatever is inside that door, it's pure evil. I firmly believe that it got to Michelle. Wherever she is, I hope she is not suffering. The apartment will get to you too, if you don't get out."

Nathan leaned back and stared down at his lap.

"I mean it, Nathan. That place is dangerous. Have you heard or seen anything in there since you moved in?"

Nathan looked up at the old woman. Should he tell her or not? If he tells her that the door opened and that he saw

Michelle in there, she would urge him to get out of the apartment. Somehow, Nathan knew that Dolores would not advise him to look for Michelle and risk his own life, despite knowing him for a very short time. But he didn't want to give her false hope that Michelle may be alive, if she wasn't already dead… or worse. He knew that if he said he saw nothing Dolores wouldn't believe him, so he decided to cast small bait to appease her.

"Yeah, I did hear something, actually. One night, I heard my grandmother's voice." He looked at Dolores, carefully observing her reaction, to see if she bought it.

"When did she pass on?" Dolores asked.

"Years ago, when I was still a teenager. She had a stroke and spent her final days half-paralyzed in the hospital. She uh… she wanted to see me, but I… I didn't go. I was too afraid to see her that way. I didn't want to have my last memories of my perfect grandmother tainted by the morbid reality. So I refused to visit her, even though she asked for me. And then she died." He felt tears welling up in his own eyes and his vision becoming blurry, as he stared morosely at the cup of tea, "The guilt still hasn't gone away, after all these years."

That story was true and he never talked to anyone about it. Mentioning it now made it more real and that previously dormant feeling of guilt resurfaced again. Dolores sighed and looked down, while Nathan used the moment to wipe his tears away. Dolores asked.

"And this voice. It mimicked your grandmother? What did it say?"

"It called out to me. It uh…" He was about to say something about the corridor, but then remembered that it would be a mistake, "It just told me to open the door. It was on a loop. It kept repeating the same sentences over and over. And then towards the end of the night it got more aggressive. And then it just stopped."

"Oh, you poor child." Dolores shook her head, wiping away her newly formed tears, "So then, why not leave the apartment? You're young, you can find a new place. Any place is better than apartment 304."

That was a good question and Nathan couldn't think of a convincing answer to throw Dolores off.

"I just… you're right, I think I will. As soon as I'm done here. Right now I have to stay in the apartment for some work-related reasons, but I'll leave as soon as I'm done."

"By the time you're done, you may end up like Michelle, Nathan." Dolores said rigidly.

Her tone then suddenly changed to a compassionate one and she said.

"If you have nowhere to go, you can stay in my apartment, until you find something better. I don't mind it, but please get out of there."

Nathan's phone started buzzing, much to his relief.

"I'm sorry, I uh. I gotta get this." he said and pulled the phone out of his pocket.

It was Sam. Never had Nathan been so happy as he was now to get a phone call from him. He immediately picked it up and stood up, walking over to the foyer.

"Hello? Sam?"

"Nathan. Hey, how you doing?" Sam asked with a serious tone, which could only mean one thing.

He was testing the waters to see how angry Nathan was over the whole medium thing. The truth was that he didn't even have time to think about it, but between not sleeping enough and being cursed by an evil apartment, being angry at Sam was the least of his worries.

"I'm great, thanks for asking. What about you?" Nathan enthusiastically answered.

"I'm… fine." Sam said carefully, "You're not angry, are you?"

"Nah, man. Why would I be?" Nathan chuckled and looked at the living room to see Dolores sipping her tea.

"Well I just thought… never mind."

"If you're talking about that whole Nigel thing, no, it's fine. We're cool." he said.

He glanced at Dolores again, who was sitting as still as a statue. Although she was occupied with her tea, she may have been eavesdropping, so he decided he had to get out of here before she asked him any more tough questions.

"Hey, listen. I took a PTO. Wanna come over? There's something important I gotta talk to you about."

"I was just about to ask you that." Sam said, "What time works for you?"

"Um… now works." Nathan said.

"Great. Alright, I'm on my way, then. There's actually something I've been meaning to talk to you about, too. See you in a bit."

"Great. See you soon, Sam."

He hung up and turned back to face Dolores. She was walking towards him from the living room to the foyer.

"I take it you have to go?" she asked with a smile.

"Yeah, I got a friend coming over." He put the phone in his pocket and propped his shoulder against the doorframe, as he said, "Listen, I really appreciate everything you told me, Dolores."

"You'll need to make a decision, sooner or later. But the longer you wait, the more the apartment is going to drain you. Keep that in mind."

"I will, thank you. And um... I'm sorry about what happened to Michelle. She sounded like a really nice girl."

"She was. And you are a nice guy, too. That's why I'm giving you a warning." She stared at him with a stern face, as if expecting a response.

Nathan smiled and said.

"Thank you."

He put on his shoes and Dolores opened the door for him. She smiled warmly and said.

"Stop by any time you like. And don't worry, I won't be ignoring you anymore when I see you. Truth be told, I grow fond of people easily. I wanted to avoid having anything to do with you, because I was afraid if you grew on me and the same thing happened to you as it did to Michelle, I'd be heartbroken."

"I really appreciate your concern, Dolores. Don't worry about me. I'm built like a tank." He winked and stepped outside.

"You be careful there, Nathan. Oh, and one last thing. Hold on."

She scurried into her living room. Within seconds, she came back with a rosary decorated with yellow beads. The cross had a crucified Christ on it. She took Nathan's hand and put the rosary in it, saying.

"I want you to hold onto this." She closed his fingers around the rosary and held it firmly with both hands, "It has helped me that night when I heard Harold. If you ever feel overwhelmed, just hold it firmly and pray. I am sure that our Lord will come to your aid in dark hours."

Nathan tentatively nodded, as a sign to Dolores that he accepted the rosary. He wasn't overly religious, like he told her and doubted any rosaries or crosses or any other religious items could protect him in a place like apartment 304, but at the moment, he was desperate enough to try anything.

"Thank you." Was all he managed to say.

Dolores let go of his hand and clasped her hands together.

"I will try to find out what I can about the other tenants who lived here before you and Michelle. There have been at least three other tenants which I saw come and go. I never dared look them up, but now that we opened that particular can of worms, I feel that it is my obligation to help you and them, if they're still out there." She smiled once more reassuringly.

"Thank you, Dolores. For everything. If you find anything out, let me know. I will do my part, too."

"I know you will. Bye for now, sweetie."

Nathan turned around and heard the door close behind him. He clutched the rosary firmly, as his head spun a thousand miles an hour with all the newfound information.

Chapter 32

"Come on in, Samuel." Nathan sardonically used Sam's full name.

"Thank you, Nathaniel." Sam nodded, as he made his way inside.

Nathan closed the door behind him and the two of them made their way into the living room.

"Want something to drink?" Nathan asked.

"Nah, I'm good." Sam waved his hand dismissively, before slumping into the sofa.

Nathan sat on the couch and for a moment, an awkward silence filled the air.

"So." Sam said, as he tapped the armrest, "You look like shit, Nate."

Nathan couldn't help but chuckle. It was obvious, but he knew that Sam knew more about what was going on than he led on. He could no longer hide this from him. He decided he would tell him everything. The last thing he wanted was to die unexpectedly while stuck in the storage and for Sam to blame himself for his friend's death.

"I know." Nathan said, "I've been uh… having some rough days lately."

"I know." Sam nodded, "What Nigel sensed over here that day when we arrived, it wasn't bullshit, was it?"

Nathan looked down and sighed.

"No. No, it wasn't bullshit." he said.

Sam propped one leg over the other and said.

"Tell me what's going on. We've known each other for years now, you can't hide this shit from me. Whatever your problem is, it's my problem, too."

Seeing Sam serious like this was an extremely rare occasion. But when he did get like this, it meant that the situation was either really grave, or he knew it was no time to joke out of respect to the other person. Of course Sam would be willing to share his problems. They were like brothers.

"And who wouldn't wanna see some ghostly shit coming from a mysterious fucking door?" Sam said, making Nathan's sentimentality fade away.

They laughed.

"Talk to me, man."

Nathan rubbed his eyes and nodded. He leaned on his knees, sitting almost at the edge of the couch.

"It's the damn door. It's always been the damn door. It opens at night, at exactly 2:19 am and stays open for one hour before closing. And it's not a storage room, it's an entire fucking corridor which stretches… far. And I've been there and at the end is this different world, this building, *my* building, but different. And the shit I've seen there keeps me up at night and I know it sounds crazy even to someone like you, but believe me that this shit is real and I'm not losing my mind. I…"

He stopped and looked at the coffee table, unable to meet Sam's gaze any longer. He recited his problems so quickly, that it made him realize how much he had been bottling it up this whole time. He couldn't tell what Sam was thinking, since his facial expression remained indifferent the entire time. That's how rare it was to see Sam serious. Nathan looked back at his friend and continued.

"And there is... someone in there. Someone or something that keeps chasing me. And I can't leave the place. And all of what I told you didn't even skim the surface. I just... I dunno...."

Sam scratched his upper lip and stared at the coffee table for a moment. He then looked back at Nathan and said.

"I believe you, Nate. Now tell me everything I need to know, in detail."

Nathan told him everything he knew about Michelle, about how he couldn't leave the apartment area, how he'd seen twisted and disgusting things inside the apartment, including the creaking woman and how he needed to find Michelle. It felt good opening up about this to someone. After he was done speaking, a lingering silence filled the room. And then Sam said.

"So, we going in tonight?"

Nathan was flabbergasted. After everything he had told Sam, he didn't think he would still want to even be near that place.

"Sam, did you even hear what I-"

"I heard you. And I'll be damned to hell if you think I'm letting you have all the fun with the spooky shit." He grinned and stood up.

Nathan stood up with him and raised his hand, protesting.

"Now wait a second. You don't understand. This place is dangerous. It's like… it's like it has a mind of its own and plays tricks on you based on your fears and insecurities. You know? Trust me, you don't want to be there."

"Nateman, listen." Sam put his hands on Nathan's shoulders, "I'm coming with you tonight, whether you want my company or not. Like I said. We're in this together. Got it?"

He put his hands down.

"Plus, I know this shit like the back of my hand. Who better to help you in this situation than Sam the Man?"

Nathan suddenly felt more encouraged at the thought of having a companion in that dark place. And there was no one he would have rather had in there than Sam.

Chapter 33

"So, let's see if we have everything." Sam said.

He flicked one flashlight on to see if it worked and then the second one. Once he was sure they were working, he took the walkie-talkie and headed towards the bedroom.

"Sam, what are you-" Nathan asked, but before he finished his question, Sam got inside the bedroom and slammed the door shut.

"Nighthawk, do you read me? Over." A crackling, distorted voice of Sam came from the other walkie-talkie on the kitchen counter.

Nathan rolled his eyes and picked it up. He pressed the button and said.

"Quit fucking around, Sam."

"Nighthawk, if you can read me, say the passcode. Over." Sam responded.

Nathan rolled his eyes and grumpily said.

"This is Nighthawk. Seagull, come in."

"Not Seagull, I told you, it's Shark." Sam said irritated, breaking out of his role.

"Okay, Snail. The radio works." Nathan replied.

Sam got back outside and said.

"We really gotta use the passcodes, Nate. If we get separated and someone snatches our equipment…"

"Okay, okay. We'll use codenames."

At any other time, Sam's nitpicking would have annoyed Nathan, but right now he knew the best course of action would be following his lead, as he was far more experienced.

"Okay, let's sync our watches." Sam said, as he began fidgeting with his wristwatch, "What is the exact time for you now?"

Nathan looked at his own watch.

"Seven thirty four, twenty five." He looked down and said.

"Okay, I'll sync it up with yours, give me a countdown five seconds before the minute is over."

"Alright."

Although Nathan thought that Sam was going to unnecessary lengths preparing with such surgical precision, he understood his skepticism. The otherworld was dangerous and every tiny step could matter. Once they synchronized their watches, Sam began outfitting the toolbelt he brought with necessary equipment, like a stack of rope, a hammer in case he needed to break something or defend himself, a small bottle of water and ready-to-use first aid kid.

Nathan would have laughed at him in any other situation, but this was no laughing matter. When he saw Sam preparing so diligently for the expedition, as if they were going into hostile enemy territory, he started contemplating whether telling him about the door was a good idea after all. He suddenly became aware of all the potential dangers that lurked inside the storage and as much as he dreaded going in there himself, he feared even more losing a friend like Sam. Maybe they could tell someone like Vincent. That man's expertise would surely save them if they got themselves in any trouble. No, Vincent had a family, a daughter. They couldn't risk his life over something as dangerous as this. Nathan did have an idea, though. He said.

"Hey, maybe we can wait for my neighbor to come back. He might have some guns we can use."

Sam clipped his belt on, testing how firmly it rested on his waist and rotated it both hands with some effort. Still looking at the belt, he said.

"I like the direction in which you're thinking. But, guns won't hurt ghosts." He looked up at Nathan.

"So, how do we defend ourselves against ghosts?" Nathan asked.

"With that." Sam pointed to the coffee table.

Nathan seriously thought for a moment that Sam was referring to lugging an entire coffee table into the corridor, until he realized he left Dolores' rosary on top of it.

"The cross? How?"

"Simple. Just point it at whatever you're facing and recite some words from the bible or some shit." Sam said, as he unclipped his belt and gently placed it back on the counter.

"Um… what words?"

"Oh, you know. You must have seen those movies like *The Exorcist* or some shit. Just say 'In the name of our lord Jesus Christ, I command you to leave', blah blah, that kind of thing. Trust me, they'll run away as soon as they see the cross."

Nathan scratched his cheek.

"And what if that doesn't work?" he asked skeptically, not at all convinced that pointing a wooden object in the shape of a cross would defend him in any way.

"Then, I'm afraid we're facing something different, something new. And possibly something more dangerous than ghosts." Sam said.

He went over to the sofa and threw himself on it.

"Do you think it'll work against the creaking woman?" Nathan asked.

"Good question. Here's what. You try to do the cross thing and if it doesn't work, I'll smash her with the hammer." Sam said.

"Sam, I'm serious. This could cost us our lives."

"Do I look like I'm fucking around, Nate? Look, I understand your concern, but this is the best we can do. Guns will do us no good and most likely blunt weapons, won't neither. So we have to rely on holy things and light."

Nathan nodded, still not fully convinced, but a little more assured.

"So, we got plenty of time until the door opens, let's take a nap to be ready."

"I don't think-"

"Dibs on the bedroom." Sam interrupted him and stood up, making his way to the bedroom.

"Oh no, no, no. You're *my* guest here. You can have the couch." Nathan put his hand on Sam's chest, effectively stopping him in his tracks.

"I'll play you rock-paper-scissors for it." Sam rubbed his hands together.

"No. The bedroom is mine." Nathan sternly said.

"Fine. But once we get this out into the public, I'm taking credit for most of the work." Sam replied and laid down on the couch, "Now shut up and let me catch some z's."

He fiddled around his cellphone for a moment, before placing it on his chest and clasping his hands together.

"Alright, alarm set. I'll wake you up in time for a meal." he said as his eyes slid closed.

Nathan shook his head and got into the bedroom. He suddenly felt overwhelmingly tired. He slumped into bed on his side, facing the closet to the right and as soon as his head hit the pillow, his eyelids began closing. He heard the door opening a moment later, followed by a batter of footsteps.

"Nathan." He heard Sam whisper his name.

"What?" Nathan asked groggily, unable to open his eyes.

He got no response.

"Go to bed, Sam." he said lazily, feeling his body sinking into the bed.

He felt Sam's weight on the edge of the bed as he sat on it.

"The couch is too rough, huh?" Nathan asked and readjusted his pillow, "Alright, you can sleep here. Just don't touch me or any nasty shit like that."

He got into a comfortable position and closed his eyes.

"Hey, Nate? Maybe we can get some holy water later!" Sam shouted.

But it didn't come from the bed. It came from the living room.

Nathan's eyes shot open widely, as he stared at the half-open wardrobe in front of him. The weight on the bed slowly began shifting, leaning towards Nathan and he was powerless to move. The bed began creaking as the person sitting on it leaned forward, getting closer and closer. Nathan saw a looming shadow on the closet in front of him, stretching thinly, towering above him.

"Yo, Nate!" The door burst open, "Did you hea-"

Nathan jumped out of bed and hit his back against the wardrobe, staring at the bed, as his heart raced rapidly. No one was on the bed.

"Nate, what's going on?" Sam asked with a confused look on his face, holding the door open.

"The… there was someone in here with me just now." He barely got the words out of his mouth.

"What?" Sam asked with a frown.

Nathan already began frantically looking under his bed and outside the window, but there was no one there, not even a trace of someone being there just now.

"Nathan, there's nobody here except us." Sam said.

"No, I heard someone. I'm positive. I… I felt their weight on the bed, I heard them call my name, someone… someone is here, I know it!" He was inconsolable.

Sam put his hands on Nathan's shoulders and said.

"Bro, bro. There's nobody fucking here, alright?" He stepped back and took a judgmental look at Nathan, "Alright, listen, I'll stay in here with you, okay?"

Nathan glanced at the bed once more and then tentatively nodded.

"Just don't get too close to me, man. No homo stuff." Sam said with a grin.

Nathan got into bed, deciding to sleep on his back this time. Although the adrenaline was keeping him wide awake, his eyelids got heavy as soon as it started subsiding.

***

"Nate, wake up." Nathan felt a firm grip on his shoulder shake him awake.

He shot up into a upright position. It took him a moment to realize that Sam was waking him up.

"It's midnight." he said, "Let's eat something."

Nathan rubbed his eyes and got up with a groan. He smelled something good from the kitchen and immediately recognized the savory aromas.

"Is that Mike's chicken nuggets?" he asked with a croaking voice.

"Sure is. We need our strength for tonight and what better to eat than some oily nuggets?" Sam grinned and opened the door of the bedroom, "Come on, gotta load up on them carbs."

He disappeared out of the room. Nathan stood up and thought to himself.

Carbs are the least of your issues in that meal.

While eating, Sam discussed tactics with Nathan once they got inside. They agreed to stay together, unless something forced them to separate. If that were the case, they were to retreat to the entrance and rethink their tactics. Sam was confident that nothing would get in their way, not even the creaking woman, but Nathan seemed skeptical about it.

He's seen the woman and whatever she was, she didn't look like anything that could be intimidated by a cross or prayer. Although Sam believed him about his ordeal, Nathan assumed that he didn't buy the whole creaking woman story. It did seem too far-fetched even for someone like Sam, and he didn't blame him for that.

They also agreed to stick with the codename usage, in the unlikely event that someone snatched their radios. Sam talked a little bit about Nigel and how his expertise would be more than useful in a place like that one, but said that Nigel would not dare step inside, as he felt extremely strong energy even outside the door.

After eating, Nathan and Sam spent some time watching TV and talking about random things, mostly to kill the time. As the time of the door opening approached, Nathan got progressively nervous and he could tell that Sam was, too. He continuously tapped his foot on the floor, which he never did – that's how Nathan even noticed it in the first place. Despite that, Sam tried masking it with his usual jokes, stories from work, etc.

At one point, Nathan said.

"You know, you don't have to do this. You can still walk away from this and I won't think any less of you."

Sam grimaced and produced a sound similar to what kids do when they stick their tongues out. He then waved his hand dismissively and said.

"Are you kidding? I *want* to see this stuff. Trust me, man. I'm going for you, but I'm also going for me."

"I just think that maybe we aren't that ready. Maybe we can call the police and just inform them of all of this." Nathan replied.

"And tell them what? That there's a magical door that opens at a specific time and leads to Narnia? They'd never believe us."

"Well, maybe they'd do something if they saw the corridor when the door opens." Nathan shrugged.

"Nah, trust me. We don't need the police. We can handle this ourselves. And once we're back, we'll be hailed as heroes. Hell, I'm already thinking of the speech I'm going to give on Jimmy Fallon's show."

"You what?" Nathan suddenly burst out laughing.

"You just keep laughing, my guy. But when we become celebrities and start getting all the chicks from the audience, you'll be thanking me that I tagged along."

"I don't think Jimmy has guests which are... I dunno, paranormal investigators, or ghost encounter survivors, whatever the hell we are." Nathan scratched his cheek.

Sam shrugged.

"There are other ones I could go for, too. Maybe Colbert. Or Ellen."

"Ellen?"

"Yeah, she likes to have funny guys. I'm a funny guy, I'd be a great fit there. I could turn a tragic ghost story into something funny, just like this." He snapped his fingers, as if to indicate what an easy task that was.

"Alright, Ed Warren, don't get ahead of yourself. We still need to survive this shit."

"We'll survive it, don't worry."

For a while, the only sound that filled the air was the reporter from the news channel. Nathan hadn't been paying attention to the news, as he was too focused on either listening to Sam's daydreaming, or thinking about his expedition ahead. He was more scared than before. It was like, the less he knew about the apartment and the more oblivious he was, the easier it was to go inside, as he didn't know what awaited him.

Now he still didn't know what awaited him, but he had a distinct impression that the apartment could throw almost anything at him and Sam, with nothing being out of its grasp of reality. He wondered if the apartment would play tricks on the two of them differently and that Sam would see something else, where Nathan saw maggots. He hoped that they wouldn't need to go through that disgusting ordeal, but the more he thought about it, he preferred maggots over the creaking woman.

Hell, he even preferred that abominable fleshy mass in the elevator over the creaking woman. Something about the unholy sight of her provoked a primordial fear within him that he never experienced before in life.

"How about some music?" Sam asked jovially, breaking the train of Nathan's thoughts.

Before Nathan could answer, Sam typed something on his phone and put it on the coffee table. The song *Born Free* began playing and Sam raised both his arms and closed his eyes, listening to the music in ecstasy. Seeing Sam's relaxed attitude, Nathan couldn't help but smile. Whether this was his friend's coping mechanism or just his way to relax before something stressful, didn't matter. After the song was over, Sam played a few similar ones which Nathan didn't recognize. And then he picked up his phone and the relaxed expression disappeared from his face.

"It's 2 am." Sam said, "Almost time. You feeling tired?"

"Not even a little." Nathan responded.

He found himself staring at the door more and more, waiting for the time to pass. It went by very slowly, with each minute taking an eternity every time he'd glance at his watch. He started to worry if the door would even open while Sam was here. A part of him started hoping that it wouldn't. Not just for Sam's sake, but for his own. His will started to falter at the thought of going inside once again and staying in his bedroom and taking a nap instead seemed a much more attractive option right now. He tried to push that to the back of his mind, since he knew how difficult it would be for him mentally to get inside the corridor, if he got too cozy with the thought of the door not opening.

"So, you ready to do this?" Sam asked.

He had become a lot quieter in the past hour or so, possibly due to a combination of sleepiness and nervousness. Or just nervousness. Nathan nodded and looked at Sam.

"Yep. Hey, listen. If anything happens to me in there… if I don't make it out…"

"Stop it. Don't get all emotional on me. We're going in, doing a recon of the situation and heading back out safely. Got it?"

"Yeah." Nathan nodded and looked back at the door.

"You said it opens at 2:19 exactly, right?"

"No, not exactly. Somewhere around 2:19 and 20 seconds."

"Does it close at the exact same time?"

"No idea. Probably. I know it closes at 3:19, so we have exactly one hour, give or take the seconds."

More silence ensued, as the two of them kept glancing at the watches. When it was 2:15, Sam insisted they get up and don their gear. Not that there was much to wear, though. Sam put on the toolbelt, which he used for the aforementioned items, while Nathan wrapped the rosary around his left wrist, grabbed the flashlight with the right hand and attached the walkie-talkie to the belt of his jeans.

"Man, I feel like we're going out on a space repair mission or something with all the stuff I'm carrying." Sam said.

"Yeah, you could've brought a hazmat suit." Nathan chuckled.

Sam looked at his watch and said

"2:17, get ready."

They stood at the ready facing the door at some distance, just in case something unexpectedly popped out when it opened.

"2:18." Sam said, intermittently looking at his watch and the door.

Nathan felt his palms getting sweaty. He hadn't felt this nervous since that one night when he took a leap of faith and kissed Natalia on their first date. That feeling of butterflies that he had in his stomach the night he kissed her was now replaced by excruciating knots and twists.

"We got 2:19 in 5, 4, 3, 2, 1."

Sam put his hand down and he and Nathan stared at the door breathlessly, in utter silence. Nathan swallowed and with such eerie silence it seemed obnoxiously loud. He felt his eyes burning from a lack of blinking, so he quickly blinked a few times to make the sensation go away.

A loud click resounded in the room. Nathan and Sam exchanged looks of bewilderment and then turned back towards the door. The creaking followed, loud enough for Nathan to feel his eardrums throbbing. More and more the door opened, revealing its omnipresent darkness. The creaking was steady in volume and pace, never faster, or louder, until the door was almost completely open. And then the sound gradually faded away with the door stopping completely, revealing the corridor in its entirety.

Sam slapped his knee and started laughing. Nathan locked eyes with him in amazement, not sure if his friend was losing his mind.

"Holy shit, Nate, the door is open!"

Nathan smiled weakly and let out a chuckle in the form of an inaudible exhale.

"Yeah, it is." he said.

"Well, let's go then." Sam gestured with his head and before Nathan had the time to say anything, his friend pointed the flashlight at the corridor and stepped over the threshold.

Afraid that Sam would rush off in excitement, Nathan followed closely behind.

Chapter 34

Nathan heard the sound of something metallic scraping far in the distance. He opened his eyes and shot up into a sitting position. He was in apartment 102. It looked way more decrepit than last time. The ceiling looked just about ready to cave in and the lights flickered, leaving Nathan intermittently between complete darkness and a brownish dim glow. The walls seemed to have all sorts of black-looking moldy substances covering them in patches. Nathan looked around.

"Sam?" he called out and got up on his feet.

He realized he was still holding his flashlight, so he began pointing it in various directions, until he realized that he was alone in the room. Panic immediately started to settle in, at the thought that he lost his best friend in this horrid place.

"Sam! Sam, where are you?!" he shouted, now frantically looking around, not caring if anyone else would hear him.

How the hell could this happen? They both entered the corridor and then… and then what happened? Nathan couldn't remember anything else. Did he pass out somewhere along the way? He then remembered that he had his walkie-talkie with him, so he grabbed it and tried contacting Sam right away.

"Sam, can you hear me?" he frantically shouted into the radio and waited for a moment.

He received only static as his response.

"Sam, are you out there? Respond."

Nothing. "Sam, this is Nathan. Are you there?"

He heard a voice, but it was so choppy that he only caught it for a split second before it abruptly cut off. It definitely sounded like Sam, though.

"Sam!" Nathan hysterically shouted into the radio, feeling a mixture of panic and hope at the same time.

He pressed the button again and opened his mouth, but said nothing. He released the button and then pressed it once more and said, this time more calmly.

"This is Nighthawk. Shark, do you read me?"

"Shark to Nighthawk. I read you. Over." Sam's voice came through clear as day.

"Okay, what the fuck, Sam?" Nathan got infuriated by Sam's strict following of protocol in a situation like this one, "Where are you?"

A pause ensued for a moment, before Sam's voice crackled over the radio again.

"Im i… me ki… room… mak… re."

"What? Sam, you cut off. Repeat what you said." Nathan shouted into the radio.

A long moment of static ensued, before another, feminine voice came through.

"You can't save him." it said raspily, making Nathan recoil in fear.

His heart started thumping fast and he shouted into the radio, calling out to Sam over and over. Just before the radio went completely silent, Sam uttered only one word with calmness and clarity.

"Basement."

"Sam? Sam! Goddammit!" Nathan almost flung the walkie-talkie across the room in frustration, but refrained, out of fear of never finding his friend again.

He attached it back to his belt and pointed the flashlight at the entrance door. It was wide open and Nathan stepped outside, not even bothering to be careful. His friend was in danger and he had to hurry. He turned to the left and started striding down the hallway, until he reached the crossroads. He took a quick look at the hellish elevator on his left.

It was closed this time, but he had no intention of calling it to go to the basement in it. Instead, he carefully pointed the flashlight down the hall to the left and once he convinced himself that no one was there, he hurriedly strode towards the stairs.

A terrifying thought crossed his mind that the corridor here would stretch on like the one from his apartment and that he may end up losing a lot of time before he found Sam. He felt panic slowly take over again, so he pushed that thought down and took a deep breath, deciding to focus on what was in front of him.

In seconds, he got to the stairs and this time, the ones leading up were blocked by rusty-looking bars. Nathan pointed his flashlight to the top and as if in response, heard a very low creak come from somewhere upstairs. He gasped and quickly moved to the right side, pointing his flashlight down the flight of stairs which led into the basement.

He couldn't see the bottom of the stairs and in his imagination, he started picturing horrible things crawling up and suddenly lunging at him. The more he stared at it, the more the darkness looked like it was going to devour him, pull him in. He was scared beyond words that could explain, not so much for himself, but for Sam. Without hesitation, he took the first step.

The steps felt slippery, so he put his right hand on the wall, as he slowly descended, careful not to tumble down. The entire time, he didn't take his eyes off the bottom, where he kept the beam of his torch pointed. The light trembled violently and as he got deeper down, he gradually started to feel colder, until he saw his breath with each exhale.

By his estimation, he was already supposed to be at the bottom.

What the fuck is this? Where's the fucking bottom?

He briefly pointed his flashlight back at the top, but realized that he saw nothing due to the lack of light upstairs. He felt like he was completely lost in the void, but it didn't matter. There was no turning back now.

The walkie-talkie crackled to life, startling Nathan so badly, that he almost slipped and fell. At first there was static, and then Sam's voice came clearly.

"Nathan? Where are you?"

Nathan quickly grabbed the walkie-talkie and pressed the button as he spoke into it.

"Sam? Sam, I'm coming down, stay there, okay?!" His voice echoed and he heard panic in his own words.

"Nathan... where am I?"

"Sam, just stay there, okay?" Nathan said and clipped his radio back to his belt, before continuing to move down, now much faster than before.

He went on for a few more minutes, before he started hearing a distinct sound of droplets coming from somewhere below him, slowly and steadily, like from a faucet which was left on. This empowered him to hurry up even more, which in turn caused him to lose balance and almost fall a few times. And then he saw another beam of flashlight below, pointed at him, bouncing up and down in the dark.

He stopped to observe it and the light mirrored the movement of his flashlight. His heart jumped into his throat at the utter realization that someone was running towards him with a flashlight. But as he stopped, the light in front of him stopped as well. With relief, he realized that it was the reflection of his own torch, so he ran down to it and sure enough, in front of him, at the very bottom of the stairs stood a sturdy-looking, metallic door. It seemed not only untouched by the decay and rot around it, but it also retained a glow, as if someone had cleaned and polished it just recently.

The door had no knob, so Nathan leaned on it with his entire weight, hoping to push it open. It opened surprisingly easily on the left side, with a creak loud enough to alert the dead. What lay in front of him was a wide corridor. It looked like the entirety of it was made from metal and was rusted beyond repair, with various colors ranging from orange to dark-red on its walls, ceiling and floor.

Nathan took a step forward, his footstep echoing on the metal surface.

"Sam? Are you in here?" he called out, his breath coming out of his mouth and disappearing.

He got no response. It was cold here, really cold and Nathan began shivering. He had to find Sam before it was too late. He started walking forward and while doing so, grabbed his walkie-talkie and spoke into it intermittently, asking Sam if he was there. Static was all he got as a response. He occasionally tried using codenames, but that didn't work either.

The corridor he was in seemed to stretch a long way and it was difficult to tell where he was exactly, since it had no landmarks, doors or anything else that he could use to orient himself. From time to time, he'd hear something that sounded like the scraping of metal, which made him cringe.

"Come on, Sam. Where are you, man?" Nathan mumbled to himself in desperation.

The further he went in, the more his adrenaline dissipated and the more he started giving room to the guilt of bringing his friend with him. If he could only turn back the clock and never tell Sam about this door… If he could only be back in Aleksei's apartment now and never sign the lease for the new apartment…

Come on, Nathan. Focus dammit, focus. Sam needs you.

After what felt like minutes of walking, Nathan heard something in the distance. Static. He didn't even need to think about it, because he recognized the static as the same sound which came from the walkie-talkie. He hurriedly strode towards the source of the sound and sure enough, there it was, on the floor. The same kind of walkie-talkie as the one he had. It was woefully facing the ceiling, producing a crackling sound.

Nathan shone his light ahead and then down at the walkie talkie. He slowly bent down and picked it up. Almost as soon as he did, the staticky noise began breaking up, like on an old radio when changing channels. And then it resumed, but in the background, there was something else. A song. And not just any song.

Although Nathan had to put the walkie-talkie up to his ear since the static drowned it out, the song that was playing was without a doubt, *Born Free.* Nathan felt shivers run down his spine and moved the radio away from his face, as if he got burned by it. He turned it off just in time for the voice to sing *as free as the grass grows* and clipped it to his belt.

"Sam, where the hell are you?" he murmured to himself and continued forward, now more scared for his friend than ever before.

He walked for a few more minutes by his estimation, until he finally saw the end of the corridor. There was another metallic door in front of him, but this one entirely contrasted the one he saw before. It was just as rusted as the walls surrounding it. It had no knob and Nathan doubted he would even be able to make it budge.

With both hands he began pushing and with a loud scraping sound, the door slowly began to open. As soon as the door began opening, he saw a sickly orange light gleaming in from inside the room, cast onto the dark rusty corridor where he was. Once the door was ajar enough for him to squeeze through, he poked his head inside and glanced around.

He saw a very plain-looking room, which had rusted-up walls like the corridor outside. A neon light illuminated the room from the center of the ceiling, casting a color which seemed similar to the rust around it. There was nothing in the room except an old hospital stretcher with a person on it, laid on his back.

"Sam!" Nathan shouted when he recognized his friend and rushed inside the room, feeling a pang of fear rise within him once again.

Please don't be dead, please don't be dead.

He stopped on the side of the musty stretcher, realizing for the first time now that it had tears in places, which revealed dirty and damaged sponges. Sam seemed like he was sleeping, but his skin was pale. Nathan grabbed him by the shoulder and shook him.

"Sam! Wake up!"

Sam jerked awake and looked at Nathan with bafflement in his eyes.

"Nathan? What the hell happened? Where are we?"

"Thank god you're okay. Holy shit. Listen, we have to get out of here."

For the time being, Nathan felt relieved. The looming danger was still here and he knew that they wouldn't be safe for long. Sam observed his surroundings for a moment, before nodding and saying.

"Uh, yeah. Okay, let's go."

He swung aside and jumped on the ground and immediately fell down, yelping in pain.

"What's wrong?" Nathan knelt down to see what was going on with his friend.

"My ankle. I twisted it when I was running through the office just now."

"The office? What are you talking about? Come on, I'll help you up." Nathan said, as he grabbed Sam's hand and helped him up.

He slung Sam's arm over his shoulder and placed his own hand on Sam's waist to help him walk. Together, they started lumbering and Sam said.

"I dunno. You just disappeared, I have no idea what happened. I got inside the storage and turned around to see if you were coming and before I knew it, I found myself back in my office."

"Your office?"

Nathan pushed the rusty door open wider with a grunt. He and Sam then walked out. Sam continued.

"Yeah, it was really strange. It's like… it's like I was really there and I was talking to my coworker Cindy."

"The one you were hitting on?" Nathan asked, as he continued helping Sam walk through the rusty corridor.

"Yeah. But we were the only ones in the office. And she'd sit at her computer and type and just answer my questions normally. But then when I would leave to sit inside my own cubicle, I'd find her there again. I thought first I was imagining things, but I just kept going and going and she was always there and the entire office looked like it was on a fucking loop."

"That's weird, man." Nathan tried acknowledging what Sam was saying, even though the only thought that raced through his mind right now was getting the hell out.

"Yeah. But that's not it. Cindy's responses were on a loop, too. Whatever I'd ask her, she'd either just shrug or smile or give me the same *aha* response while typing. And then I climbed on her desk to get a better view and I saw the exit, but when I ran towards it, it just kept repeating. And that's when shit hit the fan."

Nathan glanced sideways at his friend, before looking back forward, focusing on the corridor ahead. The left hand which he used to hold Sam's arm around his shoulder was the same hand he used for the flashlight to illuminate the path ahead. Sam said.

"Yeah. I looked and I saw this one strange guy in a suit. He was standing between cubicles, facing away from me. I tried calling out, but he didn't respond, he just fucking stood there like in some fucking trance or something. I was panicked by now and really didn't have the patience to fuck around with some psycho like that, so I grabbed him by the shoulder and spun him around. And holy shit, Nathan."

"What?" Nathan asked.

"His fucking face. It was all… wrong."

"Wrong how?"

"Like, you know how when you wear one of those overly realistic leather masks for Halloween, and if you don't put them on right, they look like your face is literally being pulled off? Well, he looked like that. His mouth was half-open and stretched to the side, so I saw all his side teeth and I saw just the bottom of his eyes, since the pupils were covered by the skin being pulled down. And he produced this terrible fucking croaking sound. It's like he was trying to speak, but couldn't. And he stretched his hand out towards me, so I ran."

"And that's how you twisted your ankle?"

"Yeah. And I have no fucking idea how I ended up in this shithole." Sam scoffed.

"I guess this apartment shows you what it wants to show you, huh?" Nathan said.

"Yeah, well. Whatever we're facing here, it ain't ghosts. You need to move out as soon as you can, Nathan. Hell, I'll trade you for your apartment."

"You found yourself in a looping office, saw a guy with a fucked up face and now you're limping through a rusted corridor in some otherworldly dimension and you still haven't had enough?" Nathan asked, forcing a chuckle.

"We need these things for a successful story. Imagine what the audience's reaction will be like when we tell them we fought off a horde of demons using only our flashlights." Sam said with intermittent grunts whenever he'd step on his foot.

"Horde of demons?" Nathan was amazed by Sam's ability to joke even during this kind of time.

"Yeah. Need a little dramatic exaggeration." he said.

Nathan didn't respond. He started getting tired and Sam was too, from the way he was slowing down, but they couldn't stop now. By his estimation, they weren't too far from the stairs. From there, it was a straight shot back to 102 and the real world. If the door happened to be closed, then they'd just wait it out.

But as he accidentally shone his light to the left, he stopped in his tracks along with Sam.

"What's wrong?" Sam asked.

Nathan pointed the light at the wall to the left and felt his legs getting cut off. Carved into the metallic surface of the wall, was a crudely written message that said *LEAVE*.

"This wasn't here before." Nathan said.

"Maybe you just missed it. Come on." Sam said.

Nathan forced himself to move his gaze away from the message and continued walking with Sam, as he said.

"No, I'm positive it wasn't here. I couldn't have just missed it, no way."

But what if he did? He was so focused on finding Sam, that it may have been possible that he just missed it, regardless of how obtrusive the scrawling was. They went on for a few more minutes when they ran into another message, this time on the right wall. It said *CANT*.

"Okay, that definitely wasn't here." Nathan said, "Let's hurry up, Sam."

"I'm trying." Sam responded.

But before they even left the previous message behind them properly, another one showed up, again on the left wall this time.

HIM.

Nathan instinctively hurried his steps and Sam tried to keep up silently, but it was obvious that his leg was hurt too badly. More and more messages kept showing up on the walls, ceiling and floor.

LEAVE HIM

CANT SAVE HIM

HE IS GONE

DIE

"Bro, you need to leave me and go." Sam said between short breaths.

"What are you talking about, Sam? I'm not leaving you, are you crazy?" Nathan scoffed at Sam's absurd suggestion.

"You need to go, otherwise we'll both be trapped here. Look, it's already 3:04 am. We'll never make it back like this." Sam said.

Nathan stopped and looked at Sam with a frown, before shaking his head and continuing to walk with him.

"We came here together, we're leaving together. You came here to help me. I'm not leaving you to be trapped or die in here."

The messages began overlapping. They were carved into the corridor so many times, that they were indecipherable in many spots. In total, they must have walked for at least ten minutes, before Nathan frustratedly said.

"This can't be right. We were already supposed to be at the exit."

"Nate, wait. I need a moment." Sam said between exhausted breaths.

"Just a little longer Sam, come on. You can do it." Nathan urged him.

"No, I really need a short break, otherwise I'll collapse." Sam said.

"Alright, alright." Nathan gently helped Sam against a wall and assisted him in sliding down in a sitting position.

One of the rusty parts of the wall caught Sam's shirt, until Nathan helped him untangle from it. Nathan sat next to Sam, feeling pretty tired himself. He wiped the beads of sweat off his forehead, as he leaned his head against the cold, metallic wall. Sam panted next to him, slowly stabilizing his breathing. He looked at Nathan after a long moment and said.

"You remember that time when we threw eggs on Mr. Birkin's house?" He smiled connivingly.

Nathan chuckled and nodded.

"Yeah. He popped our ball for accidentally throwing it into his backyard. It was your favorite ball, too."

"Uh-huh. Got it for my birthday from my mom. She knew I wanted to be a baseball player when I grew up. Too bad I didn't pursue that career, huh?"

"Who knows? You probably wouldn't have had a chance to hit on hot coworkers like Cindy then, right?"

Sam laughed.

"Remember how Mr. Birkin came running out of his house shirtless with a pitchfork? Remember how he chased us down the street?"

Nathan laughed.

"You tried reasoning with him, but he just kept running at us. Good thing he was so slow. We managed to run across the street, while all the other kids stared at us in confusion. And then they started running, too."

"And then…" Sam paused, laughing, "And then old Mr. Birkin tripped and fell, you remember that? Fell right into that mud puddle, face first."

The two of them burst out in uncontrollable laughter. Nathan thought that if anyone saw them, two guys stuck in the middle of a hellish apartment, reminiscing and laughing, they would have thought they were out of their minds. After a minute or so, when their laughter died down, Sam said.

"This all reminds me of that. We found that one alley where we hid and laughed, all exhausted from running from Mr. Birkin."

Nathan nodded, a little more serious now.

"If you hadn't yanked me then, I would've stayed frozen in place. And who knows, maybe Mr. Birkin was just crazy enough to impale me on his rusty pitchfork. You've had my back ever since."

Sam looked at Nathan and shook his head.

"Come on, Nate. You had my back, too."

Nathan put his hand on Sam's shoulder. His eyes fell on the CANT SAVE HIM message and he said.

"You know, that day when you and Nigel came. You know how Nigel hugged me and I pushed him back and told him to fuck off?"

"Yeah?" Sam curiously frowned.

"Well, he didn't just hug me. He whispered something to me." Nathan said, as his panting dissipated and his voice started to quiver, "He said: *You can't save him.*"

Sam smiled widely and said.

"I knew it. See, I told you Nigel was no phony. Damn, he's good."

A moment of silence ensued, before Sam asked.

"So you think he meant me? That you can't save *me*?"

"I don't know, but I wish he told me more, the cryptic son of a bitch."

"He probably didn't know. Usually these things just come to him, but he doesn't understand what they mean until they actually happen. So don't blame him." He swallowed loudly and looked at Nathan, "Listen. If he was right, then you have to go. You have to leave me."

Nathan shook his head.

"You're my brother, Sam. I'm not letting you die here."

Just then, the walkie-talkie started to produce static. It started as a low hum and gradually increased in volume. It got so loud, that Nathan's ears started to hurt. He quickly unclipped it from his belt and fumbled to switch it off.

"Turn it off!" Sam shouted, clasping his ears with his hands.

"I'm trying!" Nathan said, trying to flick the switch on and off, but the radio stayed on.

And then the static was suddenly replaced by a blaring *Born Free,* causing Nathan to drop the walkie-talkie. Both he and Sam clasped their ears with their hands and screamed in agony.

Nathan tried to reach for it and toss it away, but he felt himself losing balance. His vision was becoming blurry and his body got all wobbly, causing him to fall on the floor. And then everything went dark.

Chapter 35

"Sam?" Nathan mumbled groggily, as he struggled to open his eyes.

His body felt heavy, as if it was made out of lead. When he finally managed to open his eyes, his blurry vision began clearing up. He was inside the same corridor where he was with Sam before he lost consciousness. Crude messages carved all over the walls were the first thing that greeted him, along with the walkie-talkie which he dropped just before fainting.

"Sam, are you...?" He began and swiveled his head around, but Sam was nowhere to be found.

Immediately, panic began settling in and he was suddenly wide awake.

"Sam? Where are you?!" He grabbed his flashlight and got up, pointing it back and forth.

With no sense of orientation or any idea where Sam could have gone, he began running in one direction.

"You won't take him, you hear me?!" Nathan shouted into the air.

He was scared, angry, tired and fed up, all at the same time. Most of all, he was scared for his friend. If the creaking woman herself jumped in front of him in that moment, he would have tackled her and punched her until she was nothing more than a bloody pulp.

"You can't have Sam!" he shouted again and his voice echoed in the corridor.

But it wasn't an echo. It was someone else's voice. Nathan stopped in his tracks to listen and then heard it once more. A shriek, which sounded like a scream of pure, undeniable agony.

"Sam? Sam, is that you?!" Nathan shouted and began running forward recklessly.

"Nathan! Help me!" The voice shrieked at the top of their lungs.

It was definitely Sam and he sounded like he was being flayed alive.

"Sam, hold on! I'm coming!"

Nathan's jog turned into a sprint. He rushed through the corridor, panting and calling out to Sam. Sam called out to him between screams, which grew closer and louder.

"Sam, hold on! I'm almost there!" Nathan shouted in pure desperation.

No, no, no, no. Please, not him. Not Sam.

His lungs and legs burned, but he refused to stop. He had to save his friend. He was close now, just a few dozen yards and he'd be there, he knew it. But to his surprise, the corridor diverged into three different pathways. Nathan stopped and looked at all three passages, before calling out to Sam again. Sam's screams came from what Nathan thought was the left passage, so with a moment of hesitation, he began sprinting in that direction.

Before he knew it, the corridor forked again into three more passages. This time Sam sounded like he was coming from the right, so Nathan continued there. But then he reached another forking and Sam's screams sounded like they were coming from the left.

Okay, what the fuck!

He ran passage after passage, but the more he ran, the more it seemed like he was running in circles. Sam's agonizing screams were slowly fading away, too. The ear-piercing screams that he heard before were now barely audible, but not like he was moving away from the source of the sound. Rather, it sounded like Sam was losing his strength and could no longer scream so loudly.

"Sam, tell me where you are!" Nathan shouted, tears now streaming down his face.

Sam didn't respond, so Nathan continued running in the direction he thought was the right one, his sprint long-ago turned into a meager jog. He hadn't even noticed where he was going until he bumped into a person. He looked up, his heart jumping and then dropping when he realized it wasn't Sam.

In front of him stood Martin, with his palm on Nathan's chest in a stop sign. Although he was as calm as ever, he looked somewhat sad this time.

"Martin! Martin, you gotta help me! Sam is in trouble! I have to find him, please!"

Martin moved his palm to Nathan's shoulder and shook his head, as he exhaled through his nose like a disappointed teacher.

"You never should have brought your friend." he said with immense sorrow in his voice, "The apartment is angry now."

Nathan didn't fully understand what that meant, but he understood enough to know he should be afraid for his friend.

"We have to save him, please. Someone is... doing something to him, please." He was aware of the saliva hanging from his mouth like a dog's, but he didn't care in that moment about that.

"You can't save him." Martin said, "I'm sorry, Nathan. He's gone. And you have to leave for now. You made the apartment angry and if you stay, you will die along with your friend."

Nathan shook his head and said.

"No. No, I'm going to save him. If you're not going to help me, get the hell out of my-"

He tried to push Martin aside, but with a swift and elegant motion, Martin slapped Nathan's hand down and pushed him with his palm. Nathan lost balance and fell backwards, the room spinning around him. He got up, ready to punch Martin in his goddamn face, but when he got up, he was gone.

He was back in his apartment and the door was closed.

"No. No, no, no, goddammit, no!" Nathan rushed to the door.

He violently rammed it with his shoulder over and over, even as his shoulder burned with pain. He then switched to kicking, but that did nothing to budge the door, either. He grabbed the stool next to the kitchen counter and hit the door with it, but still no dice.

"FUCK!" he shouted and threw the chair across the room.

It thudded loudly against the kitchen counter and miserably fell on the floor. Nathan leaned on the door with his back and let himself slide into a sitting position. He felt his phone vibrating and he immediately pulled it out of his pocket. He saw multiple messages from an unknown number. Under the previously received message that said *Yo* CanT s%4E H*m*, there were a few lines of gibberish and under that:

YOU CAN'T SAVE HIM.

Hopeless, Nathan tried calling Sam, but no one was answering. With nothing left to give him hope of finding his friend, he dropped his phone, buried his head into his hands and started sobbing.

Chapter 36

When Nathan woke up in his bed, he felt even more tired than before his short nap. It was 6 am right now and he called the police for a welfare check on Sam. They told him to give Sam some time and if he didn't respond they would perform a welfare check.

Nathan thanked them and hung up. He wasn't sure what happened to Sam. He somehow knew with certainty that he was dead, he just didn't know if he was really *dead*, or if the apartment decided to keep him there as a plaything. He prayed that it was the first one.

The fight inside him was gone. The apartment had won. He felt daggers twisting in his heart every minute and it was as if a big black hole suddenly appeared in his life and devoured everything remaining that he loved.

If only he could turn back time. If only he could go back just ten hours and tell Sam to go home. He would chase him out with a bat if he had to, but there was no way he would let him go in there. He felt so stupid for bringing Sam with him. What in the hell was he thinking? Of course it was dangerous and of course the apartment would find a way to punish him for doing that. And now Sam was gone and he would never see him again.

He'd never get to travel the world, like he planned on doing. Or hit on his coworker Cindy, or tell Nathan paranormal stories.

He spent the first three days in bed, unable to shake himself out of the funk he currently found himself in. He barely ate anything and drifted from haunted nightmares to waking moments, which were even worse than the dreams that plagued him. At night, he heard the door opening, beckoning him, tantalizing him, but he didn't care. As far as he was concerned, Satan himself could come into his bedroom and wreak whatever torment he wanted on him.

And then on the fourth day, he heard a knock on his door. Nathan didn't even know what time it was until he entered his living room and the morning light glaring through the window burned his eyes. He looked through the peephole and saw Dolores standing outside. He didn't want any company right now, but even in his heavy depression, he knew that turning away from Dolores after barely managing to get on her good side would probably be a bad idea.

He slightly opened the door and stared at his neighbor. Dolores was looking down when Nathan opened the door, so when she saw him, her eyes widened. *Yeah, I'm a mess, lady.* She quickly tried to hide her reaction by asking.

"Hi, Nathan. Is everything okay?"

"Yeah. Can I help you?" he asked, oblivious to how unfriendly he sounded with his raspy voice, half-open door and tired gaze.

Dolores took a deep breath and asked.

"Did something happen, Nathan?"

"Nothing happened. What can I do for you, Dolores?"

She stared at him for a long moment.

"It's the door, isn't it?" she asked quietly, "It did something, didn't it?"

Nathan suddenly lost his temper. He didn't think he had it in him right now to snap, let alone argue, but he supposed that all of this has been building up inside of him for a long time.

"No, Dolores, it's not the door. Now please, leave me alone, because I need to take care of something. Thank you for your concern, though." he said the last sentence in hopes of softening the blow.

He was about to close the door, but Dolores firmly put her foot inside. She no longer looked sympathetic, but rather angry. It made Nathan recoil in surprise.

"I recognize that look. It's the same look that Michelle had, just before she went missing. Now, I already told you. There's something wrong with that door. And I already lost more than one neighbor to this room. I am *not* letting you get yourself killed, Nathan. I'll call the superintendent if I have to and I'll tell him everything, but I am not going to leave you alone, until we talk about this."

Nathan's annoyance dissipated at Dolores' words. She really wasn't going to let him go, he saw it in the determined look in her eye. He looked down at her foot and the slipper lodged inside the door. He nodded and asked.

"You wanna come in?"

Dolores shook her head.

"You know I don't. Let's talk in my place."

***

"Eat." Dolores said as she put a steaming bowl of vegetable soup on the kitchen table in front of Nathan.

Nathan looked at the pieces of carrots, broccoli and cauliflower that swam inside the hot, yellowish broth.

"I'm not hungry." He chuckled bemusedly.

Dolores put a spoon inside the bowl, which clanked against the ceramic.

"Come on, when is the last time you ate?" She straightened her back, towering over him, "You plan to starve yourself? How's that going to help anyone?"

Nathan continued staring at the bowl for a moment. He grabbed the spoon with fingers that felt far too weak for him to hold the metallic utensil and leaned forward. The smell of cooked vegetables filled his nostrils and he suddenly felt a rumble in his stomach. After the first spoonful, the nausea went away and he was able to finish the entire bowl, even drinking the remaining broth from it.

"Don't go too fast, you'll throw up. Especially if you haven't eaten in days." Dolores smirked from the seat across from Nathan.

Nathan placed the bowl back down and wiped his mouth with his forearm, not caring that he must have looked barbaric to the old lady.

"Thank you." he said as he pushed the bowl away from him.

Dolores took the bowl to the kitchen sink and placed it among the rest of the dirty dishes.

"You want some water?" she asked.

"I'm good." He responded, continuing to stare at the table where the bowl was.

Dolores slowly made her way back to the seat in front of Nathan and placed her hands in her lap. The clock from the living room ticked loudly for an awkwardly long moment. *How does she sleep with that thing here?* Nathan was aware of Dolores' eyes on him, but he refused to look up. He felt ashamed of himself. He felt like the apartment reduced him to a husk of his former self. That he was less than a man. He heard the old woman shifting in her seat.

"So, who was it?" she asked.

Nathan felt a pang of pain in his heart, but played dumb nonetheless.

"Who was what?" he asked.

"Who was it that the apartment took from you?" Dolores softly asked.

"Sam. He was my best friend. He insisted that he come with me. Inside the room, I mean. It's my fault that he's dead. And now I'll never-" He felt his lips quivering and his vision started blurring.

He blinked and felt tears forming up in his eyes.

"It's okay, let it all out. It's okay, dear." Dolores said sympathetically.

Nathan couldn't stop his tears. It was as if the floodgates opened and he sobbed in front of the old woman like a little kid, unable to control his heaving and shaking. Dolores brought tissues to him and sat back in her chair. Despite keeping such a distance, Nathan felt compassion from her end, like a caring mother.

Once he calmed down, he told her everything about the door and the otherworld inside it. He told her about

Michelle and Martin and how he saw a version of Vincent and Margery in there. He told her about the abominations he saw inside the apartment and the weird paranormal occurrences he experienced inside 304 during the daytime and how he couldn't leave the place.

He told her about Sam's death and this is when he decided to stop, because he was so overwhelmed with emotions that he felt like his heart was going to explode. The two of them sat silently for a moment, while Nathan sniffled and wiped his remaining tears. By now, the tears have dried up and he felt tired, but at least the pain was temporarily gone.

"I remember seeing Sam once." Dolores said, as she sat with her fingers crossed on the table, "He was polite. Really charming. I could see all the girls falling for his joking nature."

Nathan chuckled.

"That was him, alright. Always turned everything into a joke and was able to lighten the mood if it got too dark. And always helpful. He really wanted to help me with the apartment. He didn't wanna let me do it alone. I never should have let him."

"You can't blame yourself. You said he insisted on coming. He was your friend and if the roles were reversed, you would have done the same for him."

"But they're not reversed. He's dead and I'm alive." Nathan shook his head.

"For now." Dolores coldly said.

Nathan jerked his head up in surprise.

"How long do you think you'll stay alive in this state? A week? A month? How long until that place gets you?"

Nathan stared at her in silence with a frown. Dolores leaned back in her chair and said.

"Your friend wanted to help you get through this. And by sitting around and doing nothing, you're allowing him to die in vain. Is that what you want?"

Nathan turned his palms upright and shook his head.

"What exactly do you want me to do? I can't beat that place. It has its own fucking rules. It's just fucking with me, until it decides the time is right for it to off me."

Dolores looked down at her lap and nodded. She glanced at Nathan and said.

"I never told you everything I know about apartment 304. You've hidden the things about the door from me, but I've hidden things from you, too."

"Why?" Nathan asked.

"I didn't want you to panic. I didn't want you to do something irrational. Although now that I think about it, it was probably a mistake. And for that I am truly, deeply sorry for your friend." There was a glint in her eye and she blinked it away.

She sighed and looked at the kitchen sink, as if something interesting was there. A story was coming up, Nathan could sense it. He knew from the way she looked nowhere in particular in silence, just like she did when she told him the story of her dead husband. She was preparing herself mentally for what she was about to talk about.

"I never told you about Vincent's daughter." She began.

"Vincent's daughter? Sarah? What about her?" Nathan asked, his interest suddenly soaring.

He felt his exhaustion fading away and him returning to his old self for the time being. He knew it was only temporary, though. The loss of Sam would manifest itself through pain soon enough, but right now, he wanted to distract himself from it.

"Vincent's daughter was the first person who lived in 304."

Nathan's eyes widened.

"What?!" he asked louder than he planned, feeling his heart beginning to race.

"Her name was Sarah. She moved into this building along with Vincent and Margery. I don't know the details, but she apparently wanted some adult responsibility, so her parents allowed her to rent an apartment here for the time being. But…"

Dolores trailed off, staring to the right of the kitchen sink, deep in her thoughts. She sighed.

"Just a few months after moving in there, she went missing. Just like Michelle."

"Vincent's daughter went missing in my apartment?" Nathan couldn't believe what he was hearing.

Dolores nodded.

"No one knows what happened. She just never came back one night after going out. Not long after that, someone else moved in. Vincent never talked about Sarah's disappearance and he tried to hide it, I mean of course he did, it's Vincent. But I saw how it wrecked him. I saw how sorrowful his eyes were and… well. Let's just say that he and Margery were never the same after that."

She sniffled and used one of the tissues she held in her hand to wipe her own tears.

"But Vincent told me about Sarah. We talked about her, how she goes to college and all. He never mentioned anything about her disappearing."

Dolores shook her head.

"Vincent is a proud man. I assume he blames himself for Sarah's disappearance. Either way, on the outside, Vincent and Margery may seem like a happily married couple. But I cannot imagine what they had to go through. There's nothing worse in this world than burying your own child." Her voice trembled with that last sentence and Nathan saw that her eyes were red.

She gently wiped her tears with a tissue, sniffled and continued.

"From then on, tenant after tenant just kept coming to apartment 304. If I'm not mistaken, including Sarah and Michelle there were six tenants altogether. And none of them stayed longer than half a year."

Dolores comically blew her nose into the tissue loudly and apologized to Nathan, before continuing.

"I told you how I felt guilty about Michelle disappearing and me doing nothing to stop it. That feeling is worsened by the fact that I ignored the potential dangers of the apartment. I should have seen it right after Sarah's disappearance, but it hadn't even occurred to me that the apartment could have been the source of the problems. And then by the time I decided it was time to step in, poor Michelle was gone, too."

She shook her head and looked at Nathan with red, puffy eyes. Nathan ran his hand across his mouth and said.

"Does Vincent know about all the other tenants disappearing?"

Dolores thought for a moment.

"He knows about Michelle, that's for sure."

Something clicked in Nathan's mind. Something that didn't fit with Dolores' story. He raised an index finger.

"Wait, Vincent told me that he never knew any of the tenants from before."

Dolores scoffed and closed her eyes. She shook her head with a smile, before looking back at Nathan.

"Oh no, no. He knew Michelle. He may have known some of the other tenants, too. But I *do* know that he talked to Michelle multiple times."

That can't be. Vincent wouldn't lie to Nathan, would he? He said he didn't know any of the tenants, so maybe Dolores was confused.

"Well, maybe he talked to her, but he didn't know that she lived in apartment 304. He said he never even set foot on the third floor before I moved." Nathan said.

Dolores shook her head again.

"Oh, he knew she lived there, alright. He knew her name and he knew exactly where she lived. I guess he was trying to avoid scaring you, since you just moved in. Although he should have known better, especially him, given the circumstances."

Nathan suddenly remembered the visage he saw inside the apartment. Vincent and Michelle talking near the letterbox. Michelle tentatively asking him about something weird going on in the building and Vincent denying he knew anything about it. Maybe he was telling the truth, maybe he really didn't know anything about the supernatural things going on in the apartment. But the fact remained that he lied about knowing a tenant from 304.

Nathan suddenly remembered the second visage he saw in the apartment, the one of Margery and Vincent talking about something secretive.

If the neighbors find out that we knew something, but kept quiet-

They won't find out about it.

What the hell was that big secret? It couldn't have been Sarah, because Dolores knew about it. But maybe Vincent *did* know that something was going on in the apartment, just decided to keep quiet about it. That's the only viable reason that Nathan could think of as to why he would omit certain information from him.

"Nathan? Are you still with me?" Dolores asked.

Nathan nodded in a zombified manner.

"Yeah, I'm still here. I was just thinking about what you said. Listen, do you know anything about the other tenants?"

Dolores did her trademark head shaking. She pursed her lips and said.

"I'm afraid not. I wasn't able to find any relevant information. If they went missing and the cases were filed under missing persons, it wasn't ever on the news. I'm sorry, I wish I could help you more."

"No, you did everything you could. And I appreciate you telling me everything you know."

Dolores cleared her throat.

"About that. Don't talk to Vincent about Sarah. I think he's doing a little better these days, especially since he went fishing. He hasn't gone fishing since before his daughter went missing. I don't want you reminding him of his tragic loss."

"I understand."

There was a long moment of silence, as the ticking of the living room clock permeated the air.

"So, about Michelle." Nathan started cautiously, "Do you think there's a chance that she's… still alive? Somewhere inside the apartment?"

"For her sake, I hope not. I can't imagine having to live in that hellish place all these months. If you want to know my opinion, I think whatever is in there is trying to lure you by pretending to be Michelle. You should stay as far away as you can from that cursed place."

"I can't leave. The apartment won't let me. I have to reach apartment 304 on the other side. Maybe then I'll get some answers."

Dolores blinked at Nathan with a hint of worry in her eye. One last question raced to Nathan's mind, and he leaned back in the chair.

"Do you know who the landlord of the building is?"

Dolores looked at her lap for a moment, before woefully shaking her head.

"Sorry. I know it's a relatively young person, maybe a few years older than you. I've seen him a long time ago, talking to Sarah a couple times and that was that."

A young guy? Who could it possibly be and why would he set people up like that? Nathan suddenly felt really tired again. Dolores' silent gaze told him that she had nothing else to share, so he stood up and said.

"I, uh… I should get going. Thank you for the soup. And for telling me everything. I really appreciate it."

Dolores mirrored Nathan's movement and stood up herself. She nodded and started for the door.

"Well, you hang in there, Nathan. I know that losing a friend is very difficult." She and Nathan walked up to the door and she held it open for him.

Nathan stepped out and turned back to face her.

"The rosary I gave you, you still have it?" she asked.

Nathan flashed her a lazy grin and pulled the rosary out of his pocket. He felt a momentary cramp in his face muscles, since he hadn't smiled in days.

"Been keeping it close since you gave it to me. To tell you the truth, I'm not sure if it's doing me any good, but if anything, the voices and other occurrences are a lot less frequent inside the apartment than they were before."

Dolores smiled tiredly, as Nathan gently squeezed the rosary back into his pocket.

"Should you ever need anything Nathan, please don't hesitate to come by. We'll find a way to handle that apartment."

There was a sound of the front doors below on the first floor opening. The sound carried itself all the way up the stairs to the third floor for Nathan to hear the heavy batter of footsteps of someone walking inside and then the distinct, rough voice of his neighbor from 204 saying.

"Margery, the keys are on you?"

Nathan waved to Dolores and turned around to face his apartment. He took out his keys and pretended to fumble around with them, until he heard the door behind him closing shut. He turned around to make sure that Dolores was no longer anywhere in sight. And then he tip-toed down the hallway.

Sorry Dolores. He thought to himself. *I know you told me not to talk to Vincent about Sarah, but I need answers.*

Chapter 37

"Margery, hand me that bottle of water, will ya?" Vincent pointed at the bottle in the car door on the passenger's side.

Margery pulled out the bottle, took off the cap and handed it over to her husband.

"Thanks, Marge." Vincent said, holding the steering wheel with one hand and grabbing the bottle with the other.

He took a long sip, feeling his mustache getting drenched in the process. That was one of the annoying parts of having a stylish mustache – you always have to be careful how you eat or drink.

"Hoo boy, I was parched." he said as he handed the bottle back to Margery.

"No wonder. That final catch must have been stressful." Margery said, as she screwed the cap back on and placed the bottle back inside the car door.

"Amen to that." Vincent said, focusing his gaze on the road, "The bastards were barely biting in the past few days, but this big boy really made up for that. Think you can make something good out of him?"

"Vincent, honey. In the one hundred years we've been married, has there ever been something I wasn't able to make so that it tastes good?" Margery playfully asked, giving Vincent a smile full of yellowish teeth.

Vincent smiled back. She was old and withered, but to Vincent she was still beautiful. More so for sticking with him through thick and thin.

"You're right, Marge. Even with minimal ingredients, you always work a miracle. Your mother was an amazing cook, but she's nowhere close to you." He winked.

"Hey, what do you think about inviting Nathan over for dinner? You like hanging out with him, right?" she asked.

"Yeah. He's a real gem, that one. Smart, funny. I'm sure you'd like him. I think that's a great idea, we can invite him over."

"That is great!" Margery suddenly sounded enthusiastic.

She always loved having guests over. The apartment felt lonely with just the two of them, so having someone visit, even for just a short time, was always welcome. Vincent tried to occupy himself by doing various repairs and works around the summerhouse and apartment he owned, but he also loved going out to see his veteran buddies in bars or other places.

Some of them were in nursing homes and Vincent felt really sorry for them. That was one way he didn't want to end up in his age, having someone to take care of you while you're shitting and pissing your diapers. He would have preferred death on the battlefield as a hero.

"We should be home in half an hour or so and then we can do all the necessary preparations."

"Yeah, you need to take a shower." Margery bluntly rebutted.

"What? Come on, I don't smell that bad."

"Vince, you've been out fiddling with worms and dirt and other bait for a whole week. I could smell you before I saw you. When was the last time you showered?"

Vincent chuckled.

"I dunno. Two days ago, maybe. I think I'm still fine."

He glanced at Margery, who lowered her chin and stared at him in a judgmental glare. Vincent averted his gaze back to the road and said.

"Alright, ma'am. Shower, it is. And you do your cooking magic to impress Nathan. I already told him what an amazing cook you are, so you gotta make sure you live up to the hype."

"Oh, honey. As soon as he takes the first bite of my food, he'll want to move in with us." She chuckled, as she put her hand on Vincent's thigh.

He laughed along with her. That sentence made him feel bittersweet.

***

"Margery, are the keys on you?" Vincent asked, as he lugged all the fishing equipment inside the building.

"Let me check." she said.

She nonchalantly dug into her purse and began searching for the keys. There was a sound of items rattling, as she rummaged through them.

"Goddammit, woman. Hurry up, I can't hold this stuff for much longer." Vincent said impatiently, shaking his head at this happening for the hundredth time since they got married.

"Oh, come on now. You spent 25 years in the Corps carrying full military equipment on your back, I'm sure you can tough this one out."

Vincent outstretched the hand which he used to hold the bucket full of bait and pressed the elevator call button. It was on the same floor, so it luckily opened right away. They got inside and he placed the bucket on the floor.

"Jesus, this thing is much heavier than it was when we left."

In a moment, the elevator started ascending with a whir and seconds later, the doors opened. Margery brushed past Vincent to unlock the door, while he scooped up the things he left on the elevator floor with a groan. The doors of the elevator started closing, but he stuck his foot in the door to reopen them.

"Damn elevator. It's the 21st century and they still have elevator doors closing before you can exit."

"Well, did you expect the elevator to know you're inside?" Margery asked, as the keys jingled in her hands.

The door clicked loudly when she turned the key, as Vincent responded.

"Well it would have been nice to recognize if someone was inside, yeah. Like a sensor, or something."

Margery shot him a bemused glance, before swinging the door open and stepping aside.

"Hi, Vincent." A voice came from his left.

Vincent jerked his head in the direction of the sound and saw Nathan standing in the middle of the hallway. Vincent squinted when he saw what state the boy was in. He was pale and had heavy bags under his eyes. Despite smiling, Vincent clearly recognized the exhaustion and what he detected was worry on his face. The poor guy looked like he hadn't slept or eaten in days. Did something drastic happen to him while Vincent was gone?

"Hi there!" Margery greeted the kid with a wide and enthusiastic greet, "Can we help you?"

"Hey, Nathan. How are things going?" Vincent smiled back and tried to hide his surprise at Nathan's sudden change in appearance, "Hold on, let me just bring this stuff inside."

He ran inside and put the items on the floor near the entrance. He had a dreadful feeling washing over him all of a sudden. At first he couldn't pinpoint what exactly it was, but then he realized it was worry. Worry for Nathan. Was the kid going through something bad? Is that why he looked like shit?

"Oh, so you're Nathan?" Vincent heard Margery's voice jovially asking, "I've heard so much about you!"

Vincent stepped back outside, in time to see Nathan giving Marge a courteous smile.

"And you must be Margery." he said, "I've heard only good things about you from Vincent."

He winked at Vincent and the old man gave him a thumbs up behind Margery's back. There was a moment of awkward silence, where Margery swiveled to look at Vincent, as if asking what to do.

"Say, um… do you need any help bringing in those things?" Nathan asked.

"No, no. We're fine, son. Actually, we were going to invite you to dinner tonight, since we just got back from our fishing trip. If you don't mind waiting a little, you can come inside for a beer or two." Vincent said, expecting an angry glance from Marge, but instead, she clapped her hands together and shouted.

"Oh, yes please, Nathan. You have to stay for dinner!"

Nathan's smile flared across his face a little wider this time, making the bags under his eyes just a little more visible. He shrugged and said.

"I would love to stay for dinner!"

Chapter 38

"I would love to stay for dinner!" Nathan grinned at Margery.

The old lady's eyes lit up, as she smiled widely and said.

"Oh, that is wonderful. Vincent, Vincent." She turned around and called out to her husband, as if he wasn't standing right behind her, "We have to prepare dinner. Quick, where are the fish?"

She seemed to become frantic all of a sudden, falling over herself in a possible attempt to leave a good first impression on Nathan.

"The fish are already inside, Marge. And relax, Nathan isn't here for inspection. Right, Nate?" Vincent smiled under his bushy mustache.

"Don't worry about me, ma'am. If there's anything I can help you with-"

"Out of the question!" Margery said with a shocked look in her eye, "You just go on inside and relax with Vincent, while I get started on supper." Margery wasted no time strolling inside the apartment.

"You heard the woman. Come on." Vincent gestured with his head towards the door.

Nathan nodded and went inside and Vincent followed closely behind. Immediately, the pungent smell of fish hit him in the face. He felt like he just walked into one of the seafood sections in the supermarket where they had living fish, lobsters and other animals swimming in murky tanks, ready to be netted out and bagged at the request of the customers. He couldn't help but always wonder while he was there how the employees were able to withstand the smell for 8 hours a day.

That was until the toilet once broke in his old apartment and shit-filled water began pouring out, which Aleksei refused to fix. The smell was abysmal for the first couple of hours, but after that, it gradually faded away, until it was completely gone. When the repairmen knocked the next day and Nathan opened the door, they recoiled and put their hands over their mouths and noses.

They asked him if anyone had died in there, to which he responded with silence. They ended up fixing the toilet, but Aleksei refused to pay for it, even after Nathan showed him the receipt. That's why Nathan refused to pay for the toilet when it broke the second time just before he moved out.

"The living room is right ahead, make yourself at home, Nathan!" Margery shouted from the kitchen to the right.

Yeah, I already know where it is. He wanted to say, but didn't. The apartment looked exactly like it did in the visage he had when he went through the door. Vincent and Margery were talking about something back then and now that Nathan saw that their apartment was portrayed with such surgical accuracy, he had no doubt that the conversation he heard there was real, too.

He took off his shoes and made his way inside the living room. It wasn't unlike Dolores' apartment in terms of the design itself, only it was furnished and decorated with much more modernized items. Daylight gleamed in through the big window on the opposite end, prominently shining off the walls of the apartment, which were pristinely white, without a single speck on them. Nathan had no doubt that Margery spent hours every week keeping the place spotless, while Vincent probably chugged beer and watched TV. Or maybe Margery made him do some chores and he grumpily agreed – she did seem like the type who would order her spouse around, despite being so perky in nature.

"Go on, son. Sit wherever you like." Vincent said and put his hands on his hips authoritatively.

It sounded like an order, rather than an invitation. Nathan obliged and decided to take a seat in the middle of the couch which faced away from the window. As he did, he couldn't help but notice a photograph of a young woman on one of the shelves. She had dark hair and smiled innocently at the camera. *Sarah.*

Vincent sat with a groan on the sofa to the left of the coffee table, which sat in the middle of the room. He ran his fingers over his mustache for a moment, before looking in the direction of the kitchen.

"Marge!" He shouted, "Mind bringing me and Nathan a beer?"

"One second!" Margery shouted from the kitchen.

A moment later, she came batting down the living room with two condensation-covered cans of Budweiser. She gave one to Nathan first (even though Vincent was closer), and then the other to her husband.

"Thank you, ma'am." Nathan nodded, as he held the cold, wet can in his hand.

"I hope you like salmon, Nathan. You're not allergic to seafood, are you? Gosh. I completely forgot to ask you that, how stupid of me. If you want, I can make something else. I have a frozen chicken in the freezer, it'll take just-"

"I *love* salmon, ma'am." Nathan raised his hand and tone to interrupt Margery's quickened speaking, "If you're half as good as Vincent says you are, I'm sure whatever you make is gonna be amazing."

Margery giggled like a schoolgirl and looked at Vincent, who rolled his eyes at her.

"Well, you boys enjoy." she said and waltzed back into the kitchen.

"You should come by more often. She never brings me beer when I ask for it." Vincent connivingly grinned.

"You can get off your ass to get it yourself!" Margery shouted from the kitchen.

Nathan chuckled and popped open the can, which produced a fizzy noise. Vincent did the same and gulped down a big sip. When he was done, he made an *ahhh* sound to vocalize his satisfaction and placed the can on the coffee table. The speed at which he chugged made Nathan assume his alcohol resistance was extremely high.

"So, you've been fishing, right?" Nathan asked the old man.

"Yep. Just down Oswego Lake. I have a buddy who I go with from time to time and it's been a while since we last went fishing, so I wanted to do some catching up and relaxing. Being retired is real hard work, you know?" He winked and took another sip from his can.

Nathan took a small sip. He wanted to be completely sober for the questions he was about to ask. He didn't know how he would do it without alerting Margery to it, though. Maybe he could convince Vincent to turn on the TV, to drown out their conversation. Or maybe when Margery starts frying stuff in the kitchen, she won't hear anything anyway.

"So, anything big biting?" he asked, as he took a sip of his own beer.

Vincent leaned in and whispered.

"To this day, my biggest catch ever is in the kitchen right now."

Nathan was about to congratulate Vincent, not realizing his sarcasm, until Margery's loud voice came from the kitchen.

"I heard that, you old bastard!"

"I meant that in a good way, honey!" Vincent defensively raised his hands and shouted back.

He shook his head and looked at Nathan.

"Be careful when you decide to get married, Nathan. You don't wanna end up like me." They both laughed.

Vincent brought the can to his mouth and spun it gently in his hands, before throwing his head back and taking a gulp.

"So, what have you been up to lately, Nate?"

Nathan shrugged and threw a glance towards the foyer, before answering.

"Oh, you know. The usual. Work. Nothing much more than that. I've been working on a new project lately and it's been taking a toll on me."

Vincent nodded with a frown. He smiled and said.

"I didn't wanna say anything, but you look terrible, son. Can't you take a vacation or something?"

The distinct repetitive sound of something being cut on a wooden board came loudly from the kitchen. Nathan assumed Margery was cutting potatoes or some other vegetables. He took a sip of his beer and shook his head with his mouth full, before swallowing.

"Not right now. They're expecting some demo to be delivered, so I can't stop halfway. We got only a dozen team members and most of them have been delegated some other tasks."

"Mhm." Vincent pursed his lips, making them disappear halfway under his mustache, "Well, just don't work too hard, alright? I know what it's like. Back when I served in Iraq, I once went three days without sleeping."

Nathan widened his eyes. Here he was running on a few hours of sleep every night and felt like he was going to collapse, let alone three whole days.

"Three days?" he asked, "Without even a little rest?"

Vincent nodded slowly.

"Yep. We were on a mission and as soon as we were done, I had to replace someone on guard duty, since we were short on men. And then we were ambushed and then… well, one thing just led to another and my squad and I had to wait for backup to arrive. After it was all done, I slept for about twelve hours and would have slept twelve more had the gunshots not woken me up."

"Sounds like it was a rough time out there."

"Sometimes. It's not like Hollywood portrays it, guns blazing 24/7 while you're deployed. There's maybe five percent of the time that you're in combat and the rest of the time you're doing other normal things, like paperwork, filling up sandbags, carrying this or that, and so on."

Vincent looked at the coffee table for a moment, as if reminiscing.

"So what was it like? Not sleeping for three days, I mean." Nathan asked.

Vincent whistled and shook his head.

"Well, the first few hours after not sleeping, you feel just fine. In fact, you feel like you got way more energy than before. But this is I guess your body's response to the lack of sleep. I guess it gives you a caffeinated-kind of boost of energy to keep you alive for a little bit. After that, your focus starts to drop, you're slower… and that kind of thing can cost you your life on the battlefield."

Nathan listened attentively. He was very fascinated by the military stories that Vincent shared with him and the way the old man described it was so vivid, that Nathan clearly imagined it in his mind. Vincent continued.

"And then you start to think you see movement in the distance. It's like, you're going to see the enemy standing in the distance and you shoot at him, but when you get closer, you realize it's just a tree. That was day two. On day three, the hallucinations start."

His face turned dark, as he took another sip of his beer and then placed what Nathan assumed was an empty can on the table in front of him.

"I actively started seeing things moving around, just out of my line of sight. It really made me paranoid. One guy in my team even claimed that he heard voices, kept accusing us of saying things we never said. If backup hadn't showed up by day four, I'm pretty sure some of us would have turned on each other."

"Wow." That was all Nathan could mutter, as he listened to the story in macabre attentiveness, "So, didn't you ever get scared for your life?"

Vincent shook his head.

"Not right away, no. Adrenaline is a crazy thing. When the shooting starts, your fight or flight instinct kicks in and you don't feel afraid. But as soon as the adrenaline wears off, you start to realize how close you were to getting killed."

"And your wife never tried to talk you out of leaving the Army?"

"Marine Corps, not Army." He corrected him.

"Sorry." Nathan shyly looked at his can of beer.

"I did try it, many times." Margery suddenly appeared at the entrance of the kitchen.

She had a purse over her shoulder, as she waved her hand and said.

"But he's an extremely stubborn man. Now even more so than he was before. Luckily though, he always came back safely." She smiled at Nathan widely.

"You going somewhere, Marge?" Vincent asked.

This is my chance to talk to Vincent alone. Nathan thought, feeling a smile forming on his face. Margery looked at Vincent and said.

"Yeah, we ran out of some things, so I'm going to the store to buy them real quick while the potatoes cook. Can you do me a favor? If I'm not back in ten minutes or so, just poke your head in there and check to see if it's done and remove it from the stove, will you?"

"Sure, honey." Vincent nodded.

"And get Nathan another beer. And snacks, if he's hungry."

"Will do, Marge." Vincent groaned.

She closed the front door behind her and the only sound remaining in the room was the faint boiling of water in the kitchen.

"She's not to be messed with, that one." Vincent said, "I've been in war multiple times, but she still scares the crap out of me."

"I guess that's probably the secret of a successful marriage." Nathan grinned, to which Vincent laughed.

Now was the time. He couldn't wait any longer. Margery could be back in five or ten minutes and he really didn't want to bring up the topic in front of a sweet, old lady like her.

"Hey, um, Vincent. I wanted to ask you something."

"What's up?" Vincent said enthusiastically.

Nathan looked at the picture of Sarah. No need to swerve around the topic. He had to be direct due to the lack of time.

"Did you know anyone from the building who lived here before, called Michelle?"

Vincent's facial expression turned sour for a moment, before he frowned. Nathan could see that he was just pretending and trying to hide his shock, but he was caught in that split second of insecurity.

"Michelle, you say?" He asked, "I don't think so. I mean, I know a lot of Michelles, but I didn't know a Michelle who lived in this building."

Nathan frowned.

"Are you sure? Because she lived in my apartment before me. Blonde woman, a little younger than me. Maybe that will refresh your memory." He tried to smile to seem less hostile.

Vincent grabbed his beer can, all the while shaking his head.

"Nope. Like I told you before, I didn't know any of the previous tenants from your apartment." He took an erratic sip, which told Nathan that he was getting somewhat nervous.

"Alright, no worries. I mean, I'm just asking because Dolores, my neighbor, said she saw you talking to Michelle."

"Really? Well, if I did, I don't remember. Sorry." Vincent shrugged and took another quick, pretend-sip, avoiding Nathan's gaze.

"She said that you two really knew each other." Nathan insisted.

He was sure that Vincent was lying to him and he had no intention of backing down. Vincent stared at Nathan with a blank stare for a moment, before he snapped his fingers and pointed an index at him. He said.

"You know what, you're right. I did know a blonde woman from the building, now that you've mentioned it. But I didn't know her name was Michelle."

Nathan nodded and asked.

"So, what happened to her?" Nathan asked.

Vincent shrugged.

"No idea. She stayed here for a while I think, before moving out."

"I see." Nathan nodded, not convinced at Vincent's blatant lie.

"What's it to you, Nathan?" The old man asked sternly.

The sudden shrewd military gaze took Nathan aback, but he intended to keep going, until he got all the answers. He pointed at Sarah's picture and asked.

"Is that Sarah?"

Vincent looked at the photo and then lethargically nodded.

"Yeah. That's my baby girl."

"Where *is* Sarah, Vincent?"

Vincent hesitated for a moment, his eyes still glued to the picture. A second later he looked back at Nathan and said.

"She's off at university right now. Why?" He had a somewhat angry expression on his face now.

Nathan looked down at his lap, as he rotated the almost empty can of beer in his hand. He knew Vincent already drank his own can, but pretended to take sips to ease the awkwardness.

"Is she gonna come back home soon?" he asked confidently.

Vincent frowned. He ran his fingers across his mustache a few times, leaning on the armrest.

"What's all this about, Nathan? I don't understand why you're asking any of these questions." he asked with what sounded like a panicky chuckle.

Staring at the can, Nathan muttered.

"If the other tenants find out that we knew something…"

He looked up at Vincent to see him staring wide-eyed at Nathan with a half-open mouth.

"What did you just say?" Vincent asked, somewhat accusingly.

Nathan leaned forward and looked the old man directly in the eye. He started to feel anger slowly boiling up inside him and he could no longer contain it. Not even Vincent's scary attitude would stop him from obtaining answers.

"I know you're lying to me, Vincent. I know Sarah lived in apartment 304. And I know that just like Michelle, she went missing. Why are you hiding it, Vincent?"

Vincent stared back at Nathan without blinking, with a blank expression on his face.

"How in the hell do you know this?" he asked with a slight quiver in his voice, contrasting his iron-like posture.

Nathan looked down at his can and then back up at Vincent. He leaned back in the sofa and said.

"My best friend Sam. He, uh… he died a few days ago." He looked up at Vincent, feeling tears welling up in his eyes, but suppressed them.

Maybe he could get Vincent to fess up by getting sympathy out of him.

"Oh, geez. Nathan, I'm so sorry for your loss."

"Why did you hide things from me? I could have stopped Sam from dying." He raised his tone slightly.

Vincent opened his mouth and then sighed. He threw his head back and chugged whatever few drops remained of his beer and tossed the can on the coffee table. It fell with a loud clank and rolled for a bit, before stopping near the edge of the table. He leaned forward on his knees and stared at the table with his fingers interlaced. He ran his hand across his face and squinted for a moment. Then he shook his head and took a deep breath through his nose, before he began with a somber tone.

"Sarah was… the best thing in the world that ever happened to me and Margery. She was smart. Kind. Talented. She played two instruments, you know? She was gonna become a special ed teacher. Hell, she even volunteered around kids with special needs in kindergartens and schools, when they let her. She was… such a kind soul."

Vincent closed his eyes and shook his head.

"And then. She went missing. Only a few months after she moved into 304." He looked at Nathan with teary eyes.

"What happened?"

The old man shrugged.

"No one knows. She went out one night and just… never came back." He wiped his tears.

He looked at Nathan with an angry grimace and said, emphasizing every word aggressively.

"Just like that. My little girl went missing. And I never saw her again." He put his hand over his eyes and silently began sobbing, his shoulders heaving up and down.

Nathan began feeling a little guilty. *How the tables have turned.* He couldn't imagine what Vincent was going through, but he had to know what was going on. His life depended on it. He let Vincent sob for a while, until the old man calmed down and wiped his tears. His eyes and face were crimson and Nathan couldn't recognize the hardened military veteran in this state. If anything though, it raised his respect for the man, because it once again proved to him that he wasn't just a killing machine, but a human with emotions.

"Vincent, I'm sorry. I really didn't want to bring this up, I really didn't. But my life may depend on it. Your daughter.

Michelle. Sam. And I fear I could be next. That apartment. There's something wrong with it."

Vincent shook his head in dismay.

"I know exactly what you're thinking, Nathan. But a door is just a door. Nothing else."

"But you said that Sarah-"

"Sarah was kidnapped." Vincent interrupted Nathan with a raised tone, before lowering it again, "She went out and while she was coming back home, she had to go through a shady part of town to get here. I think... I think that's where it happened."

"Vincent, I... that door. It's-"

"It's rats. You understand? *Rats*." He emphasized the last word, giving Nathan a stern look.

Nathan knew better than to argue. The two of them sat in awkward silence for a while, Vincent staring at Sarah's photograph and Nathan feeling like shit for making the old man feel that way. But he couldn't stop now. He had more questions and he was almost out of time.

"Vincent? Dolores said she saw Sarah talking to the landlord a few times. A young guy around my age. You must have seen him, right?"

Vincent looked at Nathan tiredly, but with a composed expression.

"Landlord? Oh, no, Dolores mixed it up. That wasn't the landlord. It was Sarah's boyfriend. Good kid, that one. He really treated her well."

Nathan nodded. He felt uncomfortable asking more questions about his daughter. He instead opened to his mouth to ask how closely he knew Michelle, when the front door swung open.

"Sorry I'm late, boys. Vincent, are the potatoes okay?" Margery came in with the sound of grocery bags shuffling in the foyer.

Vincent quickly wiped away his remaining tears with a hard swipe across his face with both palms.

"Yeah, Marge. I think they're just fine." He stood up as he said so.

Margery walked in with a smile, carrying two paper bags. She glanced at the two of them and her grin dropped.

"Are you two attending a funeral or something?"

Nathan chuckled out of courtesy, but avoided Margery's gaze. She seemed to become aware of the awkward silence, so she quickly inhaled and said.

"Well anyway. Nathan, you are going to *love* the dinner I'm making. And there's dessert later."

"I'm sorry Marge, but Nate has some urgent business that he has to take care of right now. Right, Nate?" Vincent looked at Nathan with the same, stern look as before.

It almost made Nathan regret opening up the topic which he did. Almost.

"Uh, yeah. Sorry, ma'am. I just got a call from work. Gotta go back and fix an issue ASAP." he said as he stood up.

Margery's smile dropped like an anchor and she furrowed her brow as a sad expression crossed her face.

"Oh, no! You can't stay? Do you think you can join us later? I can put off starting dinner until later." She desperately tried to save the situation.

"I really can't. I'm so sorry, ma'am. And thank you so much for your hospitality." Nathan said.

Margery sighed and gave Nathan a woeful smile, before saying.

"Well, I'm so sorry that you have to go. Next time I'll be sure to chain you down until you've had one of my special meals. Don't be a stranger now, okay?"

Vincent shook Nathan's hand and leaned in closer to him. Nathan could see the remnants of still-wet beer on his mustache. As he said in a soft tone.

"Listen. I'll stop by your house in a day or two. We can watch the upcoming game and make plans for our next fishing expedition. My friend Brock and I decided to let you join the club." He smiled and winked.

Nathan smiled back and took it as a sign that Vincent wasn't angry. He probably just needed some time alone after remembering Sarah.

"Thanks, Vince. You can come by any time you want. I work from home anyway." he said.

He left the apartment feeling empty and sadder than he was at the beginning of the day. He felt another emotion stir inside him, though. Something that made his fighter instinct kick in so strongly, that it momentarily replaced the depression over the loss of his friend.

Anger.

Chapter 39

Nathan sat on the couch of his living room. He was facing the evil door, giving it a menacing look. The TV was running in the background, playing a series of commercials which Nathan wasn't paying attention to. It was midnight, so he still had some time to go until the door opened.

He kept Sam in his mind the entire time. The apartment took his best friend away from him and it was going to pay for that. It wasn't just Sam, either. Vincent lost his daughter and Dolores lost a close friend. The apartment was insidious and didn't care about the pain it brought to others. It angered Nathan and he did his best to hold onto that anger, to use it against the apartment. He had no idea what he would do, but he did prepare a kitchen knife, which he placed on the coffee table hours ago, along with the flashlight right next to it. Whoever got in his way, whether it was the creaking woman or the blobby, fleshy mass from the elevator, or the maggots, he would kill all of them.

His anger started to dissipate as the night went on and he got more tired. At around 2 am, he got up to eat the leftover protein puddings he had in his fridge, since it was the only somewhat nutritious food that would give him enough strength for what awaited him inside. *Gotta load up on them carbs.* He bitterly remembered Sam saying the night when he died. At 2 am, he continued staring at the door once more, trying to build up his dissipating anger.

It killed Sam. It killed Michelle. It killed Sarah. It has to die.

He kept chanting over and over in his mind. His thought kept coming back to the last conversation he had with Sam, how they said they always had each other's backs. Sam was a good person. He meant no harm to anyone, despite being somewhat of a prankster. And what about Sarah? She was younger and according to Vincent, talented, with a bright future ahead of her. The apartment took that away from her. Now Nathan was going to put an end to its reign of terror.

A knock resounded on the door. *Who the hell could it be now?* He tip-toed to the door and leaned in. He peeped through the hole and saw the familiar mustachy face of Vincent staring back.

Shit, what the hell is he doing here at this time? He couldn't have Vincent interrupt him now. Should he open the door? Vincent rang the doorbell. Nathan shook his head, knowing it would be suspicious if he didn't answer. He told him himself that he's always home. Plus, this could be a chance to fix what he screwed up earlier.

He rushed over to the table and grabbed the knife and flashlight. He rushed to the kitchen counter and stashed the items under it, before returning to the door. Gritting his teeth, he opened the door and forced a smile.

"Hey, Vince." he greeted him jovially, awaiting to see how the old man would respond.

"Hey, Nate. Am I interrupting you in anything?" he somberly asked.

"No, not at all. But it is kinda late. What are you doing up?"

"You know, just. Couldn't sleep, is all." Vincent shrugged.

Undoubtedly he had trouble sleeping because of the conversation he had with Nathan. Nate probably stirred up a lot of bad memories which Vincent tried really hard to bury deep and not think about. He felt guilty for making his neighbor feel that way. He couldn't just shut the door in the old man's face after what he had done. He'll let him in just for a few minutes.

"Um… you wanna come in?" he asked.

"Sure, I got time." Vincent responded somberly.

Nathan opened the door and let him in. Vincent made his way into the living room and sat on the sofa again, making Nathan assume he made himself comfortable as a guest on that particular sofa. That, or he really liked sitting on it back when Sarah lived here.

"I don't have any beer, so, um…" Nathan started awkwardly, pursing his lips and looking around.

"That's alright, I need a clear head anyway. Marge has been giving me a lot of trouble for drinking too much lately. Like I said, hell of a woman, that one." He chuckled.

"Well, she was awfully nice to me when I came over." Nathan said and sat on the couch.

"Yeah, she tends to be really good to the guests. You could set the apartment on fire and she'd find a way to circumvent the guilt to me, while telling you to relax and eat something."

They both laughed.

"Sam's grandma was like that, too. This one time we were playing on the stairs in the house and I accidentally knocked down a plant potpotted plant. There was dirt all over the place and I thought that's it, I'm screwed. His grandma is gonna kill me."

He shook his head at the bittersweet reminiscence.

"When his grandma heard the noise, she was there in seconds. And then she started yelling. But not at me. At Sam."

Vincent laughed heartily.

"I was too scared to take the blame and Sam got my back, so he just silently bit the bullet. He ended up having to clean the entire staircase, even the steps where there was no dirt. I wanted to help him, but his grandma insisted that I should just sit and drink some chocolate milk. That change in her was so bipolar, I can't even explain it. It's like, she looked at Sam and screamed at the top of her lungs. And then she looked at me and spoke with a soft lullaby-like voice."

They both laughed.

"That pretty much describes Margery, too. Although the one thing she's never going to tolerate is someone going into the kitchen and touching things without permission. She completely loses it, but not because she values things, but because she insists that *she* do all the cooking."

A brief moment of silence ensued, before Nathan looked at his watch. 2:09. He could spare a few more minutes.

"You sure you don't want anything to drink? I mean, I don't have anything alcoholic, but if you want coffee, or something-"

"No, Nathan. Thank you, though." Vincent said, "Listen, uh. I'm sorry that I hid things from you. About Sarah and this whole apartment thing, I mean."

"No, I'm sorry. I know I shouldn't have pried. I knew you lost your daughter and I asked anyway, so I'm really sorry about that."

"Well, I guess I didn't think things through. I was so used to following orders without question, that I didn't think that someone might actually try to dig something up." He glanced at the humongous TV, before looking back at Nathan, "You know, you remind me of her a lot. Of Sarah, I mean."

"Yeah?"

"Yeah. That's why I took a liking to you. The two of you would have been good friends. Hell, maybe even more than that."

Nathan started feeling a little uncomfortable at Vincent hinting at him dating his missing daughter. He decided not to share his dislike for the topic, though. He snuck a glance at his watch. 2:12. Vincent continued.

"The both of you are overachievers. You don't even need to show me your prizes and whatnot, I can already tell you're a hardworking man."

Oh boy, are you wrong, Vincent. Nathan was hard working, yeah. But not lately.

"How can you tell that?" he asked.

Vincent shrugged.

"Instinct."

A moment of pause, before he said.

"Anyway, I don't wanna get all sentimental or anything like that, but um… what I'm trying to say is… you're the kind of guy I'd gladly fight alongside on the battlefield."

The awkward feeling that Nathan had just before was now exacerbated twofold. He liked Vincent as a buddy, but right now he was in no mood for any sentimental or emotional conversations. Especially after having one with Sam just before they got separated. And the one he had with Dolores. He also felt his anger dissipating, which he considered not to work in his favor. He glanced at the watch once more. 2:14. He was almost out of time.

"Vincent, look. We're both in a bad place right now. You because of your daughter, me because of my friend. We've both been through hell. Once this is all over, we can go to a bar and get drunk together like normal human beings, not wallow in misery like this at 2 am, you know?"

"Not a chance. Marge would kill me. We can drink while fishing, though."

"Deal."

Vincent nodded and scratched his cheek.

"Alright. Well, I'll be going home now, just wanted to stop by for a few minutes." He quickly got up and strode to the middle of the room.

He glanced at the storage door for a prolonged moment, before striding towards the exit with heavy steps.

"Well, we'll be in touch." Nathan said, as he stood up to see Vincent out, "I just need to sort some things out, first."

"Yeah, I understand. Take care of yourself, Nate. Don't do anything stupid, okay?"

"Hey, that's *your* job." Nathan said with a chuckle.

He shut the door and locked it. Not half a minute later the creaking started. The all-too familiar creaking, which sent shivers down his spine, but now only angered him. He wasn't afraid. In fact, he would gladly welcome any monstrosity coming at him. The apartment would pay for what it did to Sam. And to Vincent.

He stood up and with stretched out steps, he strode over to the knife and flashlight he stowed away under the kitchen counter before opening the door to Vincent. With menacing steps, he crossed the threshold of the storage door.

Chapter 40

Almost as quickly as he stepped into the dark corridor, he was unconscious and found himself in the dilapidated apartment 102. It was even worse than last time. The light hanging from the ceiling swung back and forth, casting down a meager reddish glow onto the room – or what was left of it. The floor seemed to be replaced with worn-out tiles, which appeared to be covered in dark red liquid. The walls had old-looking, flower-decorated wallpapers, which peeled away and had its once-green and now brown color exposed, equally covered with red stains which slid down and dried up at some point. Nathan immediately assumed it was blood, but there was far too much of it on the floor and walls.

It was much darker than last time, too. His flashlight helped him orient himself, but just barely, as the beam narrowly illuminated what was ahead of him.

"You're not going to stop me." he said to the empty room, feeling his anger slowly mixing with perceptible fear.

He knew that his time for short, so he immediately stepped out of the apartment and turned left, clutching his knife so firmly, that he felt the handle digging into the palm of his hand. The corridor was pitch-black and the light barely illuminated a few feet ahead of him, revealing nothing but a damaged concrete floor and walls. He wouldn't let that dissuade him, though. He was determined to get to apartment 304 and find Michelle, if she was still there.

He strode with long steps across the corridor, the batter of his footsteps loudly echoing. If something was going to jump at him, let it jump. He was ready. Part of why he strode so quickly was precisely because of that. He wanted something to either jump at him or just leave him alone, because the suspense was slowly building up the fear in him and he didn't want that feeling to overpower the anger.

He heard a whirring sound coming from ahead, around the corner to the left, which he immediately recognized as the elevator. He wasn't sure anymore if he wanted to take the stairs or not, since both pathways seemed equally haunted. He pointed his flashlight to the left where the wall ended and then to the right. His light caught something for a split second, before it was gone.

Something skinny-looking and pale got illuminated by his torch before it skittered out of sight on all fours with a batter of bare footsteps echoing throughout the corridor. Nathan froze, his heartbeat beginning to quicken. *What in god's name was that?* It looked somewhat like the same creature he saw behind the bars on top of the staircase. Whatever it was, it didn't seem malicious. If anything, it may have been scared of Nathan.

Feeling paranoid, he shone his flashlight around, half-assured that it was just his stressed mind playing tricks on him. Except it wasn't, and he knew it. He reprimanded himself for recoiling and reminded himself to get ready to plunge the knife into whoever jumped at him. He peeked around the corner where he thought the silhouette disappeared and pointed the light around. It was futile. The only thing he was able to see was the yellow glow of the elevator button. As the whirring got louder, it was apparent that the elevator was going down.

In moments, faint light began descending upon the room and Nathan jerked his head in the direction, realizing that it was the elevator. The whirring stopped just as the light reached the bottom of the room and a loud ding resonated throughout the corridor. It took Nathan a moment to realize he was staring at one of those old-styled elevators, which had metal bars instead of a door and an interior that could be seen from the outside.

Sickly, yellowish light gleamed meagerly through the bars and upon the concrete floor outside the elevator, putting Nathan's torch to shame even with the miserable amount it managed to illuminate. With a rustling noise, the metal bars slid aside, fully revealing the interior of the elevator. It looked rusted and utterly unsafe to use, however Nathan knew that this was probably going to be his only way up. Or maybe it was a trap.

Well, bring it! He thought to himself, gladly willing to fight whatever was thrown at him. Without further hesitation, he stepped into the decrepit elevator and pressed the big button with the arrow pointing upwards, right next to the door.

He took a small step back as the rusted metal bars slid back and closed the elevator. A mechanical sound resounded and then the elevator began ascending with the same whir. It ascended slowly enough for Nathan to see the first floor disappear under his feet for a solid few seconds.

The second floor soon came into view, similar reddish light in its corridor like in room 102. The walls over there seemed somewhat rusted, similar to the walls he saw back when he was with Sam. A painful pang struck him for a moment, but he managed to push it back and focus on his task.

The second floor disappeared out of sight and the wall continued obscuring his view, while the elevator continued to ascend. The third floor came into view, the same kind of rusty hallway like on the second floor. But the elevator didn't stop.

It continued going up and Nathan began pressing the middle round button, in hopes to stop the elevator. It didn't respond, so he began slamming the button with the arrow pointing down. The elevator continued ascending, completely ignoring his commands.

"No, come on!" he shouted, as he slammed all three buttons more and more violently.

The next floor came into view and Nathan realized something as he looked at it. It was the same floor. He wouldn't have realized it, had he not seen the same curve-shaped rust on the left wall just outside the elevator. The elevator continued ascending and reached the same floor again, but this time, there was a silhouette of a person standing at the far end of the hallway. Nathan couldn't see clearly, but it looked like the person was staring right at him.

The floor disappeared under Nathan's feet and reached the floor above. It was the exact same one, only this time the figure was standing a little closer. Nathan felt his heart drop to the bottom of his stomach, as he couldn't help but simply glare at the figure, just as it glared back at him.

It disappeared out of view and a song started playing somewhere in the distance, in bad quality, but still discernible. An all-too familiar song.

As free as the wind blows, as free as the grass grows…

Nathan frantically slammed all three buttons, his legs feeling like they were cut off from the rest of his body. *No, no, no, not this, please.*

When the elevator reached the next floor, the figure was there again, even closer this time. Nathan saw a man coated in blood from head to toe. His shirt looked torn in places and his forearm had a deep gash across it, all the way to the wrist. And below his torso… Nathan's heart jumped from the pit of his stomach all the way to his throat. No, that couldn't be. He refused to believe it, it couldn't possibly be real. He recognized that toolbelt. *Born Free* started playing louder now, but in a distorted manner, with the music and voice of the singer swerving into an abysmal cacophony of unnatural sounds.

The floor disappeared out of sight along with Sam's silhouette, but then came into view again on the next floor. Sam was standing right in front of the elevator door and Nathan saw all his features clearly. He had a cut on his forehead, which made blood run down his angered face and over the remaining eye. Instead of the other eye there was a gaping, fleshy red hole. Through the tears in his clothes, Nathan saw various scratches and cuts.

And then the worst thing Nathan feared happened. The elevator stopped. Nathan backed up into the wall of the elevator, as he dared not take his eyes off Sam's menacing gaze. The lights suddenly went out, even the one on Nathan's flashlight, and everything was pitch black.

Nathan began hyperventilating, as he frantically felt the wall behind him for some support.

And then the lights returned and Nathan was staring directly at Sam inside the elevator, only inches from his face. He screamed, pressing against the wall of the elevator more tightly, while Sam only stared at him with an angry expression on his face.

"Oh, god. Sam, I'm so sorry! I never meant for this to happen!" Nathan pleaded, as tears welled up in his eyes.

Sam only stood there, not showing any signs of hearing Nathan's words.

"It's my fault." Nathan wept, "I never should have brought you here. Sam…"

Sam grinned. His teeth were red, as if he had a mouth full of blood.

"Heya, Nateman." He said in Sam's familiar voice, "Did you know that the chances of elevators detaching from the cord and collapsing are almost non-existent? The elevator has four firm attachments on top of it and as long as even one stands, there's no way the elevator will come off. See?"

He hopped up, with the grin still plastered to his face. The elevator rattled dangerously and Nathan firmly gripped the wall. A metallic, creaking noise resounded and then… the elevator began plummeting.

"Oh, whoops. Guess I was wrong. But don't worry! We still have the safety cushion at the bottom!" Sam shrugged and said a bit louder now, to drown out the sound of the elevator's scraping.

Nathan had slid down into an almost sitting position, with his back against the elevator door, bracing himself for the fall.

The lights went out again and Nathan screamed once more. When they came back, Sam was gone and the elevator was still. At the same time, the music stopped and the only thing heard in the air was Nathan's frantic panting. He looked around the elevator in confusion, expecting to see Sam somewhere right next to him.

"Sam?" he called out, but no one was there.

The elevator began ascending again with the same whirring sound from before. Nathan bent down and leaned on his knees, hyperventilating. It wasn't from fear or exhaustion, but a suddenly suffocating feeling he had in his chest. The overwhelming guilt he felt all of a sudden blocked his breathing passage and he struggled to inhale. His vision got blurry and he blinked firmly to make the tears fall from his eyes in front of his feet.

"Sam… I'm so sorry…" he said to himself, as he shook his head.

Was that really Sam? If it was, what was happening to him? Did he die a slow and painful death? Did they dig out his eye first and then cut him little by little, until he bled to death? How long did he suffer? And if he was dead, was he trapped inside the apartment as some kind of an apparition? Or was the apartment playing tricks on Nathan's mind, to use his guilt against him?

That couldn't have been Sam, no way. The thought of it all being in his head alleviated the pain a little. He took deep breaths and straightened his back.

Come on, Nathan. Come on, you pussy. Get a hold of yourself.

The elevator stopped and a loud ding resounded. At first, Nathan saw nothing in front of him. And then, bright white lights flicked on, blinding him for a split second. He instinctively shielded his eyes with his hand and upon opening them, he realized he was staring at a pristine, white corridor. It was brightly lit, which reminded Nathan of an operating room. There were no cracks or other blemishes visible, which made the apartment contrast the lower floors.

The only exception from the white walls, floor and ceiling was a large plate on the right-hand wall with the number 3 on it. *This is it.* There were doors there on both sides, too. Wooden doors with numbers on them. Even though he couldn't see it from here, Nathan took a wild guess in his mind that those were apartment doors and they started with the number 3.

The elevator door opened with a rustle, but Nathan continued standing inside of it, glancing at various flawless spots of the corridor. Even his real apartment building didn't look this sterile. That was a good thing, though. This was too perfect, too alien. It gave off the impression of an artificial environment created by someone (or something) that had no idea how unnatural it would look to humans.

It reminded Nathan of the Uncanny Valley theory, which hypothesized that robots look normally human up to a certain point. And if they cross that threshold and begin resembling humans too much, they become suspiciously weird, probably due to a lack of normalized facial expressions and emotions.

If his gut feeling was correct, this was a trap. But a trap he had to step into.

Taking a deep breath, he took the first step forward. Whatever the apartment had in store for him, it was here. He stepped outside and began walking, allowing his flashlight and knife to uselessly dangle from his hands. It was eerily quiet, but for some reason, he didn't feel like he was in any immediate danger.

He looked at the first apartment on the left. 310. Across from it on the other side was 309. The corridor was way longer than in the real world, putting good space between each apartment. Despite being so brightly lit, Nathan still couldn't see the end of the corridor, so he cautiously walked forward. 308, 307, 306. And then he saw it.

The second to last door on the left side near the end of the corridor, was open. Crimson light emanated from it in pulsating motions, beckoning Nathan. He paused for a moment and then as if guided by someone else's actions, continued walking towards the door, transfixed on it. He allowed the flashlight and knife to drop from his hand with a loud, echoing clatter, not bothering to even look at the items.

He had to get to apartment 304. As soon as he enters it, everything will be okay, he was sure of that. Nothing else mattered right now. As he got closer, he could hear the pulsating of the light, as if a giant heart was beating inside. Even if he wanted to stop now, he couldn't. Something else was controlling him and he could no longer resist his urge to enter the room. He was so close, just a few more steps and he would be in.

He could see the red light inside clearly now. It changed the color from red to bright red with each pulse and he outstretched his arm to reach it, only steps away from it. A comforting warmth washed over him, further increasing his desire to enter.

Just as his hand was about to touch the interior of the apartment, he felt something yank him back violently. He fell backwards, suddenly snapping out of his trance, the warmth from earlier replaced by a depressing cold feeling. He looked up and for a brief moment realized he was in a dark, dilapidated surrounding. A woman was kneeling above him.

"Don't go in there." she said as she shook her head, "It's what it wants you to do."

Chapter 41

The light bled from the corridor and onto the woman's tormented features. She had greasy, messy hair, which slumped over her shoulders. Her eyes were bulging and her cheeks sunken. Her facial expression showed concern as she stared down at Nathan.

Nathan couldn't help but stare at her in bafflement, unable to form any words. Just then, a loud creaking noise resounded in the corridor outside and when Nathan looked towards the direction of the sound, he saw that 304 was just across from the room he and the woman were in.

We're inside Dolores' apartment. The mixture of red and white light which emanated from the corridor and apartment 304 became increasingly darker by the second, as if coinciding with the creaking. The pristine walls began peeling away and evaporating upwards, leaving layers of rust underneath them. The door to 304 began deteriorating too, and the light pulsed with a black color one last time and maintained it frozen like that. The creaking resounded once more, much closer this time.

The woman quickly got up and swiveled her head in all directions.

"Oh, no. She's coming!" she said and reached down to Nathan with surprising speed.

She grabbed him by the shoulders and helped him up.

"Come here, quickly!" she whispered.

She led Nathan to the corner of the room, pushing him against the wall and with a quivering voice, she said.

"Whatever you do, do not make a sound. You understand? Just. Be. Quiet."

The creaking was replaced by a loud clamor of footsteps rapidly approaching. In seconds, Nathan saw the creaking woman emerge in the corridor on all fours. She violently twitched and jerked her head left and right, producing a low, momentary creaking sound whenever she'd do so.

The woman who had stopped Nathan from entering apartment 304 firmly held her hand clasped over her mouth, while facing Nathan. Nathan on the other hand, stood frozen in place as he watched in terror what the creaking woman was doing. She moved her head in various direction, prominently displaying her empty eye sockets, before she crawled out of sight. The creaking dissipated slowly in the distance.

The woman who stopped Nathan closed her eyes and sighed in relief and Nathan did the same. He shifted the weight from one foot to the other and then… something connected with his foot with a loud clank and rolled on the floor, producing an alarming noise. The creaking immediately got louder once again from down the corridor and in mere seconds, the creaking woman rushed her way inside, right into the middle of the room.

The woman who was with Nathan grabbed his forearm with a feverish grip and when Nathan jerked his head in her direction, she saw her staring right at the creaking woman with one hand over her mouth. Nathan stood still, frozen in place, afraid to even breathe.

There she stopped and with a low, creaking sound looked around in all directions. She started crawling around, violently slapping the floor and scratching it with her hands every time she pulled herself, making Nathan cringe at the sound.

She went to the other side of the room, staring at the opposite wall and then moved to the other end of the room and then back in the direction of Nathan and the girl. Nathan's heart jumped into his throat as he watched the woman approach them and stop just a few feet away from them. She creaked and jerked her head in various directions violently. She pulled herself closer with one hand and was only inches away from Nathan now.

She looked up directly at him with the black holes of her eyes and opened her mouth. A low creak escaped her mouth and Nathan felt his heart racing a million miles an hour. He trembled like a leaf on the wind, but refused to make a run. He closed his eyes and held his breath, silently praying for this to be over. Before he knew it, the woman turned around and left the room with a dragging sound, producing low creaking all along.

The lady who helped Nathan looked towards the door, listening as the creaking faded away bit by bit. When it was completely gone, she sighed audibly and said.

"Okay, I think we're safe now."

"What the hell is that thing? How do you know how to deal with it?"

"That… is my sister." the woman said somberly.

"Your sister?" Nathan widened his eyes. Now that he took a better look at her, he saw an uncanny resemblance, despite the creaking woman having no eyes.

"Who are you, exactly?" he asked.

"You don't recognize me? I guess this apartment really took a toll on me." She smiled and it made her look even older.

She sighed and said.

"I'm Michelle. And it took you long enough to find me, Nathan."

No, that couldn't be. Michelle was young, beautiful. This skinny, disgusting hag couldn't possibly be Michelle.

"I know, you expected something else." she said with a low chuckle, "I can assure you, it's me. It's this apartment. It drains you of your life with each passing second."

"Wait, you've been here this whole time? Are you even alive?"

She nodded. She put one hand on the wall and said.

"I'm getting really tired. Let's sit over there."

She pointed to her right, where an old wooden table and two rusted stools occupied one corner of the room.

"Sure. Do you need help?" Nathan asked.

She shook her head.

"No, I can manage. Let's just sit there and then we can talk."

They made their way to the chairs and Michelle looked tremendously relieved when she took her own seat. Nathan couldn't see it right away from the dark, but now that they were sitting, Nathan realized there was a small half-used candle in the middle of the table, sitting on a cracked porcelain plate. Michelle whipped out a match out of somewhere and lit up the candle. The room became illuminated enough for Nathan to see what was around him.

The entire room was covered in crudely carved messages, much like the ones he saw in the corridor back when he and Sam… Messages were erratic and incoherent, with random phrases and sentences scribbled all over the place.

WHO IS HE

CANT FIND HIM

LANDLORD

CREEEEEEAAAAAK

REMEMBER REMEMBER REMEMBER

HOW LONG

BURN

Those were only some of the messages written on the walls and Nathan averted his gaze and looked down at the table, suddenly feeling uncomfortable.

"Did you do this?" he asked, pointing to the wall behind Michelle.

She nodded tiredly. Nathan scratched the back of his head. Maybe coming here wasn't such a good idea. If this was really Michelle, was she even reliable? The entire room resembled a schizophrenic's place.

There was a squeaking sound somewhere around and Michelle immediately got alert to this, snapping out of her fatigued state. She jerked her head in the direction of the sound and Nathan followed her gaze.

On the ground nearby was a rat, squeaking and scurrying around. Faster than Nathan could comprehend, Michelle jumped off her chair and leaped towards the rat. The rat tried running away, but Michelle was amazingly quick and precise. She snatched the rat with one hand and held it in a squatting position. Through her dirty shirt, Nathan saw her spine protruding tightly.

Michelle bit into the rat, who squeaked and twitched in pain, before ceasing all movement. She bit down harder, a horrible crunching sound echoing in the room, making Nathan feel sick. He stared in disgust, as Michelle bit into the rat over and over, coating her mouth and hands in blood.

She made voracious gnawing sounds as she chewed on the dead rodent and within seconds, the whole animal was gone, bones and all. She straightened and looked at Nathan with an expression of relief on her face. When she realized how appalled and even scared Nathan was, she frowned and said.

"Oh, don't give me that disgusted look. You don't know what it's like in here. I bet you never had to go a full day without eating. Just three days without food and your stomach is going to burn so badly, that you wouldn't be able to sleep. Beggars can't be choosers, so I take whatever scraps the apartment tosses my way."

Nathan averted his gaze, suddenly feeling ashamed. She was right. He didn't know what she had to go through all this time to stay alive and if nothing changed soon, he could find himself in her shoes. Michelle took a few moments breathing steadily with her eyes closed, before opening them and sitting back down on the chair. She wiped the remaining blood off her mouth, smearing it over her hands and wrists and said.

"So, you finally got here. I can't believe you actually made it."

"Michelle, I don't understand. You went missing months ago, before I moved in. What happened?"

"You already know what happened." She scoffed, "It's the door. It lures you inside and then it traps you. And if it doesn't kill you right away, it toys with you. Feeds on you every day until you are nothing more than an empty husk. And then once it finished having its fun, it offs you."

"You went through the door, just like me. But why can't you leave?"

"You can't leave if you enter apartment 304. The apartment… it wears you down as much as it can until you get to apartment 304 on this side. And then when you're exhausted, it lures you by giving you a false sense of security. Once you enter the room from this side, there's no going back."

"So like me, you went through the old corridor and revisited the apartment every night until you reached 304?" Nathan asked.

"Old corridor?" Michelle frowned, "There was no *old* corridor for me. When the door opened, I saw a corridor, yes. But it wasn't an old one. It was the corridor in the hospital where my mother had been treated before she died. And I heard her calling to me. I was so foolish. She died years ago, but I… I thought maybe she was somehow alive. So I followed her voice into the hospital corridor. I thought I was really there, except it went on for much longer and it felt like it was on a loop. I got increasingly panicked and thought I was losing my mind and then... I saw the patient's room where my mother was staying. It was open and I heard my mother calling to me. Except when I entered it, it wasn't my mother's room. It was apartment 304."

Her voice got increasingly shaky as she spoke, remembering an obviously painful memory.

"I entered it and all the solace and comfort I felt just disappeared and I found myself in a dark place. This place. And I've been stuck here ever since."

She put her hand over her mouth and stifled a cry.

"There must be something we can do to bust you out." Nathan said.

Michelle shook her head.

"Nothing. Trust me, I tried everything and it just... nothing works. I... this apartment makes sure to trap you. It has its own rules. It took care of me quickly, but now it learned to toy with its prey. It'll get you too, Nathan. It's only a matter of time. The apartment... it... it traps you."

A shiver ran down Nathan's spine. No, he couldn't be stuck in here. He couldn't end up like Michelle. He would rather die than let that happen. He would rather slit his own throat than give the apartment the pleasure of having his living corpse to play with.

"You told me to find you here. I assume there's something you wanted me to know." he said.

Michelle nodded.

"I called you here, because you need to stop 304 from hurting other people. Right now only you can do it."

"Other people? I don't know if you've noticed, but I'm in as much trouble with the apartment as anyone else." Nathan chuckled ironically.

"I know. But you've already lost someone dear to you, didn't you? Your friend, Sam?" Michelle somberly said.

"How do you know him? Is he here? Is Sam in the apartment?"

Michelle sighed before Nathan's hope even had a chance of sparking even an ember.

"He's gone, just like the rest of us. You've seen some of them, haven't you? Some of the previous tenants?"

Nathan thought for a moment. He started sweating bullets at the utter realization that Michelle was absolutely right. The fleshy blob in the elevator, the little pale thing which scurried away, Martin… But how did Martin and Michelle's sister fit into all of this? Martin seemed oblivious to the entire thing, but he also seemed intact by the apartment.

"Michelle, do you know anyone by the name of Martin? I keep seeing him in the apartment."

Michelle frowned.

"Martin? I don't think so. Who is that?"

"Uh… I don't know, to tell you the truth. He just… he's pretty mysterious. I can't figure out his game plan." He paused for a moment, "Never mind."

There was a moment of silence, before Nathan asked.

"What about your sister? How did she get here?"

"Her name is Daniella. Before I got inside, I told her everything. About the hospital corridor, our mom's voice… She begged me not to go, but I didn't listen. She decided to follow me not long after I got trapped, but she didn't make it out of the corridor before the door closed. She remained stuck in the limbo between the two worlds and now she haunts the apartment like this… this creaking thing." She burst into tears, but quickly regained her composure.

"So, she kills any trespassers?"

"Kills? No, of course not. She tries to chase them out of the apartment."

"What?" Nathan widened his eyes.

"She never meant to harm you. She wanted to chase you away before you entered. But she failed and now you're here."

Nathan stared down at his hands. He was perplexed at the absurdity of the situation. He thought that the creaking woman, Daniella, wanted to kill him. She definitely fit the role with her appearance and the chasing. But now that he knew the truth, Nathan felt sorry for her. He couldn't imagine what it would be like, being stuck in a place like this one, as a mere shadow of your former self, cursed to haunt the place, probably forever.

A moment of silence ensued in the room. Nathan stared at the wall behind Michelle, at the plethora of messages carved into the wall. The word *landlord* caught his eye.

"Michelle, who is the landlord?" He had all but forgotten about this important fact, until he saw the messages on the walls.

"I... I don't know. I've been trying to find out when I was out there in the real world, but I just can't seem to figure it out. The information is hidden everywhere. I tried looking it up, asking around... no one knows. *No one.* Whoever it is, he did really well hiding his tracks. So that leads me to only one conclusion."

"He knew what was going on inside the apartment." Nathan finished the sentence for her.

Michelle nodded.

"Not only that, but I think he wanted this to happen. I think he threw us into the apartment as food for it."

"But why would he do that?" Nathan leaned closer.

"I don't know. I think I had some ideas before, but... I just can't remember anymore."

"And you've never met him before? My neighbor from 204, Vincent, he said he saw the landlord a couple of times here and there, when he entered the building. A young guy."

Michelle shook her head and said.

"Sorry, I don't know anything about that. When I asked Vincent about the previous tenants, he said he didn't know them. But then later I found out from Dolores that his daughter also disappeared in the apartment. Those poor people..."

"Is she here? Is Sarah inside?" Nathan ecstatically asked, hardly able to contain his excitement.

He already started imagining how he would tell Vincent that not all is lost and that his daughter was still alive inside the apartment somewhere. Then the two of them could enter the place and rescue everyone that needed rescuing. That short-lived fantasy died as soon as Michelle shook her head.

"I haven't seen her. She must be here, I just never saw her anywhere. Forget about her, though. If she really *is* here, by now I assume she's no more than a mindless zombie controlled by the apartment."

Maybe this was for the best. Now that he thought about it, he didn't want to give Vincent false hope about Sarah being alive. And he definitely didn't want him to see Sarah in a condition similar to Michelle's. Looking at Michelle, he remembered that Dolores cared about her immensely.

He took out the rosary from his pocket and presented it to her. Her eyes immediately lit up, as she stared at the thing in amazement. She outstretched her palms for Nathan to place the rosary there and said.

"This… this is Dolores', isn't it? She gave this to you! Is she okay? Please, I need to know!"

Nathan placed the rosary in her hands. She brought it to her chest, feverishly clutching it, as if her life depended on it. Nathan nodded.

"She's alive. She's wracked with guilt over your disappearance. But she's fine."

Michelle smiled and started sobbing.

"Oh, Dolores. You sweet woman, you." she said through a cascade of tears, "She was always so kind. So caring. I wish I could see her again. To tell her not to blame herself."

Nathan reached across the table and gently put his hand on her wrist, feeling the bony protrusions. Michelle winced momentarily, as if the touch burned her, which Nathan took as a sign that she hadn't had friendly human contact with anyone for a very long time.

"You still can, Michelle. Just tell me what I need to do to get us out of here."

Michelle stared at Nathan for a brief moment, her lips quivering, before she buried her hands in her face crying. Nathan pulled back and gave her some time. When she regained her composure, she wiped away her tears and said.

"There's nothing you can do to save me. But you can still save yourself."

"I already lost Sam. I won't let you die here, too. I'll find a way to save the both of us."

"No!" she sternly said, startling Nathan.

"Trust me, I tried everything. There's nothing you can do to save me." Her tone returned to its usual self and she leaned forward, her facial expression changing to a serious one, "You need to burn the apartment, Nathan."

"But won't you die, then? And everyone else in it?"

"We're already as good as dead. The ones who are still alive... the apartment is feeding off them, like I already told you. I... I keep forgetting everything. That's why I wrote all of this on the wall, to remember, but... but it's not helping! Every day I lose more and more of myself and the apartment keeps me alive just enough so it can continue feeding on me. I don't want to live like this anymore. Nathan, please. Free me and my sister. Free us all. Please…"

Michelle froze, her face stopped in a weeping grimace as the tears glistened on her bony cheeks.

"Michelle?" Nathan asked, but she remained in the same position.

He waved his hand in front of her face, but she didn't even blink.

"Now do you get it?" A voice came from behind Nathan so abruptly, that he jumped back and knocked the chair down.

He turned around and saw Martin standing in front of him, as calm as ever. Something was different about him, though. His expression wasn't as jovial as it usually was. Nathan detected a hint of sorrow in his eyes, as Martin said with a sense of finality.

"I know that you've been through a lot, Nathan. Now it's time to end it."

Nathan nodded, staring at Martin's dimly illuminated face.

"You were a tenant in apartment 304, weren't you?"

Martin quirked up his lips and looked down, thinking for a moment.

"I don't remember. Maybe I was."

"And all this fucked up shit around the building… the ruined apartments, the monsters… you don't see them, do you?"

Martin's eyebrows dropped from a raise to a frown.

"Monsters? I'm afraid I don't know what you're talking about. This building is in impeccable shape and the residents here are nothing but friendly." He spread his arms demonstratively, before letting them slap against his thighs.

"Well, I should get going. She needs me. Goodbye Nathan. It was a pleasure meeting you. Stay out of trouble, okay?"

He turned around and began walking towards the door, before turning to face Nathan once more.

"Oh? And do try to be quick, alright? I assume you may anger her."

"Who? The apartment?"

Before Nathan could respond, Martin walked out of the room and got straight into 304, into the still, black light. The door of 304 slammed shut behind him with a loud bang, startling Nathan.

His eyes started to burn so he blinked firmly, waiting for the pain to go away. When he opened them, he was back in his living room. Neatly placed next to the storage door was a gas canister and atop it sat a Zippo lighter.

Chapter 42

He would anger the apartment. That must be what Martin meant. He would anger the apartment if he burned it. Good, he wanted to anger it. He wanted to defy it in any way he possibly could. But he had to warn Dolores and Vincent. He couldn't let the other innocent tenants die in the fire. He glanced at his watch and realized it was 3:21 am.

He approached the generous gifts that were left for him by the storage door and knelt down. He put the lighter in his pocket and picked up the gas can.

"It's my turn, bitch!" he said, as he removed the lid.

The smell of gasoline immediately filled Nathan's nostrils and he had never smelled anything more beautiful. He raised the can with both hands with a grunt. It was as heavy as he expected it to be. He began swinging it towards the storage door, making sure it and the walls around it were well coated in gasoline. He then turned towards the living room and began pouring gas on the furniture.

Something slammed into his right foot and he fell sideways, dropping the gas can with a loud thud. Searing pain went through his ankle, as he looked up in time to see the gas can overturned, spilling massive amounts of liquid on the carpet. He scooted towards it on his good foot and turned it over with one swift flip, glancing over at his ankle.

He looked okay and upon looking to the left, he saw that the kitchen chair was overturned next to him.

It's trying to stop me. He thought to himself, which gave him a burst of renewed energy, allowing him to stand up despite the pain in his foot. He picked up the can and continued splashing gas everywhere, the smell permeating the air more and more with each second. He was worried about the harmful effects inhaling the fumes would have on him, so he put his shirt over his mouth and continued the grueling work.

In minutes, the bedroom, living room, kitchen and bathroom were covered in gasoline. He didn't give a shit about the damaged furniture. As far as he cared, the landlord could burn along with the apartment. He did feel a sting when he realized that his humongous TV would burn along with everything else. He's had that TV for a while and it had a sentimental value. But that wasn't important now. He would buy ten new TVs later, if he could just get rid of this hellish place.

There was only a little bit of gas left inside the canister, making it much easier to carry and splash around. He turned to the storage door and coated it with the rest of the gas. Once the can was empty, he forcefully chucked it at the door with a loud scream. He made his way to the door and peeked outside.

It was still dark and everyone was probably sleeping. He walked over to Dolores' apartment and banged on the door with his fist. Within seconds, Dolores opened the door in her night gown, still half-asleep, but with a worried expression on her face.

"Dolores!" Nathan said in a hushed tone, "You need to get out of here."

Dolores closed the door to remove the chain and then opened it widely. She stepped outside, shaking her head in a manner which said that she didn't understand what Nathan said. Nathan grabbed her by the shoulders firmly. He felt her recoil from his touch. She must have been in shock from just waking up so suddenly.

"You need to get out of here. I'm gonna burn the apartment."

Dolores pulled back with a stupefied expression, before nodding energetically, making her chin jiggle. She took a deep breath and composed herself to look more calm.

"Do what you must Nathan, but please, be careful."

"I will. Take whatever you need and go."

"I don't need anything." She put her hand gently on his wrist, "End it."

He nodded and nudged her in the direction of the stairs. Dolores strode down the hallway in her slippers, the shuffling noise echoing throughout the apartment.

"Dolores." He called out to her.

She turned around and looked at him in anticipation.

"It wasn't your fault. At least, she doesn't blame you."

Dolores put her hand over her suddenly quivering lips. She let out a sob and Nathan couldn't tell if it was out of relief or sorrow. Before he had time to comprehend it, Dolores turned around and walked over to the edge of the staircase. She gave Nathan one last look of determination, before disappearing behind the corner.

Okay, Dolores is safe. Vincent and Marge will have more than enough time before the flames reach the second floor. He thought to himself as he made his way back into 304.

He glanced around to make sure no one peeked out in the meantime. Once he was sure that the coast was clear, he walked over to the fire alarm switch near the end of the hallway. *Gotta buy them time to get out. Vincent and Margery should be long-gone by the time the apartment burns.* Using all his bottled-up anger, he swung his elbow. It connected with the glass and shattered instantly, shards of it falling on the floor. The alarm began blaring immediately, so loudly that Nathan's head began throbbing.

Fuck, that's loud.

He began walking towards apartment 304 and already saw confused and frightened faces peeking out of their apartments to see what was going on.

"Fire!" Nathan shouted, barely able to hear his own voice over the alarm, "Everybody get out! FIRE!"

He felt a little guilty suddenly. Most of the tenants would probably lose their apartments and would need to move to a new place. But if it meant that no more lives would be consumed by the evil 304, he was more than glad to make that sacrifice. He got inside his apartment and closed the door. The other tenants were preoccupied with their own escape to concern themselves with Nathan's plans.

He got to the front door and pulled out his Zippo. He opened the door and stood just outside the apartment. He flicked it on and the fire came to life, steadily dancing left and right.

It would really suck if it didn't work and I had to go borrow some matches from neighbors now. He thought to himself and suppressed a peal of hysterical laughter. What was going to happen to him after the apartment burns? He already knew the answer and he was sure, beyond a shadow of a doubt, that he would be able to leave and see the outside world once again. He should have done this long, long ago.

"Sam, this is for you." Staring directly at the storage door, he knelt down and touched the lighter to the ground.

Chapter 43

Vincent jumped from his bed at the sudden thud which came from upstairs. Old military habit. His platoon got attacked a dozen times while he was serving, so every minor noise would wake him up. Sometimes when some noise abruptly woke him up like that in the middle of the night, he'd still think he was in Iraq or Afghanistan, until his sleepy mind reminded him that he was retired. He'd usually go back to bed after it happened and fall asleep after about half an hour of tossing and turning. Other times, when he knew it would be impossible to fall asleep, he'd go out for a walk.

Not this time, though. Something was wrong, he could feel it. He didn't have any logical reasoning behind it, but his gut feeling just told him that something was off. He always believed his instinct. It kept him alive through thick and thin and he didn't see any reason why it should be wrong this time.

Moments later, his gut feeling turned out to be right, because the initial thud he heard turned into raging footsteps echoing above the ceiling. *What the hell is Nathan doing at this hour?* He glanced at his watch and his suspicions were confirmed. It was early morning, almost 3:30. He stood there listening, trying to decipher if there were any muffled screams or anything of the like coming from above. The footsteps continued erratically and Vincent assumed that it was just one person up there, doing god knows what.

Maybe he's just moving stuff around? At 3:30 am? No, that's ridiculous. Something was up and he knew it. He had to go and check it out. Margery turned from her side onto her back and blearily raised her head from her pillow.

"Vince? What's wrong? Why are you up?" She blinked a few times.

"I'm gonna check up on Nate. Something's going on up there." he said as he put on his jeans.

"What? What do you mean?" Margery asked, now more alert than a moment ago.

"I don't know. I'll be back in a few minutes, alright? Go back to sleep." He put on his sneakers, straining to hear any new noise coming from upstairs.

It ceased entirely, but Vincent took it as a bad sign. His mind raced back to his young days as a recruit, when he had first aid training. The commander lined up the recruits and asked: *Say you have three wounded soldiers on the battlefield. One of them is screaming in pain, but you don't see any injuries. The second one has a visible wound, but is screaming like the first one. The third one is unconscious. Who do you help first?*

The majority of the people, including Vincent guessed that you should help the one with the visible wound. The commander shook his head and pointed at the imaginary unconscious soldier. *These two are crying, meaning their injury isn't as severe as it may be for the one unconscious. Just because he's quiet, doesn't mean he's okay.*

The silence that ensued after the batter of footsteps upstairs very much reminded Vincent of that lesson and his stomach started filling with dread at the thought of something bad happening in 304. He got up and went over to the closet next to the bed. He opened it and pulled out his trusty baseball bat. Even in the dark, it looked as pristine as ever.

He only had to use it once against a burglar in their old home and luckily no one was hurt badly. The bat turned out to be quite sturdy and even though he could have bought a better one, he decided to keep this one, since it saved his family from the intruder. He had a gun in his drawer, but he resorted to using it only in absolutely necessary cases. He deemed this particular situation not falling in that category.

"Vincent? Why do you need that?" Margery asked.

"I'll be right back, Marge. If I'm not back in ten minutes, call the police."

He swung the bat between his fingers elegantly, before turning to the door. And just then, a loud alarm began blaring in the building.

"What the fuck?" he calmly said.

His brain recognized the sound as a fire alarm and he quickly turned back to Marge. She had a wide-eyed expression on her face, as she stared at Vincent.

"Margery, quick! We need to get out of here!"

Margery flung the bed cover aside and stood up in her night gown, frantically shouting.

"Hold on! I need to grab our things!"

"There's no time, woman!" Vincent firmly grabbed her by the arm and pushed her towards the door, "Go!"

She didn't really have a choice, anyway. Vincent nudged her to the door and as soon as she opened the entrance door, the alarm became so loud, that Vincent's head began throbbing. *Still less noisy than using an RPG.* He thought to himself and pushed Margery towards the stairs. Other tenants from floors 2 and 3 were already pushing past each other, rushing downstairs, some of them half-dressed, others carrying certain items of what Vincent thought were valuable belongings.

Once he and Margery got to the stairs, he leaned towards her and said.

"You go on ahead! I have to get Nathan!"

"But Vincent-"

"Just go! I'll be there in a minute!" He could hardly even discern his own voice over the sound of the alarm.

Margery began running down the stairs clumsily, while he started running up to the third floor. Almost as soon as he reached the end of the stairwell, he bumped into an older lady. It was Dolores.

"Vincent!" she shouted, "We have to get out! There's a fire!"

"Where's Nathan?" Vincent asked.

"He's in his apartment, he'll come join us as soon as he's done." Dolores retorted.

"What the hell is he doing there?" Vincent frowned.

"What he should have done a long time ago." Dolores said with a serious expression.

Vincent stared at her for a moment, before looking to the right. He smelled something coming from down the hall and his nose immediately perceived it as gasoline. A horrible realization hit him like a ton of bricks. *Nathan wants to burn the building down.*

"Vincent, come on, we have to get-"

Before Dolores managed to finish her sentence, Vincent swung his bat and hit her across the temple. Dolores fell backwards and tumbled down the stairs, stopping only when her back hit the wall and she slumped in an awkward position. She opened her mouth and probably produced a moaning sound, but Vincent couldn't hear her. *She's still alive.*

He got down to her and stopped above her, gripping his bat firmly, irritated with the old woman. Dolores tried to get up, but she couldn't. She was old and stuck in a position which she would need help out of. Hell, maybe she even broke a few bones.

"Vincent, what are you-" she asked, but didn't finish her sentence.

Vincent grabbed the bat with both hands.

"It was all an accident, Dolores. That's all it was, nothing personal." he said, as he raised the bat and brought it down on the old lady.

Chapter 44

Will I go to prison for arson? What if someone gets killed and I get charged with murder? Nathan thought to himself as he held the lighter just inches above the gasoline-soaked carpet. He really didn't want to go to prison. But in the end, was that really such a bad punishment comparing to what he was going through now?

Fuck it.

Before he managed to finish that thought, he felt a heavy blow on the back of his head. He found himself in a sense of vertigo, as he stumbled forward, losing balance. His ears were ringing and the room around him was spinning. As if through a tunnel, he heard a voice shouting, but he couldn't make out the words.

He turned over on his back and raised his head. The angry voice was clearing up now and he managed to understand bits of what it was saying. That's when the pain in his head came, throbbing and pulsating, like someone was cutting open his skull with a rusted knife.

"What the fuck do you think you're doing, Nathan?!" Vincent stood menacingly above him at the entrance.

He wore a tank top and held a baseball bat in his hand. Even with his spinning vision, Nathan could see the ripped muscles standing out in his arms and shoulders, as he flailed the bat viciously. He had an expression of anger on his face. No, anger was too mellow for what Vincent was right now. This was pure, utter, menacing hatred. As scary as the old man was in his natural state, this one was unimaginably worse. The old man was a war veteran and probably killed a bunch of enemy soldiers. What would stop him from killing Nathan, too?

"Vincent?" Nathan groaned, "What are you doing?"

He scooted backwards and clambered up to his feet. He almost fell back down due to the room still slightly spinning, but a few seconds on his feet allowed his vision to clear up and his balance to restore.

"What am *I* doing? Are you trying to burn down my apartment, Nathan?!"

He swung the bat sideways, but Nathan took a step back. Vincent's bat connected with the TV, breaking the screen and producing a crackling noise. Nathan raised his hands in a stop sign and took a few steps back, as he said in a panic.

"Whoa, whoa, Vincent, calm down! I'm not trying to burn your apartment, just apartment 304. Listen, there's something wrong with-"

"I know there's something wrong, Nathan. It's my fucking apartment!"

"What?" Nathan frowned, trying to urge his brain to comprehend what Vincent just said, despite the throbbing headache.

His head pulsated with pain immensely, but he was mostly able to ignore it due to the adrenaline which slowly started to build up in him.

"You? You're the landlord? And you knew all this time what's going on in here, didn't you? Didn't you?!"

It was him. He was responsible for Sam's death. And everyone else who'd died in 304. He felt anger suddenly enveloping him and as if guided by someone else's actions, he lunged at the old man. Vincent effortlessly sidestepped and grabbed him by the neck under his arm. With a swift motion, he tossed Nathan aside, making him tumble onto the coffee table.

He hit his calf on the edge of the table and immediately, pain surged through his leg. He gritted his teeth, expecting the pain to come, but the adrenaline must have shielded him from the worst of it. Vincent raised the bat above his head with a violent cry. Nathan rolled off the table just in time for Vincent to bring down the bat with a loud thud.

Nathan crawled to the other side of the room, propping himself with his back on the sofa while in a sitting position. *There's no way I can take him down, he's too strong. I need to figure something else out.* He knew that he was almost out of time. The fire department would be here soon.

"Why'd you have to do it, Nathan?! You were like a son to me!" Vincent hysterically shouted.

"You tried to kill me! You allowed me to stay in here, even though you knew what was going on!" While he spoke, he frantically looked around for any objects he could use to his advantage.

"I tried to protect you! But you had to go on and stick your nose where it didn't belong! And so you got your friend killed!"

This refueled Nathan's rage. He stood up and shouted.

"Don't you fucking dare!" He lunged at Vincent again, but the old man punched him, effectively knocking him back down.

He's just toying with me. He could have easily killed me by now.

"First you got your friend killed! And then Dolores!" Vincent shouted.

Nathan propped himself up on his hands, but Vincent kicked him in the face, the impact sending Nathan flying and falling on his back. The blinding rage that he felt almost immediately dissipated and was replaced with a sense of rising dread, coupled with a burning pain in his face. He spat out some blood on the side and turned his head towards Vincent.

"What did you do to Dolores? Where is she?!"

"She told you too much, Nate. I couldn't risk her doing that for the future tenants. So she had an accident while running down the stairs."

"You crazy son of a bitch! She was innocent in all this!" Nathan shouted, as he leaned on his elbows, scooting back to the sofa.

"No, Nate! You don't understand!" Vincent's eyes flared up even more and he took a menacing step towards Nathan, gripping the baseball bat so firmly that his knuckles turned white.

"It was an accident!" Vincent shouted, as he swung the bat sideways.

He hit the already broken TV, which created another crack on the screen.

Vincent turned to face Nathan, red in the face.

"It was *her* fault! How was I supposed to know she would suffocate in there?!"

"Vincent, just calm down. What are you talking about?" Nathan raised one hand in a stop sign, while holding himself up on the other.

He looked around again and saw the little Buddha statue that his mother gave him, splayed on the floor to his right. He looked at Vincent. There was no way he would be able to reach the figurine and swing it at the old man before he stopped him. Vincent sobbed, as he flailed the bat around.

"It wasn't my fault!" He repeated.

"You did something to Sarah, didn't you?" Nathan asked as calmly as he could, trying to distract him.

Vincent snapped out of his sorrowful state at this question and returned to his angry behavior.

"It was an accident! That's all it was!" he shouted.

Suddenly, Nathan's head started hurting again and his vision got dark. He felt like he was in a place with no space and time, as he saw images flashing in front of him, like in a dream. He saw Vincent sitting on the sofa of the living room in 304. The room was dimly illuminated by the kitchen light and even in the dimness, Nathan saw some objects around which didn't belong to him. The kitchen light was casting shadows on Vincent's face, making him look much older than he was. He had a worried look on his face, as he fidgeted with his fingers and rocked back and forth.

The sound of a key being inserted into the lock resounded and Vincent snapped his head towards the entrance door. Muffled voices filled the air and as the door swung open, a young couple was in front, kissing and saying goodbye to each other. Vincent stood up and strode over to the door. The man, who was facing the apartment saw Vincent first and pulled away from the young girl.

He adjusted his glasses awkwardly, as he cleared his throat.

"Oh, hello, sir." he said politely, but with visible fear on his face.

Even before he spoke up, Nathan recognized him.

Martin?

The girl noticed Martin's expression and turned around, her smiling face turning into one of utter surprise.

"Dad! What are you doing here?" she asked with a high-pitched tone, obviously caught off guard.

Vincent put his hands on his hips and spoke to Martin.

"Son, Sarah has to go. You go on home, now."

"Yes, sir." Martin timidly nodded.

He glanced at Sarah and then back at the old man again. He was obviously aware of Vincent's penetrating gaze, so he simply said to Sarah.

"I'll call you tomorrow, okay?" Before anyone could say anything else, he turned on his heel and took off.

"Bye." Sarah said, but he was already gone.

She closed the door and turned to face Vincent.

"Dad, what are you thinking entering my apartment like that?"

"Where have you been all this time? Do you have any idea what time it is?!" He slightly raised his tone, becoming red in the face.

It was the same expression that Nathan had seen just now, when he was swinging his bat, but a lot less mild.

"I lost track of time. What's the big deal? All the other girls stayed later, too."

"I don't care what other girls are doing, you understand me?! When I give you a curfew, I expect you to follow it, do you understand?!"

Sarah looked down at her shoes, holding her purse in front of herself.

"I'm sorry." She muttered under her breath.

"What exactly are you sorry about? Are you sorry about being two hours late? Or are you sorry about bringing a guy back home? Don't you remember my rule about no boys in the apartment?! What exactly were you planning on doing with him?" Vincent's tone gradually rose.

"That's none of your business!" she angrily retorted.

She opened the front door and stepped aside, as she said.

"Please, get out of my apartment. We'll talk about things tomorrow, once you've had a chance to cool down."

Vincent looked down and took a step towards the door, visibly calmer. Instead of walking through, he slammed the door shut and locked it. Sarah recoiled in surprise, as Vincent walked over to the storage door and swung it open, the red color returning to his face. Nathan could see partly inside. It was just a storage. It had a shelf on the opposite wall and various tools, all neatly stacked. A grey wall which was similar to the corridor he saw, but there was no corridor.

Vincent walked over to the surprised Sarah and grabbed her by the wrist firmly. He began dragging her towards the storage closet, as she tried resisting him.

"Dad, what are you doing?! Let me go!"

"You never listen. You need to be disciplined." Vincent said calmly, but Nathan could see the anger on his face, despite him trying to hide it.

He effortlessly pushed Sarah inside and slammed the door shut with a loud bang. Sarah banged on the door, but Vincent held it firmly with one hand, while locking the door with the other.

"See what you're making me do?! You're going… to stay in there… until… you've learned… some manners!"

Sarah pleaded with him to let her out, crying and screaming. Vincent looked at his wristwatch and said calmly, as he put the key in his pocket.

"Right now it's 2:19 am. I will be back at 3:19 to let you out. You think about your actions and by the time I'm back, you better be ready to make a change!"

Not uttering another word, he walked out of the apartment and closed the door, ignoring Sarah's knocking and crying. Sarah continued pleading, until her voice got hoarse and her strength dissipated. Her screams turned into whimpers, which slowly turned into gasps for air, which gradually faded away. Then, there was nothing but silence for a prolonged moment, as Nathan glanced around the room, waiting for something to happen.

Then, Vincent burst inside the room loudly, startling Nathan.

"Alright, 3:19. You ready to come out and talk?"

He leaned on the wall next to the door and waited for a response. When none came, he knocked on the door loudly and said.

"Hey! Don't you fall asleep on me now, you hear?!"

Sarah didn't respond. Vincent put his hand into his pocket and pulled out the storage key.

"Goddamn disrespectful kid!" he mumbled to himself, as he put the key into the lock and turned it.

The door clicked loudly and Vincent swung the door open.

"Sarah, when I address you, then yo-" he started shouting, but stopped mid-sentence.

The storage room was no longer there. What Vincent was staring at was a long corridor, with red, fleshy walls, which enclosed on the corridor itself, pulsating and writhing slowly. Black tendrils poked out of the walls, flailing in the air like worms on a fishing hook. Vincent stared in disbelief at the living amalgamation, his eyes violently darting in all directions.

"Sarah?!" he called out to her.

Two fleshy tendrils shot from the darkness in his direction, but he was faster. He ducked just in time before the pointy end of the tendril hit his head and slammed the door shut.

It closed on the tendril, which writhed and wiggled furiously, before retreating into the corridor. Vincent shut the door hastily and stepped back, panting and wide-eyed. A bang resounded on the door, making him jump.

He stared at the door in bafflement for a brief moment, before getting with his back to the wall next to the door, as if taking cover. He grabbed the doorknob and held it firmly, staring at the door, beads of sweat running down his wrinkled forehead. With a swift motion, he turned the knob, but nothing happened. He tried again and when that didn't work, he got in front of the door and actively pushed it with his shoulder.

"Sarah… no… What have I done?" he said defeated, holding both hands on the door and his head down.

The room started changing slightly. Objects disappeared from the shelves, leaving the place visibly emptier. Vincent himself faded out of the apartment and the lighting changed, making it clear that sunlight gleamed in through the window this time. The entrance door opened and Martin timidly stepped inside, tentatively looking around.

"Sarah?" he asked in a hushed tone, tip-toeing to the middle of the living room.

He confusedly looked around the living room, facing the coffee table. The storage door began opening slowly, but Martin seemed unaware of it. Nathan felt dread rising in him, and he watched in horror as the darkness inside the corridor slowly got revealed.

Martin turned around and noticed the open door. He leaned forward, cocking his head left and right.

"Sarah? Are you in there?" he began walking towards the door.

Nathan wanted to scream at Martin not to go inside, but his senses seemed to be taken away from him. He had no mouth and he couldn't say anything. He couldn't move to pull Martin back, so he was forced to watch in terror as Martin stepped inside. *You fool, get out of there!* Nathan futilely thought to himself, but it was too late.

"Sarah?" he called out to her one more time.

And then the door slammed shut. The entire room went completely dark, until Nathan was once again enveloped in a sense of vertigo. Moments later, his vision slowly returned and he was once again faced with the gasoline-soaked room, while Vincent menacingly stood above him with the bat in his hand.

"It was you." Nathan said, "You did it. You killed her!"

"Don't you fucking dare, Nathan!" Vincent said angrily, "It was an accident!"

"You locked her up in that storage room and the apartment killed her!"

Vincent laughed.

"You still don't understand, do you Nathan? The apartment didn't kill her. Sarah *is* the apartment. When she died in there, her rage and her sorrow lived and went on to create this… this monster in the storage room. It's pure evil and it's hungry.", He took a step towards Nathan, "But it's still my daughter. And I won't let you kill her."

He raised his bat with a look of pure determination and anger in his eyes. *This is it. He won't hesitate to kill me.*

"VINCENT!" A shriek came from the door.

Vincent turned around, just in time to see Margery standing there, with a confused look on her face.

"Vincent, what are you doing?" she asked fearfully.

"Margery! What are you doing here?! I told you to get out!" Vincent shouted.

"Dolores fell down the stairs, she needs help, but I can't move her!"

"She's still alive?" Vincent asked with a frustrated look on his face.

This is my chance.

Nathan fumbled for the Buddha figurine and swung it in the direction of Vincent's head. He never stood a chance, because Vincent saw it coming before Nathan was even done grabbing the statuette. He hit Nathan's arm, effectively making him drop the figurine. Pain jolted through his arm, joining in the already present pain in his head and face.

He didn't even have time to process that, before Vincent swung his bat once more. Nathan raised his hands and ducked instinctively, making the bat connect with his shoulder. He lost balance and fell on his side, silently thanking god for not getting hit over the head again.

When he looked up, Vincent stared down at Nathan, holding the bat limply in his hand. *If only I could jump and snatch the bat away from him.* But there was no way he would be able to do that. With no other hope, Nathan looked at Margery, who looked like she was witnessing something incomprehensible. He shouted.

"Margery, get help! Vincent's the one who attacked Dolores!"

"Shut up!" Vincent shot Nathan a stern look.

Margery darted her eyes from Nathan to Vincent with a look of confusion in her eyes.

"Don't listen to him, Marge. He's deluded. He wanted to burn down our apartment." Vincent said.

"Nathan, is this true?" Margery nervously held her chubby hands close to her chest.

"Vincent killed Sarah, Margery! He locked her up in the storage and allowed her to die!"

Margery had a bemused look on her face, as she averted her gaze from Nathan and looked down. She looked back up at Nathan, looking confused, as if she was thinking over what to say next.

"Oh, god. You knew, didn't you?" Nathan asked, "You knew he killed her and you allowed him to bring more tenants here!"

All three stayed silent for a moment, before Margery looked up at Vincent pleadingly and asked.

"Vincent, we have to go to the police. Before this situation gets worse than it already is."

"Marge, think! If we go to the police, I'll go to prison. And then you'll be all alone. You already lost Sarah. You're going to lose me, too. Is that what you really want?" he uttered the final sentence in a manipulatively gentle tone.

Margery stared at Vincent with eyes glistening from unshed tears. Vincent took a menacing step towards her and grabbed her by the back of the neck. He said in a soft tone.

"Hey. Hey, listen to me. I never meant to hurt our baby. It was all just an accident, okay? You believe me, right Marge?"

Margery glanced at Nathan for a brief moment. Nathan tried catching her eye contact to appeal to her, but Vincent was so close to her, that she had no choice but to stare at him. Nathan looked around, but no other objects were close now. He could lunge at the old man again, but he would just be overpowered again. Vincent said to Margery.

"We can continue our old lives. We can go on like nothing ever happened. You just have to trust me, okay honey?"

Come on Margery, do something, dammit.

Margery's lips quivered for a moment, before she looked at Nathan and said.

"I'm sorry, Nathan. I'm really sorry."

Nathan felt his heart drop to his stomach, as Vincent turned around to face him. He spun the bat in his hands like he was about to start playing baseball and said.

"Turn around, Marge. You don't wanna see this."

Margery turned around and put her hands on her ears, her back heaving up and down from sobbing. Vincent took a few steps towards Nathan and said.

"You didn't have to do this, Nathan. We could have figured something out. I planned on warning you about the whole thing and finding someone else to replace you. But you ruined it, son."

He raised the bat above his head, ready to bring it down on Nathan. Nathan saw the storage door opening with his peripheral vision. He imagined the loud creaking sound filling the room, but it was drowned out by the fire alarm. Almost as soon as the door opened, a bony, gray hand reached out and grabbed at the carpet, prominently displaying its jagged fingernails.

Daniella.

The creaking woman emerged at an rapid pace and lunged at Margery. The old woman screamed loudly enough to drown out any other noise momentarily and that caught Vincent's attention. Daniella lay on top of Margery, holding one bony hand on her chest and the other on her cheek. Margery silently sobbed, as she remained completely still.

"Margery! Get off her, you freak!" Vincent turned his attention to Daniella, holding his bat firmly, ready to strike.

The creaking woman slowly turned her head in Vincent's direction.

"Oh, my god." Vincent's grip on the bat seemed to loosen when he saw Daniella's face, "What the hell is this thing?"

Daniella creaked, turning her head back to Margery. She gently ran the hand which was on her chest upwards, until she was holding Margery by the cheeks with both hands.

"Please…" Margery sobbed, her lips quivering.

Daniella began creaking louder and louder, until it was all Nathan could hear. And then everything went black for a moment and he experienced the same sense of vertigo from before. He was without a body, floating in air, but he recognized the room.

304. It was empty and when the front door opened, Margery waltzed inside, carrying a bottle of water and a homemade sandwich. She gently closed the door behind her, tip-toeing to the storage.

"Sarah? Sweetheart? Are you awake?" she said, leaning one ear against the door, "I brought you some food and water."

"Mom?" Sarah's muffled voice came from inside the storage, "Mom, let me out, please."

"Sweetie, I can't do that. Your dad is very angry. He's asleep downstairs right now, so I brought you some food in case you're hungry."

"I just want to get out of here. It's so dark in here. Please, let me out."

Margery walked over to the kitchen counter and placed the bottle of water and sandwich on top of it. She strode over to the storage and pulled a key out of her pocket. She put the key into the keyhole and said.

"I can't let you out. It's almost 3 am right now, so just hold on a little longer. A little over twenty minutes, okay?"

She turned the key and the lock echoed loudly in the room. She pushed the door open, to reveal a teary-eyed, makeup-smeared Sarah standing in front of her, a look of grief on her face.

"I made you your favorite sandwich. I even cut the crust off, just the way you like it." Margery said.

She went over to take the sandwich and when she turned around, she saw Sarah taking a step out of the storage room. A look of worry washed over Margery's face, as she quickly paced over to her daughter and said.

"No, no, no, sweetie. You can't leave the storage room. Your dad will be really angry if you do that."

"I don't care what he thinks. I'm moving out right now." Sarah said, wiping away the remnants of her tears.

She walked past her mother and over to the kitchen counter. She grabbed the bottle, uncapped it and took a few big swigs of the water.

"Honey, no. You can't leave. Just twenty more minutes and you'll be out, I promise." Margery said pleadingly, walking after Sarah.

"No, Mom. It's not just getting locked in. It's his constant need to control everything. You guys bought this place for me, but I feel like I'm still living with you. I have to leave."

"But where will you even go?"

"I'll move in with Martin."

Margery shook her head.

"Sarah, sweetie. No, you can't do that. Your father would be devastated. He'd-"

"I don't care what he thinks!" Sarah raised her tone, before calming down, "I'm leaving, Mom. You can't stop me."

"Sarah, you have to go back inside the storage room. Just twenty more minutes, okay. Please. Just go back in the storage." Margery looked like she was on the verge of crying, as she pleaded with Sarah in desperation.

"No." Sarah retorted briskly.

She tried walking past her mom, but Margery stepped in front of her, putting her hands in front of herself and pleading with her. The two of them began shouting over each other, Sarah ordering her to step aside, Margery pleading with her to go back into the storage room. Their arguing escalated and before they knew it, Margery lost her temper and went from pleading to hysterically ordering Sarah.

"Just go back in the storage!" Margery shouted loudly one final time and shoved Sarah.

It all happened so fast. Sarah tumbled backwards and lost her balance. She slammed her head on the kitchen counter with a loud cracking noise and fell on the floor. She remained limp, her eyes vacantly staring at the ceiling, as suddenly a deafening silence enveloped the room.

Margery stared at the body of her daughter on the floor with her mouth gaped open, looking as if she was trying to process what was in front of her. And then she started gasping for air, as if suffocating. She put her hand over her mouth and hyperventilated, before she started sobbing.

Everything else happened as if on fast-forward. Margery kneeling over Sarah's body and crying, looking around for something, grabbing Sarah under her arms and dragging her over to the storage, locking her back inside, crying some more and then subtly exiting the apartment.

Everything went black again and when Nathan's vision returned, he was back in the room with Daniella lying on top of a sobbing Margery and Vincent looking around confusedly.

"You… you killed her…" Vincent said in a stupor, staring at Margery, "You killed her…"

Margery could do nothing but continue crying, as Daniella's void eyes incessantly stared into the old woman.

"Vincent… please…" she mouthed, her voice drowned out by the blaring of the alarm and the creaking.

This seemed to snap Vincent out of his trance and he gripped his bat firmly again.

"Get off my wife!" he shouted and swung the bat.

Daniella did a flailing kind of motion with one hand - Nathan couldn't see what - and the next thing he knew, Vincent flew backwards at a force impossible to comprehend, all the way to the wall above the couch, sliding down on the floor in the process.

Margery screamed and thrashed against her captor and Daniella began creaking louder and faster. Still holding Margery's head, she twisted her head. A loud snap resounded in the room and Margery's screams instantaneously cut off. Her arms and legs fell limply to the floor, as she stared in Nathan's direction, her eyes having the same vacant look as Sarah's had when she broke her neck.

"Margery! Oh, my god!" Vincent shouted and shot up to his feet.

The creaking woman was too fast and before Vincent could take another swing, she tackled him to the ground with a loud creaking sound. Vincent dropped the bat and struggled against her, but despite her frame, she overpowered him easily. She grabbed him by the head and viciously smashed it onto the floor over and over, until his arms went limp and a smear of blood appeared on the carpet under Vincent's head.

She then pushed her fingers into his eyes hard. Blood spurted out of Vincent's eyes, as he twitched and screamed, clawing at Daniella's arms in futility. The strength at which she did it made Nathan grateful that he didn't engage her head-on back when he entered the apartment all angry. Once she managed to dig her bony thumbs into his eyes enough, she stepped back, now for the first time standing upright. She looked at Nathan with her empty eye sockets, as if awaiting his next move.

Vincent rolled on the ground left and right, holding his bloodied eye sockets and screaming in pain. Nathan stood up and grabbed the blood-stained baseball bat. Vincent had ceased screaming and was now hyperventilating and whimpering. Nathan stopped above him, gripping the baseball bat firmly, unspeakable rage overwhelming him. He thought about Sam, Michelle, Daniella, Sarah and everyone else who died in the apartment because of him. He thought about Vincent trying to kill Nathan in cold blood.

"You murdering piece of shit." he calmly said.

Vincent helped himself up to his knees with great effort and held out one hand in front of himself, facing slightly to the right of Nathan. Nathan looked at his ruined eyes and the broken frame which this once-strong man had and felt no pity.

"Nathan… Nathan… wait…" he said breathlessly.

He stumbled forward, but stopped himself from falling face-first by putting his hand on the floor.

"Wait Nathan… Please… I'm sorry…"

He was crying, or at least that's what it sounded like, but if any tears came out, they could only be the blood which already ran down his cheeks.

"I'm so-"

He never managed to finish that sentence, because Nathan swung the bat with both hands at full strength, making it connect with Vincent's temple. The old man fell sideways and raised his hand, pleading, but Nathan ignored him. He smashed his fingers with the bat, the sound of bones cracking heard despite the alarm that was still blaring out in the hallway. Vincent pulled his hand back and Nathan then hit him over the head again.

And again. And again. He kept hitting despite the crushing sound which Vincent's skull made with each bash. He continued hitting even after his head was an unrecognizable pulp of blood and brain matter, scattered messily over the carpet. The whole time, Daniella stood by the side and watched.

When he was done, he dropped the bat and beheld his artwork. Daniella slowly approached Vincent's body and grabbed him by the foot. She then lazily turned towards Margery's body and grabbed a clump of her hair with her skeletal fingers. She turned her head in Nathan's direction one more time, producing a low creaking sound, before heading towards the storage door and slowly dragging the two bodies into the corridor with almost no effort, leaving a trail of blood from Vincent's head in the path. Almost as soon as the bodies were through the door, the door slammed shut and Nathan knew it was time to leave.

Epilogue

It took him a moment to find the lighter on the ground near the entrance. The flame immediately spread like a tsunami with an igniting sound. Nathan felt the heat upon his face right away. He watched with relish as apartment 304 burned, destroying what had been his prison since the day he arrived. He wanted to watch the place get destroyed for the pain it caused him, but he knew he had no choice but to go.

The flames danced all around the room, causing things to slowly melt away and fall over in the room. When the first minor explosion resounded somewhere in the apartment, Nathan knew he could no longer wait there. He rushed to the stairwell, ignoring the sounds of glass breaking, pipes bursting and embers crackling. He swung around the stairwell and stopped in his tracks.

Dolores' body was splayed sideways on the floor between the third and second floor. Her head was propped against the wall and her eyes closed. She would have looked like she was sleeping, had it not been for the dried blood which caked her forehead.

"Dolores, no..." Nathan rushed down the steps and knelt in front of her.

Guilt began taking him over, overwhelmingly like it did the night Sam died. He sighed and began smelling the distinct smell of smoke. If he didn't get out of here right now, he would probably suffocate.

"Dolores, I'm so sorry. This is my fault." he said.

Reluctantly, he stood up and began down the stairs. He glanced at Dolores' lifeless body one last time, before rushing down the stairs. He got to the entrance just in time to see it burst open violently. He recoiled momentarily, until he realized that a group of firefighters stood there.

Not even dignifying him of a brisk glance, they rushed past Nathan with fire extinguishers. Nathan looked back to see them climbing up the steps to the second floor. A thought crossed his mind that he may be blamed for Dolores' murder, especially with Vincent and Margery gone, but he tried to push that thought to the back of his mind, telling himself he would figure out a believable story later.

He got out of the building and into the parking lot. Never before has fresh air felt so welcoming. A crowd of people stood in front of the building, most of them in their pajamas or night gowns, worriedly staring at the burning building and murmuring amongst each other, while firefighters buzzed here and there, shouting orders to each other.

"Third floor's gone!" Nathan heard one of the firefighters shout to his colleagues.

Nathan got all the way to the back of the crowd, in order to take a better look at the building. He watched in relish as the flames on the third floor danced and fluttered on the wind. Apartment 304 was engulfed in flames, but the adjacent apartments looked beyond saving, too.

"It started in that apartment up there!" One of the firefighters shouted.

"That's apartment 304!" One of the tenants shouted back.

"Where's the tenant? Tenant from 304, are you here?" The firefighter shouted, glancing over the heads of the tenants.

"Yeah, that's me!" Nathan raised his hand.

There was no point in hiding himself. He was probably already suspicious enough as it was.

The firefighter kept swiveling his head left and right, while the tenants exchanged glanced between each other.

"Tenant from 304! Are you out here?!" The firefighter repeated.

Nathan was about to shout louder, when the sound of glass breaking resounded from one of the windows on the third floor.

"Everybody, step back! It's dangerous here!" The firefighter ordered fervently.

It took the group of people a moment before they started moving to the back of the parking lot. Nathan was about to leave the place entirely, when he saw something in the window of 304.

There was a figure standing there, right in the flame, staring right at him. As the flames fluttered and momentarily moved away from the window, Nathan saw Michelle standing there, no longer looking skinny and gaunt, but appearing rather healthy and in clean clothes.

It was then that he started seeing figures in other windows with his peripheral vision. He darted his eyes from figure to figure, recognizing most of them. Martin stood in the window of 302, then there was Daniella, and many other people he didn't know, who he assumed were other tenants.

One figure in particular caught his eye when he looked at one of the apartments on the second floor. A young man around his age with casual wear and an all-too familiar, contagious smile.

"Sam." Nathan mumbled to himself breathlessly.

"Come on, this way!" The voice of one of the firefighters shouting right next to Nathan as he ran past him with a colleague grabbed his attention.

He jerked his head in the direction of the voice and then back at the building. The figures in the windows were gone, leaving only an already-charring building with flames gyrating and spreading in the windows.

With a sense of finality, Nathan turned around and exited the apartment complex, not looking back. The crowd rushed around him, people flocking on the street to see what was going on. None of them paid attention to Nathan, as decrepit and beaten down as he looked.

He stopped halfway down the street, relief and sorrow overwhelming him. It was over, but at what cost? Sam was dead. Dolores was dead. Vincent and Margery deserved to die for the horrible things they did, but did they really deserve to die in such a gruesome way?

Nathan suddenly started feeling woozy. His head began spinning and his vision was getting darker. He started hyperventilating, as his body began to give out on him. The last thing he thought before everything went completely dark was:

That's one hell of a panic attack.

***

He heard distant, muffled voices. He couldn't make out what they were saying, even as they grew gradually by the second. He smelled smoke and ash. He shot his eyes open, disoriented and confused. He propped himself up and for a very long moment he couldn't comprehend where he was.

All around him were charred walls and burnt and destroyed furniture and décor. He looked around the blackened room and realized he was on a half-burnt bed. The sheets, although almost completely destroyed, were intact in certain places. His heart began pumping immediately and he jumped down from his bed, frenetically looking around the room.

His eyes fell on the badly damaged picture frame which lay face-down on top of a desk. He didn't even need to look at it to know what it was. As he glanced at the scorched door, a terrifying realization hit him.

My bedroom. This is my bedroom.

The muffled voices permeated the air and based on what he could tell, they were coming from the living room. He rushed to the door and grabbed the knob. He had to pull hard in order to get the door to open, as it seemed to be stuck somewhere in the frame. He practically sprinted outside and was met with an unexpected sight.

He hadn't even thought about it, but now that he was looking at the rest of the apartment, it made sense that it too, would be burnt as much as the living room. The once-pristine walls and ceiling were covered in soot, while the furniture and electronics lay completely or partially destroyed by the sweeping fires. Nathan couldn't help but notice how the gigantic TV was melted in place, with only an amalgamation of the once recognizable behemoth hanging on the wall. The only thing that remained intact however, perfectly well-preserved and still in its full glory, was the storage door.

"What the hell?" Nathan said to himself.

The voices were still muffled, but much louder here. It was evident that they were coming from outside the front door. Ignoring the strangeness of the situation, Nathan strode over to the charred entrance and looked through the peephole. He immediately saw the face of a police officer standing in front, facing away from the door.

"No, still nothing new regarding that." he said to the person who was out of sight.

"And the other tenants?" The officer asked.

"All okay."

Nathan grabbed the doorknob and tried to turn it. It wouldn't budge. He knocked on the door.

"Officers! Hey, I'm in here!"

"So, what do you think happened here exactly?" The police officer asked, entirely oblivious to Nathan's pounding on the door.

"No idea. It's the strangest shit I've seen in a while." The other cop said.

Nathan banged louder on the door, shouting and calling out to the policemen. They didn't give him any more attention than they would to a nearby insect. In his desperation, he turned around, looking for something he could do.

The window.

As he ran over to the living room window, Jessica's words from when she first showed him the apartment echoed in his mind.

The fire escape is here, but let's hope you don't need to use it.

He happened to glance outside the window and noticed that the parking lot which used to be filled with cars was now almost entirely empty, with the exception of a couple of cars and one police cruiser. Nathan placed his hands on the rim of the window and pulled it up. It wouldn't budge.

He tried pulling harder, but to no avail. He ran over to the kitchen counter, where the toppled-over bar stool still lay on the floor forlornly. He picked it up and with a furious scream, chucked it in the direction of the window. He expected to hear a loud glass-shattering noise, followed by the stool clattering over the railing of the fire escape.

Instead, the sound that came was a dull thump, followed by the stool falling on the floor. The window was intact.

"What?" Nathan stared in awe at the scene before him.

Did he miss? He walked over to the stool, picked it up and with all his force, swung it towards the window with both hands. He felt the impact bounce back into his hands. The window didn't have so much as a scratch on it. Nathan stared, dumbstruck at the sudden invincibility of the escape routes.

The muffled conversation of the police officers continued outside and Nathan quickly went into his bedroom, trying the same escape method through the window, which yielded the exact same results. Defeated, he slumped down on his bed, feeling numb. It was the similar feeling that he had the night Sam died. There was nothing, just a void that begged to be filled with something, anything, even if it was pain.

The muffled conversation of the police officers outside reminded Nathan that the cops were still there and it urged him to get up and overhear what they were talking about. When he got to the door, he glanced through the peephole, not bothering to grab their attention anymore. He knew it was futile.

"So, what now?" The officer who was out of sight asked.

"Nothing. The forensics found nothing salvageable on the crime scene, so we file another missing persons report and that's that." The other officer shrugged.

"Man, there is something seriously messed up going on with this apartment, I tell you."

"Don't start with that shit again."

"Well, how would you explain all the tenants going missing then?"

"We don't know if all of them went missing. The last one could still show up."

"After what? One month since the fire? Come on, he couldn't have just disappeared. The detectives said the cameras never caught him leaving apartment 304."

A month?!

"Well, that doesn't mean it can't be logically explained. Thing is, he probably set the fire and ran off via the fire escape."

The other officer scoffed, before asking.

"So, what about the building?"

"Nothing. Only the third floor was damaged, the rest of the building is alright. Investors wanna fix this place up, so I reckon that it'll be open real soon and new tenants can start moving in."

"Just like that, huh?"

"Just like that."

The officer moved out of sight. The sound of footsteps ensued, slowly fading away, until they were gone. Nathan noticed that he had been holding his breath almost the entire time. His mind couldn't process what was going on. With no other thing to do, he began slowly pacing around the room, the panic that he felt before slowly building up, threatening to take full control.

Was he dead? Was he dreaming? He pinched himself to wake up, but was still there. Was he going to stay trapped in here until he died of starvation or thirst? Or was he going to be trapped here for an eternity?

Just when he thought things couldn't get any worse, a sound came from behind him. An all-too familiar, dreadful, steady sound, which he had heard so many nights before. The creaking was slow and loud, as if announcing its glorious opening to Nathan – or tantalizing him with it.

He slowly turned around, feeling like he was on the verge of going crazy. He saw the door opening, revealing the dark corridor inside.

Make it stop, make it stop, make it stop.

He kept chanting in his mind, wanting this to be over. When the door was widely open, the creaking stopped and silence ensued, which Nathan found to be as unnerving as the creaking itself.

He took shallow breaths, as he slowly moved toward the corridor, taking small, timid steps. He stopped at the edge of the threshold, peering into the darkness ahead. Somehow, the darkness looked thicker than before and he expected something sinister to suddenly lunge at him. He stared at it longer than he liked. When he finally decided that more of his sanity would be drained if he continued staring, he decided it was time to get away from it, anywhere, even if it was the charred room he once called a bedroom.

Just when he was about to turn and leave, a voice came from the corridor, echoing from somewhere far inside all the way to apartment 304.

"Come on in, Mr. Adventurer. I have a very rare treasure map over here!" His grandma's voice toyed with him.

"G-grandma?" he asked with a quivering voice.

"Come on, Nateman. We got a lot of exploring to do if we're gonna run into some ghosts and shit." It was Sam, clear as day.

"Sam? Is that you?" Nathan asked.

And then another voice came through. Vincent's.

"Come join us, son. I got a cold beer with your name on it." he said with his usual, laid-back tone.

Nathan continued staring into the darkness wide-eyed. He opened his mouth to say something, but no words came through.

"Come on, Nathan! You gonna keep us waiting all day?" Sam asked.

Nathan looked to the right at the entrance. And then to the left, past the burned-up furniture and toward the intact window.

"Over here, Mr. Adventurer!" his grandma called out, making Nathan snap his head back towards the corridor.

He thought for a few minutes pondering his options.

After a long moment of hesitation, he stepped inside.

THE END

Thank you for purchasing my book. As a token of gratitude, you can get a free book here.

Huge thanks for reading my book. If you enjoyed it, I would appreciate it if you left a review on the Amazon product page. Your review will help me grow and allow me to continue expanding my writing career.

Free Excerpts

Radio Tower

The branches whipped at her face and exposed arms, while the cold furiously bit her skin. She had twisted her ankle earlier and was now limping painfully, but she knew that she couldn't stop. They would catch her if she did. The forest was dark and the cacophony of the chirping birds and crickets was more than welcome after the days of hell she had been through prior to this. Despite the myriad of noises that swirled around her, her own panting was loud enough to drown out the sounds of the forest.

She kept glancing behind to make sure there was no one at her heels. She was cold, tired and her lungs were burning from the long run she had endured from the peak down to this point of the hill. She decided to slow down from her sprint into a jog and then gradually into a fast walk. As she made her way down the elevation, her head suddenly started throbbing. She ignored it, but it was becoming persistent, like a mosquito that would incessantly come back to taunt you after you unsuccessfully flailed your arms at it.

Soon, there was a deafening buzzing in her ears and her vision got blurry. She tried to push forward, but the pain was too much. She stopped and leaned on her knees, shutting her eyes firmly in hopes that the pain would pass soon. She couldn't waste much time, or they would find her.

After an intense moment of agony, the headache gradually abated and she opened her eyes to see the blur slowly clearing away. She sighed in relief and straightened her back. And then suddenly there was a snap of a branch somewhere behind her, no more than a dozen feet away.

She gasped and instinctively ducked behind the nearest tree, jerking her head in the direction of the sound. There were two bright beams of light penetrating the darkness between the rows of trees, bouncing up and down. The shuffling of leaves could now be heard, coming from the direction of the flashlights. And then the voices wafted over on the breeze.

"See anything?" A rough, male voice echoed.

"Nothing yet. She must have come through here, though." The other one responded.

The flashlight beams started moving towards her, the shuffling of leaves slowly drawing louder and closer. The woman darted back behind the massive trunk, with her back against the tree, facing away from the lights. She clasped her mouth with her scratched palm to stop herself from screaming. Every panicked breath she took sent a stinging pain to her wounded hand, but she refused to put it down.

"She couldn't have gotten far." The rough male voice said again, now only a few feet away from her.

She saw with her peripheral vision the light bouncing up and down to her right, illuminating the trees ahead, too close for comfort.

"We can't go that far." The other voice responded.

There was another shuffle of leaves and a snap of a branch, as one of the men evidently took another step closer.

"Yeah, but we can't let her get away." The first voice responded.

The woman put her other hand over her mouth now as well, tears streaming silently down her face. Her hands were trembling so badly, that she had to press hard against her mouth. She resisted the urge to let go and take a deep breath.

"She can't go anywhere. Come on, let's go back. The others will catch her." The second voice said and another set of footsteps on the leaves ensued, this time moving in the opposite direction.

There was a moment of silence before the other person veered off and followed his friend, seemingly with silent agreement. The gleam of flashlight beams disappeared and the forest was dark now again and completely silent. The woman waited for what felt like a whole minute, before she put her hands down and very slowly exhaled through her mouth, like a pregnant woman going through labor, her breath trembling from the cold and fear thrumming through her body. She gathered enough courage to peek around the tree and saw the two lights off in the distance, moving further away with each passing second. This lifted her spirits a little and she realized it was time to continue moving.

She slowly stood up, her left ankle throbbing with pain even more now that it had gotten cold. She took one tentative step, then another, and another, until she had a steady pace. The terrain was uneven and unpredictable and the area too dark, so she took extra caution, testing the ground with her good foot first while using the surrounding trees as support. Luckily, the path she took slowly led downhill, which took some pressure off her ankle. Soon enough, the forest was brimming again with sounds of animals and insects and she felt safer, knowing that she managed to put some distance between herself and her pursuers. Despite that, she glanced behind from time to time and listened for any potential human activities. She had come too far to be caught now.

She was so tired, but she couldn't stop now, she couldn't be too far away from town. Before she even managed to finish that thought, she saw faint lights below in the distance. These were not flashlight beams, but she rather immediately recognized them as streetlights. With renewed hope, she hurried down the hill, forgetting about her injured leg. She had to find help immediately and warn the people. As she got closer to the bottom of the hill, she realized there was a road up ahead, with cozy looking houses of a suburban area. She knew this place very well.

She limped across the uneven grassy ground, almost twisting her ankle again in the process. She stopped at the edge of the tree line, scanning the area from left to right and then vice versa. No one was outside. That was good, but she wasn't sure if anyone would be on the lookout for her. What that man back in the woods said about 'the others catching her' put her on edge. Just to be on the safe side, she decided to stick to the shadows of the grassy area under the trees and then run across the street, while hunched over to avoid detection.

It was pretty late and everyone seemed to be asleep, but she had to be careful nonetheless. She glanced to the far left at her neighbor's house. Maybe she could go to her? No, it was too dangerous. Things may have changed since the last time they saw each other and her neighbor could potentially be a threat now. Even if nothing changed, she could unintentionally be putting her neighbor in jeopardy. She couldn't risk that.

As she stood at the corner of one of the houses, she noticed that house number 39 had a new resident. She noticed this from the barely visible figurine decorations on the bedroom window upstairs. This could be a good thing, she thought. Whoever was in there was new in the town. That means he might be willing to help her. She couldn't trust anyone else.

Tentatively, she ran up to the house and glanced behind herself, to see if anyone had seen her. She approached the window squinting into the living room and tried to peer inside, but the curtains were pulled closed. She ducked down and skeptically looked behind her once more, unable to shake the uneasy feeling of being watched. The streetlight illuminated her clearly, so she felt like a sitting duck out here in the open, but she had no choice. She couldn't go to just anyone for help. The new resident was her best bet.

She gently knocked on the window three times. She looked around once more to make sure no one had magically appeared behind her. She knocked five more times, a little louder this time, not taking her eyes off the road and the lined-up houses. She waited a little bit, probably around thirty seconds, but to her it felt like an eternity. She knocked again, more frantically this time.

She continued beating on the window intermittently, trying to do it gently enough to avoid anyone outside from hearing the noise, but loudly enough for the owner of the house to hear. She started to get more desperate. Her thighs were burning from squatting down for too long, so she dared to stand up and lean in against the window with one palm, while knocking with the knuckles of her other hand. If anyone outside managed to see her, they'll think she's crazy.

But that was the least of her worries right now. She continued knocking, slowly losing hope that the person living inside would wake up, or that he was even home. Just as she was about to step back and look for another way out, the drapes slid sideways and she came face to face with a man in his mid-twenties.

The man screamed, the barrier between them muffling his yelp as he stepped back, clearly startled by the disturbing-looking woman. Her heart started racing, as she placed the palm of her other hand on the window as well. The man stared at her wide-eyed, with a look of palpable confusion on his face. She didn't recognize him, so she deduced he must have been new to the town. The poor guy had no idea what he had gotten himself into.

When she realized that the man was frozen in place and had no intention of getting any closer, she decided she had to capture his attention before anyone saw her. She reckoned she only had a short amount of time before he called the police.

"Please, you have to help me! If they find me, they'll take me back. I can't go back there, please!" she frantically recited with a trembling voice, her face so close to the window that it fogged up the glass with each breath she took.

The man seemed equally confused, his facial expression vacillating from scared to somewhat baffled. She realized how crazy the whole situation must seem to him. He had probably just woken up from a deep sleep and to see a dirty, scared-to-death, rambling woman at his window probably wasn't an everyday occurrence for him.

"Please, they're looking for me." The woman whispered loudly enough for the man to hear her.

The man looked like he was weighing his options. He was staring at her, eyeing her up and down with a frown.

"Please." She muttered again, feeling her lips quiver.

For a moment, a terrifying thought crossed her mind that he might call the others. The man ran his hand across his mouth and gave her a slight nod. He rushed to the right where the entrance door was. The woman's hopes soared and she ran to the front door, just in time to hear it unlocking. The door swung open and the man stood in front of her, looking visibly distressed now.

"It's not safe here, we have to get out! Please, we have to go now!" she pleaded breathlessly.

She wanted to say a million things at once, but what came out of her mouth instead was a bunch of incoherent words. The man frowned in confusion and shook his head.

"Wait, I don't understand." he uttered.

"There's no time, we have to-" she started, but before she managed to finish her sentence, a sound on her right interrupted her.

She looked to her right and saw a vehicle coming down the street. *Oh no.* Her terror surged even more so when she realized it was a police cruiser. She jerked her head back to face the man and feeling fear like she'd never felt before, she shouted.

"Oh no, it's them. They found me!"

The Grayson Legacy

"Uh… Blaire?" Alex sounded distraught.

"Shhh, not now." She said, trying to focus on the lock.

"Someone's coming." Alex said.

That grabbed Blaire's attention. She looked to the left in his direction and saw him peeking around the corner. He turned back to her and said.

"I think it's the same guy from before. I see his light at the far end."

"Is he coming this way?" Blaire asked, still holding the lockpicks steadily.

"No, not yet."

"Okay, keep an eye out."

She turned back to the lock and continued picking it. When she got to the third pin, she heard Alex's voice again.

"Oh shit. He's coming this way."

"Hold on, I got it." Blaire said impatiently, feeling her heart beginning to race.

She tried to focus only on the lock and nothing more. If her hands started trembling, she could forget about picking the lock.

"Blaire, hurry up." Alex whispered with more agitation in his voice.

Blaire looked to the left and saw Alex with his back against the wall. The first, faint gleam of whatever light the person at the stairs was carrying appeared around the corner. It was getting brighter by the second.

Blaire raked the fourth pin, trying to adjust the driver pins with the shear line. Alex grabbed the flashlight on the ground and pointed it at the door. Blaire felt the pins align and slowly began rotating the tensioner wrench.

The lock clicked and Blaire immediately removed the wrench and the pick from the lock, pushing the door open.

"Inside, hurry!" She whispered.

She looked to the left long enough to see the light brightly illuminating the corner of the corridor, before jumping inside. Alex followed closely behind, practically bumping into her and closing the door behind him.

Blaire stood in silence in the unseen room, while Alex crouched by the door and held one hand on the knob, probably afraid that it would produce a sound of he let go. His other hand cradled the flashlight close to his body, pointed at himself to prevent the light from appearing.

The muffled sound of footsteps resounded once again and the light bathed the crack at the bottom of the door. A pair of feet appeared, but just as quickly as they appeared, they disappeared, along with any vestiges of light that the person carried, leaving the two trespassers in utter darkness.

A very long moment of the two of them staring at each other in silence passed, before Blaire casually said.

"See? Told you I got it. Come on, give me my flashlight."

Alex outstretched his hand, the beam of light pointing next to Blaire, but recoiled and pulled his hand back slightly. Blaire noticed that he was wide-eyed, and that he was staring at something over her shoulder. She immediately shot around to see what he was looking at and her heart jumped into her throat.

She was staring at a pink canopy bed on the other end of the bedroom. The curtains were pulled over, but since they were thin, she was able to see through them. On the bed, propped up with their back against the bedframe was the silhouette of a person, facing Blaire and Alex. The person wasn't moving, which prompted Blaire to freeze in place herself.

It felt like an eternity, until Alex finally spoke up, breaking the silence.

"Maybe... maybe she's sleeping?"

Blaire slightly turned her head to the right where Alex was, but kept her gaze fixated on the figure.

"No, not sleeping." She said with a trembling voice as she shook her head, "Her head is up. Sh-she's awake."

Alex took a step forward and raised one hand in a surrender sign, holding the flashlight still pointed at the bed.

"Ma'am, we're not gonna hurt you. We're just here to pick something up and we'll be on our way, okay?"

The person didn't budge. Alex continued taking slow and deliberate steps towards her, going to the left around the bed. The entire time, he kept the flashlight trained on the bed, the shadow of the silhouette sitting on it dancing along with the beam of light in the opposite direction.

"Ma'am?" Alex asked again, now significantly slowing down.

Blaire felt a chill run down her spine. She still couldn't will herself to move. There was something really unnerving about the way the person on the bed was still. Blaire would have preferred if the woman just jumped up and began screaming at them and threatening to call the police.

This on the other hand, felt like watching a horror movie and waiting for a jumpscare to happen.

Alex put his free hand forward and grabbed the curtain of the bed from the left side.

"Please be careful." Blaire uttered in a timorous tone.

Alex yanked the curtain to the right with a loud zipping sound and quickly backed away, still pointing the flashlight at the person. This whole time, the person hadn't moved an inch, not even when Alex moved the curtains.

Final notes

Thank you for reading my book. If you enjoyed it, I would appreciate it if you left a review on the Amazon Product page. Reviews can greatly help me reach more audience and expand my writing career, which in turn will allow me to give you more stories such as this one.

Printed in Great Britain
by Amazon